Dr Robin Cook, a graduate of the Columbia University medical school, finished his postgraduate medical training at Harvard. The author of many bestselling novels, most recently *Chromosome 6* and *Invasion,* he lives and works in Florida.

Also by Robin Cook

ROBIN COOK

contagion

PAN BOOKS

First published 1995 by G. P. Putnam's Sons, New York

First published in Great Britain 1996 by Macmillan

This edition published 1997 by Pan Books
an imprint of Macmillan Publishers Ltd
25 Eccleston Place, London SW1W 9NF
Basingstoke and Oxford

Associated companies throughout the world

ISBN 0 330 34755 1

Copyright © Robin Cook 1995

7 9 8

A CIP catalogue record for this book is available from
the British Library.

Phototypeset by Intype London Ltd
Printed by Mackays of Chatham PLC, Chatham, Kent

FOR PHYLLIS,
STACY, MARILYN,
DAN, VICKY,
AND BEN

Our leaders should reject market values as a framework for health care and the market-driven mess into which our health system is evolving.

JEROME P. KASSIRER, M.D.
New England Journal of Medicine
Vol. 333, No. 1, p. 50, 1995

I would like to thank all my friends and colleagues who are always graciously willing to field questions and offer helpful advice. Those whom I'd particularly like to acknowledge for *Contagion* are:

DR. CHARLES WETLI, Forensic Pathologist and Medical Examiner

DR. JACKI LEE, Forensic Pathologist and Medical Examiner

DR. MARK NEUMAN, Virologist and Virology Laboratory Director

DR. CHUCK KARPAS, Pathologist and Laboratory Supreme Commander

JOE COX, Esquire, Lawyer and Reader

FLASH WILEY, Esquire, Lawyer, Fellow Basketball Player, and Rap Consultant

JEAN REEDS, Social Worker, Critic, and Fabulous Sounding Board

contagion

PROLOGUE

PROLOGUE

June 12, 1991, dawned a near-perfect, late-spring day as the sun's rays touched the eastern shores of the North American continent. Most of the United States, Canada, and Mexico expected clear, sunny skies. The only meteorological blips were a band of potential thunderstorms that was expected to extend from the plains into the Tennessee Valley and some showers that were forecasted to move in from the Bering Strait over the Seward Peninsula in Alaska.

In almost every way this June twelfth was like every other June twelfth, with one curious phenomenon. Three incidents occurred that were totally unrelated, yet were to cause a tragic intersection of the lives of three of the people involved.

11:36 A.M.
Deadhorse, Alaska

"Hey! Dick! Over here," shouted Ron Halverton. He waved frantically to get his former roommate's attention. He didn't dare leave his Jeep in the brief chaos at the tiny airport. The morning 737 from Anchorage had just landed and the security people were strict about unattended vehicles in the loading area. Buses and vans were waiting for the tourists and the returning oil company personnel.

Hearing his name and recognizing Ron, Dick waved back and then began threading his way through the milling crowd.

Ron watched Dick as he approached. Ron hadn't seen him since they'd graduated from college the year before, but Dick appeared just as he always did: the picture of normality with his Ralph Lauren shirt and windbreaker jacket, Guess jeans, and a small knapsack slung over his shoulder. Yet Ron knew the real Dick: the ambitious, aspiring microbiologist who would think nothing of flying all the way from Atlanta to Alaska with the hope of finding a new microbe. Here was a guy who loved bacteria and viruses. He collected the stuff the way other people collected baseball cards. Ron smiled and shook his head as he recalled that Dick had even had petri dishes of microbes in their shared refrigerator at the University of Colorado.

When Ron had met Dick during their freshman year, it had taken a bit of time to get used to him. Although he was an indubitably faithful friend, Dick had some peculiar and unpredictable quirks. On the one hand he was a fierce competitor in intramural sports and surely the guy you wanted with you if you mistakenly wandered into the wrong part of town, yet on the other hand he'd been unable to sacrifice a frog in first-year biology lab.

Ron found himself chuckling as he remembered another surprising and embarrassing moment involving Dick. It was during their sophomore year when a whole group had piled into a car for a weekend ski trip. Dick was driving and accidentally ran over a rabbit. His response had been to break down in tears. No one had known what to say. As a result some people began to talk behind Dick's back, especially when it became common knowledge that he would pick up cockroaches at the fraternity house and deposit them outside instead of squishing them and flushing them down the toilet as everybody else did.

As Dick came alongside the Jeep, he tossed his bag into the backseat before grasping Ron's outstretched hand.

They greeted each other enthusiastically.

"I can't believe this," Ron said. "I mean, you're here! In the Arctic."

"Hey, I wouldn't have missed this for the world," Dick said. "I'm really psyched. How far is the Eskimo site from here?"

Ron looked nervously over his shoulder. He recognized several of the security people. Turning back to Dick, he lowered his voice. "Cool it," he murmured. "I told you people are really sensitive about this."

"Oh, come on," Dick scoffed. "You can't be serious."

"I'm dead serious," Ron said. "I could get fired for leaking this to you. No fooling around. I mean, we got to do this hush-hush or we don't do it at all. You're to tell no one, ever! You promised!"

"All right, all right," Dick said with a short, appeasing laugh. "You're right. I promised. I just didn't think it was such a big deal."

"It's a very big deal," Ron said firmly. He was beginning to think he'd made a mistake inviting Dick to visit, despite how much fun it was to see him.

"You're the boss," Dick said. He gave his friend a jab on the shoulder. "My lips are sealed forever. Now chill out and relax." He swung himself into the Jeep. "But let's just buzz out there straightaway and check out this discovery."

"You don't want to see where I live first?" Ron asked.

"I have a feeling I'll be seeing that more than I care to," he said with a laugh.

"I suppose it's not a bad time while everybody is preoccupied with the Anchorage flight and screwing around with the tourists." He reached forward and started the engine.

They drove out of the airport and headed northeast on the only road. It was gravel. To talk they had to shout over the sound of the engine.

"It's about eight miles to Prudhoe Bay," Ron said, "but we'll be turning off to the west in another mile or so. Remember, if anybody stops us, I'm just taking you to the new oilfield."

Dick nodded. He couldn't believe his friend was so uptight about this thing. Looking around at the flat, marshy monotonous tundra and the overcast gunmetal gray sky, he wondered if the place was getting to Ron. He guessed life was not easy on the alluvial plain of Alaska's north slope. To lighten the mood he said: "Weather's not bad. What's the temperature?"

"You're lucky," Ron said. "There was some sun earlier, so it's in the low fifties. This is as warm as it gets up here. Enjoy it while it lasts. It'll probably flurry later today. It usually does. The perpetual joke is whether it's the last snow of last winter or the first snow of next winter."

Dick smiled and nodded but couldn't help but think that if the people up there considered that funny, they were in sad shape.

A few minutes later Ron turned left onto a smaller, newer road, heading northwest.

"How did you happen to find this abandoned igloo?" Dick asked.

"It wasn't an igloo," Ron said. "It was a house made out of peat blocks reinforced with whalebone. Igloos were only made as temporary shelters, like when people went out hunting on the ice. The Inupiat Eskimos lived in peat huts."

"I stand corrected," Dick said. "So how'd you come across it?"

"Totally by accident," Ron said. "We found it when we were bulldozing for this road. We broke through the entrance tunnel."

"Is everything still in it?" Dick asked. "I worried about that flying up here. I mean, I don't want this to be a wasted trip."

"Have no fear," Ron said. "Nothing's been touched. That I can assure you."

"Maybe there are more dwellings in the general area," Dick suggested. "Who knows? It could be a village."

Ron shrugged. "Maybe so. But no one wants to find out. If anybody from the state got wind of this they'd stop construction on our feeder pipeline to the new field. That would be one huge disaster, because we have to have the feeder line functional before winter, and winter starts in August around here."

Ron began to slow down as he scanned the side of the road. Eventually he pulled to a stop abreast of a small cairn. Putting a hand on Dick's arm to keep him in his seat, he turned to look back down the road. When he was convinced that no one was coming, he climbed from the Jeep and motioned for Dick to do the same.

Reaching back into the Jeep, he pulled out two old and soiled anoraks and work gloves. He handed a set to Dick. "You'll need these," he explained. "We'll be down below the permafrost." Then he reached back into the Jeep for a heavy-duty flashlight.

"All right," Ron added nervously. "We can't be here long. I don't want anybody coming along the road and wondering what the hell is going on."

Dick followed Ron as he headed north away from the road. A cloud of mosquitoes mystically materialized and attacked them mercilessly. Looking ahead, Dick could see a fog bank about a half mile away and guessed it marked the coast of the Arctic Ocean. In all other directions there was no relief from the monotony of the flat, windswept, featureless tundra that extended to the horizon. Overhead seabirds circled and cried raucously.

A dozen steps from the road, Ron stopped. After one last glance for approaching vehicles, he bent down and grabbed the edge of a sheet of plywood that had been painted to match the variegated colors of the surrounding tundra. He pulled the wood aside to reveal a hole four feet deep. In the north wall of the hole was the entrance to a small tunnel.

"It looks as if the hut was buried by ice," Dick said.

Ron nodded. "We think that pack ice was blown up from the beach during one of the ferocious winter storms."

"A natural tomb," Dick said.

"Are you sure you want to do this?" Ron asked.

"Don't be silly," Dick said while he donned the parka and pulled on the gloves. "I've come thousands of miles. Let's go."

Ron climbed into the hole and then bent down on all

fours. Lowering himself, he entered the tunnel. Dick followed at his heels.

As Dick crawled, he could see very little save for the eerie silhouette of Ron ahead of him. As he moved away from the entrance, the darkness closed in around him like a heavy, frigid blanket. In the failing light he noticed his breath crystalizing. He thanked God that he wasn't claustrophobic.

After about six feet the walls of the tunnel fell away. The floor also slanted downward, giving them an additional foot of headroom. There were about three and a half feet of clearance. Ron moved to the side and Dick crawled up next to him.

"It's colder than a witch's tit down here," Dick said.

Ron's flashlight beam played into the corners to illuminate short vertical struts of beluga rib bones.

"The icc snapped those whalebones like they were toothpicks," Ron said.

"Where are the inhabitants?" Dick asked.

Ron directed his flashlight beam ahead to a large, triangular piece of ice that had punched through the ceiling of the hut. "On the other side of that," he said. He handed the flashlight to Dick.

Dick took the flashlight and started crawling forward. As much as he didn't want to admit it, he was beginning to feel uncomfortable. "You're sure this place is safe?" hc questioned.

"I'm not sure of anything," Ron said. "Just that it's been like this for seventy-five years or so."

It was a tight squeeze around the block of dirty ice in the center. When Dick was halfway around he shone the light into the space beyond.

Dick caught his breath while a little gasp issued from

his mouth. Although he thought he'd been prepared, the image within the flashlight beam was more ghoulish than he'd expected. Staring back at him was the pale visage of a frozen, bearded Caucasian male dressed in furs. He was sitting upright. His eyes were open and ice blue, and they stared back at Dick defiantly. Around his mouth and nose was frozen pink froth.

"You see all three?" Ron called from the darkness.

Dick allowed the light to play around the room. The second body was supine, with its lower half completely encased in ice. The third body was positioned in a manner similar to the first, propped up against a wall in a half-sitting position. Both were Eskimos with characteristic features, dark hair, and dark eyes. Both also had frozen pink froth around their mouths and noses.

Dick shuddered through a sudden wave of nausea. He hadn't expected such a reaction, but it passed quickly.

"You see the newspaper?" Ron called.

"Not yet," Dick said as he trained his light on the floor. He saw all sorts of debris frozen together, including bird feathers and animal bones.

"It's near the bearded guy," Ron called.

Dick shone the light at the frozen Caucasian's feet. He saw the Anchorage paper immediately. The headlines were about the war in Europe. Even from where he was he could see the date: April 17, 1918.

Dick wriggled back into the antechamber. His initial horror had passed. Now he was excited. "I think you were right," he said. "It looks like all three died of pneumonia, and the date is right on."

"I knew you'd find it interesting," Ron said.

"It's more than interesting," Dick said. "It could be the chance of a lifetime. I'm going to need a saw."

The blood drained from Ron's face. "A saw," he repeated with dismay. "You've got to be joking."

"You think I'd pass up this chance?" Dick questioned. "Not on your life. I need some lung tissue."

"Jesus H. Christ!" Ron murmured. "You'd better promise again not to say anything about this ever!"

"I promised already," Dick said with exasperation. "If I find what I think I'm going to find, it will be for my own collection. Don't worry. Nobody's going to know."

Ron shook his head. "Sometimes I think you're one weird dude."

"Let's get the saw," Dick said. He handed the flashlight to Ron and started for the entrance.

6:40 P.M.
O'Hare Airport, Chicago

Marilyn Stapleton looked at her husband of twelve years and felt torn. She knew that the convulsive changes that had racked their family had impacted most on John, yet she still had to think about the children. She glanced at the two girls who were sitting in the departure lounge and nervously looking in her direction, sensing that their life as they knew it was in the balance. John wanted them to move to Chicago where he was starting a new residency in pathology.

Marilyn redirected her gaze to her husband's pleading face. He'd changed over the last several years. The confident, reserved man she had married was now bitter and insecure. He had shed twenty-five pounds, and his once ruddy, full cheeks had hollowed, giving him a lean, haggard look consistent with his new personality.

Marilyn shook her head. It was hard to recall that just

two years previously they had been the picture of the successful suburban family with his flourishing ophthalmology practice and her tenured position in English literature at the University of Illinois.

But then the huge health-care conglomerate AmeriCare had appeared on the horizon, sweeping through Champaign, Illinois, as well as numerous other towns, gobbling up practices and hospitals with bewildering speed. John had tried to hold out but ultimately lost his patient base. It was either surrender or flee, and John chose to flee. At first he'd looked for another ophthalmology position, but when it became clear there were too many ophthalmologists and that he'd be forced to work for AmeriCare or a similar organization, he'd made the decision to retrain in another medical speciality.

"I think you would enjoy living in Chicago," John said pleadingly. "And I miss you all terribly."

Marilyn sighed. "We miss you, too," she said. "But that's not the point. If I give up my job the girls would have to go to an inner-city public school. There's no way we could afford private school with your resident's salary."

The public-address system crackled to life and announced that all passengers holding tickets for Champaign had to be on board. It was last call.

"We've got to go," Marilyn said. "We'll miss the flight."

John nodded and brushed away a tear. "I know," he said. "But you will think about it?"

"Of course I'll think about it," Marilyn snapped. Then she caught herself. She sighed again. She didn't mean to sound angry. "It's all I'm thinking about," she added softly.

Marilyn lifted her arms and embraced her husband. He hugged her back with ferocity.

"Careful," she wheezed. "You'll snap one of my ribs."

"I love you," John said in a muffled voice. He'd buried his face in the crook of her neck.

After echoing his sentiments, Marilyn broke away and gathered Lydia and Tamara. She gave the boarding passes to the ticket agent and herded the girls down the ramp. As she walked she glanced at John through the glass partition. As they turned into the jetway she gave a wave. It was to be her last.

"Are we going to have to move?" Lydia whined. She was ten and in the fifth grade.

"I'm not moving," Tamara said. She was eleven and strong-willed. "I'll move in with Connie. She said I could stay with her."

"And I'm sure she discussed that with her mother," Marilyn said sarcastically. She was fighting back tears she didn't want the girls to see.

Marilyn allowed her daughters to precede her onto the small prop plane. She directed the girls to their assigned seats and then had to settle an argument about who was going to sit alone. The seating was two by two.

Marilyn answered her daughters' impassioned entreaties about what the near future would bring with vague generalities. In truth, she didn't know what was best for the family.

The plane's engines started with a roar that made further conversation difficult. As the plane left the terminal and taxied out toward the runway, she put her nose to the window. She wondered how she would have the strength to make a decision.

A bolt of lightning to the southwest jolted Marilyn

from her musing. It was an uncomfortable reminder of
her disdain for commuter flights. She did not have the
same confidence in small planes as she did in regular jets.
Unconsciously she cinched her seat belt tighter and again
checked her daughters'.

During the takeoff Marilyn gripped the armrests with
a force that suggested she thought her effort helped the
plane get aloft. It wasn't until the ground had significantly receded that she realized she'd been holding her
breath.

"How long is Daddy going to live in Chicago?" Lydia
called across the aisle.

"Five years," Marilyn answered. "Until he finishes his
training."

"I told you," Lydia yelled to Tamara. "We'll be old
by then."

A sudden bump made Marilyn reestablish her death
grip on her armrests. She glanced around the cabin. The
fact that no one was panicking gave her some solace.
Looking out the window, she saw that they were entirely
enveloped in clouds. A flash of lightning eerily lit up the
sky.

As they flew south the turbulence increased, as did the
frequency of the lightning. A terse announcement by
the pilot that they would try to find smoother air at a
different altitude did little to assuage Marilyn's rising
fears. She wanted the flight to be over.

The first sign of real disaster was a strange light that
filled the plane, followed instantly by a tremendous
bump and vibration. Several of the passengers let out
half-suppressed screams that made Marilyn's blood run
cold. Instinctively she reached over and pulled Tamara
closer to her.

The vibration increased in intensity as the plane began an agonizing roll to the right. At the same time the sound of the engines changed from a roar to an earsplitting whine. Sensing that she was being pressed into her seat and feeling disoriented in space, Marilyn looked out the window. At first she didn't see anything but clouds. But then she looked ahead and her heart leaped into her throat. The earth was rushing up at them at breakneck speed! They were flying straight down . . .

10:40 P.M.
Manhattan General Hospital, New York City

Terese Hagen tried to swallow, but it was difficult; her mouth was bone dry. A few minutes later her eyes blinked open, and for a moment she was disoriented. When she realized she was in a surgical recovery room it all came back to her in a flash.

The problem had started without warning that evening just before she and Matthew were about to go out to dinner. There had been no pain. The first thing she was aware of was wetness, particularly on the inside of her thigh. Going into the bathroom, she was dismayed to find that she was bleeding. And it wasn't just spotting. It was active hemorrhaging. Since she was five months pregnant, she was afraid it spelled trouble.

Events had unfolded rapidly from that point. She'd been able to reach her physician, Dr. Carol Glanz, who offered to meet her at the Manhattan General's emergency room. Once there, Terese's suspicions had been confirmed and surgery scheduled. The doctor had said that it appeared as if the embryo had implanted in one of her tubes instead of the uterus — an ectopic pregnancy.

Within minutes of her regaining consciousness, one of the recovery-room nurses was at her side, reassuring her that everything was fine.

"What about my baby?" Terese asked. She could feel a bulky dressing over her disturbingly flat abdomen.

"Your doctor knows more about that than I do," the nurse said. "I'll let her know you are awake. I know she wants to talk with you."

Before the nurse left, Terese complained about her dry throat. The nurse gave her some ice chips, and the cool fluid was a godsend.

Terese closed her eyes. She guessed that she dozed off, because the next thing she knew was that Dr. Carol Glanz was calling her name.

"How do you feel?" Dr. Glanz asked.

Terese assured her she was fine thanks to the ice chips. She then asked about her baby.

Dr. Glanz took a deep breath and reached out and put her hand on Terese's shoulder. "I'm afraid I have double bad news," she said.

Terese could feel herself tense.

"It was ectopic," Dr. Glanz said, falling back on doctor jargon to make a difficult job a bit easier. "We had to terminate the pregnancy and, of course, the child was not viable."

Terese nodded, ostensibly without emotion. She had expected as much and had tried to prepare herself. What she wasn't prepared for was what Dr. Glanz said next.

"Unfortunately the operation wasn't easy. There were some complications, which was why you were bleeding so profusely when you came into the emergency room. We had to sacrifice your uterus. We had to do a hyster-ectomy."

At first Terese's brain was unable to comprehend what she'd been told. She nodded and looked expectantly at the doctor as if she anticipated more information.

"I'm sure this is very upsetting for you," Dr. Glanz said. "I want you to understand that everything was done that could have been done to avoid this unfortunate outcome."

Sudden comprehension of what she'd been told jolted Terese. Her silent voice broke free from its bounds and she cried: "No!"

Dr. Glanz squeezed her shoulder in sympathy. "Since this was to be your first child, I know what this means to you," she said. "I'm terribly sorry."

Terese groaned. It was such crushing news that for the moment she was beyond tears. She was numb. All her life she had assumed she would have children. It had been part of her identity. The idea that it was impossible was too difficult to grasp.

"What about my husband?" Terese managed. "Has he been told?"

"He has," Dr. Glanz said. "I spoke to him as soon as I'd finished the case. He's downstairs in your room, where I'm sure you'll be going momentarily."

There was more conversation with Dr. Glanz, but Terese remembered little of it. The combined realization that she'd lost her child and would never be able to have another was devastating.

A quarter hour later an orderly arrived to wheel her to her room. The trip went quickly; she was oblivious to her surroundings. Her mind was in turmoil; she needed reassurance and support.

When she reached her room, Matthew was on his cellular phone. As a stockbroker, it was his constant companion.

The floor nurses expertly transferred Terese to her bed and hung her IV on a pole behind her head. After making sure all was in order and encouraging her to call if she needed anything, they left.

Terese looked over at Matthew, who had averted his gaze as he finished his call. She was concerned about his reaction to this catastrophe. They had been married for only three months.

With a definitive click Matthew flipped his phone closed and slipped it into his jacket pocket. He turned to Terese and stared at her for a moment. His tie was loosened and his shirt collar unbuttoned.

She tried to read his expression but couldn't. He was chewing the inside of his cheek.

"How are you?" he asked finally with little emotion.

"As well as can be expected," Terese managed. She desperately wanted him to come to her and hold her, but he kept his distance.

"This is a curious state of affairs," he said.

"I'm not sure I know what you mean," Terese said.

"Simply that the main reason we got married has just evaporated," Matthew said. "I'd say your planning has gone awry."

Terese's mouth slowly dropped open. Stunned, she had to struggle to find her voice. "I don't like your implication," she said. "I didn't get pregnant on purpose."

"Well, you have your reality and I have mine," Matthew said. "The problem is: What are we going to do about it?"

Terese closed her eyes. She couldn't respond. It had been as if Matthew had plunged a knife into her heart. She knew from that moment that she didn't love him. In fact she hated him . . .

CHAPTER ONE

Wednesday, 7:15 A.M., March 20, 1996
New York City

"Excuse me," Jack Stapleton said with false civility to the darkly complected Pakistani cabdriver. "Would you care to step out of your car so we can discuss this matter fully?"

Jack was referring to the fact that the cabdriver had cut him off at the intersection of Forty-sixth Street and Second Avenue. In retaliation Jack had kicked the cab's driver-side door when they had both stopped at a red light at Forty-fourth Street. Jack was on his Canondale mountain bike that he used to commute to work.

This morning's confrontation was not unusual. Jack's daily route included a hair-raising slalom down Second Avenue from Fifty-ninth Street to Thirtieth Street at breakneck speed. There were frequent close calls with trucks and taxicabs and the inevitable arguments. Anyone else would have found the trip nerve-racking. Jack loved it. As he explained to his colleagues, it got his blood circulating.

Choosing to ignore Jack until the light turned green, the Pakistani cabdriver then cursed him soundly before speeding off.

"And to you too!" Jack yelled back. He accelerated standing up until he reached a speed equal to the traffic.

Then he settled onto the seat while his legs pumped furiously.

Eventually he caught up with the offending cabdriver, but Jack ignored him. In fact, he whisked past him, squeezing between the taxi and a delivery van.

At Thirtieth Street Jack turned east, crossed First Avenue, and abruptly turned into the loading bay of the Office of the Chief Medical Examiner for the City of New York. Jack had been working there for five months, having been offered a position as an associate medical examiner after finishing his pathology residency and a year's fellowship in forensics.

Jack wheeled his bike past the security office and waved at the uniformed guard. Turning left, he passed the mortuary office and entered the morgue itself. Turning left again, he passed a bank of refrigerated compartments used to store bodies prior to autopsy. In a corner where simple pine coffins were stored for unclaimed bodies heading for Hart Island, Jack parked his bike and secured it with several Kryptonite locks.

The elevator took Jack up to the first floor. It was well before eight in the morning and few of the daytime employees had arrived. Even Sergeant Murphy wasn't in the office assigned to the police.

Passing through the communications room, Jack entered the ID area. He said hello to Vinnie Amendola, who returned the greeting without looking up from his newspaper. Vinnie was one of the mortuary techs who worked with Jack frequently.

Jack also said hello to Laurie Montgomery, one of the board-certified forensic pathologists. It was her turn in the rotation to be in charge of assigning the cases that had come in during the night. She'd been at the Office of the Chief Medical Examiner for four and a half years. Like Jack, she was usually one of the first to arrive in the morning.

"I see you made it into the office once again without having to come in feet first," Laurie said teasingly. She was referring to Jack's dangerous bike ride. "Coming in feet first" was office vernacular for arriving dead.

"Only one brush with a taxi," Jack said. "I'm accustomed to three or four. It was like a ride in the country this morning."

"I'm sure," Laurie said without belief. "Personally I think you are foolhardy to ride your bike in this city. I've autopsied several of those daredevil bicycle messengers. Every time I see one in traffic I wonder when I'll be seeing him in the pit." The "pit" was office vernacular for the autopsy room.

Jack helped himself to coffee, then wandered over to the desk where Laurie was working.

"Anything particularly interesting?" Jack asked, looking over her shoulder.

"The usual gunshot wounds," Laurie said. "Also a drug overdose."

"Ugh," Jack said.

"You don't like overdoses?"

"Nah," Jack said. "They're all the same. I like surprises and a challenge."

"I had a few overdoses that fit into that category during my first year," Laurie said.

"How so?"

"It's a long story," Laurie said evasively. Then she pointed to one of the names on her list. "Here's a case you might find interesting: Donald Nodelman. The diagnosis is unknown infectious disease."

"That would certainly be better than an overdose," Jack said.

"Not in my book," Laurie said. "But it's yours if you want it. Personally I don't care for infectious disease cases, never have and never will. When I did the external exam earlier, it gave me the creeps. Whatever it was, it was an aggressive bug. He's got extensive subcutaneous bleeding."

"Unknowns can be a challenge," Jack said. He picked up the folder. "I'll be glad to do the case. Did he die at home or in an institution?"

"He was in a hospital," Laurie said. "He was brought in from the Manhattan General. But infectious disease wasn't his admitting diagnosis. He'd been admitted for diabetes."

"It's my recollection that the Manhattan General is an AmeriCare hospital," Jack said. "Is that true?"

"I think so," Laurie said. "Why do you ask?"

"Because it might make this case personally rewarding," Jack said. "Maybe I'll be lucky enough for the diagnosis to be something like Legionnaires' disease. I couldn't think of anything more enjoyable than giving AmeriCare heartburn. I'd love to see that corporation squirm."

"Why's that?" Laurie asked.

"It's a long story," Jack said with an impish smile. "One of these days we should have a drink and you can tell me about your overdoses and I'll tell you about me and AmeriCare."

Laurie didn't know if Jack's invitation was sincere or not. She didn't know much about Jack Stapleton beyond his work at the medical examiner's office; her understanding was that no one else did either. Jack was a superb forensic pathologist, despite the fact that he'd only recently finished his training. But he didn't socialize much, and he was never very personally revealing in his small talk. All Laurie knew was that he was forty-one, unmarried, entertainingly flippant, and came from the Midwest.

"I'll let you know what I find," Jack said as he headed toward the communications room.

"Jack, excuse me," Laurie called out.

Jack stopped and turned around.

"Would you mind if I gave you a bit of advice," she said hesitantly. She was speaking impulsively. It wasn't like her, but she appreciated Jack and hoped that he would be working there for some time.

Jack's impish smile returned. He stepped back to the desk. "By all means," he said.

"I'm probably speaking out of turn," Laurie said.

"Quite the contrary," Jack said. "I honor your opinion. What's on your mind?"

"Just that you and Calvin Washington have been at odds," Laurie said. "I know it's just a clash of personalities, but Calvin has had a long-standing relationship with the Manhattan General, as AmeriCare does with the mayor's office. I think you should be careful."

"Being careful hasn't been one of my strong points for five years," Jack said. "I have utmost respect for the deputy chief. Our only disagreement is that he believes rules to be carved in stone while I see them as guidelines. As for AmeriCare, I don't care for their goals or methods."

"Well, it's not my business," Laurie said. "But Calvin keeps saying he doesn't see you as a team player."

"He's got a point there," Jack said. "The problem is

that I've developed an aversion to mediocrity. I'm honored to work with most people around here, especially you. However, there are a few whom I can't deal with, and I don't hide it. It's as simple as that."

"I'll take that as a compliment," Laurie said.

"It was meant as one," Jack said.

"Well, let me know what you find on Nodelman," Laurie said. "Then I'll have at least one more case for you to do."

"My pleasure," Jack said. He turned and headed for the communications room. As he walked past Vinnie, he snatched away his paper.

"Come on, Vinnie," Jack said. "We're going to get a jump on the day."

Vinnie complained but followed. While trying to retrieve his paper he collided with Jack, who had abruptly stopped outside of Janice Jaeger's office. Janice was one of the forensic investigators, frequently referred to as PAs or physician's assistants. Her tour of duty was the graveyard shift, from eleven to seven. Jack was surprised to find her still in her office. A petite woman with dark hair and dark eyes, she was obviously tired.

"What are you still doing here?" Jack asked.

"I've got one more report to finish."

Jack held up the folder in his hand. "Did you or Curt handle Nodelman?"

"I did," Janice said. "Is there a problem?"

"Not that I know about yet," Jack said with a chuckle. He knew Janice to be extremely conscientious, which made her ideal for teasing. "Was it your impression the cause of death was a nosocomial infection?"

"What the hell is a 'nosocomical infection'?" Vinnie asked.

"It's an infection acquired in a hospital," Jack explained.

"It certainly seems so," Janice said. "The man had been in the hospital five days for his diabetes before developing symptoms of an infectious disease. Once he got them, he died within thirty-six hours."

Jack whistled in respect. "Whatever the bug was, it certainly was virulent."

"That's what worried the doctors I spoke with," Janice said.

"Any laboratory results from microbiology?" Jack questioned.

"Nothing has grown out," Janice said. "Blood cultures were negative as of four o'clock this morning. The terminal event was acute respiratory distress syndrome, or ARDS, but sputum cultures have been negative as well. The only positive thing was the gram stain of the sputum. That showed gram-negative bacilli. That made people think of pseudomonas, but it hasn't been confirmed."

"Any question of the patient being immunologically compromised?" Jack asked. "Did he have AIDS or had he been treated with anti-metabolites?"

"Not that I could ascertain," Janice said. "The only problem he had listed was diabetes and some of the usual sequelae. Anyway, it's all in the investigative report if you'd care to read it."

"Hey, why read when I can get it from the horse's mouth?" Jack said with a laugh. He thanked Janice and headed for the elevator.

"I hope you are planning to wear your moon suit," Vinnie said. The moon suit, the completely enclosed, impervious outfit complete with a clear plastic face mask, was designed for maximum protection. Air was forced into the suit by a fan worn at the small of the back, pulling air through a filter before circulating it within the headpiece. That provided enough ventilation to breathe but guaranteed sauna-like temperatures inside. Jack detested the setup.

As far as Jack was concerned the moon suit was bulky, restrictive, uncomfortable, hot, and unnecessary. He'd not worn one throughout his training. The problem was that the New York chief, Dr. Harold Bingham, had decreed that the suits be used. Calvin, the deputy chief, was intent on enforcing it. Jack had endured several confrontations as a result.

"This might be the first time the suit is indicated," Jack said to Vinnie's relief. "Until we know what we are dealing with we have to take all precautions. After all, it could be something like Ebola virus."

Vinnie stopped in his tracks. "You really think it's possible?" he asked, his eyes opened wide.

"Not a chance," Jack said. He slapped him on the back. "Just kidding."

"Thank God," Vinnie said. They started walking again.

"But maybe plague," Jack added.

Vinnie stopped again. "That would be just as bad," he said.

Jack shrugged his shoulders. "All in a day's work," he said. "Come on, let's get it over with."

They changed into scrubs, and then while Vinnie put on his moon suit and went into the autopsy room, Jack went through the contents of Nodelman's folder. It had a case work sheet, a partially completed death certificate, an inventory of medical-legal case records, two sheets for autopsy notes, a telephone notice of death as received that night by communications, a completed identification sheet, Janice's investigative report, a sheet for the autopsy report, and a lab slip for HIV antibody analysis.

Despite having spoken with Janice, Jack read her report carefully as he always did. When he was finished he went into the room next to the pine coffins and put on his moon suit. He took his ventilation unit from where it had been charging and hooked himself up. Then he set out for the autopsy room on the other side of the morgue.

Jack cursed the suit as he walked past most of the 126 refrigerated compartments for bodies. Being encased in the contraption put him in a bad mood, and he eyed his surroundings with a jaundiced eye. The morgue had been state of the art at one time, but it was now in need of repair and upgrading. With its aged, blue tile walls and stained cement floor it looked like a set for an old horror movie.

There was an entrance to the autopsy room directly from the hallway, but that wasn't used any longer except to bring bodies in and out. Instead Jack entered through a small anteroom with a washbasin.

By the time Jack entered the autopsy room Vinnie had Nodelman's body on one of the eight tables and had assembled all the equipment and paraphernalia necessary to do the case. Jack positioned himself on the patient's right, Vinnie on the left.

"He doesn't look so good," Jack said. "I don't think he's going to make it to the prom." It was hard to talk in the moon suit, and he was already perspiring.

Vinnie, who never quite knew how to react to Jack's

irreverent comments, didn't respond even though the corpse did look terrible.

"This is gangrene on his fingers," Jack said. He lifted one of the hands and examined the almost-black fingertips closely. Then he pointed to the man's shriveled genitals. "That's gangrene on the end of his penis. Ouch! That must have hurt. Can you imagine?"

Vinnie held his tongue.

Jack carefully examined every inch of the man's exterior. For Vinnie's benefit he pointed out the extensive subcutaneous hemorrhages on the man's abdomen and legs. He told him it was called purpura. Then Jack mentioned there were no obvious insect bites. "That's important," he added. "A lot of serious diseases are transmitted by arthropods."

"Arthropods?" Vinnie questioned. He never knew when Jack was joking.

"Insects," Jack said. "Crustaceans aren't much of a problem as disease vectors."

Vinnie nodded appreciatively, although he didn't know any more than he had when he'd asked the question. He made a mental note to try to remember to look up the meaning of "arthropods" when he had an opportunity.

"What are the chances whatever killed this man is contagious?" Vinnie asked.

"Excellent, I'm afraid," Jack said. "Excellent."

The door to the hallway opened and Sal D'Ambrosio, another mortuary tech, wheeled in another body. Totally absorbed in the external exam of Mr. Nodelman, Jack did not look up. He was already beginning to form a differential diagnosis.

A half hour later six of the eight tables were occupied

by corpses awaiting autopsies. One by one the other
medical examiners on duty that day began to arrive.
Laurie was first, and she came over to Jack's table.

"Any ideas yet?" she asked.

"Lots of ideas but nothing definitive," Jack said. "But
I can assure you this is one virulent organism. I was
teasing Vinnie earlier about its being Ebola. There's a
lot of disseminated intravascular coagulation."

"My God!" Laurie exclaimed. "Are you serious?"

"No, not really," Jack said. "But from what I've seen
so far it's still possible, just not probable. Of course
I've never seen a case of Ebola, so that should tell you
something."

"Do you think we ought to isolate this case?" Laurie
asked nervously.

"I can't see any reason to," Jack said. "Besides, I've
already started, and I'll be careful to avoid throwing any
of the organs around the room. But I'll tell you what
we should do: alert the lab to be mighty careful with
the specimens until we have a diagnosis."

"Maybe I'd better ask Bingham's opinion," Laurie
said.

"Oh, that would be helpful," Jack said sarcastically.
"Then we'll have the blind leading the blind."

"Don't be disrespectful," Laurie said. "He is the
chief."

"I don't care if he's the Pope," Jack said. "I think I
should just get it done, the sooner the better. If Bingham
or even Calvin gets involved it will drag on all morning."

"All right," Laurie said. "Maybe you're right. But let
me see any abnormality. I'll be on table three."

Laurie left to do her own case. Jack took a scalpel

from Vinnie and was about to make the incision when he noticed Vinnie had moved away.

"Where are you going to watch this from, Queens?" Jack asked. "You're supposed to be helping."

"I'm a little nervous," Vinnie admitted.

"Oh, come on, man," Jack said. "You've been at more autopsies than I have. Get your Italian ass over here. We've got work to do."

Jack worked quickly but smoothly. He handled the internal organs gently and was meticulously careful about the use of instruments when either his or Vinnie's hands were in the field.

"Whatcha got?" Chet McGovern asked, looking over Jack's shoulder. Chet was also an associate medical examiner, having been hired in the same month as Jack. Of all the colleagues he'd become the closest to Jack, since they shared both a common office and the social circumstance of being single males. But Chet had never been married and at thirty-six, he was five years Jack's junior.

"Something interesting," Jack said. "The mystery disease of the week. And it's a humdinger. This poor bastard didn't have a chance."

"Any ideas?" Chet asked. His trained eye took in the gangrene and the hemorrhages under the skin.

"I got a lot of ideas," Jack said. "But let me show you the internal, I'd appreciate your opinion."

"Is there something I should see?" Laurie called from table three. She'd noticed Jack conversing with Chet.

"Yeah, come on over," Jack said. "No use going through this more than once."

Laurie sent Sal to the sink to wash out the intestines on her case, then stepped over to table one.

"The first thing I want you to look at is the lymphatics

I dissected in the throat," Jack said. He had retracted the skin of the neck from the chin to the collarbone.

"No wonder autopsies take so long around here," a voice boomed in the confined space.

All eyes turned toward Dr. Calvin Washington, the deputy chief. He was an intimidating six-foot-seven, two-hundred-and-fifty-pound African-American man who'd passed up a chance to play NFL football to go to medical school.

"What the hell is going on around here?" he demanded half in jest. "What do you people think this is, a holiday?"

"Just pooling resources," Laurie said. "We've got an unknown infectious case that appears to be quite an aggressive microbe."

"So I heard," Calvin said. "I already got a call from the administrator over at the Manhattan General. He's justly concerned. What's the verdict?"

"A bit too soon to tell," Jack said. "But we've got a lot of pathology here."

Jack quickly summarized for Calvin what was known of the history and pointed out the positive findings on the external exam. Then he started back on the internal, indicating the spread of the disease along the lymphatics of the neck.

"Some of these nodes are necrotic," Calvin said.

"Exactly," Jack said. "In fact most of them are necrotic. The disease was spreading rapidly through the lymphatics, presumably from the throat and bronchial tree."

"Airborne, then," Calvin said.

"It would be my first guess," Jack admitted. "Now look at the internal organs."

Jack presented the lungs and opened the areas where he'd made slices.

"As you can see, this is pretty extensive lobar pneumonia," Jack said. "There's a lot of consolidation. But there is also some necrosis, and I believe early cavitation. If the patient had lived longer, I think we would be seeing some abscess formation."

Calvin whistled. "Wow," he said. "All this was happening in the face of massive IV antibiotics."

"It's worrisome," Jack agreed. He carefully slid the lungs back into the pan. He didn't want them sloshing around, potentially throwing infective particles into the air. Next he picked up the liver and gently separated its cut surface.

"Same process," he announced, pointing with his fingers to areas of early abscess formation. "Just not as extensive as with the lungs." Jack put the liver down and picked up the spleen. There were similar lesions throughout the organ. He made sure everyone saw them.

"So much for the gross," Jack said as he carefully replaced the spleen in the pan. "We'll have to see what the microscopic shows, but I actually think we'll be relying on the lab to give us the definitive answer."

"What's your guess at this point?" Calvin asked.

Jack let out a short laugh. "A guess it would have to be," he said. "I haven't seen anything pathognomonic yet. But its fulminant character should tell us something."

"What's your differential diagnosis?" Calvin asked. "Come on, Wonderboy, let's hear it."

"Ummmm," Jack said. "You're kinda putting me on the spot. But okay, I'll tell you what's been going

through my head. First, I don't think it could be pseudomonas as suspected at the hospital. It's too aggressive.
It could have been something atypical like strep group
A or even staph with toxic shock, but I kinda doubt it,
especially with the gram stain suggesting it was a bacillus.
So I'd have to say it is something like tularemia or
plague."

"Whoa!" Calvin exclaimed. "You're coming up with
some pretty arcane illnesses for what was apparently a
hospital-based infection. Haven't you heard the phrase
about when you hear hoofbeats you should think of
horses, not zebras?"

"I'm just telling you what's going through my mind.
It's just a differential diagnosis. I'm trying to keep an
open mind."

"All right," Calvin said soothingly. "Is that it?"

"No, that's not it," Jack said. "I'd also consider that
the gram stain could have been wrong and that would
let in not only strep and staph but meningococcemia as
well. And I might as well throw in Rocky Mountain
spotted fever and hantavirus. Hell, I could even throw
in the viral hemorrhagic fevers like Ebola."

"Now you're getting out in the stratosphere," Calvin
said. "Let's come back to reality. If I made you guess
which one it is right now with what you know, what
would you say?"

Jack clucked his tongue. He had the irritated feeling
he was being put back in medical school, and that Calvin,
like many of his medical-school professors, was trying to
make him look bad.

"Plague," Jack said to a stunned audience.

"Plague?" Calvin questioned with surprise bordering
on disdain. "In March? In New York City? In a

hospitalized patient? You got to be out of your mind."

"Hey, you asked me for one diagnosis," Jack said. "So I gave it to you. I wasn't responding by probabilities, just pathology."

"You weren't considering the other epidemiological aspects?" Calvin asked with obvious condescension. He laughed. Then, talking more to the others than Jack, he said: "What the hell did they teach you out there in the Chicago boonies?"

"There are too many unknowns in this case for me to put a lot of weight on unsubstantiated information," Jack said. "I didn't visit the site. I don't know anything about the deceased's pets, travel, or contact with visitors. There are a lot of people coming and going in this city, even in and out of a hospital. And there are certainly more than enough rats around here to support the diagnosis."

For a moment a heavy silence hung over the autopsy room. Neither Laurie nor Chet knew what to say. Jack's tone made them both uncomfortable, especially knowing Calvin's stormy temperament.

"A clever comment," Calvin said finally. "You're quite good at double entendre. I have to give you credit there. Perhaps that's part of pathology training in the Midwest."

Both Laurie and Chet laughed nervously.

"All right, smartass," Calvin continued. "How much are you willing to put on your diagnosis of plague?"

"I didn't know it was customary to gamble around here," Jack said.

"No, it's not common to gamble, but when you come

up with a diagnosis of plague, I think it's worthwhile to make a point of it. How about ten dollars?"

"I can afford ten dollars," Jack said.

"Fine," Calvin said. "With that settled, where's Paul Plodgett and that gunshot wound from the World Trade Center?"

"He's down on table six," Laurie said.

Calvin lumbered away and for a moment the others watched him. Laurie broke the silence. "Why do you try to provoke him?" she asked Jack. "I don't understand. You're making it more difficult for yourself."

"I can't help it," Jack said. "He provoked me!"

"Yeah, but he's the deputy chief and it's his prerogative," Chet said. "Besides, you were pushing things with a diagnosis of plague. It certainly wouldn't be on the top of my list."

"Are you sure?" Jack asked. "Look at the black fingers and toes on this patient. Remember, it was called the black death in the fourteenth century."

"A lot of diseases can cause such thrombotic phenomena," Chet said.

"True," Jack said. "That's why I almost said tularemia."

"And why didn't you?" Laurie asked. In her mind tularemia was equally improbable.

"I thought plague sounded better," Jack said. "It's more dramatic."

"I never know when you are serious," Laurie said.

"Hey, I feel the same way," Jack said.

Laurie shook her head in frustration. At times it was hard to have a serious discussion with Jack. "Anyway," she said, "are you finished with Nodelman? If you are, I've got another case for you."

"I haven't done the brain yet," Jack said.

"Then get to it," Laurie said. She walked back to table three to finish her own case.

CHAPTER TWO

Wednesday, 9:45 A.M., March 20, 1996
New York City

Terese Hagen stopped abruptly and looked at the closed door to the "cabin," the name given to the main conference room. It was called the cabin because the interior was a reproduction of Taylor Heath's Squam Lake house up in the wilds of New Hampshire. Taylor Heath was the CEO of the hot, up-and-coming advertising firm Willow and Heath, which was threatening to break into the rarefied ranks of the advertising big leagues.

After making sure she was not observed, Terese leaned toward the door and put her ear against it. She heard voices.

With her pulse quickening, Terese hurried down the hall to her own office. It never took long for her anxiety to soar. She'd only been in the office five minutes and already her heart was pounding. She didn't like the idea of a meeting she didn't know about being held in the cabin, the CEO's habitual domain. In her position as the creative director of the firm, she felt she had to know everything that was going on.

The problem was that a lot was going on. Taylor Heath had shocked everybody with his previous month's announcement that he planned to retire as CEO and was designating Brian Wilson, the current president, to succeed him. That left a big question mark about who would succeed Wilson. Terese was in the running. That was for sure. But so was Robert Barker, the firm's executive director of accounts. And on top of that, there was always the worry that Taylor would pick someone from outside.

Terese pulled off her coat and stuffed it into the closet. Her secretary, Marsha Devons, was on the phone so Terese dashed to her desk and scanned the surface for any telltale message; but there was nothing except a pile of unrelated phone messages.

"There's a meeting in the cabin," Marsha called from the other room after hanging up the phone. She appeared in the doorway. She was a petite woman with raven-black hair. Terese appreciated her because she was intelligent, efficient, and intuitive – all the qualities lacking in the year's previous four secretaries. Terese was tough on her assistants, since she expected commitment and performance equivalent to her own.

"Why didn't you call me at home?" Terese demanded.

"I did, but you'd already left," Marsha said.

"Who's at the meeting?" Terese barked.

"It was Mr. Heath's secretary who called," Marsha said. "She didn't say who would be attending. Just that your presence was requested."

"Was there any indication what the meeting is about?" Terese asked.

"No," Marsha said simply.

"When did it start?"

"The call came through at nine," Marsha said.

Terese snatched up her phone and punched in Colleen Anderson's number. Colleen was Terese's most trusted art director. She was currently heading up a team for the National Health Care account.

"You know anything about this meeting in the cabin?" Terese asked as soon as Colleen was on the line.

Colleen didn't, only that it was going on.

"Damn!" Terese said as she hung up.

"Is there a problem?" Marsha asked solicitously.

"If Robert Barker has been in there all this time with Taylor, there's a problem," Terese said. "That prick never misses a beat to put me down."

Terese snatched the phone again and redialed Colleen. "What's the status on National Health? Do we have any comps or anything I can show right now?"

"I'm afraid not," Colleen said. "We've been brainstorming, but we don't have anything zippy like I know you want. I'm looking for a home run."

"Well, goose your team," Terese said. "I have a sneaking suspicion I'm most vulnerable with National Health."

"No one's been sleeping down here," Colleen said. "I can assure you of that."

Terese hung up without saying good-bye. Snatching up her purse, she ran down the hall to the ladies' room and positioned herself in front of the mirror. She pushed her Medusa's head of highlighted tight curls into a semblance of order, then reapplied some lipstick and a bit of blush.

Stepping back, she surveyed herself. Luckily she'd chosen to wear one of her favorite suits. It was dark blue wool gabardine and seriously severe, hugging her narrow frame like a second skin.

Satisfied with her appearance, Terese hustled to the cabin door. After a deep breath she grasped the knob, turned it, and entered.

"Ah, Miss Hagen," Brian Wilson said, glancing at his

watch. He was sitting at the head of a rough-hewn plank table that dominated the room. "I see you're now indulging in banker's hours."

Brian was a short man with thinning hair. He vainly tried to camouflage his bald spot by combing his side hair over it. As per usual he was attired in a white shirt and tie, loosened at the neck, giving him the appearance of a harried newspaper publisher. To complete the journalistic look, his sleeves were rolled up above his elbows and a yellow Dixon pencil was tucked behind his right ear.

Despite the catty comment, Terese liked and respected Brian. He was an able administrator. He had a patented derogatory style, but he was equally demanding of himself.

"I was in the office last night until one a.m.," Terese said. "I certainly would have been here for this meeting if someone had been kind enough to let me know about it."

"It was an impromptu meeting," Taylor called out. He was standing near the window, in keeping with his laissez-faire management style. He preferred to hover above the group like an Olympian god, watching his demigods and mere mortals hammer out decisions.

Taylor and Brian were opposite in most ways. Where Brian was short, Taylor was tall. Where Brian was balding, Taylor had a dense halo of silver-gray hair. Where Brian appeared as the harried newspaper columnist always with his back against the wall, Taylor was the picture of sophisticated tranquillity and sartorial splendor. Yet no one doubted Taylor's encyclopedic grasp of the business and his uncanny ability to maintain strategic goals in the face of daily tactical disaster and controversy.

Terese took a seat at the table directly across from her nemesis, Robert Barker. He was a tall, thin-faced man with narrow lips who seemed to take a cue from Taylor in regard to his dress. He was always attired nattily in dark silk suits and colorful silk ties. The ties were his trademark. Terese could not remember ever having seen the same tie twice.

Next to Robert was Helen Robinson, whose presence made Terese's racing heart beat even a little faster. Helen worked under Robert as the account executive assigned specifically to National Health. She was a strikingly attractive twenty-five-year-old woman with long, chestnut-colored hair that cascaded to her shoulders, tanned skin even in March, and full, sensuous features. Between her intelligence and looks she was a formidable adversary.

Also sitting at the table was Phil Atkins, the chief financial officer, and Carlene Desalvo, the corporate director of account planning. Phil was an impeccably precise man with his perennial three-piece suit and wire-rimmed glasses. Carlene was a bright, full-figured woman who always dressed in white. Terese was mildly surprised to see both of them at the meeting.

"We've got a big problem with the National Health account," Brian said. "That's why this meeting was called."

Terese's mouth went dry. She glanced at Robert and detected a slight but infuriating smile. Terese wished to God she'd been there since the beginning of the meeting so she could have known everything that had been said.

Terese was aware of trouble with National Health. The company had called for an internal review a month ago, which meant that Willow and Heath had to come up with a new advertising campaign if they expected to keep the account. And everybody knew they had to keep the account. It had mushroomed to somewhere around forty million annually and was still growing. Health-care advertising was in the ascendancy, and would hopefully fill the hole vacated by cigarettes.

Brian turned to Robert. "Perhaps you could fill Terese in on the latest developments," he said.

"I defer to my able assistant, Helen," Robert said, giving Terese one of his condescending smiles.

Helen moved forward in her seat. "As you know, National Health has had misgivings about its advertising campaign. Unfortunately their displeasure has increased. Just yesterday their figures came in for the last open subscriber period. The results weren't good. Their loss of market share to AmeriCare in the New York metropolitan area has increased. After building the new hospital, this is a terrible blow."

"And they blame our ad campaign for that?" Terese blurted out. "That's absurd. They only made a twenty-five-point buy with our sixty-second commercial. That was not adequate. No way."

"That may be your opinion," Helen said evenly. "But I know it is not National Health's."

"I know you are fond of your 'Health care for the modern era' campaign, and it is a good tag line," Robert said, "but the fact of the matter is that National Health has been losing market share from the campaign's inception. These latest figures are just consistent with the previous trend."

"The sixty-second spot has been nominated for a Clio," Terese countered. "It's a damn good commercial. It's wonderfully creative. I'm proud of my team for having put it together."

"And indeed you should be," Brian interjected. "But it is Robert's feeling that the client is not interested in our winning a Clio. And remember, as the Benton and Bowles agency held, 'If it doesn't sell, it isn't creative.' "

"That's equally absurd," Terese snapped. "The campaign is solid. It's just that the account people couldn't get the client to buy adequate exposure. There should have been 'flights' on multiple local stations at a bare minimum."

"With all due respect, they would have bought more time if they'd liked the commercial," Robert said. "I don't think they were ever sold on the idea of 'them versus us,' ancient medicine versus modern medicine. I mean it was humorous, but I don't know if they were convinced the viewer truly associated the ancient methods with National Health Care's competitors, particularly AmeriCare. My personal opinion is that it went over people's heads."

"Your real point is that National Health Care has a very specific type of advertising it wants," Brian said. "Tell Terese what you told me just before she came in here."

"It's simple," Robert said, making an open gesture with his hands. "They want either 'talking heads' discussing actual patient experiences, or a celebrity spokesperson. They couldn't care less whether their ad wins a Clio or any of the other awards. They want results. They want market share, and I want to give it to them."

"Am I hearing that Willow and Heath wants to turn its back on its successes and become a mere vendor shop?" Terese asked. "We're on the edge of becoming one of the big-league firms. And how did we get here? We got here by doing quality advertising. We've carried on in the Doyle-Dane-Bernback tradition. If we start letting clients dictate that we turn out slop, we're doomed."

"What I'm hearing is the usual conflict between the account executive and the creative," Taylor said, interrupting the increasingly heated discussion. "Robert, you think Terese is this self-indulgent child who is bent on alienating the client. Terese, you think Robert is this shortsighted pragmatist who wants to throw out the baby with the bathwater. The trouble is you are both right and both wrong at the same time. You have to use each other as a team. Stop arguing and deal with the problem at hand."

For a moment everyone was quiet. Zeus had spoken and everyone knew he was on target as usual.

"All right," Brian said finally. "Here's our reality. National Health is a vital client to our long-term stability. Thirty-odd days ago it asked for an internal review, which we expected in a couple of months. They now have told us they want it next week."

"Next week!" Terese all but shouted. "My God." It took months to put together a new campaign and pitch it.

"I know that will put the creatives under a lot of pressure," Brian said. "But the reality is National Health is the boss. The problem is that after our pitch, if they are not satisfied, they'll set up an outside review. The account will then be up for grabs, and I don't have to remind you that these health-care giants are going to be the advertising cash cows of the next decade. All the agencies are interested."

"As chief financial officer I think I should make it clear what the loss of the National Health account would do to our bottom line," Phil Atkins said. "We'll have to put off the restructuring because we won't have the funds to buy back our junk bonds."

"Obviously it is in all our best interests that we do not lose the account," Brian said.

"I don't know if it is possible to put together a pitch for next week," Terese said.

"You have anything you can show us at the moment?" Brian asked.

Terese shook her head.

"You must have something," Robert said. "I assume you have a team working on it." The smile had returned to the corners of his mouth.

"Of course we have a team on National Health," Terese said. 'But we haven't had any 'big ideas' to date. Obviously we thought we had several more months."

"Perhaps you might assign some additional personnel," Brian said. "But I'll leave that up to your judgment." Then to the rest of the group he said: "For now we'll adjourn this meeting until we have something from Creative to look at." He stood up. Everybody else did the same.

Dazed, Terese stumbled out of the cabin and descended to the agency's main studio on the floor below.

Willow and Heath had reversed a trend that began during the seventies and eighties when New York advertising firms had experienced a diaspora to varying chic sections of the city like TriBeCa and Chelsea. The agency returned to the old stamping ground of Madison Avenue, taking over several floors of a modest-sized building.

Terese found Colleen at her drawing board.

"What's the scoop?" Colleen asked. "You look pale."

"Trouble!" Terese exclaimed.

Colleen had been Terese's first hire. She was her most reliable art director. They got along famously both professionally and socially. Colleen was a milky-white-skinned strawberry blonde with a smattering of pale freckles over an upturned nose. Her eyes were a deep blue, a much stronger hue than Terese's. She favored oversized sweatshirts that somehow seemed to accentuate rather than hide her enviable figure.

"Let me guess," Colleen said. "Has National Health pushed up the deadline for the review?"

"How'd you know?"

"Intuition," Colleen said. "When you said 'trouble,' that's the worst thing I could think of."

"The Robert-and-Helen sideshow brought information that National Health has lost more market share to AmeriCare despite our campaign."

"Damn!" Colleen said. "It's a good campaign and a great sixty-second commercial."

"You know it and I know it," Terese said. "Problem is that it wasn't shown enough. I have an uncomfortable suspicion that Helen undermined us and talked them out of the two-hundred- to three-hundred-point TV commercial buy they had initially intended to make. That would have been saturation. I know it would have worked."

"I thought you told me you had pulled out the stops to guarantee National Health's market share would go up," Colleen said.

"I did," Terese said. "I've done everything I could think of and then some. I mean, it's my best sixty-second spot. You told me yourself."

Terese rubbed her forehead. She was getting a headache. She could still feel her pulse clanging away at her
temples.

"You might as well tell me the bad news," Colleen
said. She put down her drawing pencil and swung around
to face Terese. "What's the new time frame?"

"National Health wants us to pitch a new campaign
next week."

"Good Lord!" Colleen said.

"What do we have so far?" Terese asked.

"Not a lot."

"You must have some tissues or some preliminary
executions," Terese said. "I know I haven't been giving
you any attention lately since we've had deadlines with
three other clients. But you have had a team working
on this for almost a month."

"We've been having strategy session after strategy session," Colleen said. "A lot of brainstorming, but no big
idea. Nothing's jumped out and grabbed us. I mean, I
have a sense of what you are looking for."

"Well, I want to see what you have," Terese said. "I
don't care how sketchy or preliminary. I want to see
what the team has been doing. I want to see it today."

"All right," Colleen said without enthusiasm. "I'll get
everybody together."

CHAPTER THREE

Susanne Hard had never liked hospitals.

A scoliotic back had kept her in and out of them as a child. Hospitals made her nervous. She hated the sense that she was not in control and that she was surrounded by the sick and the dying.

Susanne was a firm believer in the adage If something can go wrong, it will go wrong. She felt this way particularly in relation to hospitals. Indeed, on her last admission, she'd been carted off to urology to face some frightful procedure before she'd finally been able to convince a reluctant technician to read the name on her wristband. They'd had the wrong patient.

On her present admission Susanne wasn't sick. The previous night her labor had started with her second child. In addition to her back problem, her pelvis was distorted, making a normal vaginal delivery impossible. As with her first child, she had to have a cesarean section.

Since she'd just undergone abdominal surgery, her doctor insisted that she stay at least a few days. No amount of cajoling on Susanne's part had been successful in convincing the doctor otherwise.

Susanne tried to relax by wondering what kind of child she'd just birthed. Would he be like his brother, Allen, who had been a wonderful baby? Allen had slept through the night almost from day one. He'd been a delight, and now that he was three and already exerting independence, Susanne was looking forward to a new baby. She thought of herself as a natural mother.

With a start, Susanne awoke. She'd surprised herself by nodding off. What had awakened her was a white-clad figure fiddling with the IV bottles that hung from a pole at the head of her bed.

"What are you doing?" Susanne asked. She felt paranoid about anybody doing anything she didn't know about.

"Sorry to have awakened you, Mrs. Hard," a nurse said. "I was just hanging up a new bottle of fluid. Yours is just about out."

Susanne glanced at the IV snaking into the back of her hand. As an experienced hospital patient, she suggested that it was time for the IV to come out.

"Maybe I should check on that," the nurse said. She then waltzed out of the room.

Tilting her head back, Susanne looked at the IV bottle to see what it was. It was upside down, so she couldn't read the label.

She started to turn over, but a sharp pain reminded her of her recently sutured incision. She decided to stay on her back.

Gingerly she took a deep breath. She didn't feel any discomfort until right at the end of the inspiration.

Closing her eyes, Susanne tried again to calm down. She knew that she still had a significant amount of drugs "on board" from the anesthesia, so sleep should be easy. The trouble was, she didn't know if she wanted to be asleep with so many people coming in and out of her room.

A very soft clank of plastic hitting plastic drifted out of the background noise of the hospital and caught Susanne's attention. Her eyes blinked open. She saw an orderly off to the side by the bureau.

"Excuse me," Susanne called.

The man turned around. He was a handsome fellow in a white coat over scrubs. From where he was standing, Susanne could not read his name tag. He appeared surprised to be addressed.

"I hope I didn't disturb you, ma'am," the young man said.

"Everybody is disturbing me," Susanne said without malice. "It's like Grand Central Station in here."

"I'm terribly sorry," the man said. "I can always return later if it would be more convenient."

"What are you doing?" Susanne asked.

"Just filling your humidifier," the man said.

"What do I have a humidifier for?" Susanne said. "I didn't have one after my last cesarean."

"The anesthesiologists frequently order them this time of year," the man said. "Right after surgery, patients' throats are often irritated from the endotracheal tube. It's usually helpful to use a humidifier for the first day or even the first few hours. In what month did you have your last cesarean?"

"May," Susanne said.

"That's probably the reason you didn't have one then," the man said. "Would you like me to return?"

"Do what you have to do," Susanne said.

No sooner had the man left than the original nurse

returned. "You were right," she said. "The orders were to pull the IV as soon as the bottle was through."

Susanne merely nodded. She felt like asking the nurse if missing orders was something she did on a regular basis. Susanne sighed. She wanted out of there.

After the nurse had removed the IV, Susanne managed to calm herself enough to fall back asleep. But it didn't last long. Someone was nudging her arm.

Susanne opened her eyes and looked into the face of another smiling nurse. In the foreground and between them was a five-cc syringe.

"I've got something for you," the nurse said as if Susanne were a toddler and the syringe candy.

"What is it?" Susanne demanded. She instinctively pulled away.

"It's the pain shot you requested," the nurse said. "So roll over and I'll give it to you."

"I didn't request a pain shot," Susanne said.

"But of course you did," the nurse said.

"But I didn't," Susanne said.

The nurse's expression changed to exasperation like a cloud passing over the sun. "Well then, it's doctor's orders. You are supposed to have a pain shot every six hours."

"But I don't have much pain," Susanne said. "Only when I move or breathe deeply."

"There you are," the nurse said. "You have to breathe deeply, otherwise you'll get pneumonia. Come on now, be a good girl."

Susanne thought for a moment. On the one hand she felt like being contrary. On the other hand she wanted to be taken care of and there was nothing inherently wrong with a pain shot. It might even make her sleep better.

"Okay," Susanne said.

Gritting her teeth, she managed to roll to the side as the nurse bared her bottom.

CHAPTER FOUR

Wednesday, 2:05 P.M., March 20, 1996

"You know, Laurie's right," Chet McGovern said.

Chet and Jack were sitting in the narrow office they shared on the fifth floor of the medical examiner's building. They both had their feet up on their respective gray metal desks. They'd finished their autopsies for the day, eaten lunch, and were now supposedly doing their paperwork.

"Of course she's right," Jack agreed.

"But if you know that, why do you provoke Calvin? It's not rational. You're not doing yourself any favors. It's going to affect your promotion up through the system."

"I don't want to rise up in the system," Jack said.

"Come again?" Chet asked. In the grand scheme of medicine, the concept of not wanting to get ahead was heresy.

Jack let his feet fall off the desk and thump onto the floor. He stood up, stretched, and yawned loudly. Jack was a stocky, six-foot man accustomed to serious physical activity. He found that standing at the autopsy table and sitting at a desk tended to cause his muscles to cramp, particularly his quadriceps.

"I'm happy being a low man on the totem pole," Jack said, cracking his knuckles.

"You don't want to become board certified?" Chet asked with surprise.

"Ah, of course I want to be board certified," Jack said. "But that's not the same issue. As far as I'm concerned, becoming board certified is a personal thing. What I don't care about is having supervisory responsibility. I just want to do forensic pathology. To hell with bureaucracy and red tape."

"Jesus," Chet remarked, letting his own feet fall to the floor. "Every time I think I get to know you a little, you throw me a curveball. I mean, we've been sharing this office for almost five months. You're still a mystery. I don't even know where the hell you live."

"I didn't know you cared," Jack teased.

"Come on," Chet said. "You know what I mean."

"I live on the Upper West Side," Jack said. "It's no secret."

"In the seventies?" Chet asked.

"A bit higher," Jack said.

"Eighties?"

"Higher."

"You're not going to tell me higher than the nineties, are you?" Chet asked.

"A tad," Jack said. "I live on a Hundred and Sixth Street."

"Good grief," Chet exclaimed. "You're living in Harlem."

Jack shrugged. He sat down at his desk and pulled out one of his unfinished files. "What's in a name?" he said.

"Why in the world live in Harlem?" Chet asked. "Of all the neat places to live in and around the city, why live there? It can't be a nice neighborhood. Besides, it must be dangerous."

"I don't see it that way," Jack said. "Plus there are a lot of playgrounds in the area and a particularly good one right next door. I'm kind of a pickup basketball nut."

"Now I know you are crazy," Chet said. "Those playgrounds and those pickup games are controlled by neighborhood gangs. That's like having a death wish. I'm afraid we might see you in here on one of the slabs even without the mountain bike heroics."

"I haven't had any trouble," Jack said. "After all, I paid for new back-boards and lights and I buy the balls. The neighborhood gang is actually quite appreciative and even solicitous."

Chet eyed his officemate with a touch of awe. He tried to imagine what Jack would look like out running around on a Harlem neighborhood blacktop. He imagined Jack would certainly stand out racially with his light brown hair cut in a peculiar Julius Caesar-like shag. Chet wondered if any of the other players had any idea about Jack, like the fact that he was a doctor. But then Chet acknowledged that he didn't know much more.

"What did you do before you went to medical school?" Chet asked.

"I went to college," Jack said. "Like most people who went to medical school. Don't tell me you didn't go to college."

"Of course I went to college," Chet said. "Calvin is right: you are a smartass. You know what I mean. If you just finished a pathology residency, what did you do in the interim?" Chet had wanted to ask the question for months, but there had never been an opportune moment.

"I became an ophthalmologist," Jack said. "I even had a practice out in Champaign, Illinois. I was a conventional, conservative suburbanite."

"Yeah, sure, just like I was a Buddhist monk." Chet laughed. "I mean I suppose I can see you as an ophthalmologist. After all, I was an emergency-room physician for a few years until I saw the light. But you conservative? No way."

"I was," Jack insisted. "And my name was John, not Jack. Of course, you wouldn't have recognized me. I was heavier. I also had longer hair, and I parted it along the right side of my head the way I did in high school. And as far as dress was concerned, I favored glen-plaid suits."

"What happened?" Chet asked. Chet glanced at Jack's black jeans, blue sports shirt, and dark blue knitted tie.

A knock on the doorjamb caught both Jack's and Chet's attention. They turned to see Agnes Finn, head of the micro lab, standing in the doorway. She was a small, serious woman with thick glasses and stringy hair.

"We just got something a little surprising," she said to Jack. She was clutching a sheet of paper in her hand. She hesitated on the threshold. Her dour expression didn't change.

"Are you going to make us guess or what?" Jack asked. His curiosity had been titillated, since Agnes did not make it a point to deliver lab results.

Agnes pushed her glasses higher onto her nose and handed Jack the paper. "It's the fluorescein antibody screen you requested on Nodelman."

"My word," Jack said after glancing at the page. He handed it to Chet.

Chet looked at the paper and then leaped to his feet. "Holy crap!" he exclaimed. "Nodelman had the god-damn plague!"

"Obviously we were taken aback by the result," Agnes said in her usual monotone. "Is there anything else you want us to do?"

Jack pinched his lower lip while he thought. "Let's try to culture some of the incipient abscesses," he said. "And let's try some of the usual stains. What's recommended for plague?"

"Giemsa's or Wayson's," Agnes said. "They usually make it possible to see the typical bipolar 'safety pin' morphology."

"Okay, let's do that," Jack said. "Of course, the most important thing is to grow the bug. Until we do that, the case is only presumptive plague."

"I understand," Agnes said. She started from the room.

"I guess I don't have to warn you to be careful," Jack said.

"No need," Agnes assured him. "We have a class-three hood, and I intend to use it."

"This is incredible," Chet said when they were alone. "How the hell did you know?"

"I didn't," Jack said. "Calvin forced me to make a diagnosis. To tell the truth, I thought I was being facetious. Of course, the signs were all consistent, but I still didn't imagine I had a snowball's chance in hell of being right. But now that I am, it's no laughing matter. The only positive aspect is that I win that ten dollars from Calvin."

"He's going to hate you for that," Chet said.

"That's the least of my worries," Jack said. "I'm stunned. A case of pneumonic plague in March in New York City, supposedly contracted in a hospital! Of course, that can't be true unless the Manhattan General is supporting a horde of infected rats and their fleas. Nodelman had to have had contact with some sort of infected animal. It's my guess he was traveling recently." Jack snatched up the phone.

"Who are you calling?" Chet asked.

"Bingham, of course," Jack said as he punched the numbers. "There can't be any delay. This is a hot potato I want out of my hands."

Mrs. Sanford picked up the extension but informed Chet that Dr. Bingham was at City Hall and would be all day. He had left specific instructions he was not to be bothered since he'd be closeted with the mayor.

"So much for our chief," Jack said. Without putting down the receiver, he dialed Calvin's number. He didn't have any better luck. Calvin's secretary told him that Calvin had had to leave for the day. There was an illness in the family.

Jack hung up the phone and drummed his fingers on the surface of the desk.

"No luck?" Chet asked.

"The entire general staff is indisposed," Jack said. "We grunts are on our own." Jack suddenly pushed back his chair, got up, and started out of the office.

Chet bounded out of his own chair and followed. "Where are you going?" he asked. He had to run to catch up with Jack.

"Down to talk to Bart Arnold," Jack said. He got to the elevator and hit the Down button. "I need more .

information. Somebody has to figure out where this plague came from or this city's in for some trouble."

"Hadn't you better wait for Bingham?" Chet asked. "That look in your eye disturbs me."

"I didn't know I was so transparent," Jack said with a laugh. "I guess this incident has caught my interest. It's got me excited."

The elevator door opened and Jack got on. Chet held the door from closing. "Jack, do me a favor and be careful. I like sharing the office with you. Don't ruffle too many feathers."

"Me?" Jack questioned innocently. "I'm Mister Diplomacy."

"And I'm Muammar el Qaddafi," Chet said. He let the elevator door slide closed.

Jack hummed a perky tune while the elevator descended. He was definitely keyed up, and he was enjoying himself. He smiled when he remembered telling Laurie that he'd hoped Nodelman turned out to have something with serious institutional consequences like Legionnaires' disease so he could give AmeriCare some heartburn. Plague was ten times better. And on top of sticking it to AmeriCare, he'd have the pleasure of collecting his ten bucks from Calvin.

Jack exited on the first floor and went directly to Bart Arnold's office. Bart was the chief of the PAs, or physician's assistants. Jack was pleased to catch him at his desk.

"We've got a presumptive diagnosis of plague. I've got to talk with Janice Jaeger right away," Jack said.

"She'll be sleeping," Bart said. "Can't it wait?"

"No," Jack said.

"Bingham or Calvin know about this?" Bart asked.

"Both are out, and I don't know when they'll be back," Jack said.

Bart hesitated a moment, then opened up the side drawer of his desk. After looking up Janice's number, he made the call. When she was on the line, he apologized for having awakened her and explained that Dr. Stapleton needed to speak with her. He handed the phone to Jack.

Jack apologized as well and then told her about the results on Nodelman. Any sign of sleepiness in Janice's voice disappeared instantly.

"What can I do to help?" she asked.

"Did you find any reference to travel in any of the hospital records?" Jack asked.

"Not that I recall," Janice said.

"Any reference to contact with pets or wild animals?" Jack asked.

"Negative," Janice said. "But I can go back there tonight. Those questions were never specifically asked."

Jack thanked her and told her that he'd be looking into it himself. He handed the phone back to Bart and hurried back to his own office.

Chet looked up as Jack dashed in. "Learn anything?" he asked.

"Not a thing," Jack said happily. He pulled out Nodelman's folder and rapidly shuffled through the pages until he found the completed identification sheet. On it were phone numbers for the next of kin. With his index finger marking Nodelman's wife's number, Jack made the call. It was an exchange in the Bronx.

Mrs. Nodelman answered on the second ring.

"I'm Dr. Stapleton," Jack said. "I'm a medical examiner for the City of New York."

At that point Jack had to explain the role of a medical

examiner, because even the archaic term "coroner" didn't register with Mrs. Nodelman.

"I'd like to ask you a few questions," Jack said once Mrs. Nodelman understood who he was.

"It was so sudden," Mrs. Nodelman said. She had started to cry. "He had diabetes, that's true. But he wasn't supposed to die."

"I'm very sorry for your loss," Jack said. "But did your late husband do any recent traveling?"

"He went to New Jersey a week or so ago," Mrs. Nodelman said. Jack could hear her blow her nose.

"I was thinking of travel to more distant destinations," Jack said. "Like to the Southwest or maybe India."

"Just to Manhattan every day," Mrs. Nodelman said.

"How about a visitor from some exotic locale?" Jack asked.

"Donald's aunt visited in December," Mrs. Nodelman said.

"And where is she from?"

"Queens," Mrs. Nodelman said.

"Queens," Jack repeated. "That's not quite what I had in mind. How about contact with any wild animals? Like rabbits."

"No," Mrs. Nodelman said. "Donald hated rabbits."

"How about pets?" Jack asked.

"We have a cat," Mrs. Nodelman said.

"Is the cat sick?" Jack asked. "Or has the cat brought home any rodents?"

"The cat is fine," Mrs. Nodelman said. "She's a house cat and never goes outside."

"How about rats?" Jack asked. "Do you see many

rats around your house? Have you seen any dead ones lately?"

"We don't have any rats," Mrs. Nodelman said indignantly. "We live in a nice, clean apartment."

Jack tried to think of something else to ask, but for the moment nothing came to mind. "Mrs. Nodelman," he said, "you've been most kind. The reason I'm asking you these questions is because we have reason to believe that your husband died of a serious infectious disease. We think he died of plague."

There was a brief silence.

"You mean bubonic plague like they had in Europe long ago?" Mrs. Nodelman asked.

"Sort of," Jack said. "Plague comes in two clinical forms, bubonic and pneumonic. Your husband seems to have had the pneumonic form, which happens to be the more contagious. I would advise you to go to your doctor and inform him of your potential exposure. I'm sure he'll want you to take some precautionary antibiotics. I would also advise you to take your pet to your vet and tell him the same thing."

"Is this serious?" Mrs. Nodelman asked.

"It's very serious," Jack said. He then gave her his phone number in case she had any questions later. He also asked her to call him if the vet found anything suspicious with the cat.

Jack hung up the phone and turned to Chet. "The mystery is deepening," he said. Then he added cheerfully: "AmeriCare is going to have some severe indigestion over this."

"There's that facial expression again that scares me," Chet said.

Jack laughed, got up, and started out of the room.

"Where are you going now?" Chet asked nervously.

"To tell Laurie Montgomery what's going on," Jack said. "She's supposed to be our supervisor for today. She has to be apprised."

A few minutes later Jack returned.

"What'd she say?" Chet asked.

"She was as stunned as we were," Jack said. He grabbed the phone directory before taking his seat. He flipped open the pages to the city listings.

"Did she want you to do anything in particular?" Chet asked.

"No," Jack said. "She told me to tread water until Bingham is informed. In fact she tried to call our illustrious chief, but he's still incommunicado with the mayor."

Jack picked up the phone and dialed.

"Who are you calling now?" Chet asked.

"The Commissioner of Health, Patricia Markham," Jack said. "I ain't waiting."

"Good grief!" Chet exclaimed, rolling his eyes. "Hadn't you better let Bingham do that? You'll be calling his boss behind his back."

Jack didn't respond. He was busy giving his name to the commissioner's secretary. When she told him to hold on, he covered the mouthpiece with his hand and whispered to Chet: "Surprise, surprise, she's in!"

"I guarantee Bingham is not going to like this," Chet whispered back.

Jack held up his hand to silence Chet. "Hello, Commissioner," Jack said into the phone. "Howya doing. This is Jack Stapleton here, from over at the ME's office."

Chet winced at Jack's breezy informality.

"Sorry to spoil your day," Jack continued, "but I felt

I had to call. Dr. Bingham and Dr. Washington are momentarily unavailable and a situation has developed that I believe you should know about. We've just made a presumptive diagnosis of plague in a patient from Manhattan General Hospital."

"Good Lord!" Dr. Markham exclaimed loud enough for Chet to hear. "That's frightening, but only one case, I trust."

"So far," Jack said.

"All right, I'll alert the City Board of Health," Dr. Markham said. "They'll take over and contact the CDC. Thanks for the warning. What was your name again?"

"Stapleton," Jack said. "Jack Stapleton."

Jack hung up with a self-satisfied smile on his lips. "Maybe you should sell short your AmeriCare stock," he told Chet. "The Commissioner sounds concerned."

"Maybe you'd better brush up on your résumé," Chet said. "Bingham is going to be pissed."

Jack whistled while he leafed through Nodelman's file until he came up with the investigative report. Once he had located the name of the attending physician, Dr. Carl Wainwright, he wrote it down. Then he got up and put on his leather bomber jacket.

"Uh oh," Chet said. "Now what?"

"I'm going over to the Manhattan General," Jack said. "I think I'll make a site visit. This case is too important to leave up to the generals."

Chet swung around in his chair as Jack went through the door.

"Of course, you know that Bingham doesn't encourage us MEs doing site work," Chet said. "You'll be adding insult to injury."

"I'll take my chances," Jack said. "Where I was trained it was considered necessary."

"Bingham thinks it's the job of the PAs," Chet said. "He's told us that time and again."

"This case is too interesting for me to pass up," Jack called from down the hall. "Hold down the fort. I won't be long."

CHAPTER FIVE

Wednesday, 2:50 P.M., March 20, 1996

It was overcast and threatening rain, but Jack didn't mind. Regardless of the weather, the vigorous bike ride uptown to the Manhattan General was a pleasure after having stood all morning in the autopsy room imprisoned inside his moon suit.

Near the hospital's front entrance Jack located a sturdy street sign to lock his mountain bike to. He even locked up his helmet and bomber jacket with a separate wire lock that also secured the seat.

Standing within the shadow of the hospital, Jack glanced up at its soaring facade. It had been an old, respected, university-affiliated, proprietary hospital in its previous life. AmeriCare had gobbled it up during the fiscally difficult times the government had unwittingly created in health care in the early 1990s. Although Jack knew revenge was far from a noble emotion, he savored the knowledge that he was about to hand AmeriCare a public relations bomb.

Inside Jack went to the information booth and asked about Dr. Carl Wainwright. He learned that the man was an AmeriCare internist whose office was in the attached professional building. The receptionist gave Jack careful directions.

Fifteen minutes later, Jack was in the man's waiting

room. After Jack flashed his medical examiner's badge, which looked for all intents and purposes like a police badge, the receptionist wasted no time in letting Dr. Wainwright know he was there. Jack was immediately shown into the doctor's private office, and within minutes the doctor himself appeared.

Dr. Carl Wainwright was prematurely white-haired and slightly stooped over. His face, however, was youthful with bright blue eyes. He shook hands with Jack and motioned for him to sit down.

"It's not every day we're visited by someone from the medical examiner's office," Dr. Wainwright said.

"I'd be concerned if it were," Jack said.

Dr. Wainwright looked confused until he realized Jack was kidding. Dr. Wainwright tittered. "Right you are," he said.

"I've come about your patient Donald Nodelman," Jack said, getting right to the point. "We have a presumptive diagnosis of plague."

Dr. Wainwright's mouth dropped open. "That's impossible," he said when he'd recovered enough to speak.

Jack shrugged. "I guess it's not," he said. "Fluorescein antibody for plague is quite reliable. Of course, we haven't yet grown it out."

"My goodness," Dr. Wainwright managed. He rubbed a nervous palm across his face. "What a shock."

"It is surprising," Jack agreed. "Especially since the patient had been in the hospital for five days before his symptoms started."

"I've never heard of nosocomial plague," Dr. Wainwright said.

"Nor have I," Jack said. "But it was pneumonic

plague, not bubonic, and as you know the incubation period is shorter for pneumonic, probably only two to three days."

"I still can't believe it," Dr. Wainwright said. "Plague never entered my thoughts."

"Anybody else sick with similar symptoms?" Jack asked.

"Not that I know of," Dr. Wainwright said, "but you can rest assured that we will find out immediately."

"I'm curious about this man's lifestyle," Jack said. "His wife denied any recent travel or visitors from areas endemic to plague. She also doubted he'd come in contact with wild animals. Is that your understanding as well?"

"The patient worked in the garment district," Dr. Wainwright said. "He did bookkeeping. He never traveled. He wasn't a hunter. I'd been seeing him frequently over the last month, trying to get his diabetes under control."

"Where was he in the hospital?" Jack asked.

"On the medical ward on the seventh floor," Dr. Wainwright said. "Room seven-oh-seven. I remember the number specifically."

"Single room?" Jack asked.

"All our rooms are singles," Dr. Wainwright said.

"That's a help," Jack said. "Can I see the room?"

"Of course," Dr. Wainwright said. "But I think I should call Dr. Mary Zimmerman, who's our infection-control officer. She's got to know about this immediately."

"By all means," Jack said. "Meanwhile, would you mind if I went up to the seventh floor and looked around?"

"Please," Dr. Wainwright said as he gestured toward the door. "I'll call Dr. Zimmerman and we'll meet you up there." He reached for the phone.

Jack retraced his route back to the main hospital building. He took the elevator to the seventh floor, which he found was divided by the elevator lobby into two wings. The north wing housed internal medicine while the south wing was reserved for OB-GYN. Jack pushed through the doors that led into the internal-medicine division.

As soon as the swinging door closed behind Jack, he knew that word of the contagion had arrived. A nervous bustle was apparent, and all the personnel were wearing newly distributed masks. Obviously Wainwright had wasted no time.

No one paid Jack any attention as he wandered down to room 707. Pausing at the door, Jack watched as two masked orderlies wheeled out a masked and confused patient clutching her belongings who was apparently being transferred. As soon as they were gone, Jack walked in.

Seven-oh-seven was a nondescript hospital room of modern design; the interior of the old hospital had been renovated in the not-too-distant past. The metal furniture was typical hospital issue and included a bed, a bureau, a vinyl-covered chair, a night table, and a variable-height bed table. A TV hung from an arm attached to the ceiling.

The air-conditioning apparatus was beneath the window. Jack went over to it, lifted the top, and looked inside. A hot-water and a chill-water pipe poked up through the concrete floor and entered a thermostated fan unit that recirculated room air. Jack detected no holes large enough for any type of rodent, much less a rat.

Stepping into the bathroom, Jack glanced around at the sink, toilet, and shower. The room was newly tiled. There was an air return in the ceiling. Bending down, he opened the cabinet below the sink; again there were no holes.

Hearing voices in the other room, Jack stepped back through the door. It was Dr. Wainwright clutching a mask to his face. He was accompanied by two women and a man, all of whom were wearing masks. The women were attired in the long, white professorial coats Jack associated with medical-school professors.

After handing Jack a mask, Dr. Wainwright made the introductions. The taller woman was Dr. Mary Zimmerman, the hospital's infection-control officer and head of the like-named committee. Jack sensed she was a serious woman who felt defensive under the circumstances. As she was introduced, she informed him that she was a board-certified internist with subspecialty training in infectious disease.

Not knowing how to respond to this revelation, Jack complimented her.

"I did not have an opportunity to examine Mr. Nodelman," she added.

"I'm certain you would have made the diagnosis instantly had you done so," Jack said, consciously trying to keep sarcasm out of his voice.

"No doubt," she said.

The second woman was Kathy McBane, and Jack was happy to turn his attention to her, especially since Ms. McBane had a warmer demeanor than her committee chairwoman. He learned she was an RN supervisor and a member of the Infection Control Committee. It was usual for such a committee to have representatives from most if not all the hospital departments.

The man was George Eversharp. He was dressed in a heavy cotton twill blue uniform. As Jack suspected, he was the supervisor of the department of engineering and was also a member of the Infection Control Committee.

"We certainly are indebted to Dr. Stapleton for his rapid diagnosis," Dr. Wainwright said, trying to lighten the atmosphere.

"Just a lucky guess," Jack said.

"We've already begun to react," Dr. Zimmerman said in a deadpan voice. "I've ordered a list to be drawn up of possible contacts to start chemoprophylaxis."

"I think that is wise," Jack said.

"And as we speak, the clinical computer is searching our current patient database for symptom complexes suggestive of plague," she continued.

"Commendable," Jack said.

"Meanwhile we have to discover the origin of the current case," she said.

"You and I are thinking along the same lines," Jack said.

"I'd advise you to wear your mask," she added.

"Okay," Jack said agreeably. He held it up to his face.

Dr. Zimmerman turned to Mr. Eversharp. "Please continue with what you were saying about the air flow."

Jack listened as the engineer explained that the ventilation system in the hospital was designed so that there was a flow from the hall into each room and then its bathroom. The air was then filtered. He also explained that there were a few rooms where the air flow could be reversed for patients with compromised immune systems.

"Is this one of those rooms?" Dr. Zimmerman asked.

"It is not," Mr. Eversharp said.

"So there is no freak way plague bacteria could have gotten into the ventilation system and infected just this room?" Dr. Zimmerman asked.

"No," Mr. Eversharp said. "The air induction in the hall goes into all these rooms equally."

"And the chances of bacteria floating out of this room into the hall would be low," Dr. Zimmerman said.

"Impossible," Mr. Eversharp said. "The only way it could leave would be on some sort of vector."

"Excuse me," a voice called. Everyone turned to see a nurse standing in the doorway. She, too, had a mask pressed against her face. "Mr. Kelley would like you all to come to the nurses' station."

Dutifully everyone started from the room. As Kathy McBane stepped in front of him, Jack got her attention. "Who's Mr. Kelley?" he asked.

"He's the hospital president," Ms. McBane said.

Jack nodded. As he walked he nostalgically reminisced that the head of the hospital used to be called an administrator and was frequently a person who'd had medical training. That was back when patient care was paramount. Now that business was king and the goal was profit, the name had changed to president.

Jack was looking forward to meeting Mr. Kelley. The hospital president was the on-site representative of AmeriCare, and giving him a headache was the equivalent of giving AmeriCare a headache.

The atmosphere at the nurses' station was tense. Word of the plague had spread like wildfire. Everyone who worked on the floor and even some of the ambulatory patients now knew they had been potentially exposed. Charles Kelley was doing his best to reassure them. He told them there was no risk and that everything was under control.

"Yeah, sure!" Jack scoffed under his breath. Jack looked with disgust at this man who had the gall to utter such patently false platitudes. He was intimidatingly tall, a good eight inches taller than Jack's six feet. His handsome face was tanned and his sandy-colored hair was streaked with pure, golden blond as if he'd just returned from a Caribbean vacation. From Jack's perspective, he looked and sounded more like an unctuous car salesman than the business manager that he was.

As soon as Kelley saw Jack and the others approach, he motioned for them to follow him. Breaking off his consoling speech, he made a bee-line for the safety of the utility room behind the nurses' station.

As Jack squeezed in behind Kathy McBane, he noticed Kelley wasn't alone. He was being shadowed by a slightly built man with a lantern jaw and thinning hair. In sharp contrast to Kelley's sartorial splendor, this second man was dressed in a threadbare, cheap sports coat over slacks that appeared never to have been pressed.

"God, what a mess!" Kelley said angrily to no one in particular. His demeanor had metamorphosed instantly from slippery salesman to sardonic administrator. He took a paper towel and wiped his perspiring brow. "This is not what this hospital needs!" He crumpled the towel and threw it into the trash. Turning to Dr. Zimmerman and in contrast to what he'd just said out in the nurses' station, he asked her if they were taking a risk just being on the floor.

"I sincerely doubt it," Dr. Zimmerman said. "But we'll have to make certain."

Turning to Dr. Wainwright, Kelley said: "No sooner had I heard about this disaster than I learned you already knew about it. Why didn't you inform me?"

Dr. Wainwright explained that he'd just heard the news from Jack and had not had time to call. He explained he thought it was more important to call Dr. Zimmerman to get corrective measures instituted. He then proceeded to introduce Jack.

Jack stepped forward and gave a little wave. He was unable to suppress a smile. This was the moment he knew he'd savor.

Kelley took in the chambray shirt, the knitted tie, and the black jeans. It was a far cry from his own Valentino silk suit. "Seems to me the Commissioner of Health mentioned your name when she called me," Kelley said. "As I recall, she was impressed you'd made the diagnosis so quickly."

"We city employees are always glad to be of service," Jack said.

Kelley gave a short, derisive laugh.

"Perhaps you'd like to meet one of your dedicated fellow city employees," Kelley said. "This is Dr. Clint Abelard. He's the epidemiologist for the New York City Board of Health."

Jack nodded to his mousy colleague, but the epidemiologist didn't return the greeting. Jack got the sense that his own presence was not wholly appreciated. Interdepartmental rivalry was a fact of bureaucratic life he was just beginning to appreciate.

Kelley cleared his throat and then spoke to Wainwright and Zimmerman. "I want this whole episode kept as low-key as possible. The less that's in the media the better. If any reporter tries to talk with either of you, send them to me. I'll be gearing up the PR office to do damage control."

"Excuse me," Jack said, unable to restrain himself from interrupting. "Corporate interests aside, I think you should concentrate on prevention. That means treating contacts and ascertaining where the plague bacteria came from. I think you have a mystery on your hands here, and until that's solved, the media is going to have a field day no matter what damage control you attempt."

"I wasn't aware anyone asked your opinion," Kelley said scornfully.

"I just felt you could use a little direction," Jack said. "You seemed to be wandering a bit far afield."

Kelley's face reddened. He shook his head in disbelief. "All right," he said, struggling to control himself. "With your clairvoyance, I suppose you already have an idea of its origin."

"I'd guess rats," Jack said. "I'm sure there are lots of rats around here." Jack had been waiting to use that comment since it had had such a good effect with Calvin that morning.

"We have no rats here at the Manhattan General," Kelley spluttered. "And if I hear that you've said anything like that to the media, I'll have your head."

"Rats are the classical reservoir for the plague," Jack said. "I'm sure they're around here if you know how to recognize them, I mean find them."

Kelley turned to Clint Abelard. "Do you think rats had anything to do with this case of plague?" he demanded.

"I have yet to begin my investigation," Dr. Abelard said. "I wouldn't want to hazard a guess, but I find it hard to believe that rats could have been involved. We're on the seventh floor."

"I'd suggest you start trapping rats," Jack said. "Start in the immediate neighborhood. The first thing to find out is if plague has infiltrated the local urban rodent population."

"I'd like to switch the conversation away from rats," Kelley said. "I would like to hear about what we should do for people who had direct contact with the deceased."

"That's my department," Dr. Zimmerman said. "Here's what I propose . . ."

While Dr. Zimmerman spoke, Clint Abelard motioned for Jack to accompany him out to the nurses' station.

"I'm the epidemiologist," Clint said in an angry, forced whisper.

"I've never disputed the fact," Jack said. He was surprised and confused by the vehemence of Clint's reaction.

"I'm trained to investigate the origin of diseases in the human community," he said. "It's my job. You, on the other hand, are a coroner . . ."

"Correction," Jack said. "I'm a medical examiner with training in pathology. You, as a physician, should know that."

"Medical examiner or coroner, I couldn't care less what term you guys use for yourselves," Clint said.

"Hey, but I do," Jack said.

"The point is that your training and your responsibility involve the dead, not the origin of disease."

"Wrong again," Jack said. "We deal with the dead so that they speak to the living. Our goal is to prevent death."

"I don't know how to make it much plainer to you,"

Clint said with exasperation. "You told us a man died of plague. We appreciate that, and we didn't interfere in your work. Now it is for me to figure out how he got it."

"I'm just trying to help," Jack said.

"Thank you, but if I need your help I'll ask for it," Clint said and strode off toward room 707.

Jack watched Clint's figure recede, when a commotion behind him attracted his attention. Kelley had emerged from the utility room and was immediately besieged by the people he'd been speaking with earlier. Jack was impressed by how quickly his plastic smile returned and with what ease he sidestepped all questions. Within seconds, he was on his way down the hall toward the elevators and the safety of the administrative offices.

Dr. Zimmerman and Dr. Wainwright stepped out of the utility room deep in conversation. When Kathy McBane appeared, she was alone. Jack intercepted her.

"Sorry to have been the bearer of bad news," Jack offered.

"Don't be sorry," Kathy said. "From my point of view, we owe you a vote of thanks."

"Well, it's an unfortunate problem," Jack said.

"I'd guess it's the worst since I've been on the Infection Control Committee," she said. "I thought last year's outbreak of hepatitis B was bad. I never dreamed we'd ever see plague."

"What is the Manhattan General's experience in regard to nosocomial infections?" Jack asked.

Kathy shrugged. "Pretty much the equivalent of any large tertiary-care hospital," she said. "We've had our methicillin-resistant staph. Of course, that's an ongoing problem. We even had klebsiella growing in a canister of surgical scrub soap a year ago. That resulted in a whole series of postoperative wound infections until it was discovered."

"How about pneumonias?" Jack asked. "Like this case."

"Oh, yeah, we've had our share of them too," Kathy said with a sigh. "Mostly it's been pseudomonas, but two years ago we had an outbreak of Legionella."

"I hadn't heard about that," Jack said.

"It was kept quiet," Kathy said. "Luckily no one died. Of course, I can't say that about the problem we had just five months ago in the surgical intensive care. We lost three patients to enterobacterial pneumonia. We had to close the unit until it was discovered that some of our nebulizers had become contaminated."

"Kathy!" a voice called out sharply.

Both Jack and Kathy abruptly turned to see Dr. Zimmerman had come up behind them.

"That is confidential information," Dr. Zimmerman lectured.

Kathy started to say something but then thought better of it.

"We have work to do, Kathy," Dr. Zimmerman said. "Let's go to my office."

Suddenly abandoned, Jack debated what he should do. For a moment he considered going back to room 707, but after Clint's tirade, he thought it best to leave the man alone. After all, Jack had intended to provoke Kelley, not Clint. Then he got an idea: It might be instructive to visit the lab. As defensively as Dr. Zimmerman had responded, Jack thought it was the lab that should have been chagrined. They were the ones who missed the diagnosis.

After inquiring about the location of the lab, Jack took the elevator down to the second floor. Flashing his medical examiner's badge again produced immediate results. Dr. Martin Cheveau, the lab director, materialized and welcomed Jack into his office. He was a short fellow with a full head of dark hair and pencil-line mustache.

"Have you heard about the case of plague?" Jack asked once they were seated.

"No, where?" Martin questioned.

"Here at the Manhattan General," Jack said. "Room seven-oh-seven. I posted the patient this morning."

"Oh, no!" Martin moaned. He sighed loudly. "That doesn't sound good for us. What was the name?"

"Donald Nodelman," Jack said.

Martin swung around in his seat and accessed his computer. The screen flashed all Nodelman's laboratory results for the duration of his admission. Martin scrolled through until he got to the microbiology section.

"I see we had a sputum gram stain showing weakly gram-negative bacilli," Martin said. "There's also a culture pending that was negative for growth at thirty-six hours. I guess that should have told us something, especially where I see pseudomonas was suspected. I mean, pseudomonas would have grown out without any trouble way before thirty-six hours."

"It would have been helpful if Giemsa's or Wayson's stain had been used," Jack said. "The diagnosis could have been made."

"Exactly," Martin said. He turned back to Jack. "This is terrible. I'm embarrassed. Unfortunately, it's an example of the kind of thing that's going to happen more and more often. Administration has been forcing us to cut costs and downsize even though our workload has gone up. It's a deadly combination, as this case of plague proves. And it's happening all over the country."

"You've had to let people go?" Jack asked. He thought that the clinical lab was one place hospitals actually made money.

"About twenty percent," Martin said. "Others we've had to demote. In microbiology we don't have a supervisor any longer; if we had, he probably would have caught this case of plague. With the operating budget we've been allotted we can't afford it. Our old supervisor got demoted to head tech. It's discouraging. It used to be we strove for excellence in the lab. Now we strive for 'adequate,' whatever that means."

"Does your computer say which tech did the gram stain?" Jack asked. "If nothing else, we could turn this episode into a teaching experience."

"Good idea," Martin said. He faced the computer and accessed data. The tech's identity was in code. Suddenly he turned back to Jack.

"I just remembered something," he said. "My head tech thought of plague in relation to a patient just yesterday and asked me what I thought. I'm afraid I discouraged him by telling him the chances were somewhere on the order of a billion to one."

Jack perked up. "I wonder what made him think of plague?"

"I wonder too," Martin said. Reaching over to his intercom system, he paged Richard Overstreet. While they waited for the man to arrive, Martin determined that Nancy Wiggens had signed out on the original gram stain. Martin paged her as well.

Richard Overstreet appeared within minutes. He was

a boyish, athletic-looking individual with a shock of auburn hair that fell across his forehead. The hair had a habit of slipping over his eyes. Richard was ever pushing it back with his hand or throwing it back with a snap of his head. He wore a white jacket over surgical scrubs; his jacket pockets were crammed with test tubes, tourniquets, gauze pads, lab chits, and syringes.

Martin introduced Richard to Jack, then asked him about the short discussion they'd had about plague the day before.

Richard seemed embarrassed. "It was just my imagination getting the best of me," he said with a laugh.

"But what made you think of it?" Martin asked.

Richard swept his hair from his face and for a moment left his hand on the top of his head while he thought. "Oh, I remember," he said. "Nancy Wiggens had gone up to get a sputum culture and drawn the man's blood. She told me how sick he was and that he appeared to have some gangrene on the tips of his fingers. She said his fingers were black." Richard shrugged. "It made me think of the black death."

Jack was impressed.

"Did you follow up on it at all?" Martin asked.

"No," Richard said. "Not after what you'd said about the probability. As behind as we are in the lab, I couldn't take the time. All of us, including me, have been out drawing blood. Is there some kind of problem?" Richard asked.

"A big problem," Martin said. "The man did have plague. Not only that, but he's already dead."

Richard literally staggered. "My God!" he exclaimed.

"I hope you encourage safety with your techs," Jack said.

"Absolutely," Richard said, regaining his composure. "We have biosafety cabinets, both type two and three. I try to encourage my techs to use one or the other, especially with obviously serious infectious cases. Personally I like the type three, but some people find using the thick rubber gloves too clumsy."

At that moment Nancy Wiggens appeared. She was a shy woman who appeared more like a teenager than a college graduate. She could barely look Jack in the eye as they were introduced. She wore her dark hair parted down the middle of her head, and like that of her immediate boss, Richard, it constantly fell across her eyes.

Martin explained to her what had happened. She was as shocked as Richard had been. Martin assured her she was not being blamed but that they should all try to learn from the experience.

"What should I do about my exposure?" she questioned. "I was the one who got the specimen as well as the one who processed it."

"You'll probably be taking tetracycline by mouth or streptomycin IM," Jack said. "The hospital infection-control officer is working on that at the moment."

"Uh oh!" Martin voiced under his breath but loud enough for the others to hear. "Here comes our fearless leader and the chief of the medical staff, and both look unhappy."

Kelley swept into the room like an irate general after a military defeat. He towered over Martin with his hands on his hips and his reddened face thrust forward. "Dr. Cheveau," he began with a scornful tone. "Dr. Arnold here tells me you should have made this diagnosis before . . ."

Kelley stopped mid-sentence. Although he was content to ignore the two microbiology techs, Jack was a different story.

"What in God's name are you doing down here?" he demanded.

"Just helping out," Jack replied.

"Aren't you overstepping your mandate?" he suggested venomously.

"We like to be thorough in our investigations," Jack said.

"I think you have more than exhausted your official capacity," Kelley snapped. "I want you out of here. After all, this is a private institution."

Jack got to his feet, vainly trying to look the towering Kelley in the eye. "If AmeriCare thinks it can do without me, I think I'll run along."

Kelley's face turned purple. He started to stay something else but changed his mind. Instead he merely pointed toward the door.

Jack smiled and waved to the others before taking his leave. He was pleased with his visit. As far as he was concerned, it couldn't have gone better.

CHAPTER SIX

Wednesday, 4:05 P.M., March 20, 1996

Susanne Hard was looking through the small, round window of the door to the elevator lobby with rapt attention. The end of the corridor was as far as she was allowed to go on her ambulation. She'd been walking with little steps while supporting her freshly sutured abdomen. As unpleasant as the exercise was, she knew from experience that the sooner she mobilized herself, the sooner she'd be in a position to demand release.

What had caught her attention out in the elevator lobby was the disturbing amount of traffic coming in and out of the medical ward as well as the nervous demeanor of the staff. Susanne's sixth sense told her that something was wrong, especially with most of the people wearing masks.

Before she could put a finger on the cause of the apparent stir, a literal chill passed through her like an icy arctic wind. Turning around, she expected to feel a draft. There wasn't any. Then the chill returned, causing her to tense and shiver until it had passed. Susanne looked down at her hands. They had turned bone white.

Increasingly anxious, Susanne started back to her room. Such a chill could not be a good sign. As an experienced patient she knew there was always the fear of a wound infection.

By the time she entered her room she had a headache behind her eyes. As she climbed back into bed, the headache spread over the top of her head. It wasn't like any headache she'd ever had before. It felt as if someone were pushing an awl into the depths of her brain.

For a few panicky moments Susanne lay perfectly still, hoping that whatever had seemed wrong was now all right. But instead a new symptom developed: the muscles of her legs began to ache. Within minutes she found herself writhing in the bed, vainly trying to find a position that afforded relief.

Close on the heels of the leg pain came an overall malaise that settled over her like a stifling blanket. It was so enervating that she could barely reach across her chest for the nurse's call button. She pressed it and let her arm fall limply back to the bed.

By the time the nurse came into the room, Susanne had developed a cough that chafed her already irritated throat.

"I feel sick," Susanne croaked.

"How so?" the nurse questioned.

Susanne shook her head. It was even hard to talk. She felt so terrible she didn't know where to begin.

"I have a headache," she managed.

"I believe you have a standing order of pain medication," the nurse said. "I'll get it for you."

"I need my doctor," Susanne whispered. Her throat felt as bad as when she'd first awakened from the anesthesia.

"I think we should try the pain medicine before we call your doctor," the nurse said.

"I feel cold," Susanne said. "Terribly cold."

The nurse put a practiced hand on Susanne's forehead,

then pulled it back in alarm. Susanne was burning up. The nurse took the thermometer from its container on the bedside table and stuck it into Susanne's mouth. While she waited for the thermometer to equilibrate, she wrapped a blood-pressure cuff around Susanne's arm. The blood pressure was low.

She then took the thermometer out of Susanne's mouth. When she saw what the reading was, she let out a little gasp of surprise. It was 106° Fahrenheit.

"Do I have a fever?" Susanne questioned.

"A little one," the nurse said. "But everybody is going to be fine. I'll go and give your doctor a call."

Susanne nodded. A tear came to the corner of her eye. She didn't want this kind of complication. She wanted to go home.

CHAPTER SEVEN

"Do you honestly think that Robert Barker deliberately sabotaged our ad campaign?" Colleen asked Terese as they descended the stairs. They were on their way to the studio where Colleen wanted to show Terese what the creative team had put together for a new National Health campaign.

"There's not a doubt in my mind," Terese said. "Of course, he didn't do it himself. He had Helen do it by talking National Health out of buying adequate exposure time."

"But he'd be shooting himself in the foot. If we lose the National Health account and we can't restructure, then his employee participation units are worth the same as ours: zilch."

"Screw his employee participation units," Terese said. "He wants the presidency, and he'll do anything to get it."

"God, bureaucratic infighting disgusts me," Colleen said. "Are you sure you want the presidency?"

Terese stopped dead on the stairs and looked at Colleen as if she'd just blasphemed. "I can't believe you said that."

"But you've complained yourself that the more

administrative duties you have, the less time you can spend on creativity."

"If Barker gets the presidency he'll screw up the whole company," Terese said indignantly. "We'll start kowtowing to clients, and there goes creativity and quality in one fell swoop. Besides, I want to be president. It's been my goal for five years. This is my chance, and if I don't get it now, I'll never get it."

"I don't know why you're not happy with what you've already accomplished," Colleen said. "You're only thirty-one and you're already creative director. You should be content and do what you are good at: doing great ads."

"Oh, come on!" Terese said. "You know we advertising people are never satisfied. Even if I make president I'll probably start eyeing CEO."

"I think you should cool it," Colleen said. "You're going to burn out before you're thirty-five."

"I'll cool it when I'm president," Terese said.

"Yeah, sure!" Colleen said.

Once in the studio Colleen directed her friend into the small separate room that was affectionately called the "arena." This was where pitches were rehearsed. The name came from the arenas of ancient Rome where Christians were thrown to the lions. At Willow and Heath the Christians were the low-level creatives.

"You got a film?" Terese questioned. In the front of the room a screen had been pulled down over the chalkboards. At best she thought she'd be looking at sketchy storyboards.

"We threw together a 'ripomatic,'" Colleen explained. A ripomatic was a roughly spliced together amalgam of previously shot video that had been "stolen" from other projects to give a sense of a commercial.

Terese was encouraged. She'd not expected video.

"Now I'm warning you, this is all very preliminary," Colleen added.

"Save the disclaimers," Terese said. "Run what you have."

Colleen waved to one of her underlings. The lights dimmed and the video started. It ran for a hundred seconds. It depicted a darling four-year-old girl with a broken doll. Terese recognized the footage immediately. It was part of a spot they'd done the year before for a national toy chain to promote the company's generous return policy. Colleen had cleverly made it appear as if the child were bringing the doll to the new National Health hospital. The tag line was "We cure anything anytime."

As soon as the video stopped, the lights came on. For a few moments no one spoke. Finally Colleen broke the silence. "You don't like it," she said.

"It's cute," Terese admitted.

"The idea is to make the doll reflect different illnesses and injuries in different commercials," Colleen said. "Of course, we'd have the child speak and extol the virtues of National Health in the video versions. In print we'd make sure the picture told the story."

"The problem is it's too cute," Terese said. "Even if I think it has some merit, I'm sure the client won't like it, since Helen via Robert would certainly trivialize it."

"It's the best that we've come up with so far," Colleen said. "You'll have to give us some direction. We need a creative brief from you; otherwise we'll just keep wandering all over the conceptual landscape. Then there will be no more chance to put anything together for next week."

"We have to come up with something that sets National Health apart from AmeriCare even though we know they are equivalent. The challenge is finding that one idea," Terese said.

Colleen motioned for her assistant to leave. Once she had, Colleen took a chair and put it in front of Terese's. "We need more of your direct involvement," she said.

Terese nodded. She knew Colleen was right, but Terese felt mentally paralyzed. "The problem is that it's hard to think with this presidency situation hanging over me like the sword of Damocles."

"I think you've got yourself in overdrive," Colleen said. "You're a ball of nerves."

"So what else is new?" Terese said.

"When was the last time you went out for dinner and a few drinks?" Colleen said.

Terese laughed. "I haven't had time for anything like that for months."

"That's my point," Colleen said. "No wonder your creative juices aren't flowing. You need to relax. Even if it's just for a few hours."

"You really think so?" Terese asked.

"Absolutely," Colleen said. "In fact we're going out tonight. We'll go to dinner and we'll have a few drinks. We'll even try not to talk about advertising for one night."

"I don't know," Terese voiced. "We've got this deadline . . ."

"That's exactly my point," Colleen said. "We need to blow the tubes and clear out the cobwebs. Maybe then we'll come up with that big idea. So don't argue. I'm not taking no for an answer."

CHAPTER EIGHT

Wednesday, 4:35 P.M., March 20, 1996

Jack navigated his mountain bike between the two Health and Hospital Corporation mortuary vans parked at the receiving bay at the medical examiner's office and rode directly into the morgue. Under normal circumstances he'd have dismounted by then and walked the bike, but he was in too good a mood.

Jack parked his bike by the Hart Island coffins, locked it up, then whistled on his way to the elevators. He waved to Sal D'Ambrosio as he passed the mortuary office.

"Chet, my boy, how are you?" Jack asked as he breezed into their shared fifth-floor office.

Chet laid his pen down on his desk and turned to face his officemate. "The world's been in here looking for you. What have you been doing?"

"Indulging myself," Jack said. He peeled off his leather jacket and draped it over the back of his desk chair before sitting down. He surveyed his row of files, deciding which one to attack first. His in-basket had a newly replenished pile of lab results and PA reports.

"I wouldn't get too comfortable," Chet said. "One of those looking for you was Bingham himself. He told me to tell you to come directly to his office."

"How nice," Jack said. "I was afraid he'd forgotten about me."

"I wouldn't be so flippant about it," Chet said. "Bingham was not happy. And Calvin stopped by as well. He'd like to see you, too, and smoke was coming out of his ears."

"Undoubtedly he's eager to pay me my ten dollars," Jack said. He got up from his desk and patted Chet on the shoulder. "Don't worry about me. I have a strong survival instinct."

"You could have fooled me," Chet said.

As Jack descended in the elevator, he was curious how Bingham would handle the current situation. Since Jack had started working at the ME office, he'd had only sporadic contact with the chief. The day-to-day administrative problems were all handled by Calvin.

"You can go right in," Mrs. Sanford said without even looking up from her typing. Jack wondered how she knew it was he.

"Close the door," Dr. Harold Bingham commanded.

Jack did as he was told. Bingham's office was spacious with a large desk set back under high windows covered with ancient venetian blinds. At the opposite end of the room was a library table with a teaching microscope. A glass-fronted bookcase lined the far wall.

"Sit down," Bingham said.

Dutifully Jack sat.

"I'm not sure I understand you," Bingham said in his deep, husky voice. "You apparently made a rather brilliant diagnosis of plague today and then foolishly took it upon yourself to call my boss, the Commissioner of Health. Either you are a completely apolitical creature or you have a self-destructive streak."

"It's probably a combination of the two," Jack said.

"You're also impertinent," Bingham said.

"That's part of the self-destructive streak," Jack said. "On the positive side, I'm honest." He smiled.

Bingham shook his head. Jack was testing his ability to control himself. "Just so I can try to understand," he said as he entwined the fingers of his shovel-like hands, "did you not think that I would find it inappropriate for you to call the commissioner before talking with me?"

"Chet McGovern suggested as much," Jack said. "But I was more concerned about getting the word out. Ounce of prevention is worth a pound of cure, especially if we're looking at a potential epidemic."

There was a moment of silence while Bingham considered Jack's statement, which he had to admit contained a modicum of validity. "The second thing I wanted to discuss was your visit to the Manhattan General. Frankly, your decision to do this surprises me. During your orientation I know you were told that our policy is to rely on our excellent PAs to do site work. You do remember that, don't you?"

"Certainly I remember," Jack said. "But I felt that the appearance of plague was unique enough to demand a unique response. Besides, I was curious."

"Curious!" Bingham blurted out. He momentarily lost control. "That's the lamest excuse for ignoring established policy I've heard in years."

"Well, there was more," Jack admitted. "Knowing the General was an AmeriCare hospital, I wanted to go over there and rub it in a little. I'm not fond of AmeriCare."

"What in heaven's name do you have against Ameri-Care?" Bingham asked.

"It's a personal thing," Jack said.

"Would you care to elaborate?" Bingham asked.

"I'd rather not," Jack said. "It's a long story."

"Suit yourself," Bingham said irritably. "But I'm not going to tolerate your going over there flashing your medical examiner badge for some personal vendetta. That's an egregious misuse of official authority."

"I thought our mandate was to get involved in anything that could affect public health," Jack said. "Certainly a case of plague falls under that rubric."

"Indeed," Bingham pronounced. "But you had already alerted the Commissioner of Health. She in turn alerted the City Board of Health, who immediately dispatched the chief epidemiologist. You had no business being over there, much less causing trouble."

"What kind of trouble did I cause?" Jack asked.

"You managed to irritate hell out of both the administrator and the city epidemiologist," Bingham roared. "Both of them were mad enough to lodge official complaints. The administrator called the mayor's office, and the epidemiologist called the commissioner. Both of these public servants can be considered my boss, and neither one of them was pleased, and both of them let me know about it."

"I was just trying to be helpful," Jack said innocently.

"Well, do me a favor and don't try to be helpful," Bingham snapped. "Instead I want you to stay around here where you belong and do the work you were hired to do. Calvin informed me that you have a lot of cases pending."

"Is that it?" Jack asked when Bingham paused.

"For now," Bingham said.

Jack got up and headed for the door.

"One last thing," Bingham said. "Remember that you are on probation for the first year."

"I'll keep that in mind," Jack said.

Leaving Bingham's office, Jack passed Mrs. Sanford and went directly across to Calvin Washington's office. The door was ajar. Calvin was busy at his microscope.

"Excuse me," Jack called out. "I understand you were looking for me."

Calvin turned around and eyed Jack. "Have you been in to see the chief yet?" he growled.

"Just came from there," Jack said. "It's reassuring to be in such demand around here."

"Dispense with your smartass talk," Calvin said. "What did Dr. Bingham say?"

Jack told Calvin what had been said and that Bingham had concluded by reminding him that he was on probation.

"Damn straight," Calvin said. "I think you'd better shape up or you'll be out looking for work."

"Meanwhile I have one request," Jack said.

"What is it?" Calvin asked.

"How about that ten dollars you owe me," Jack said.

Calvin stared back at Jack, amazed that under the circumstances Jack had the gall to ask for the money. Finally Calvin rolled to the side in his seat, withdrew his wallet, and pulled out a ten-dollar bill.

"I'll get this back," Calvin vowed.

"Sure you will," Jack said as he took the bill.

With the money comfortably in his pocket, Jack returned upstairs to his office. As he entered he was surprised to find Laurie leaning against Chet's desk. Both she and Chet looked at Jack with expectant concern.

"Well?" Chet questioned.

"Well what?" Jack asked. He squeezed by the others to plop down in his seat.

"Are you still employed?" Chet asked.

"Seems that way," Jack said. He started going through the lab reports in his in-basket.

"You'd better be careful," Laurie advised as she started for the door. "They can fire you at their pleasure during your first year."

"So Bingham reminded me," Jack said.

Pausing at the threshold, Laurie turned back to face Jack. "I almost got fired my first year," she admitted.

Jack looked up at her. "How come?" he asked.

"It had to do with those challenging overdose cases I mentioned this morning," Laurie said. "Unfortunately, while I followed up on them I got on the wrong side of Bingham."

"Is that part of that long story you alluded to?" Jack asked.

"That's the one," Laurie said. "I came this close to being fired." She held up her thumb and index finger about a quarter inch apart. "It was all because I didn't take Bingham's threats seriously. Don't make the same mistake."

As soon as Laurie had gone Chet wanted a verbatim recounting of everything Bingham had said. Jack related what he could remember, including the part about the mayor and the Commissioner of Health calling Bingham to complain about him.

"The complaints were about you specifically?" Chet asked.

"Apparently," Jack said. "And here I was being the Good Samaritan."

"What in God's name did you do?" Chet asked.

"I was just being my usual diplomatic self," Jack said. "Asking questions and offering suggestions."

"You're crazy," Chet said. "You almost got yourself fired for what? I mean, what were you trying to prove?"

"I wasn't trying to prove anything," Jack said.

"I don't understand you," Chet said.

"That seems to be a universal opinion," Jack said.

"All I know about you is that you were an ophthalmologist in a former life and you live in Harlem to play street basketball. What else do you do?"

"That about sums it up," Jack said. "Apart from working here, that is."

"What do you do for fun?" Chet asked. "I mean, what kind of social life do you have? I don't mean to pry, but do you have a girlfriend?"

"No, not really," Jack said.

"Are you gay?"

"Nope. I've just sorta been out of commission for a while."

"Well, no wonder you're acting so weird. I tell you what. We're going out tonight. We'll have some dinner, maybe have a few drinks. There's a comfortable bar in the neighborhood where I live. It will give us time to talk."

"I haven't felt like talking much about myself," Jack said.

"All right, you don't have to talk," Chet said. "But we're going out. I think you need some normal human contact."

"What's normal?" Jack questioned.

CHAPTER NINE

Wednesday, 10:15 P.M., March 20, 1996

Chet turned out to be extraordinarily resolute. No matter what Jack said, he insisted that they have dinner together. Finally Jack relented, and just before eight he'd ridden his bike across Central Park to meet Chet in an Italian restaurant on Second Avenue.

After dinner Chet had been equally insistent about Jack's accompanying him for a few drinks. Feeling beholden to his officemate since Chet had insisted on paying for the dinner, Jack had gone along. Now, as they mounted the steps to the bar, Jack was having second thoughts. For the past several years he'd been in bed by ten and up by five. At ten-fifteen after a half bottle of wine, he was fading fast.

"I'm not sure I'm up for this," Jack said.

"We're already there," Chet complained. "Come on in. We'll just have one beer."

Jack leaned back to look at the facade of the bar. He didn't see a name. "What's this place called?" he asked.

"The Auction House," Chet said. "Get your ass in here." He was holding open the door.

To Jack the interior looked vaguely like his grandmother's living room back in Des Moines, Iowa, except for the mahogany bar itself. The furniture was an odd mishmash of Victorian, and the drapes were long and droopy. The high ceiling was brightly colored embossed tin.

"How about sitting here," Chet suggested. He pointed toward a small table set in the window overlooking Eighty-ninth Street.

Jack complied. From where he was sitting Jack had a good view of the room, which he now noted had a high-gloss hardwood floor, not the usual for a bar. There were about fifty people in the room either standing at the bar or sitting on the couches. They were all well dressed and appeared professional. There was not one backward baseball cap in the group. The mix was about even between male and female.

Jack mused that perhaps Chet had been right to have encouraged him to come out. Jack had not been in such a "normal" social environment in several years. Maybe it was good for him. Having become a loner carried its burdens. He wondered what these attractive people were saying to one another as their easy conversations drifted back to him in a babble of voices. The problem was he had zero confidence he could add to any of the discussions.

Jack's eyes wandered to Chet, who was at the bar, supposedly getting them each a beer. Actually he was in a conversation with a well-endowed, long-haired blonde in a stylish sweatshirt over tight jeans. Accompanying her was a svelte woman in a revealingly simple dark suit. She was not participating in the conversation, preferring to concentrate on her glass of wine.

Jack envied Chet's outgoing personality and the ease with which he indulged in social intercourse. During dinner he'd spoken of himself with utter ease. Among the things Jack learned was that Chet had recently broken off a long-term relationship with a pediatrician and hence was what he called "in between" and available.

While Jack was eyeing his officemate, Chet turned toward him. Almost simultaneously the two women did the same, and then they all laughed. Jack felt his face flush. They were obviously talking about him.

Chet broke away from the bar and headed in Jack's direction. Jack wondered if he should flee or merely dig his fingernails into the tabletop. It was obvious what was coming.

"Hey, sport," Chet whispered. He purposefully positioned himself directly between Jack and the women. "See those two chicks at the bar?" He pointed into his own abdomen to shield the gesture from his new acquaintances. "What do you think? Pretty good, huh? They're both knockouts and guess what? They want to meet you."

"Chet, this has been fun, but . . ." Jack began.

"Don't even think about it," Chet said. "Don't let me down now. I'm after the one in the sweatshirt."

Sensing that resistance would have required considerably more energy than capitulation, Jack allowed himself to be dragged to the bar. Chet made the introductions.

Jack could immediately see what Chet saw in Colleen. She was Chet's equal in terms of blithe repartee. Terese, on the other hand, was a foil for them both. After the introductions, she'd given Jack a once-over with her pale blue eyes before turning back to the bar and her glass of wine.

Chet and Colleen fell into spirited conversation. Jack looked at the back of Terese's head and wondered what the hell he was doing. He wanted to be home in bed, and instead he was being abused by someone as unsociable as himself.

"Chet," Jack called out after a few minutes. "This is a waste of time."

Terese spun around. "Waste of time? For whom?"

"For me," Jack said. He gazed curiously at the raw-boned yet sensuously lipped woman standing in front of him. He was taken aback by her vehemence.

"What about for me?" Terese snapped. "Do you think it's a rewarding experience to be pestered by men on the prowl?"

"Wait just one tiny second!" Jack said, with his own ire rising. "Don't flatter yourself. I ain't on the prowl. You can be damn sure about that. And if I were I sure wouldn't . . ."

"Hey, Jack," Chet called out. "Cool it."

"You, too, Terese," Colleen said. "Relax. We're out here to enjoy ourselves."

"I didn't say boo to this lady and she's jumping all over me," Jack explained.

"You didn't have to say anything," Terese said.

"Calm down, you guys." Chet stepped between Jack and Terese, but eyed Jack. "We're out here for some normal contact with fellow human beings."

"Actually, I think I should go home," Terese said.

"You're staying right here," Colleen ordered. She turned to Chet. "She's wound up like a piano wire. That's why I insisted she come out: try to get her to relax. She's consumed by her work."

"Sounds like Jack here," Chet said. "He has some definite antisocial tendencies."

Chet and Colleen were talking as if Jack and Terese couldn't hear, yet they were standing right next to them, staring off in different directions. Both were irritated but both felt foolish at the same time.

Chet and Colleen got a round of drinks and handed them out as they continued to talk about their respective friends.

"Jack's social life revolves around living in a crack neighborhood and playing basketball with killers," Chet said.

"At least he has a social life," Colleen said. "Terese lives in a co-op with a bunch of octogenarians. Going to the garbage chute is the high point of a Sunday afternoon at home."

Chet and Colleen laughed heartily, took long pulls on their respective beers, and then launched into a conversation about a play both of them had seen on Broadway.

Jack and Terese ventured a few fleeting looks at each other as they nursed their own drinks.

"Chet mentioned you were a doctor; are you a specialist?" Terese asked finally. Her tone had mellowed significantly.

Jack explained about forensic pathology. Overhearing this part of the conversation, Chet joined in.

"We're in the presence of one of the future's best and brightest. Jack here made the diagnosis of the day. Against everyone else's impression, he diagnosed a case of plague."

"Here in New York?" Colleen asked with alarm.

"At the Manhattan General," Chet said.

"My God!" Terese exclaimed. "I was a patient there once. Plague is awfully rare isn't it?"

"Most definitely," Jack said. "A few cases are reported each year in the U.S., but they usually occur in the wilds of the west and during the summer months."

"Is it terribly contagious?" Colleen asked.

"It can be," Jack said. "Especially in the pneumonic form which this patient had."

"Are you worried about having gotten it?" Terese asked. Unconsciously she and Colleen had moved a step backward.

"No," Jack said. "And even if we had, we wouldn't be communicative until after we got pneumonia. So you don't have to stand across the room from us."

Feeling embarrassed, both women stepped closer. "Is there any chance this could turn into an epidemic here in the city?" Terese asked.

"If plague bacteria has infected the urban rodent population, particularly the rats, and if there are adequate rat fleas, it could develop into a problem in the ghetto areas of the city," Jack said. "But chances are it would be self limited. The last real outbreak of plague in the U.S. occurred in 1919 and there were only twelve cases. And that was before the antibiotic era. I don't anticipate there is going to be a current epidemic, especially since the Manhattan General is taking the episode extremely seriously."

"I trust you contacted the media about this case of plague," Terese said.

"Not me," Jack said. "That's not my job."

"Shouldn't the public be alerted?" Terese asked.

"I don't think so," Jack said. "By sensationalizing it, the media could make things worse. The mere mention of the word 'plague' can evoke panic, and panic would be counterproductive."

"Maybe," Terese said. "But I bet people would feel differently if there was a chance they could avoid coming down with plague if they were forewarned."

"Well, the question is academic," Jack said. "There's no way that the media could avoid hearing about this. It'll be all over the news. Trust me."

"Let's change the subject," Chet said. "What about you guys? What do you do?"

"We're art directors in a relatively large ad agency," Colleen said. "At least I'm an art director. Terese was an art director. Now she's part of the front office. She's creative director."

"Impressive," Chet said.

"And in a strange way we're currently tangentially involved with medicine," she added.

"What do you mean you are involved with medicine?" Jack asked.

"One of our big accounts is National Health," Terese said. "I imagine you've heard of them."

"Unfortunately," Jack said. His tone was flat.

"You have a problem with our working with them?" Terese asked.

"Probably," Jack said.

"Can I ask why?"

"I'm against advertising in medicine," Jack said. "Especially the kind of advertising these new health care conglomerates are engaged in."

"Why?" Terese asked.

"First of all, the ads have no legitimate function except to increase profits by expanding enrollment. They're nothing but exaggerations, half-truths, or the hyping of superficial amenities. They have nothing to do with the quality of health care. Secondly, the advertising costs a ton of money, and it's being lumped into administrative costs. That's the real crime: It's taking money away from patient care."

"Are you finished?" Terese asked.

"I could probably think up some more reasons if I gave it some thought," Jack said.

"I happen to disagree with you," Terese said with a fervor that matched Jack's. "I think all advertising draws distinctions and fosters a competitive environment which ultimately benefits the consumer."

"That's pure rationalization," Jack said.

"Time out, you guys," Chet said, stepping between Jack and Terese for the second time. "You two are getting out of control again. Let's switch the topic of conversation. Why don't we talk about something neutral, like sex or religion."

Colleen laughed and gave Chet a playful swat on the shoulder.

"I'm serious," Chet said while laughing with Colleen. "Let's discuss religion. It's been getting short shrift lately in bars. Let's have everybody tell what they grew up as. I'll be first . . ."

For the next half hour they indeed did discuss religion, and Jack and Terese forgot their emotional outburst. They even found themselves laughing since Chet was a raconteur of some wit.

At eleven-fifteen Jack happened to glance at his watch and did a double take. He couldn't believe it was so late.

"I'm sorry," he said, interrupting the conversation. "I've got to go. I've got a bicycle ride ahead of me."

"A bike?" Terese questioned. "You ride a bike around this city?"

"He's got a death wish," Chet said.

"Where do you live?" Terese asked.

"Upper West Side," Jack said.

"Ask him how 'upper,' " Chet dared.

"Exactly where?" Terese asked.

"One-oh-six a Hundred and Sixth Street," Jack said. "To be precise."

"But that's in Harlem," Colleen said.

"I told you he has a death wish," Chet said.

"Don't tell me you're going to ride across the park at this hour," Terese said.

"I move pretty quickly," Jack said.

"Well, I think it's asking for trouble," Terese said. She bent down and picked up her briefcase that she'd set on the floor by her feet. "I don't have a bike, but I do have a date with my bed."

"Wait a second, you guys," Chet said. "Colleen and I are in charge. Right, Colleen?" He put his arm loosely around Colleen's shoulder.

"Right!" Colleen said to be agreeable.

"We've decided," Chet said with feigned authority, "that you two can't go home unless you agree to have dinner tomorrow night."

Colleen shook her head as she ducked away from Chet's arm. "I'm afraid we're not available," she said. "We've got an impossible deadline, so we'll be putting in some serious overtime."

"Where were you thinking of having dinner?" Terese asked.

Colleen looked at her friend with surprise.

"How about right around the corner at Elaine's," Chet said. "About eight o'clock. We might even see a couple of celebrities."

"I don't think I can . . ." Jack began.

"I'm not listening to any excuses from you," Chet said, interrupting. "You can bowl with that group of nuns another night. Tomorrow you're having dinner with us."

Jack was too tired to think. He shrugged.

"It's decided, then?" Chet said.

Everyone nodded.

Outside of the bar the women climbed into a cab. They offered Chet a ride home, but he said he lived in the neighborhood.

"Are you sure you don't want to leave that bike here for the night?" Terese asked Jack, who'd finished removing his panoply of locks.

"Not a chance," Jack said. He threw a leg over his bike and powered out across Second Avenue, waving over his head.

Terese gave the cabdriver the address of the first stop, and the taxi made a left onto Second Avenue and accelerated southward. Colleen, who'd kept her eye on Chet out the back window, turned to face her boss.

"What a surprise," she said. "Imagine meeting two decent men at a bar. It always seems to happen when you least expect it."

"They were nice guys," Terese agreed. "I suppose I was wrong about them being out at the meat market, and thank God they didn't spout off about sports or the stock market. Generally that's all men in this city can talk about."

"What tweaks my funny bone is that my mother has forever been encouraging me to meet a doctor," Colleen said with a laugh.

"I don't think either one of them is a typical doctor," Terese said. "Especially Jack. He's got a strange attitude.

He's awfully bitter about something, and seems a bit foolhardy. Can you imagine riding a bike around this city?"

"It's easier than thinking about what they do. Can you imagine dealing with dead people all day?"

"I don't know," Terese said. "Mustn't be too different than dealing with account executives."

"I have to say you shocked me when you agreed to have dinner tomorrow night," Colleen said. "Especially with this National Health disaster staring us in the face."

"But that's exactly why I did agree," Terese said. She flashed Colleen a conspiratorial smile. "I want to talk some more with Jack Stapleton. Believe it or not, he actually gave me a great idea for a new ad campaign for National Health! I can't imagine what his reaction would be if he knew. With his philistine attitude about advertising, he'd probably have a stroke."

"What's the idea?" Colleen asked eagerly.

"It involves this plague thing," Terese said. "Since AmeriCare is National Health's only real rival, our ad campaign merely has to take advantage of the fact that AmeriCare got plague in its main hospital. As creepy as the situation is, people should want to flock to National Health."

Colleen's face fell. "We can't use plague," she said.

"Hell, I'm not thinking of using plague specifically," Terese said. "Just emphasizing the idea of National Health's hospital being so new and clean. The contrary will be evoked by inference, and it will be the public who will make the association with this plague episode. I know what the Manhattan General is like. I've been there. It might have been renovated, but it's still an old structure. The National Health hospital is the antithesis.

I can see ads where people are eating off the floor at National Health, suggesting it's that clean. I mean, people like the idea that their hospital is new and clean, especially now with all the hullabaloo about bacteria making a comeback and becoming antibiotic-resistant."

"I like it," Colleen said. "If that doesn't increase National Health Care's market share vis-à-vis Ameri-Care, nothing will."

"I even have thought up a tag line," Terese said smugly. "Listen: 'We deserve your trust: Health is our middle name.' "

"Excellent! I love it!" Colleen exclaimed. "I'll get the whole team working on it bright and early."

The cab pulled up to Terese's apartment. The women did a high-five before Terese got out.

Leaning back into the cab, Terese said: "Thanks for getting me to go out tonight. It was a good idea for lots of reasons."

"You're welcome," Colleen said, flashing a thumbs-up sign.

CHAPTER TEN

As a man of habit, Jack arrived in the vicinity of the medical examiner's office at the same time each day, give or take five minutes. This particular morning he was ten minutes late since he'd awakened with a slight hangover. He'd not had a hangover in so long, he'd completely forgotten how miserable it made him feel. Consequently he'd stayed in the shower a few minutes longer than usual, and on the slalom down Second Avenue, he'd kept his speed to a more reasonable level.

Crossing First Avenue, Jack saw something he'd never seen before at that time of day. There was a TV truck with its main antennae extended sitting in front of the medical examiner's building.

Changing his direction a little, he cruised around the truck. No one was in it. Looking up at the front door to the ME's office, he saw a group of newspeople clustered just over the threshold.

Curious as to what was going on, Jack hustled around to the entrance bay, stashed his bike in the usual place, and went up to the ID room.

As usual Laurie and Vinnie were in their respective seats. Jack said hello but continued through the room to peek out into the lobby area. It was as crowded as he'd ever seen it.

"What the hell's going on?" Jack asked, turning back to Laurie.

"You of all people should know," she said. She was busy making up the day's autopsy schedule. "It's all about the plague epidemic!"

"Epidemic?" Jack questioned. "Have there been more cases?"

"You haven't heard?" Laurie asked. "Don't you watch morning TV?"

"I don't have a TV," Jack admitted. "In my neighborhood owning one is just inviting trouble."

"Well, two victims came in to us during the night," Laurie said. "One is for sure plague, or at least presumptive since the hospital did its own fluorescein antibody and it was positive. The other is suspected, since clinically it seemed to be plague despite a negative fluorescein antibody. In addition to that, as I understand it, there are several febrile patients who have been quarantined."

"This is all happening at the Manhattan General?" Jack asked.

"Apparently," Laurie said.

"Were these cases direct contacts with Nodelman?" Jack asked.

"I haven't had time to look into that," Laurie said. "Are you interested? If you are, I'll assign them to you."

"Of course," Jack said. "Which one is the presumptive plague?"

"Katherine Mueller," Laurie said. She pushed the patient's folder toward Jack.

Sitting on the edge of the desk where Laurie was working, Jack opened the folder. He leafed through the papers until he found the investigative report. He pulled it out and began reading. He learned the woman had

been brought into the Manhattan General emergency
room at four o'clock in the afternoon acutely ill with
what was diagnosed to be a fulminant case of plague.
She'd died nine hours later despite massive antibiotics.

Jack checked on the woman's place of employment
and wasn't surprised with what he learned. The woman
worked at the Manhattan General. Jack assumed she had
to have been a direct contact of Nodelman. Unfortunately the report did not indicate in what department
she worked, Jack guessed either nursing or lab.

Reading on in the report, Jack silently complimented
Janice Jaeger's work. After the conversation he'd had
with her the day before by phone, she added information
about travel, pets, and visitors. In the case of Mueller it
was all negative.

"Where's the suspected plague?" Jack asked Laurie.

Laurie pushed a second folder toward him.

Jack opened the second file and was immediately
surprised. The victim neither worked at the Manhattan
General nor had obvious contact with Nodelman. Her
name was Susanne Hard. Like Nodelman, she'd been a
patient in the General, but not on the same ward as
Nodelman. Hard had been on the OB-GYN ward after
giving birth! Jack was mystified.

Reading further, Jack learned that Hard had been in
the hospital for twenty-four hours when she'd experienced sudden high fever, myalgia, headache, overwhelming malaise, and progressive cough. These symptoms
had come on about eighteen hours after undergoing a
cesarean section during which she delivered a healthy
child. Eight hours after the symptoms appeared, the
patient was dead.

Out of curiosity Jack looked up Hard's address,

remembering that Nodelman had lived in the Bronx. But Hard had not lived in the Bronx. She had lived in Manhattan on Sutton Place South, hardly a ghetto neighborhood.

Reading on, Jack learned that Hard had not traveled since she'd become pregnant. As far as pets were concerned, she owned an elderly but healthy poodle. Concerning visitors, she had entertained a business associate of her husband's from India three weeks previously who was described as being healthy and well.

"Is Janice Jaeger still here this morning?" Jack asked Laurie.

"She was about fifteen minutes ago when I passed her office," Laurie said.

Jack found Janice where she'd been the previous morning.

"You are a dedicated civil servant," Jack called out from the threshold.

Janice looked up from her work. Her eyes were red from fatigue. "Too many people dying lately. I'm swamped. But tell me: Did I ask the right questions on the infectious cases last night?"

"Absolutely," Jack said. "I was impressed. But I do have a couple more."

"Shoot," Janice said.

"Now, where's the OB-GYN ward in relation to the medical ward?"

"They're right next to each other," Janice said. "Both are on the seventh floor."

"No kidding," Jack said.

"Is that significant?" Janice asked.

"I haven't the slightest idea," Jack admitted. "Do

patients from the OB ward mix with those on the medical ward?"

"You got me there," Janice admitted. "I don't know, but I wouldn't imagine so."

"Nor would I," Jack said. But if they didn't, then how did Susanne Hard manage to get sick? Something seemed screwy about this plague outbreak. Facetiously he wondered if a bunch of infected rats could be living in the ventilation system on the seventh floor.

"Any other questions?" Janice asked. "I want to get out of here, and I have this last report to finish."

"One more," Jack said. "You indicated that Katherine Mueller was employed by the General but you didn't say for what department. Do you know if she worked for nursing or for the lab?"

Janice leafed through her night's notes and came up with the sheet on which she'd recorded Mueller's information. She quickly glanced through it and then looked back up at Jack. "Neither," she said. "She worked in central supply."

"Oh, come on!" Jack said. He sounded disappointed.

"I'm sorry," Janice said. "That's what I was told."

"I'm not blaming you," Jack said with a wave of his hand. "It's just that I'd like there to be some sort of logic to all this. How would a woman in central supply get into contact with a sick patient on the seventh floor? Where's central supply?"

"I believe it's on the same floor with the operating rooms," Janice said. "That would be the third floor."

"Okay, thanks," Jack said. "Now get out of here and get some sleep."

"I intend to," Janice said.

Jack wandered back toward the ID room, thinking

that nothing seemed to be making much sense. Usually the course of a contagious illness could be easily plotted sequentially through a family or a community. There was the index case, and the subsequent cases extended from it by contact, either directly or through a vector like an insect. There wasn't a lot of mystery. That wasn't the case so far with this plague outbreak. The only unifying factor was that they all involved the Manhattan General.

Jack absently waved to Sergeant Murphy, who'd apparently just arrived in his cubbyhole office off the communications room. The ebullient Irish policeman waved back with great enthusiasm.

Jack slowed his walk while his mind churned. Susanne Hard had come down with symptoms after being only in the hospital for a day. Since the incubation period for plague was generally thought to be two days at a minimum, she would have been exposed prior to coming into the hospital. Jack went back to Janice's office.

"One more question," Jack called out to her. "Do you happen to know whether the Hard woman visited the hospital in the days prior to her admission?"

"Her husband said no," Janice said. "I asked that question specifically. Apparently she hated the hospital and only came in at the very last minute."

Jack nodded. "Thanks," he said, even more preoccupied. He turned and started back toward the ID room. That information made the situation more baffling, requiring him to postulate that the outbreak had occurred almost simultaneously in two, maybe three locations. That wasn't probable. The other possibility was that the incubation period was extremely short, less than twenty-four hours. That would mean Hard's illness was a nosocomial infection, as he suspected

Nodelman's was as well as Mueller's. The problem with that idea was that it would suggest a huge, overwhelming infecting dose, which also seemed unlikely. After all, how many sick rats could be in a ventilation duct all coughing at the same time?

In the ID room Jack wrestled the sports page of the *Daily News* away from a reluctant Vinnie and dragged him down to the pit to begin the day.

"How come you always start so early?" Vinnie complained. "You're the only one. Don't you have a life?"

Jack swatted him in the chest with Katherine Mueller's folder. "Remember the saying 'The early bird gets the worm'?"

"Oh, barf," Vinnie said. He took the folder from Jack and opened it. "Is this the one we're doing first?" he asked.

"Might as well move from the known to the unknown," Jack said. "This one had a positive fluorescein antibody test to plague, so zip up tight in your moon suit."

Fifteen minutes later Jack began the autopsy. He spent a good deal of time on the external exam, looking for any signs of insect bites. It wasn't an easy job, since Katherine Mueller was an overweight forty-four-year-old with hundreds of moles, freckles, and other minor skin blemishes. Jack found nothing he was sure was a bite, although a few lesions looked mildly suspicious. To be on the safe side he photographed them.

"No gangrene on this body," Vinnie commented.

"Nor purpura," Jack said.

By the time Jack started on the internal exam, a number of the other staff had arrived in the autopsy room and half of the tables were in use. There were a few comments about Jack becoming the local plague expert, but Jack ignored them. He was too engrossed.

Mueller's lungs appeared quite similar to Nodelman's, with extensive lobar pneumonia, consolidation, and early stages of tissue death. The woman's cervical lymphatics were also generally involved, as were the lymph nodes along the bronchial tree.

"This is just as bad or worse than Nodelman," Jack said. "It's frightening."

"You don't have to tell me," Vinnie said. "These infectious cases are the kind that make me wish I'd gone into gardening."

Jack was nearing the end of the internal exam when Calvin came through the door. There was no mistaking his huge silhouette. He was accompanied by another figure who was half his size. Calvin came directly to Jack's table.

"Anything out of the ordinary?" Calvin asked, while peering into the pan of internal organs.

"Internally this case is a repeat of yesterday's," Jack said.

"Good," Calvin said, straightening up. He then introduced Jack to his guest. It was Clint Abelard, the city epidemiologist.

Jack could make out the man's prominent jaw, but because of the reflection off the plastic face mask, he couldn't see the fellow's squirrelly eyes. He wondered if he was still as cantankerous as he'd been the day before.

"According to Dr. Bingham you two have already met," Calvin said.

"Indeed," Jack said. The epidemiologist did not respond.

"Dr. Abelard is trying to discern the origin of this plague outbreak," Calvin explained.

"Commendable," Jack said.

"He's come to us to see if we can add any significant information," Calvin said. "Perhaps you could run through your positive feelings."

"My pleasure," Jack said. He started with the external exam, indicating skin abnormalities he thought could have been insect bites. Then he showed all the gross internal pathology, concentrating on the lungs, lymphatics, liver, and spleen. Throughout the entire discourse, Clint Abelard stayed silent.

"There you have it," Jack said as he finished. He put the liver back into the pan. "As you can see it's a severe case, as was Nodelman's, and it's no wonder both patients died so quickly."

"What about Hard?" Clint asked.

"She's next," Jack said.

"Mind if I watch?" Clint asked.

Jack shrugged. "That's up to Dr. Washington," he said.

"No problem," Calvin said.

"If I may ask," Jack said, "have you come up with a theory where this plague came from?"

"Not really," Clint said gruffly. "Not yet."

"Any ideas?" Jack asked, trying to keep sarcasm out of his voice. It seemed Clint was in no better humor than he had been the day before.

"We're looking for plague in the area's rodent population," Clint said condescendingly.

"Splendid idea," Jack said. "And just how are you doing that?"

Clint paused as if he didn't want to divulge any state secrets.

"The CDC is helping," he said finally. "They sent someone up here from their plague division. He's in charge of the trapping and analysis."

"Any luck so far?" Jack asked.

"Some of the rats caught last night were ill," Clint said. "But none with plague."

"What about the hospital?" Jack asked. He persisted despite Clint's apparent reluctance to talk. "This woman we've just autopsied worked in central supply. Seems likely her illness was nosocomial like Nodelman's. Do you think she got it from some primary source in and around the hospital, or do you think she got it from Nodelman?"

"We don't know," Clint admitted.

"If she got it from Nodelman," Jack asked, "any ideas of a possible route of transmission?"

"We've checked the hospital's ventilation and air-conditioning system carefully," Clint said. "All the HEPA filters were in place and had been changed appropriately."

"What about the lab situation?" Jack asked.

"What do you mean?" Clint said.

"Did you know that the chief tech in micro actually suggested plague to the director of the lab purely from his clinical impression, but the director talked him out of following up on it?"

"I didn't know that," Clint mumbled.

"If the chief tech had followed up on it he would have made the diagnosis and appropriate therapy could have been started," Jack said. "Who knows; it could have saved a life. The problem is that the lab has been downsizing because of pressure from AmeriCare to save a few bucks, and they don't have a microbiology supervisor position. It got eliminated."

"I don't know anything about all that," Clint said. "Besides, the case of plague still would have occurred."

"You're right," Jack said. "One way or the other you still have to come up with the origin. Unfortunately, you don't know any more than you did yesterday." Jack smiled inside his mask. He was getting a bit of perverse pleasure out of putting the epidemiologist on the spot.

"I wouldn't go that far," Clint muttered.

"Any sign of illness in the hospital staff?" Jack asked.

"There are several nurses who are febrile and who are quarantined," Clint said. "As of yet there is no confirmation of them having plague, but it is suspected. They were directly exposed to Nodelman."

"When will you be doing Hard?" Calvin asked.

"In about twenty minutes," Jack said. "As soon as Vinnie gets things turned around."

"I'm going around to check on some other cases," Calvin said to Clint. "You want to stay here with Dr. Stapleton or do you want to come with me?"

"I think I'll go with you, if you don't mind," Clint said.

"By the way, Jack," Calvin said before leaving. "There's a bevy of media people upstairs crawling all over the outer office like bloodhounds. I don't want you giving any unauthorized press conferences. Any information coming from the ME's office comes from Mrs. Donnatello and her PR assistant."

"I wouldn't dream of talking to the press," Jack assured him.

Calvin wandered to the next table. Clint stayed at his heels.

"It didn't sound as if that guy wanted to talk with you," Vinnie said to Jack when Calvin and Clint were far enough away. "Not that I can blame him."

"That little mouse has been spleeny since I first met him," Jack said. "I don't know what his problem is. He's kinda a weird duck, if you ask me."

"Now there's the pot calling the kettle black," Vinnie said.

CHAPTER ELEVEN

"Mr. Lagenthorpe, can you hear me?" Dr. Doyle called to his patient. Donald Lagenthorpe was a thirty-eight-year-old African-American oil engineer who had a chronic problem with asthma. That morning, just after three a.m., he'd awakened with progressive difficulty breathing. His prescribed home remedies had not interrupted the attack, and he'd come into the emergency room of the Manhattan General at four. Dr. Doyle had been called at quarter to five after the usual emergency medications had had no effect.

Donald's eyes blinked open. He hadn't been sleeping, just trying to rest. The ordeal had been exhausting and frightening. The feeling of not being able to catch his breath was torture, and this episode had been the worst he'd ever experienced.

"How are you doing?" Dr. Doyle inquired. "I know what you have been through. You must be very tired." Dr. Doyle was one of those rare physicians who were able to empathize with all his patients with a depth of understanding suggesting he suffered from all the same conditions.

Donald nodded his head, indicating that he was okay. He was breathing through a face mask that made conversation difficult.

"I want you to stay in the hospital for a few days," Dr. Doyle said. "This was a difficult attack to break."

Donald nodded again. No one had to tell him that.

"I want to keep you on the IV steroids for a little while longer," Dr. Doyle explained.

Donald lifted the face mask off his face. "Couldn't I get the steroids at home?" he suggested. As thankful as he was about the hospital's having been there in his hour of need, he much preferred the idea of going home now that his breathing had returned to normal. At home he knew he could at least get some work done. As was always the case, this asthma attack had come at a particularly inconvenient time. He was supposed to go back to Texas the following week for more fieldwork.

"I know you don't want to be in the hospital," Dr. Doyle said. "I'd feel the same way. But I think it is best under the circumstances. We'll get you out just as soon as possible. Not only do I want to continue giving you IV steroids, but I want you breathing humidified, clean, nonirritating air. I also want to follow your peak expiratory flow rate carefully. As I explained to you earlier, it is still not completely back to normal."

"How many days do you estimate I'll have to be in here?" Donald asked.

"I'm sure it will only be a couple," Dr. Doyle said.

"I've got to go back to Texas," Donald explained.

"Oh?" Dr. Doyle said. "When were you there last?"

"Just last week," Donald said.

"Hmm," Dr. Doyle said while he thought. "Were you exposed to anything abnormal while you were there?"

"Just Tex-Mex cuisine," Donald said, managing a smile.

"You haven't gotten any new pets or anything like

that, have you?" Dr. Doyle asked. One of the difficulties of managing someone with chronic asthma was determining the factors responsible for triggering attacks. Frequently it was allergenic.

"My girlfriend got a new cat," Donald said. "It has made me itch a bit the last few times I've been over there."

"When was the last time?" Dr. Doyle asked.

"Last night," Donald admitted. "But I was home just a little after eleven, and I felt fine. I didn't have any trouble falling asleep."

"We'll have to look into it," Dr. Doyle said. "Meanwhile I want you in the hospital. What do you say?"

"You're the doctor," Donald said reluctantly.

"Thank you," Dr. Doyle said.

CHAPTER TWELVE

Thursday, 9:45 A.M., March 21, 1996

"For chrissake!" Jack murmured under his breath as he was about to start the autopsy on Susanne Hard. Clint Abelard was hovering behind him like a gnat, constantly switching his weight from one leg to the other.

"Clint, why don't you step around the table and stand on the other side," Jack suggested. "You'll be able to see much better."

Clint took the suggestion and stood with his arms behind his back opposite from Jack.

"Now don't move," Jack mumbled to himself. Jack didn't like Clint hanging around, but he had no choice.

"It's sad when you see a young woman like this," Clint said suddenly.

Jack looked up. He hadn't expected such a comment from Clint. It seemed too human. He had struck Jack as an unfeeling, moody bureaucrat.

"How old is she?" Clint asked.

"Twenty-eight," Vinnie said from the head of the table.

"From the looks of her spine she didn't have an easy life," Clint said.

"She had several major back surgeries," Jack said.

"It's a double tragedy since she'd just given birth," Clint said. "Now the child is motherless."

"It was her second child," Vinnie said.

"I suppose I shouldn't forget her husband," Clint said. "It must be upsetting to lose your spouse."

A knifelike stab of emotion went down Jack's spine. He had to fight to keep from reaching across the table and yanking Clint off his feet. Abruptly he left the table and exited to the washroom. He heard Vinnie call after him, but he ignored him. Instead Jack leaned on the edge of the sink and tried to calm himself. He knew that getting angry with Clint was an unreasonable reaction; it was nothing but pure, unadulterated transference. But understanding the origin did not lessen the irritation. It always irked Jack when he heard such clichés from people who truly had no idea.

"Is there a problem?" Vinnie asked. He'd stuck his head through the door.

"I'll be there in a second," Jack said.

Vinnie let the door close.

As he was there, Jack washed and regloved his hands. When he was finished he returned to the table.

"Let's get this show on the road," he said.

"I've looked the body over," Clint said. "I don't see anything that looks like an insect bite, do you?"

Jack had to restrain himself from subjecting Clint to a lecture like the one Clint had given to him. Instead, he merely proceeded with his external exam. Only after he'd finished did he speak.

"No gangrene, no purpura, and no insect bites as far as I can see," Jack said. "But by just looking at her I can see some of her cervical lymph nodes are swollen."

Jack pointed out the finding to Clint, who then nodded in agreement.

"That's certainly consistent with plague," Clint said.

Jack didn't answer. Instead he took a scalpel from Vinnie and quickly made the typical Y-shaped autopsy incision. The bold cruelty of the move jolted Clint. He took a step back.

Jack worked quickly but with great care. He knew that the less the internal organs were disturbed, the less chance that any of the infecting microbes would be aero-solized.

When Jack had the organs out, he turned his attention first to the lungs. Calvin had drifted over at this point and towered behind Jack as he made his initial cuts into the obviously diseased organ. Jack spread open the lung like a butterfly.

"Lots of bronchopneumonia and early tissue necrosis," Calvin said. "Looks pretty similar to Nodelman."

"I don't know," Jack said. "Seems to me there is an equal amount of pathology but less consolidation. And look at these nodal areas. They almost look like early granulomas with caseation."

Clint listened to this pathological jargon with little interest or comprehension. He remembered the terms from medical school, but had long since forgotten their meaning. "Does it look like plague?" he asked.

"Consistent," Calvin said. "Let's look at the liver and the spleen."

Jack carefully pulled these organs from the pan and sliced into them. As he'd done with the lung, he spread open their cut surfaces so everyone could see. Even Laurie had stepped over from her table.

"Lots of necrosis," Jack said. "Certainly just as viru-lent a case as with Nodelman or with the case I did earlier."

"Looks like plague to me," Calvin said.

"But why was the fluorescein antibody negative?" Jack said. "That's telling me something, especially combined with the lung appearance."

"What's with the lungs?" Laurie asked.

Jack moved the liver and the spleen aside and showed Laurie the cut surface of the lung. He explained what he thought of the pathology.

"I see what you mean now that you mention it," Laurie said. "It is different from Nodelman. His lungs definitely had more consolidation. This looks more like some sort of horribly aggressive TB."

"Whoa!" Calvin said. "This isn't TB. No way."

"I don't think Laurie was suggesting it was," Jack said.

"I wasn't," Laurie agreed. "I was just using TB as a way of describing these infected areas."

"I think it is plague," Calvin said. "I mean, I wouldn't if we hadn't just had a case from the same hospital yesterday. Chances are it is plague regardless of what their lab said."

"I don't think it is," Jack said. "But let's see what our lab says."

"How about double or nothing with that ten dollars," Calvin said. "Are you that sure?"

"No, but I'll take you up on it. I know how much the money means to you."

"Are we finished here?" Clint asked. "If so, I think I'll be going."

"I'm essentially finished," Jack said. "I'll do a little more on the lymphatics, and then I'll be obtaining samples for the microscope. You won't be missing anything if you take off now."

"I'll head out with you," Calvin said.

Calvin and Clint disappeared through the door to the washroom.

"If you don't think this case is plague, what do you think it is?" Laurie asked, looking back at the woman's corpse.

"I'm embarrassed to tell you," Jack said.

"Come on," Laurie urged. "I won't tell anybody."

Jack looked at Vinnie. Vinnie held up his hands. "My lips are sealed."

"Well, I'd have to fall back on my original differential I had for Nodelman," Jack said. "To narrow it down more than that, I have to again go out on thin ice. If it isn't plague, the nearest infectious disease both pathologically and clinically is tularemia."

Laurie laughed. "Tularemia in a twenty-eight-year-old postpartum female in Manhattan?" she questioned. "That would be pretty rare, although not as rare as your diagnosis yesterday of plague. After all, she could have a hobby of rabbit hunting on weekends."

"I know it's not very probable," Jack said. "Once again I'm relying totally on the pathology and the fact that the test for plague was negative."

"I'd be willing to bet a quarter," Laurie said.

"Such a spender!" Jack joked. "Fine! We'll bet a quarter."

Laurie returned to her own case. Jack and Vinnie turned their attention back to Susanne Hard. While Vinnie did his tasks, Jack finished the lymphatic dissection he wanted to do, then took the tissue samples he felt appropriate for microscopic study. When the samples were all in the proper preservatives and appropriately labeled, he helped Vinnie suture the corpse.

Leaving the autopsy room, Jack properly dealt with his isolation equipment. After plugging in his rechargeable ventilator battery, he took the elevator up to the third floor to see Agnes Finn. He found her sitting in front of a stack of petri dishes examining bacterial cultures.

"I've just finished another infectious case that's suspected plague," he told her. "All the samples will be coming up shortly. But there is a problem. The lab over at the Manhattan General claims the patient tested negative. Of course, I want to repeat that, but at the same time I want you to rule out tularemia, and I want it done as quickly as possible."

"That's not easy," she said. "Handling *Francisella tularensis* is hazardous. It's very contagious to laboratory workers if it gets into the air. There is a fluorescein antibody stain for tularemia, but we don't have it."

"How do you make the diagnosis, then?" Jack asked.

"We have to send any samples out," she said. "Because of the risk of handling the bacteria the reagents are generally kept only at reference labs where the personnel are accustomed to dealing with the microbe. There is such a lab here in the city."

"Can you send it right away?" Jack asked.

"We'll messenger it over as soon as it gets here," she said. "If I call and put a rush on it, we'll have a preliminary result in less than twenty-four hours."

"Perfect," Jack said. "I'll be waiting. I've got ten dollars and twenty-five cents riding on the outcome."

Agnes gave Jack a look. He considered explaining, but feared he'd sound even more foolish. Instead he fled upstairs to his office.

CHAPTER THIRTEEN

"I'm liking it more and more," Terese said. She straightened up from Colleen's drawing board. Colleen was showing her tissues that her team had comped up just that morning using the theme they'd discussed the night before.

"The best thing is that the concept is consistent with the Hippocratic oath," Colleen said. "Particularly the part about never doing harm to anyone. I love it."

"I don't know why we didn't think about it before," Terese said. "It's such a natural. It's almost embarrassing that it took this damn plague epidemic to make us think of it. Did you catch what's happening on morning TV?"

"Three deaths!" Colleen said. "And several people sick. It's terrible. In fact, it scares me to death."

"I had a headache from the wine last night when I woke up this morning," Terese said. "The first thing that went through my mind was whether I had the plague or not."

"I thought the same thing," Colleen said. "I'm glad you admitted it. I was too embarrassed."

"I hope to hell those guys were right last night," Terese said. "They seemed pretty damn confident it wasn't going to be a big problem."

"Are you worried being around them?" Colleen asked.

"Oh, it's gone through my mind," Terese admitted. "But as I said, they were so confident. I can't imagine their acting that way if there were any risk."

"Are we still on for dinner tonight?" Colleen asked.

"By all means," Terese said. "I have a sneaking suspicion that Jack Stapleton will turn out to be an unknowing fountain of ad ideas. He might be bitter about something, but he's sharp and opinionated, and he certainly knows the business."

"I can't believe how well this is working out," Colleen said. "I was a lot more drawn to Chet; he's fun and open and easy to talk with. I have enough problems of my own, so I'm not attracted to the anguished, brooding type."

"I didn't say anything about being attracted to Jack Stapleton," Terese said. "That's something else entirely."

"What's your gut reaction to this idea of using Hippocrates himself in one of our ads?"

"I think it has fantastic potential," Terese said. "Run with it. Meanwhile I'm going to head upstairs and talk with Helen Robinson."

"Why?" Colleen asked. "I thought she was the enemy."

"I'm taking to heart Taylor's admonition that we creatives and the account people should work together," Terese said breezily.

"Yeah, sure! Likely story!"

"Seriously," Terese said. "There's something I'd like her to do. I need a fifth column. I want Helen to confirm that National Health is clean when it comes to nosocomial or hospital-based infections. If their record is atrocious, the whole campaign could backfire. Then, not only would I lose my bid for the presidency, but you and I would probably be out selling pencils."

"Wouldn't we have heard by this time?" Colleen asked. "I mean, they've been clients for a number of years."

"I doubt it," Terese said. "These health-care giants are loath to publicize anything that might adversely affect their stock price. Surely a bad record in regard to noso-comial infections would do that."

Terese gave Colleen a pat on the shoulder and told her to keep cracking the whip, then headed for the stairwell.

Terese emerged breathless onto the administrative floor, having taken the stairs two at a time. From there she marched directly toward the carpeted realm of the account executives. Her mood was soaring; it was the absolute antithesis of the anxiety and dread of the day before. Her intuition told her she was onto something big with National Health and would soon be scoring a deserved triumph. . .

As soon as the impromptu meeting with Terese had ended and Terese had disappeared around the corner, Helen returned to her desk and put a call in to her main contact at National Health Care. The woman wasn't immediately available, but Helen didn't expect her to be. Helen merely left her name and number with a request to be called as soon as possible.

With the call accomplished Helen took a brush from her desk and ran it through her hair several times in front of a small mirror on the inside of her closet door.

Once she was satisfied with her appearance, she walked out of her office and headed down to Robert Barker's.

"You have a minute?" Helen called to him from his open door.

"For you I have all day," Robert said. He leaned back in his chair.

Helen stepped into the room and turned to close the door. As she did so, Robert surreptitiously turned over the photo of his wife that stood on the corner of the desk. His wife's stern stare made him feel guilty whenever Helen was in his office.

"I just had a visitor," Helen said as she came into the room. As was her custom she sat cross-legged on the arm of one of the two chairs facing Robert's desk.

Robert felt perspiration appear along his hairline in keeping with his quickening pulse. From his vantage point, Helen's short skirt afforded him a view of her thigh that didn't stop.

"It was our creative director," Helen continued. She was very conscious of the effect she was having on her boss, and it pleased her. "She asked me to get some information for her."

"What kind of information?" Robert asked. His eyes didn't move, nor did he blink. It was as if he were hypnotized.

Helen explained what Terese wanted and described the brief conversation about the plague outbreak. When Robert didn't respond immediately, she stood up. That broke the trance. "I tried to tell her not to use it as the basis of an ad campaign," Helen added, "but she thinks it's going to work."

"Maybe you shouldn't have said anything," Robert remarked. He loosened his shirt and took a breath.

"But it's a terrible idea," Helen said. "I couldn't think of anything more tasteless."

"Exactly," Robert said. "I'd like her to propose a tasteless campaign."

"I see your point," Helen said. "I didn't think of that on the spur of the moment."

"Of course not," Robert said. "You're not as devious as I am. But you're a quick study. The problem with the idea about nosocomial infection in general is that it could be a good one. There might possibly be a legitimate difference between National Health and AmeriCare."

"I could always tell her the information wasn't available," Helen said. "After all, it might not be."

"There is always risk in lying," Robert said. "She might already have the information and be testing us to make us look bad. No, go ahead and see what you can find out. But let me know what you learn and what you pass on to Terese Hagen. I want to keep a step ahead of her."

CHAPTER FOURTEEN

"Hey, sport, how the hell are you?" Chet asked Jack as Jack scooted into their shared office and dumped several folders onto his cluttered desk.

"Couldn't be better," Jack said.

Thursday had been a paper day for Chet, meaning he'd been at his desk and not in the autopsy room. Generally the associate medical examiners only did autopsies three days a week. The other days they spent collating the voluminous paperwork necessary to "sign out" a case. There was always material that needed to be gathered from PA investigators, the lab, the hospital or local doctors, or the police. Plus each doctor had to read the microscopic slides the histology lab processed on every case.

Jack sat down and pushed some of the paper debris away from the center of the desk to give him some room to work.

"You feel all right this morning?" Chet asked.

"A little wobbly," Jack admitted. He rescued his phone from beneath lab reports. Then he opened up one of the folders he'd just brought in with him and began searching through the contents. "And you?"

"Perfect," Chet said. "But I'm accustomed to a little

wine and such. Remembering those chicks helped, particularly Colleen. Hey, we still on for tonight?"

"I was going to talk to you about that," Jack said.

"You promised," Chet said.

"I didn't exactly promise," Jack said.

"Come on," Chet pleaded. "Don't let me down. They're expecting both of us. They might not stay if only I show up."

Jack glanced over at his officemate.

"Come on," Chet repeated. "Please!"

"All right, for chrissake," Jack said. "Just this once. But I truly don't understand why you think you need me. You do fine by yourself."

"Thanks, buddy," Chet said. "I owe you one."

Jack found the ID sheet that had the phone numbers for Maurice Hard, Susanne's husband. There was both a home number and an office number. He dialed the home.

"Who you calling?" Chet asked.

"You are a nosy bastard," Jack said jokingly.

"I've got to watch over you so you don't get yourself fired," Chet said.

"I'm calling the spouse of another curious infectious case," Jack said. "I just did the post, and it's got me bewildered. Clinically it looked like plague, but I don't think it was."

A housekeeper picked up the phone. When Jack asked for Mr. Hard, he was told Mr. Hard was at the office. Jack dialed the second number. This time it was answered by a secretary. Jack had to explain who he was and was then put on hold. "I'm amazed," Jack said to Chet, his hand over the receiver. "The man's wife just died and he's at work. Only in America!"

Maurice Hard came on the line. His voice was strained. He was obviously under great stress. Jack was tempted to tell the man he knew something of what he was feeling, but something made him hold back. Instead he explained who he was and why he was calling.

"Do you think I should talk to my lawyer first?" Maurice asked.

"Lawyer? Why your lawyer?"

"My wife's family is making ridiculous accusations," Maurice said. "They're suggesting I had something to do with Susanne's death. They're crazy. Rich, but crazy. I mean, Susanne and I had our ups and downs, but we never would have hurt each other, no way."

"Do they know your wife died of an infectious disease?" Jack questioned.

"I've tried to tell them," Maurice said.

"I don't know what to say," Jack said. "It's really not my position to advise you about your personal legal situation."

"Well, hell, go ahead and ask your questions," Maurice said. "I can't imagine it would make any difference. But let me ask you a question first. Was it plague?"

"That still has not been determined," Jack said. "But I'll call you as soon as we know for sure."

"I'd appreciate that," Maurice said. "Now, what are your questions?"

"I believe you have a dog," Jack said. "Is the dog healthy?"

"For a seventeen-year-old dog he's healthy," Maurice said.

"I'd like to encourage you to take the pet to your vet and explain that your wife died of a serious infectious disease. I want to be sure the dog isn't carrying the illness, whatever it was."

"Is there a chance of that?" Maurice asked with alarm.

"It's small, but there is a chance," Jack said.

"Why didn't the hospital tell me that?" he demanded.

"That I can't answer," Jack said. "I assume they talked to you about taking antibiotics."

"Yeah, I've already started," Maurice said. "But it bums me out about the dog. I should have been informed."

"There's also the issue of travel," Jack said. "I was told your wife didn't do any recent traveling."

"That's right," Maurice said. "She was pretty uncomfortable with her pregnancy, especially with her back problem. We haven't gone anywhere except to our house up in Connecticut."

"When was the last visit to Connecticut?" Jack asked.

"About a week and a half ago," Maurice said. "She liked it up there."

"Is it rural?" Jack asked.

"Seventy acres of fields and forest land," Maurice said proudly. "Beautiful spot. We have our own pond."

"Did your wife ever go out into the woods?" Jack asked.

"All the time," Maurice said. "That was her main enjoyment. She liked to feed the deer and the rabbits."

"Were there many rabbits?" Jack asked.

"You know rabbits," Maurice said. "Every time we went up there there were more of them. I actually thought they were a pain in the neck. In the spring and summer they ate all the goddamn flowers."

"Any problem with rats?"

"Not that I know of," Maurice said. "Are you sure this is all significant?"

"We never know," Jack said. "What about your visitor from India?"

"That was Mr. Svinashan," Maurice said. "He's a business acquaintance from Bombay. He stayed with us for almost a week."

"Hmm," Jack said, remembering the plague outbreak in 1994 in Bombay. "As far as you know, he's healthy and well?"

"As far as I know," Maurice said.

"How about giving him a call," Jack suggested. "If he's been sick, let me know."

"No problem," Maurice said. "You don't think he could have been involved, do you? After all, his visit was three weeks ago."

"This episode has baffled me," Jack admitted. "I'm not ruling anything out. What about Donald Nodelman? Did you or your wife know him?"

"Who's he?" Maurice asked.

"He was the first victim in this plague outbreak," Jack said. "He was a patient in the Manhattan General. I'd be curious if your wife might have visited him. He was on the same floor."

"In OB-GYN?" Maurice questioned with surprise.

"He was on the medical ward on the opposite side of the building. He was in the hospital for diabetes."

"Where did he live?"

"The Bronx," Jack said.

"I doubt it," Maurice said. "We don't know anyone from the Bronx."

"One last question," Jack said. "Did your wife happen

to visit the hospital during the week prior to her admission?"

"She hated hospitals," Maurice said. "It was difficult to get her to go even when she was in labor."

Jack thanked Maurice and hung up.

"Now who you calling?" Chet asked as Jack dialed again.

"The husband of my first case this morning," Jack said. "At least we know this case had plague for sure."

"Why don't you let the PAs make these calls?" Chet asked.

"Because I can't tell them what to ask," Jack said. "I don't know what I'm looking for. I just have this suspicion that there is some missing piece of information. Also I'm just plain interested. The more I think about this episode of plague in New York in March, the more unique I think it is."

Mr. Harry Mueller was a far cry from Mr. Maurice Hard. He was devastated by his loss and had trouble speaking despite a professed willingness to be cooperative. Not wishing to add to the man's burden, Jack tried to be quick. After corroborating Janice's report of no pets or travel and no recent visitors, Jack went through the same question concerning Donald Nodelman as he had with Maurice.

"I'm certain my wife did not know this individual," Harry said, "and she rarely met any patients directly, especially sick patients."

"Did your wife work in central supply for a long time?" Jack asked.

"Twenty-one years," Harry said.

"Did she ever come down with any illness that she thought she'd contracted at the hospital?" Jack asked.

"Maybe if one of her co-workers had a cold," Harry said. "But nothing more than that."

"Thank you, Mr. Mueller," Jack said. "You've been most kind."

"Katherine would have wanted me to help," Harry said. "She was a good person."

Jack hung up the phone but left his hands drumming on the receiver. He was agitated.

"Nobody, including me, has any idea what the hell is going on here," he said.

"True," Chet said. "But it's not your worry. The cavalry has already arrived. I heard that the city epidemiologist was over here observing this morning."

"He was here all right," Jack said. "But it was in desperation. That little twerp hasn't the foggiest notion of what's going on. If it weren't for the CDC's sending someone up here from Atlanta, nothing would be happening. At least someone's out there trapping rats and looking for a reservoir."

Suddenly Jack pushed back from the desk, got up, and pulled on his bomber jacket.

"Uh-oh!" Chet said. "I sense trouble. Where are you going?"

"I'm heading back to the General," Jack said. "My gut sense tells me the missing information is over there at the hospital, and by God I'm going to find it."

"What about Bingham?" Chet said nervously.

"Cover for me," Jack said. "If I'm late for Thursday conference, tell him . . ." Jack paused as he tried to think up some appropriate excuse, but nothing came to mind. "Oh, screw it," he said. "I won't be that long. I'll be back way before conference. If anybody calls, tell them I'm in the john."

Ignoring further pleas to reconsider, Jack left and rode uptown. He arrived in less than fifteen minutes and locked his bike to the same signpost as the day before.

The first thing Jack did was take the hospital elevator up to the seventh floor and reconnoiter. He saw how the OB-GYN and medical wards were completely separate without sharing any common facilities like lounges or lavatories. He also saw that the ventilation system was designed so as to preclude any movement of air from one ward to the other.

Pushing through the swinging doors into the OB-GYN area, Jack walked down to the central desk.

"Excuse me," he said to a ward secretary. "Does this ward share any personnel with the medical ward across the elevator lobby?"

"No, not that I know of," the young man said. He looked about fifteen with a complexion that suggested he had yet to shave. "Except, of course, cleaning people. But they clean all over the hospital."

"Good point," Jack said. He hadn't thought of the housekeeping department. It was something to consider. Jack then asked which room Susanne Hard had occupied.

"Can I ask what this is in reference to?" the ward clerk asked. He had finally noticed that Jack was not wearing a hospital ID. Hospitals all require identification badges of their employees, but then frequently do not have the personnel to enforce compliance.

Jack took out his ME badge and flashed it. It had the desired effect. The ward secretary told Jack that Mrs. Hard had been in room 742.

Jack started out for the room, but the ward clerk

called out to him that it was quarantined and temporarily sealed.

Believing that viewing the room would not have been enlightening anyway, Jack left the seventh floor and descended to the third, which housed the surgical suites, the recovery room, the intensive-care units, and central supply. It was a busy area with a lot of patient traffic.

Jack pushed through a pair of swinging doors into central supply and was confronted by an unmanned counter. Beyond the counter was an immense maze of floor-to-ceiling metal shelving laden with all the sundry equipment and supplies needed by a large, busy hospital. In and out of the maze moved a team of people attired in scrubs, white coats, and hats that looked like shower caps. A radio played somewhere in the distance.

After Jack had stood at the counter for a few minutes, a robust and vigorous woman caught sight of him and came over. Her name tag said "Gladys Zarelli, Supervisor." She asked if he needed some help.

"I wanted to inquire about Katherine Mueller," Jack said.

"God rest her soul," Gladys said. She made the sign of the cross. "It was a terrible thing."

Jack introduced himself by displaying his badge, then questioned whether she and her co-workers were concerned that Katherine had died of an infectious disease.

"Of course we're concerned," she said. "Who wouldn't be? We all work closely with one another. But what can you do? At least the hospital is concerned as well. They have us all on antibiotics, and thank God, no one is sick."

"Has anything like this ever happened before?" Jack asked. "What I mean is, a patient died of plague just the day before Katherine. That suggests that Katherine could very well have caught it here at the hospital. I don't mean to scare you, but those are the facts."

"We're all aware of it," Gladys said. "But it's never happened before. I imagine it's happened in nursing, but not here in central supply."

"Do you people have any patient contact?" Jack asked.

"Not really," Gladys said. "Occasionally we might run up to the wards, but it's never to see a patient directly."

"What was Katherine doing the week before she died?" Jack asked.

"I'll have to look that up," Gladys said. She motioned for Jack to follow her. She led Jack into a tiny, windowless office where she cracked open a large, cloth-bound daily ledger.

"Assignments are never too strict," Gladys said. Her finger ran down a row of names. "We all kinda pitch in as needed, but I give some basic responsibility to some of the more senior people." Her finger stopped, then moved across the page. "Okay, Katherine was more or less in charge of supplies to the wards."

"What does that mean?" Jack asked.

"Whatever they needed," Gladys said. "Everything except drugs and that sort of stuff. That comes from pharmacy."

"You mean like things for the patients' rooms?" Jack asked.

"Sure, for the rooms, for the nurses' station, every-thing," Gladys said. "This is where it all comes from. Without us the hospital would grind to a halt in twenty-four hours."

"Give me an example of the things you deal with for the rooms," Jack said.

"I'm telling you, everything!" Gladys said with a touch of irritation in her voice. "Bedpans, thermometers, humidifiers, pillows, pitchers, soap. Everything."

"You wouldn't have any record of Katherine going up to the seventh floor during the last week or so, would you?"

"No," Gladys said. "We don't keep records like that. I could print out for you everything sent up there, though. That we have a record of."

"Okay," Jack said. "I'll take what I can get."

"It's going to be a lot of stuff," Gladys warned as she made an entry into her computer terminal. "Do you want OB-GYN or medical or both?" she asked.

"Medical," Jack said.

Gladys nodded, pecked at a few more keys on her terminal, and soon her printer was cranking away. In a few minutes she handed Jack a stack of papers. He glanced through them. As Gladys had suggested there were a lot of items. The length of the list gave Jack respect for the logistics of running the institution.

Leaving central supply, Jack descended a floor and wandered into the lab. He did not feel he was making any progress, but he refused to give up. His conviction remained that there was some major missing piece of information. He just didn't know where he would find it.

Jack asked the same receptionist to whom he'd shown his badge the day before for directions to microbiology, which she gave him without question.

Jack walked unchallenged through the extensive lab. It was an odd feeling to see so much impressive equipment running unattended. It reminded Jack of the director's lament the day before that he'd been forced to cut his personnel by twenty percent.

Jack found Nancy Wiggens working at a lab bench plating bacterial cultures.

"Howdy," Jack said. "Remember me?"

Nancy glanced up and then back at her work.

"Of course," she said.

"You guys made the diagnosis on the second plague case just fine," he said.

"It's easy when you suspect it," Nancy said. "But we didn't do so well on the third case."

"I was going to ask you about that," Jack said. "What did the gram stain look like?"

"I didn't do it," Nancy said. "Beth Holderness did. Would you like to talk with her?"

"I would," Jack said.

Nancy slid off her stool and disappeared. Jack took the opportunity to glance around at the microbiology section of the lab. He was impressed. Most labs, particularly microbiology labs, had an invariable clutter. This lab was different. It appeared highly efficient with everything crystal-clean and in its place.

"Hi, I'm Beth!"

Jack turned to find himself before a smiling, outgoing woman in her mid-twenties. She exuded a cheerleader-like zeal that was infectious. Her hair was tightly permed and radiated away from her face as if charged with static electricity.

Jack introduced himself and was immediately charmed by Beth's natural conversation. She was one of the friendliest women he'd ever met.

"Well, I'm sure you didn't come here to gab," Beth said. "I understand you are interested in the gram stain on Susanne Hard. Come on! It's waiting for you."

Beth literally grabbed Jack by the sleeve and pulled

him around to her work area. Her microscope was set up with Hard's slide positioned on its platform and the illuminator switched on.

"Sit yourself right here," Beth said as she guided Jack's lower half onto her stool. "How is that? Low enough?"

"It's perfect," Jack said. He leaned forward and peered into the eye-pieces. It took a moment for his eyes to adapt. When they did, he could see the field was filled with reddish-stained bacteria.

"Notice how pleomorphic the microbes are," a male voice commented.

Jack looked up. Richard, the head tech, had materialized and was standing to Jack's immediate left, almost touching him.

"I didn't mean to be such a bother," Jack said.

"No bother," Richard said. "In fact, I'm interested in your opinion. We still haven't made a diagnosis on this case. Nothing has grown out, and I presume you know that the test for plague was negative."

"So I heard," Jack said. He put his eyes back to the microscope and peered in again. "I don't think you want my opinion. I'm not so good at this stuff," he admitted.

"But you do see the pleomorphism?" Richard said.

"I suppose," Jack said. "They're pretty small bacilli. Some of them almost look spherical, or am I looking at them on end?"

"I believe you are seeing them as they are," Richard said. "That's more pleomorphism than you see with plague. That's why Beth and I doubted it was plague. Of course, we weren't sure until the fluorescein antibody was negative."

Jack looked up from the scope. "If it's not plague, what do you think it is?"

Richard gave a little embarrassed laugh. "I don't know."

Jack looked at Beth. "What about you? Care to take a chance?"

Beth shook her head. "Not if Richard won't," she said diplomatically.

"Can't someone even hazard a guess?" Jack asked.

Richard shook his head. "Not me. I'm always wrong when I guess."

"You weren't wrong about plague," Jack reminded him.

"That was just lucky," Richard said. He flushed.

"What's going on here?" an irritated voice called out.

Jack's head swung around in the opposite direction. Beyond Beth was the director of the lab, Martin Cheveau. He was standing with his legs apart, his hands on his hips, and his mustache quivering. Behind him was Dr. Mary Zimmerman, and behind her was Charles Kelley.

Jack got to his feet. The lab techs slunk back. The atmosphere was suddenly tense. The lab director was clearly irate.

"Are you here in an official capacity?" Martin demanded. "If so, I'd like to know why you didn't have the common courtesy to come to my office instead of sneaking in here? We have a crisis unfolding in this hospital, and this lab is in the middle of it. I am not about to brook interference from anyone."

"Whoa!" Jack said. "Calm down." He hadn't expected this blowup, especially from Martin, who had been so hospitable the day before.

"Don't tell me to calm down," Martin snapped. "What the devil are you doing here, anyway?"

"I'm just doing my job, investigating the deaths of Katherine Mueller and Susanne Hard," Jack said. "I hardly think I'm interfering. In fact I thought I was being rather discreet."

"Is there something in particular you are looking for in my lab?" Martin demanded.

"I was just going over a gram stain with your capable staff," Jack said.

"Your official mandate is to determine the cause and the manner of death," Dr. Zimmerman said, pushing her way in front of Martin. "You've done that."

"Not quite," Jack corrected. "We haven't made a diagnosis on Susanne Hard." He returned the infection-control officer's beady stare. Since she wasn't wearing the mask she'd had on the day before, Jack was able to appreciate how stern her thin-lipped face was.

"You haven't made a specific diagnosis in the Hard case," Dr. Zimmerman corrected, "but you have made a diagnosis of a fatal infectious disease. Under the circumstances I think that is adequate."

"Adequate has never been my goal in medicine," Jack said.

"Nor mine," Dr. Zimmerman shot back. "Nor is it for the Centers for Disease Control or the City Board of Health, who are actively investigating this unfortunate incident. Frankly your presence here is disruptive."

"Are you sure they don't need a little help?" Jack asked. He couldn't hold back the sarcasm.

"I'd say your presence is more than disruptive," Kelley said. "In fact, you've been downright slanderous. You could very well be hearing from our lawyers."

"Whoa!" Jack said again, lifting his hands as if to fend

off a bodily attack. "Disruptive I can at least comprehend. Slanderous is ridiculous."

"Not from my point of view," Kelley said. "The
supervisor in central supply said you told her Katherine
Mueller had contracted her illness on the job."

"And that has not been established," Dr. Zimmerman
added.

"Uttering such an unsubstantiated statement is
defamatory to this institution and injurious to its repu-
tation," Kelley snapped.

"And could have a negative impact on its stock value,"
Jack said.

"And that too," Kelley agreed.

"The trouble is I didn't say Mueller had contracted
her illness on the job," Jack said. "I said she could have
done so. There's a big difference."

"Mrs. Zarelli told us you told her it was a fact," Kelley
said.

"I told her 'those were the facts' referring to the
possibility," Jack said. "But look, we're quibbling. The
real fact is that you people are overly defensive. It makes
me wonder about your nosocomial infection history.
What's the story there?"

Kelley turned purple. Given the man's intimidating
size advantage, Jack took a protective step backward.

"Our nosocomial infection experience is none of your
business," Kelley sputtered.

"That's something I'm beginning to question," Jack
said. "But I'll save looking into it for another time. It's
been nice seeing you all again. Bye."

Jack broke off from the group and strode away. He
heard sudden movement behind him and cringed, half
expecting a beaker or some other handy piece of

laboratory paraphernalia to sail past his ear. But he reached the door to the hallway without incident. Descending a floor, he unlocked his bike and headed south.

Jack weaved in and out of the traffic, marveling at his latest brush with AmeriCare. Most confusing was the sensitivity of the people involved. Even Martin, who'd been friendly the day before, now acted as if Jack were the enemy. What could they all be hiding? And why hide it from Jack?

Jack didn't know who at the hospital had alerted the administration of his presence, but he had a good idea who would be informing Bingham that he'd been there. Jack entertained no illusions about Kelley complaining about him again.

Jack wasn't disappointed. As soon as he came in the receiving bay, the security man stopped him.

"I was told to tell you to go directly to the chief's office," the man said. "Dr Washington himself gave me the message."

As Jack locked his bike, he tried to think of what he was going to say to Bingham. Nothing came to mind.

While ascending in the elevator, Jack decided he'd switch to offense since he couldn't think of any defense. He was still formulating an idea when he presented himself in front of Mrs. Sanford's desk.

"You're to go right in," Mrs. Sanford said. As usual she didn't look up from her work.

Jack stepped around her desk and entered Bingham's office. Immediately he saw that Bingham wasn't alone. Calvin's huge hulk was hovering near the glass-fronted bookcase.

"Chief, we have a problem," Jack said earnestly. He

moved over to Bingham's desk and gave it a tap with his fist for emphasis. "We don't have a diagnosis on the Hard case, and we got to give it to them ASAP. If we don't we're going to look bad, especially the way the press is all stirred up about the plague. I even went all the way over to the General to take a look at the gram stain. Unfortunately, it didn't help."

Bingham regarded Jack curiously with his rheumy eyes. He'd been about to lambaste Jack; now he demurred. Instead of speaking he removed his wire-rimmed spectacles and absently cleaned them while he considered Jack's words. He glanced over at Calvin. Calvin responded by stepping up to the desk. He wasn't fooled by Jack's ruse.

"What the hell are you talking about?" Calvin demanded.

"Susanne Hard," Jack said. "You remember. The case you and I have the ten-dollar double-or-nothing bet on."

"A bet!" Bingham questioned. "Is there gambling going on in this office?"

"Not really, Chief," Calvin said. "It was just a way of making a point. It's not routine."

"I should hope not," Bingham snapped. "I don't want any wagering around here, especially not in regard to diagnosis. That's not the kind of thing I'd like to see in the press. Our critics would have a field day."

"Getting back to Susanne Hard," Jack said. "I'm at a loss as to how to proceed. I'd hoped that by talking directly to the hospital lab people I might have made some headway, but it didn't work. What do you think I should do now?" Jack wanted the conversation to move away from the gambling issue. It might divert Bingham, but Jack knew he'd have hell to pay with Calvin later on.

"I'm a little confused," Bingham said. "Just yesterday I specifically told you to stay around here and get your backload of cases signed out. I especially told you to stay the hell away from the Manhattan General Hospital."

"That was if I were going there for personal reasons," Jack said. "I wasn't. This was all business."

"Then how the hell did you manage to get the administrator all bent out of shape again?" Bingham demanded. "He called the damn mayor's office for the second day in a row. The mayor wants to know if you have some sort of mental problem or whether I have a mental problem for hiring you."

"I hope you reassured him we're both normal," Jack said.

"Don't be impertinent on top of everything else," Bingham said.

"To tell you the honest truth," Jack said, "I haven't the slightest idea why the administrator got upset. Maybe the pressure of this plague episode has gotten to everybody over there, because they're all acting weird."

"So now everyone seems weird to you," Bingham said.

"Well, not everyone," Jack admitted. "But there's something strange going on, I'm sure of it."

Bingham looked up at Calvin, who shrugged and rolled his eyes. He didn't understand what Jack was talking about. Bingham's attention returned to Jack.

"Listen," Bingham said. "I don't want to fire you, so don't make me. You're a smart man. You have a future in this field. But I'm warning you, if you willfully disobey me and continue to embarrass us in the community, I'll have no other recourse. Tell me you understand."

"Perfectly," Jack said.

"Fine," Bingham said. "Then get back to your work, and we'll see you later in conference."

Jack took the cue and instantly disappeared.

For a moment Bingham and Calvin remained silent, each lost in his own thoughts.

"He's an odd duck," Bingham said finally. "I can't read him."

"Nor can I," Calvin said. "His saving grace is that he is smart and truly a hard worker. He's very committed. Whenever he's on autopsy, he's always the first one in the pit."

"I know," Bingham said. "That's why I didn't fire him on the spot. But where does this brashness come from? He has to know it rubs people the wrong way, yet he doesn't seem to care. He's reckless, almost self-destructive, as he admitted himself yesterday. Why?"

"I don't know," Calvin said. "Sometimes I get the feeling it's anger. But directed at what? I haven't the foggiest. I've tried to talk with him a few times on a personal level, but it's like squeezing water out of a rock."

CHAPTER FIFTEEN

Thursday, 8:30 P.M., March 21, 1996

Terese and Colleen climbed out of the cab on Second Avenue between Eighty-ninth and Eighty-eighth Streets a few doors away from Elaine's and walked to the restaurant. They couldn't get out right in front because of several limos inconveniently double-parked.

"How do I look?" Colleen asked as they paused under the canvas awning. She'd pulled off her coat for Terese's inspection.

"Too good," Terese said, and she meant it. Colleen had discarded her signature sweatshirt and jeans for a simple black dress that revealed her ample bust to perfection. Terese felt dowdy by comparison. She still had on her tailored suit that she'd worn to work that day, not having found time to go home to change.

"I don't know why I'm so nervous," Colleen admitted.

"Relax," Terese said. "With that dress Dr. McGovern doesn't stand a chance."

Colleen gave their names to the maître d' who immediately indicated recognition. He motioned for the women to follow him. He started to the rear.

It was an obstacle course of sorts to weave among the densely packed tables and scurrying waiters. Terese had the sensation of being in a fishbowl. Everyone, male and female alike, gave them the once-over as they passed.

The men were at a tiny table squeezed into the far corner. They got to their feet as the women approached. Chet held out Colleen's chair. Jack did the same for Terese. The women draped their coats over the backs of the chairs before sitting down.

"You men must know the owner to have gotten such a great table," Terese said.

Chet, who misinterpreted Terese's remark as a compliment, bragged he'd been introduced to Elaine a year previously. He explained she was the woman seated at the cash register at the end of the bar.

"They tried to seat us up in the front," Jack said. "But we declined. We thought you women wouldn't like the draft from the door."

"How thoughtful," Terese said. "Besides, this is so much more intimate."

"You think so?" Chet questioned. His face visibly brightened. They were, in reality, packed in like proverbial sardines.

"How could you question her?" Jack asked Chet. "She's so sincere."

"All right, enough!" Chet said good-naturedly. "I might be dense, but eventually I catch on."

They ordered wine and appetizers from the waiter who'd immediately appeared after the women had arrived. Colleen and Chet fell into easy conversation. Terese and Jack continued to be teasingly sarcastic with each other, but eventually the wine blunted their witticisms. By the time the main course was served, they were conversing congenially.

"What's the inside scoop on the plague situation?" Terese asked.

"There were two more deaths at the General," Jack said. "Plus a couple of febrile nurses are being treated."

"That was in the morning news," Terese said. "Anything new?"

"Only one of the deaths was actually plague," Jack said. "The other resembled plague clinically, but I personally don't think it was."

Terese stopped a forkful of pasta midway to her mouth. "No?" she questioned. "If it wasn't plague, what was it?"

Jack shrugged. "I wish I knew," he said. "I'm hoping the lab can tell me."

"The Manhattan General must be in an uproar," Terese said. "I'm glad I'm not a patient there now. Being in the hospital is scary enough under the best of circumstances. With the worry of diseases like plague around, it must be terrible."

"The administration is definitely agitated," Jack said. "And for good reason. If it turns out the plague originated there, it will be the first modern episode of nosocomial plague. That's hardly an accolade as far as the hospital is concerned."

"This concept of nosocomial infections is new to me," Terese said. "I'd never thought much about it before you and Chet talked about this current plague problem last night. Do all hospitals have such problems?"

"Absolutely," Jack said. "It's not common knowledge, but usually five to ten percent of hospitalized patients fall victim to infections contracted while they are in the hospital."

"My God!" Terese said. "I had no idea it was such a widespread phenomenon."

"It's all over," Chet agreed. "Every hospital has it, from the academic ivory tower to the smallest community hospital. What makes it so bad is that the hospital is the worst place to get an infection because many of the bugs hanging out there are resistant to antibiotics."

"Oh, great!" Terese said cynically. After she thought for a moment she asked, "Do hospitals differ significantly in their infection rates?"

"For sure," Chet said.

"Are these rates known?" Terese said.

"Yes and no," Chet said. "Hospitals are required by the Joint Commission of Accreditation to keep records of their infection rates, but the rates aren't released to the public."

"That's a travesty!" Terese said with a surreptitious wink at Colleen.

"If the rates go over a certain amount the hospital loses its accreditation," Chet said. "So all is not lost."

"But it's hardly fair to the public," Terese said. "By not having access to those rates people can't make their own decisions about which hospitals to patronize."

Chet opened his hands palms up like a supplicant priest. "That's politics," he said.

"I think it's awful," Terese said.

"Life's not fair," Jack said.

After dessert and coffee Chet and Colleen began campaigning to go someplace where there was dancing, like the China Club. Both Terese and Jack were disinclined. Chet and Colleen tried their best to change their minds, but they soon gave up.

"You guys go," Terese said.

"Are you sure?" Colleen asked.

"We wouldn't want to hold you back," Jack said.

Colleen looked at Chet.

"Let's go for it," Chet said.

Outside the restaurant Chet and Colleen happily piled into a cab. Jack and Terese waved as they drove off.

"I hope they enjoy themselves," Terese said. "I couldn't have thought of anything worse. Sitting in a smoke-filled nightclub assaulted by music loud enough to damage my ears is not my idea of pleasure."

"At least we've finally found something we can agree on," Jack said.

Terese laughed. She was beginning to appreciate Jack's sense of humor. It wasn't too dissimilar from her own.

For a moment of self-conscious indecision they stood at the curbside, each looking in a different direction. Second Avenue was alive with revelers despite a nippy temperature in the high thirties. The air was clear and the sky cloudless.

"I think the weatherman forgot it was the first day of spring," Terese said. She jammed her hands into her coat pockets and hunched up her shoulders.

"We could walk around the corner to that bar where we were last night," Jack suggested.

"We could," Terese said. "But I have a better idea. My agency is over on Madison. It's not too far away. How about a quick visit?"

"You're inviting me to your office despite knowing how I feel about advertising?" Jack asked.

"I thought it was only medical advertising you were against," Terese said.

"The truth is I'm not particularly fond of advertising

in general," Jack said. "Last night Chet jumped in before I had a chance to say it."

"But you're not opposed to it per se?" Terese questioned.

"Just the medical kind," Jack said. "For the reasons I gave."

"Then how about a quick visit? We do a lot more than just medical advertising. You might find it enlightening."

Jack tried to read the woman behind the soft, pale blue eyes and sensuous mouth. He was confused because the vulnerability they suggested wasn't in sync with the no-nonsense, goal-oriented, driven woman he suspected she was.

Terese met his stare head-on and smiled back coquettishly. "Be adventuresome!" she challenged.

"Why do I have the feeling you have an ulterior motive?" Jack asked.

"Probably because I do," Terese freely admitted. "I'd like your advice on a new ad campaign. I wasn't going to admit you'd been a stimulus for a new idea, but tonight during dinner I changed my mind about telling you."

"I don't know whether to feel used or complimented," Jack said. "How did I happen to give you an idea for an ad?"

"All this talk about plague at the Manhattan General Hospital," Terese said. "It made me think seriously about the issue of nosocomial infection."

Jack considered this statement for a moment. Then he asked, "And why did you change your mind about telling me and asking my advice?"

"Because it suddenly dawned on me that you might actually approve of the campaign," Terese said. "You told me the reason you were against advertising in medi-cine was because it didn't address issues of quality. Well, ads concerning nosocomial infections certainly would."

"I suppose," Jack said.

"Oh, come on," Terese said. "Of course it would. If a hospital was proud of its record, why not let the public know?"

"All right," Jack said. "I give up. Let's see this office of yours."

Having made the decision to go, there was the prob-lem of Jack's bike. At that moment it was locked to a nearby No Parking sign. After a short discussion they decided to leave the bike and go together in a cab. Jack would rescue the bike later on his way home.

With little traffic and a wildly fast and reckless Russian-émigré taxi driver, they arrived at Willow and Heath's building in minutes. Jack staggered out of the rear of the taxi.

"God!" he said. "People accuse me of taking a risk riding my bike in this city. It's nothing like riding with that maniac."

As if to underline Jack's statement, the cab shot away from the curb and disappeared up Madison Avenue with its tires screeching.

At ten-thirty the office building was locked up tight. Terese used her night key, and they entered. Their heels echoed noisily in the lonely marble hallway. Even the whine of the elevator seemed loud in the stillness.

"Are you here often after hours?" Jack asked.

Terese laughed cynically. "All the time," she said. "I practically live here."

They rode up in silence. When the doors opened Jack was shocked to find the floor brightly illuminated and bustling with activity as if it were midday. Toiling figures bent over many of the innumerable drawing boards.

"What do you have, two shifts?" Jack asked.

Terese laughed again. "Of course not," she said. "These people have been here since early this morning. Advertising is a competitive world. If you want to make it, you have to put in your time. We have several reviews coming up."

Terese excused herself and walked over to a woman at a nearby drawing table. While they conversed, Jack's eyes roamed the expansive space. He was surprised there were so few partitions. There was only a handful of separate rooms, which shared a common wall with the bank of elevators.

"Alice is going to bring in some material," Terese said when she rejoined Jack. "Why don't we go into Colleen's office?"

Terese led him into one of the rooms and turned on the lights. It was tiny, windowless, and claustrophobic when compared to the vast undivided space. It was also cluttered with papers, books, magazines, and videotapes. There were several easels set up with thick pads of drawing paper.

"I'm sure Colleen won't mind if I clear away a little area on her desk," Terese said as she moved aside stacks of orange-colored tracing paper. Gathering up an armload of books, she set them on the floor. No sooner had she finished than Alice Gerber, another of Terese's associates, appeared.

After making introductions, Terese had Alice run through a number of the potential commercial ideas they'd comped up that day.

Jack found himself interested more in the process than

the content. He'd never stopped to think about how TV commercials were made, and he came to appreciate the creativity involved and the amount of work.

It took Alice a quarter hour to present what she'd brought in. When she was finished, she gathered up the tissues and looked at Terese for further instructions. Terese thanked her and sent her back to her drawing board.

"So there you have it," Terese said to Jack. "Those're some of the ideas stemming from this nosocomial infection tissue. What do you think?"

"I'm impressed with how hard you work on this sort of thing," Jack said.

"I'm more interested in your reaction to the content," Terese said. "What do you think of the idea of Hippocrates coming into the hospital to award it the 'do no harm' medal?"

Jack shrugged. "I don't flatter myself to think I have the ability to intelligently critique a commercial."

"Oh, give me a break," Terese said, rolling her eyes to the ceiling. "I just want your opinion as a human being. This isn't an intellectual quiz. What would you think if you saw this commercial on the TV, say when you were watching the Super Bowl?"

"I'd think it was cute," Jack admitted.

"Would it make you think the National Health hospital might be a good place to go, since its nosocomial infection rates were low?"

"I suppose," Jack said.

"All right," Terese said, trying to keep herself calm. "Maybe you have some other ideas. What else could we do?"

Jack pondered for a few minutes. "You could do something about Oliver Wendell Holmes and Joseph Lister."

"Wasn't Holmes a poet?" Terese asked.

"He was also a doctor," Jack said. "He and Lister probably did more for getting doctors to wash their hands when going from patient to patient than anybody. Well, Semmelweis helped too. Anyway, handwashing was probably the most important lesson that needed to be learned to prevent hospital-based infections."

"Hmm," Terese said. "That sounds interesting. Personally, I love period pieces. Let me tell Alice to get someone to research it."

Jack followed Terese out of Colleen's office and watched her talk with Alice. It only took her a few minutes.

"Okay," Terese said, rejoining Jack. "She'll start the ball rolling. Let's get out of here."

In the elevator Terese had another suggestion. "Why don't we take a run over to your office," she said. "It's only fair now that you have seen mine."

"You don't want to see it," Jack said. "Trust me."

"Try me."

"It's the truth," Jack said. "It's not a pretty place."

"I think it would be interesting," Terese persisted. "I've only seen a morgue in the movies. Who knows, maybe it will give me some ideas. Besides, seeing where you work might help me understand you a little more."

"I'm not sure I want to be understood," Jack said.

The elevator stopped and the doors opened. They walked outside. They paused at the curb.

"What do you say? I can't imagine it would take too long, and it's not terribly late."

"You are a persistent sort," Jack commented. "Tell me: Do you always get your way?"

"Usually," Terese admitted. Then she laughed. "But I prefer to think of myself as tenacious."

"All right," Jack said finally. "But don't say I didn't warn you."

They caught a taxi. After Jack gave the destination the driver looped around and headed south on Park Avenue.

"You give me the impression of being a loner," Terese said.

"You're very perspicacious," Jack said.

"You don't have to be so caustic," Terese said.

"For once I wasn't," Jack said.

The lambent reflections of the streetlights played over their faces as they regarded each other in the half-light of the taxi.

"It's difficult for a woman to know how to feel around you," Terese said.

"I could say the same," Jack said.

"Have you ever been married?" Terese said. "That is, if you don't mind me asking."

"Yes, I was married," Jack said.

"But it didn't work out?" Terese said leadingly.

"There was a problem," Jack admitted. "But I don't really care to talk about it. How about you? Were you ever married?"

"Yes, I was," Terese said. She sighed and looked out her window. "But I don't like talking about it either."

"Now we have two things we agree on," Jack said. "We both feel the same about nightclubs and talking about our former marriages."

Jack had given directions to be dropped off at the Thirtieth Street entrance of the medical examiner's office. He was glad to see that both mortuary vans were gone. He thought their absence was a sign that there wouldn't be any fresh corpses lying around on gurneys. Although Terese had insisted on the visit, he was afraid of offending her sensibilities unnecessarily.

Terese said nothing as Jack led her past the banks of refrigerated compartments. It wasn't until she saw all the simple pine coffins that she spoke. She asked why they were there.

"They're for the unclaimed and unidentified dead," Jack said. "They are buried at city expense."

"Does that happen often?" Terese asked.

"All the time," Jack said.

Jack took her back to the area of the autopsy room. He opened the door to the washroom. Terese leaned in but didn't enter. The autopsy room was visible through a windowed door. The stainless-steel dissecting tables glistened ominously in the half-light.

"I expected this place to be more modern," she said. She was hugging herself to keep from touching anything.

"At one time it was," Jack said. "It was supposed to have been renovated, but it didn't happen. Unfortunately the city is always in some kind of budgetary crisis, and few politicians balk at pulling money away from here. Adequate funding for normal operating expenses is hard to come by, much less money to update the facility. On the other hand we do have a new, state-of-the-art DNA lab."

"Where's your office?" Terese asked.

"Up on the fifth floor," Jack said.

"Can I see it?" she asked.

"Why not?" Jack said. "We've come this far."

They walked back past the mortuary office and waited for the elevator.

"This place is a little hard to take, isn't it?" Jack said.

"It has its gruesome side," Terese admitted.

"We who work here often forget the effect it has on laypeople," Jack said, though he was impressed with the degree of equanimity Terese had demonstrated.

The elevator arrived and they got on. Jack pressed the fifth floor, and they started up.

"How did you ever decide on this kind of career?" Terese asked. "Did you know back in medical school?"

"Heavens, no," Jack said. "I wanted something clean, technically demanding, emotionally fulfilling, and lucrative. I became an ophthalmologist."

"What happened?" Terese asked.

"My practice got taken over by AmeriCare," Jack said. "Since I didn't want to work for them or any similar corporation, I retrained. It's the buzzword these days for superfluous medical specialists."

"Was it difficult?" Terese asked.

Jack didn't answer immediately. The elevator arrived on the fifth floor and the doors opened.

"It was very difficult," Jack said as he started down the hall. "Mostly because it was so lonely."

Terese hazarded a glance in Jack's direction. She'd not expected him to be the type to complain of loneliness. She'd assumed he was a loner by choice. While she was looking, Jack furtively wiped the corner of an eye with his knuckle. Could there have been a tear? Terese was mystified.

"Here we are," Jack announced. He opened his office door with his key and flipped on the light.

The interior was worse than Terese had expected. It

was tiny and narrow. The furniture was gray metal and old, and the walls were in need of paint. There was a single, filthy window positioned high on the wall.

"Two desks?" Terese questioned.

"Chet and I share this space," Jack explained.

"Which desk is yours?"

"The messy one," Jack said. "This plague episode has put me farther behind than usual. I'm generally behind because I'm rather compulsive about my reports."

"Dr. Stapleton!" a voice called out.

It was Janice Jaeger, the PA investigator.

"Security told me you were here when I just came through the receiving bay," she said after being introduced to Terese. "I've been trying to reach you at home."

"What's the problem?" Jack asked.

"The reference lab called this evening," Janice said. "They ran the fluorescein antibody on Susanne Hard's lung tissue as you requested. It was positive for tularemia."

"Are you kidding?" Jack took the paper from Janice and stared at it with disbelief.

"What's tularemia?" Terese asked.

"It's another infectious disease," Jack said. "It's similar in some ways to plague."

"Where was this patient?" Terese asked, although she suspected the answer.

"Also at the General," Jack said. He shook his head. "I truly can't believe it. This is extraordinary!"

"I've got to get back to work," Janice said. "If you need me to do anything just let me know."

"I'm sorry," Jack said. "I didn't mean to have you stand here. Thanks for getting this to me."

"No problem," Janice said. She waved and headed back to the elevators.

"Is tularemia as bad as plague?" Terese asked.

"It's hard to make comparisons," Jack said. "But it's bad, particularly the pneumonic form, which is highly contagious. If Susanne Hard were still here she could tell us exactly how bad it is."

"Why are you so surprised?" Terese asked. "Is it as rare as plague?"

"Probably not," Jack said. "It's seen in a wider area in the U.S. than plague, particularly in southern states like Arkansas. But like plague it's not seen much in the winter, at least not up here in the north. Here it's a late-spring and summer problem, if it exists at all. It needs a vector, just like plague. Instead of the rat flea it's usually spread by ticks and deerflies."

"Any tick or deerfly?" Terese asked. Her parents had a cabin up in the Catskills where she liked to go in the summer. It was isolated and surrounded by forest and fields. There were plenty of ticks and deerflies.

"The reservoir for the bacteria is small mammals like rodents and especially rabbits," Jack said. He started to elaborate but quickly stopped. He'd suddenly recalled that afternoon's conversation with Susanne's husband, Maurice. Jack remembered being told that Susanne liked to go to Connecticut, walk in the woods, and feed wild rabbits!

"Maybe it was the rabbits," Jack mumbled.

"What are you talking about?" Terese asked.

Jack apologized for thinking out loud. Shaking himself out of a momentary daze, he motioned for Terese to follow him into his office and to take Chet's chair. He described his phone conversation with Susanne's husband and explained about the importance of wild rabbits in relation to tularemia.

"Sounds incriminating to me," Terese said.

"The only problem is that her exposure to the Connecticut rabbits was almost two weeks ago," Jack mused. He drummed his fingers on his telephone receiver. "That's a long incubation period, especially for the pneumonic form. Of course, if she didn't catch it in Connecticut, then she had to catch it here in the city, possibly at the General. Of course, nosocomial tularemia doesn't make any more sense than nosocomial plague."

"One way or the other the public has to know about this," Terese said. She nodded towards his hand on the phone. "I hope you are calling the media as well as the hospital."

"Neither," Jack said. He glanced at his watch. It was still before midnight. He picked up the phone and dialed. "I'm calling my immediate boss. The politics of all this are his bailiwick."

Calvin picked up on the first ring but mumbled as if he'd been asleep. Jack cheerfully identified himself.

"This better be important," Calvin growled.

"It is to me," Jack said. "I wanted you to be first to know you owe me another ten dollars."

"Get outta here," Calvin boomed. The grogginess had disappeared from his voice. "I hope to God this isn't some kind of sick joke."

"No joke," Jack assured him. "The lab just reported it in tonight. The Manhattan General had a case of tularemia in addition to its two cases of plague. I'm as surprised as anyone."

"The lab called you directly?" Calvin said.

"Nope," Jack said. "One of the PAs just gave it to me."

"Are you in the office?" Calvin asked.

"Sure am," Jack said. "Working my fingers to the bone."

"Tularemia?" Calvin questioned. "I'd better read up on it. I don't think I've ever seen a case."

"I read up on it just this afternoon," Jack admitted.

"Make sure there are no leaks from our office," Calvin said. "I won't call Bingham tonight, because there's nothing to be done at the moment. I'll let him know first thing in the morning, and he can call the commissioner, and she can call the Board of Health."

"Okay," Jack said.

"So you are going to keep it a secret," Terese said angrily as Jack hung up the receiver.

"It's not my doing," Jack said.

"Yeah, I know," Terese said sarcastically. "It's not your job."

"I already got myself in trouble over the plague episode for calling the commissioner on my own," Jack said. "I don't see any benefit by doing it again. Word will be out in the morning through the proper channels."

"What about people over at the General who are suspected of having plague?" Terese questioned. "They might have this new disease. I think you should let everyone know tonight."

"That's a good point," Jack said. "But it doesn't really matter. The treatment for tularemia is the same as the treatment for plague. We'll wait until morning. Besides, it's only a few hours away."

"What if I alerted the press?" Terese asked.

"I'll have to ask you not to do that," Jack said. "You

heard what my boss said. If it were investigated, the source would come back to me."

"You don't like advertising in medicine and I don't like politics in medicine," Terese said.

"Amen," Jack said.

CHAPTER SIXTEEN

Despite having gone to bed much later than usual for the second night in a row, Jack was wide awake at five-thirty Friday morning. He began mulling over the irony of a case of tularemia appearing in the middle of a plague outbreak. It was a curious coincidence, especially since he'd made the diagnosis. It was a feat certainly worth the ten dollars and twenty-five cents that he stood to win from Calvin and Laurie.

With his mind churning, Jack recognized the futility of trying to go back to sleep. Consequently he got up, ate breakfast, and was on his bike before six. With less traffic than usual, he got to work in record time.

The first thing Jack did was to visit the ID room to look for Laurie and Vinnie. Both had yet to arrive. Passing back through communications, he knocked on Janice's door. She appeared even more beleaguered than usual.

"What a night," she said.

"Busy?" Jack asked.

"That's an understatement," she said. "Especially with these added infectious cases. What's going on over there at the General?"

"How many today?" Jack asked.

"Three," Janice said. "And not one of them tested

positive for plague even though that's their presumed diagnosis. Also, all three were fulminant cases. The people all died within twelve or so hours after their first symptoms. It's very scary."

"All of these recent infectious cases have been fulminant," Jack commented.

"Do you think these three new ones are tularemia?" Janice asked.

"There's a good chance," Jack said. "Especially if they tested negative for plague as you say. You didn't mention Susanne's diagnosis to anyone, did you?"

"I had to bite my tongue, but I didn't," Janice said. "I'd learned in the past by sore experience that my role is to gather information, not give it out."

"I have to learn the same lesson," Jack said. "Are you finished with these three folders?"

"They're all yours," Janice said.

Jack carried the folders back to the ID room. Since Vinnie had not arrived Jack made the coffee in the communal pot. Mug in hand, he sat down and began going through the material.

Almost immediately he stumbled into something curious. The first case was a forty-two-year-old woman by the name of Maria Lopez. What was surprising was that she worked in central supply of the Manhattan General Hospital! Not only that, but she had worked on the same shift as Katherine Mueller!

Jack closed his eyes and tried to think of how two people from central supply could possibly have come down with two different fatal infectious diseases. As far as he was concerned, it could not be a coincidence. He was convinced their illnesses had to be work-related. The question was how?

In his mind's eye, Jack revisited central supply. He could picture the shelving and the aisles, even the outfits the employees wore. But nothing came to mind as a way for the employees to come in contact with contagious bacteria. Central supply had nothing to do with the disposal of hospital waste or even soiled linen, and as the supervisor had mentioned, workers there had little or no contact with patients.

Jack read the rest of Janice's investigative report. As she'd done with the cases since Nodelman, she included information about pets, travel, and visitors. For Maria Lopez, none of the three seemed a factor.

Jack opened the second folder. The patient's name was Joy Hester. In this case Jack felt there was little mystery. She'd been an OB-GYN nurse and had had significant exposure to Susanne Hard just prior to and after the onset of Susanne's symptoms. The only thing that bothered Jack was recalling that he'd read that person-to-person transmission of tularemia rarely occurred.

The third case was Donald Lagenthorpe, a thirty-eight-year-old petroleum engineer who'd been admitted to the hospital the previous morning. He'd come in through the ER with a refractory bout of asthma. He'd been treated with IV steroids and bronchodilators as well as humidified air and bed rest. According to Janice's notes, he'd shown steady improvement and had even been campaigning to be released, when he'd had the sudden onset of severe frontal headache.

The headache had started in the late afternoon and was followed by shaking chills and fever. There was also an increase in cough and exacerbation of his asthmatic symptoms despite the continued treatment. At that point he was diagnosed to have pneumonia, which was confirmed by X ray. Curiously enough, however, a gram stain of his sputum was negative for bacteria.

Myalgia also had become prominent. Sudden abdominal pain and deep tenderness had suggested a possible appendicitis. At seven-thirty in the evening Lagenthorpe had undergone an appendectomy, but the appendix proved to be normal. After the surgery his situation became progressively grave with apparent multisystem failure. His blood pressure dropped and became unresponsive to treatment. Urine output became negligible.

Reading on in Janice's report, Jack learned that the patient had visited isolated oil rigs in Texas the previous week and had literally been tramping around in desert conditions. Jack also learned that Mr. Lagenthorpe's girl-friend had recently obtained a pet Burmese cat. But he'd not been exposed to any visitors from exotic places.

"Wow! You're here early!" Laurie Montgomery exclaimed.

Jack was shocked out of his concentration in time to see Laurie sweep into the ID room and drape her coat over the desk she used for early-morning duties. It was the last day of her current rotation as supervisor in charge of determining which of the previous night's cases should be autopsied and who would do them. It was a thankless task that none of the board-certified doctors enjoyed.

"I've got some bad news for you," Jack said.

Laurie paused on her way into communications; a shadow passed over her usually bright, honey-complected face.

Jack laughed. "Hey, relax," he said. "It's not that bad. It's just that you owe me a quarter."

"Are you serious?" she asked. "The Hard case was tularemia?"

"The lab reported a positive fluorescein antibody last night," Jack said. "I think it's a firm diagnosis."

"It's a good thing I didn't bet any more than a quarter," Laurie said. "You are amassing some impressive statistics in the infectious arena. What's your secret?"

"Beginner's luck," Jack said. "By the way, I have three of last night's cases here. They're all infectious and all from the General. I'd like to do at least two of them."

"I can't think of any reason why not," Laurie said. "But let me run over to communications and get the rest."

The moment Laurie left, Vinnie made his appearance. His face was a pasty color and his heavily lidded eyes were red. From Jack's perspective he appeared as if he belonged in one of the coolers downstairs.

"You look like death warmed over," Jack said.

"Hangover," Vinnie remarked. "I went to a buddy's bachelor party. We all got whacked."

Vinnie tossed his newspaper on a desk and went over to the cupboard where the coffee was stored.

"In case you haven't noticed," Jack said, "the coffee is already made."

Vinnie had to stare at the coffee machine with its full pot for several beats until his tired mind comprehended that his current efforts were superfluous.

"How about starting on this instead?" Jack said. He pushed the Maria Lopez folder over to Vinnie. "Might as well get set up. Remember, the early bird . . ."

"Hold the clichés," Vinnie said. He took the folder and let it fall open in his hands. "Frankly, I'm not in the mood for any of your sappy sayings. What bugs me is that you can't come in here when everybody else does."

"Laurie's here," Jack reminded him.

"Yeah, but this is her week for scheduling. You don't have any excuse." He briefly read portions of the folder. "Wonderful! Another infectious case! My favorite! I should have stayed in bed."

"I'll be done in a few minutes," Jack said.

Vinnie irritably snapped up his newspaper and headed downstairs.

Laurie reappeared with an armful of folders and dumped them on her desk. "My, my, but we do have a lot of work to do today," she said.

"I've already sent Vinnie down to get prepared for one of these infectious cases," Jack said. "I hope I'm not overstepping my authority. I know you haven't looked at them yet, but all of them are suspected plague but tested negative. At a minimum I think we have to make a diagnosis."

"No question," Laurie said. "But I should still go downstairs and do my external. Come on, I'll do it right away, and you can get started." She grabbed the master list of all the previous night's deaths.

"What's the story on this first case you want to do?" Laurie asked as they walked.

Jack gave her a quick synopsis of what he knew about Maria Lopez. He emphasized the coincidence of her being employed in central supply at the General. He reminded her that the plague victim from the day before had also worked in that department. They boarded the elevator.

"That's kinda strange, isn't it?" Laurie asked.

"It is to me," Jack agreed.

"Do you think it's significant?" Laurie asked. The elevator bumped to a stop, and they got off.

"My intuition tells me it is," Jack said. "That's why I'm eager to do the post. For the life of me, I can't figure out what the association could be."

As they passed the mortuary office Laurie beckoned to Sal. He caught up to them, and she handed him her master list. "Let's see the Lopez body first," she said.

Sal took the list, referred to his own, then stopped at compartment 67, opened the door, and slid out the tray.

Maria Lopez, like her co-worker, Katherine Mueller, was an overweight female. Her hair was stringy and dyed a peculiar reddish orange. Several IVs were still in place. One was taped to the right side of her neck, the other to her left arm.

"A fairly young woman," Laurie commented.

Jack nodded. "She was only forty-two."

Laurie held Maria Lopez's full-body X ray up to the ceiling light. Its only abnormality was patchy infiltration in her lungs.

"Go to it," Laurie said.

Jack turned on his heels and headed toward the room where his moonsuit ventilator was charging.

"Of the other two cases you had upstairs, which one would you want to do if you only do one?" Laurie called after him.

"Lagenthorpe," Jack said.

Laurie gave him a thumbs-up.

Despite his hangover, Vinnie had been his usual efficient self in setting up the autopsy on Maria Lopez. By the time Jack read over the material in Maria's folder for the second time and had climbed into his moon suit, all was ready.

With no distractions from anyone in the pit besides himself and Vinnie, Jack was able to concentrate. He spent an inordinate amount of time on the external exam. He was determined to find an insect bite if there had been one. He was not successful. As with Mueller, there were a few questionable blemishes, which he photographed, but none he felt were bites.

Jack's concentration was inadvertently aided by Vinnie's hangover. Preferring to nurse his headache, Vinnie remained silent, sparing Jack his usual quips and running commentary on sports trivia. Jack reveled in the thought-provoking silence.

Jack handled the internal exam the same way he'd handled those of the previous infectious cases. He was extraordinarily careful to avoid unnecessary movement of the organs to keep bacterial aerosolization to a minimum.

As the autopsy progressed, Jack's overall impression was that Lopez's case mirrored that of Susanne Hard, not Katherine Mueller. Hence, his preliminary diagnosis remained tularemia, not plague. This only highlighted his confusion of how two women from central supply had managed to catch these illnesses while other more exposed hospital workers had avoided them.

When he finished with the internal exam and had taken the samples he wanted, he put aside a special sample of lung to take up to Agnes Finn. Once he had similar samples from Joy Hester and Donald Lagenthorpe, he planned to have them all sent immediately to the reference lab to be tested for tularemia.

By the time Jack and Vinnie had commenced stitching up Maria Lopez, they began to hear voices in the washroom and out in the hall.

"Here come the normal, civilized people," Vinnie commented.

Jack didn't respond.

Presently the door to the washroom opened. Two figures entered in their moon suits and ambled over to Jack's table. It was Laurie and Chet.

"Are you guys finished already?" Chet said.

"It's not my doing," Vinnie said. "The mad biker has to start before the sun is up."

"What do you think?" Laurie asked. "Plague or tularemia?"

"My guess is tularemia," Jack said.

"That will be four cases if these other two are tularemia as well," Laurie said.

"I know," Jack said. "It's weird. Person-to-person spread is supposed to be rare. It doesn't make a lot of sense, but that seems par for the course with these recent cases."

"How is tularemia spread?" Chet asked. "I've never seen a case."

"It's spread by ticks or direct contact with an infected animal, like a rabbit," Jack said.

"I've got you scheduled for Lagenthorpe next," Laurie told Jack. "I'm going to do Hester myself."

"I'm happy to do Hester was well," Jack said.

"No need," Laurie said. "There aren't that many autopsies today. A lot of last night's deaths didn't need to be posted. I can't let you have all the fun."

Bodies began arriving. They were being pushed into the autopsy room by other mortuary techs and lifted onto their designated tables. Laurie and Chet moved off to do their own cases.

Jack and Vinnie returned to their suturing. When they

were finished, Jack helped Vinnie move the body onto a gurney. Then Jack asked how quickly Vinnie could have Lagenthorpe ready to go.

"What a slave driver," Vinnie complained. "Aren't we going to have coffee like everybody else?"

"I'd rather get it over with," Jack said. "Then you can have coffee for the rest of the day."

"Bull," Vinnie said. "I'll be reassigned back in here helping someone else."

Still complaining, Vinnie pushed Maria Lopez out of the autopsy room. Jack wandered over to Laurie's table. Laurie was engrossed in the external exam but straightened when she caught sight of Jack.

"This poor woman was thirty-six," Laurie said wistfully. "What a waste."

"What have you found? Any insect bites or cat scratches?"

"Nothing except a shaving nick on her lower leg," Laurie said. "But it's not inflamed, so I'm convinced it's incidental. There is something interesting. She had definite eye infections."

Laurie carefully lifted the woman's eyelids. Both eyes were deeply inflamed, although the corneas were clear.

"I can also feel enlarged preauricular lymph nodes," Laurie said. She pointed to visible lumps in front of the patient's ears.

"Interesting," Jack commented. "That's consistent with tularemia, but I didn't see it on the other cases. Give a yell if you come across anything else unusual."

Jack stepped over to Chet's table. He was happily engrossed in a multiple gunshot wound case. At the moment he was busy photographing the entrance and exit wounds. When he saw Jack he handed the camera to Sal, who was helping him, and pulled Jack aside.

"How was your time last night?" Chet asked.

"This is hardly the best time to discuss it," Jack said. Conversation in the moon suits was difficult at best.

"Oh, come on," Chet said. "I had a blast with Colleen. After the China Club we went back to her pad on East Sixty-sixth."

"I'm happy for you," Jack said.

"What did you guys end up doing?" Chet asked.

"You wouldn't believe me if I told you," Jack said.

"Try me," Chet challenged. He leaned closer to Jack.

"We went over to her office, and then we came over here to ours," Jack said.

"You're right," Chet said. "I don't believe you."

"The truth is often difficult to accept," Jack said.

Jack used Vinnie's arrival with Lagenthorpe's corpse as an excuse to return to his table. Jack pitched in to help set up the case because it was preferable to further grilling by Chet. Besides, it made it possible to start the case that much sooner.

On the external exam the most obvious abnormality was the freshly sutured, two-inch-long appendectomy incision. But Jack quickly discovered more pathology. When he examined the corpse's hands he found subtle evidence of early gangrene on the tips of his fingers. He found some even fainter evidence of the same process on the man's earlobes.

"Reminds me of Nodelman," Vinnie said. "It's just less, and he doesn't have any on his pecker. Do you think it's plague again?"

"I don't know," Jack said. "Nodelman didn't have an appendectomy."

Jack spent twenty minutes diligently searching the rest of the body for any signs of insect or animal bites. Since Lagenthorpe was a moderately dark-skinned African-American, this was more difficult than it had been with the considerably lighter-skinned Lopez.

Although Jack's diligence didn't reward him with any bite marks, it did make it possible for him to appreciate another subtle abnormality. On Lagenthorpe's palms and soles there was a faint rash. Jack pointed it out to Vinnie, but Vinnie said he couldn't see it.

"Tell me what I'm looking for," Vinnie said.

"Flat, pinkish blotches," Jack said. "Here's more on the underside of the wrist."

Jack held up Lagenthorpe's right arm.

"I'm sorry," Vinnie said. "I don't see it."

"No matter," Jack said. He took several photographs even though he doubted the rash would show up. The flash often washed out such subtle findings.

As Jack continued the external exam he found himself progressively mystified. The patient had come in with a presumed diagnosis of pneumonic plague, and externally he resembled a plague victim, as Vinnie had pointed out. Yet there were discrepancies. The record indicated he'd had a negative test for plague, which made Jack suspect tularemia.

But tularemia seemed implausible because the patient's sputum test had shown no free bacteria. To complicate things further, the patient had had severe enough abdominal symptoms to suggest appendicitis, which he proved not to have. And on top of that he had a rash on his palms and soles.

At that point Jack had no idea what he was dealing

with. As far as he was concerned, he doubted the case was either plague or tularemia!

Starting the internal exam, he immediately came across strong presumptive evidence that substantiated his belief. The lymphatics were minimally involved.

Slicing open the lung, Jack also detected a difference even on gross from what he'd expect to see in either plague or tularemia. To Jack's eye Lagenthorpe's lung resembled heart failure more than it did infection. There was plenty of fluid but little consolidation.

Turning to the other internal organs, Jack found almost all of them involved in the pathological process. The heart seemed acutely enlarged, as were the liver, the spleen, and the kidneys. Even the intestines were engorged, as if they had stopped functioning.

"Got something interesting?" a husky voice demanded.

Jack had been so absorbed, he hadn't noticed that Calvin had nudged Vinnie aside.

"I believe I do," Jack managed.

"Another infectious case?" another gruff voice asked.

Jack's head swung around to his left. He'd recognized the voice immediately, but he had to confirm his suspicion. He was right. It was the chief!

"It came in as a presumed plague," Jack said. He was surprised to see Bingham; the chief rarely came into the pit unless it was a highly unusual case or one that had immediate political ramifications.

"Your tone suggests you don't think it is," Bingham said. He leaned over the open body and glanced in at the swollen, glistening organs.

"You are very perceptive, sir," Jack said. He made a

specific effort to keep his patented sarcasm from his voice. This was one time he meant the compliment.

"What do you think you have?" Bingham asked. He poked the swollen spleen gingerly with his gloved hand. "This spleen looks huge."

"I haven't the faintest idea," Jack said.

"Dr. Washington informed me this morning that you'd made an impressive diagnosis on a case of tularemia yesterday," Bingham said.

"A lucky guess," Jack said.

"Not according to Dr. Washington," Bingham said. "I'd like to compliment you. Following on the heels of your astute and rapid diagnosis of the case of plague, I'm impressed. I'm also impressed you left it up to me to inform the proper authorities. Keep up the good work. You make me happy I didn't fire you yesterday."

"Now that's a backhanded compliment," Jack said. He chuckled, and so did Bingham.

"Where's the Martin case?" Bingham asked Calvin.

Calvin pointed. "Table three, sir," he said. "Dr. McGovern's doing it. I'll be over in a second."

Jack watched Bingham long enough to see Chet's double take when he recognized the chief. Jack turned back to Calvin. "My feelings are hurt," he said jokingly. "For a moment I thought the chief came all the way down here and suited up just to pay me a compliment."

"Dream on," Calvin said. "You were an afterthought. He really came down about that gunshot wound Dr. McGovern is doing."

"Is it a problem case?" Jack asked.

"Potentially," Calvin said. "The police claim the victim was resisting arrest."

"That's not so uncommon," Jack said.

"The problem is whether the bullets went in the front or the back," Calvin said. "Also there were five of them. That's a bit heavy-handed."

Jack nodded. He understood all too well and was glad he wasn't doing the case.

"The chief didn't come down here to compliment you, but he did it just the same," Calvin said. "He was impressed about the tularemia, and I have to admit I was too. That was a rapid and clever diagnosis. It's worth ten bucks. But I'll tell you something: I didn't appreciate that little ruse you pulled in the chief's office yesterday about our bet. You might have confused the chief for a moment, but you didn't fool me."

"I assumed as much," Jack said. "That's why I changed the subject so quickly."

"I just wanted you to know," Calvin said. Leaning over Lagenthorpe's open corpse, he pushed on the spleen just as Bingham had done. "The chief was right," he said. "This thing is swollen."

"So's the heart and just about everything else," Jack said.

"What's your guess?" Calvin asked.

"This time I don't even have a guess," Jack admitted. "It's another infectious disease, but I'm only willing to bet it's not plague or tularemia. I'm really starting to question what they are doing over there at the General."

"Don't get carried away," Calvin said. "New York is a big city and the General is a big hospital. The way people move around today and with all the flights coming into Kennedy day in and day out, we can see any disease here, any time of the year."

"You've got a point," Jack conceded.

"Well, when you have an idea what it is, let me know," Calvin said. "I want to win that twenty dollars back."

After Calvin left, Vinnie moved back into place. Jack took samples from all the organs and Vinnie saw to it that they were placed in preservative and properly labeled. After all the samples had been taken, they both sutured Lagenthorpe's incision.

Leaving Vinnie to take care of the body, Jack wandered over to Laurie's table. He had her show him the cut surfaces of the lungs, liver, and spleen. The pathology mirrored that of Lopez and Hard. There were hundreds of incipient abscesses with granuloma formation.

"Looks like another case of tularemia," Laurie said.

"I can't argue with you," Jack said. "But this issue of person-to-person spread being so rare bugs me. I don't know how to explain it."

"Unless they all were exposed to the same source," Laurie said.

"Oh sure!" Jack exclaimed scornfully. "They all happened to go to the same spot in Connecticut and feed the same sick rabbit."

"I'm just suggesting the possibility," Laurie complained.

"I'm sorry," Jack said. "You're right. I shouldn't jump on you. It's just that these infectious disease cases are driving me bananas. I feel like I'm missing something important, and yet I have no idea what it could be."

"What about Lagenthorpe?" Laurie asked. "Do you think he had tularemia as well?"

"No," Jack said. "He seems to have had something completely different, and I have no idea what."

"Maybe you are getting too emotionally involved," Laurie suggested.

"Could be," Jack said. He was feeling a bit guilty about wishing the worst for AmeriCare regarding the first case. "I'll try to calm down. Maybe I should go do more reading on infectious diseases."

"That's the spirit," Laurie said. "Instead of stressing yourself out, you should treat these cases as an opportunity to learn. After all, that's part of the fun of this job."

Jack tried vainly to peer through Laurie's plastic face mask to get an idea of whether she was being serious or just mocking him. Unfortunately with all the reflections from the overhead lights, he couldn't tell.

Leaving Laurie, Jack stopped briefly at Chet's table. Chet was not in a good mood.

"Hell," he said. "It's going to take me all day to trace these bullet paths the way Bingham suggested. If he wants to be this particular, I wonder why he doesn't do the case himself."

"Yell if you need any help," Jack said. "I'll be happy to come down and lend a hand."

"I might do that," Chet said.

Jack disposed of his protective gear, changed into his street clothes, and made sure his ventilation charger was plugged in. Then he got the autopsy folders for Lopez and Lagenthorpe. From Hester's folder he looked up her next of kin. A sister was listed whose address was the same as the deceased. Jack surmised they were roommates. He copied down the phone number.

Next Jack sought out Vinnie, whom he found coming out of the walk-in cooler where he'd just deposited Lagenthorpe's corpse.

"Where are all the samples from our two cases?" Jack asked.

"I got 'em all under control," Vinnie said.

"I want to take them upstairs myself," Jack said.

"Are you sure?" Vinnie asked. Running up the samples to the various labs was always an excuse for a coffee break.

"I'm positive," Jack said.

Once he was armed with all the samples plus the autopsy folders Jack set out for his office. But he made two detours. The first was to the microbiology lab, where he sought out Agnes Finn.

"I was impressed with your diagnosis of tularemia," Agnes said.

"I'm getting a lot of compliments out of that one," Jack said.

"Got something for me today?" Agnes asked, eyeing Jack's armful of samples.

"I do, indeed," Jack said. He found the appropriate sample from Lopez and put it on the corner of Agnes's desk. "This is another probable tularemia. Another sample will come up from a case Laurie Montgomery is doing as we speak. I want them both tested for tularemia."

"The reference lab is very eager to follow up on the Hard case, so that won't be difficult. I should have results back today. What else?"

"Well, this one is a mystery," Jack said. He put several samples from Lagenthorpe on Agnes's desk. "I don't have any idea what this patient had. All I know is that it's not plague, and it's not tularemia."

Jack went on to describe the Lagenthorpe case, giving Agnes all the positive findings. She was especially interested that no bacteria had been reported on the gram stain of the sputum.

"Have you thought of virus?" Agnes asked.

"As much as my limited infectious disease knowledge would allow," Jack admitted. "Hantavirus crossed my mind, but there was not a lot of hemorrhage."

"I'll start some viral screenings with tissue cultures," Agnes said.

"I plan to do some reading and maybe I'll have another idea," Jack said.

"I'll be here," Agnes assured him.

Leaving microbiology, Jack went up to the fifth-floor histology lab.

"Wake up, girls, we have a visitor," one of the histology techs shouted. Laughter echoed around the room.

Jack smiled. He always enjoyed visiting histology. The entire group of women who worked there always seemed to be in the best of moods. Jack was particularly fond of Maureen O'Conner, a busty redhead with a devilish twinkle in her eye. He was pleased when he saw her round the corner of the lab bench, wiping her hands on a towel. The front of her lab coat was stained a rainbow of colors.

"Well now, Dr. Stapleton," she said in her pleasant brogue. "What can we do for the likes of you?"

"I need a favor," Jack said.

"A favor, he says," Maureen repeated. "You hear that, girls? What should we ask in return?"

More laughter erupted. It was common knowledge that Jack and Chet were the only two unmarried male doctors, and the histology women liked to tease them.

Jack unloaded his armful of sample bottles, separating Lagenthorpe's from Lopez's.

"I'd like to do frozen sections on Lagenthorpe," he

said. "Just a few slides from each organ. Of course, I want a set of the regular slides as well."

"What about stains?" Maureen asked.

"Just the usual," Jack said.

"Are you looking for anything in particular?" Maureen inquired.

"Some sort of microbe," Jack said. "But that's all I can tell you."

"We'll give you a call," Maureen said. "I'll get right on it."

Back in his office, Jack went through his messages. There was nothing of interest. Clearing a space in front of himself, he set down Lopez's and Lagenthorpe's folders intending to dictate the autopsy findings and then call the next of kin. He even intended to call the next of kin of the case Laurie was doing. But instead he caught sight of his copy of Harrison's textbook of medicine.

Pulling out the book, Jack cracked it open to the section on infectious disease and began reading. There was a lot of material: almost five hundred pages. But he was able to scan quickly since much of it was information he'd committed to memory at some point in his professional career.

Jack had gotten to the chapters on specific bacterial infections when Maureen called. She said that the frozen section slides were ready. Jack immediately walked down to the lab to retrieve them. He carried them back to his office and moved his microscope to the center of the desk.

The slides were organized by organ. Jack looked at the sections of the lung first. What impressed him most was the amount of swelling of the lung tissue and the fact that he saw no bacteria.

Looking at the heart sections, he could immediately see why the heart had appeared swollen. There was a massive amount of inflammation, and the spaces between the heart muscle cells were filled with fluid.

Switching to a higher power of magnification, Jack immediately appreciated the primary pathology. The cells lining the blood vessels that coursed through the heart were severely damaged. As a result, many of these blood vessels had become occluded with blood clots, causing multiple tiny heart attacks!

With a shot of adrenaline coursing through his own circulation from the excitement of discovery, Jack quickly switched back to the section of lung. Using the same high power he saw identical pathology in the walls of the tiny blood vessels, a finding he hadn't noticed on his first examination.

Jack exchanged the lung section with one from the spleen. Adjusting the focus, he saw the same pathology. Obviously it was a significant finding, one that immediately suggested a possible diagnosis.

Jack pushed back from his desk and made a quick trip back to the micro lab and sought out Agnes. He found her at one of the lab's many incubators.

"Hold up on the tissue cultures of Lagenthorpe," he said breathlessly. "I got some new information you're going to love."

Agnes regarded him curiously through her thick glasses.

"It's an endothelial disease," Jack said excitedly. "The patient had an acute infectious disease without bacteria seen or cultured. That should have given it away. He also had the faintest beginnings of a rash that included his palms and soles. Plus he'd been suspected of having appendicitis. Guess why?"

"Muscle tenderness," Agnes said.

"Exactly," Jack said. "So what does that make you think of?"

"Rickettsia," Agnes said.

"Bingo," Jack said, and he punched the air for emphasis. "Good old Rocky Mountain spotted fever. Now, can you confirm it?"

"It's as difficult as tularemia," Agnes said. "We'll have to send it out again. There is a direct immunofluorescent technique, but we don't have the reagent. But I know the city reference lab has it, because there was an outbreak of Rocky Mountain spotted fever in the Bronx in eighty-seven."

"Get it over there right away," Jack said. "Tell them we want a reading as soon as they can get it to us."

"Will do," Agnes said.

"You're a doll," Jack said.

He started for the door. Before he got there Agnes called out to him: "I appreciate you letting me know about this as soon as you did," she said. "Rickettsias are extremely dangerous for us lab workers. In an aerosol form it is highly contagious. It's as bad or worse than tularemia."

"Needless to say, be careful," Jack told her.

CHAPTER SEVENTEEN

Friday, 12:15 P.M., March 22, 1996

Helen Robinson brushed her hair with quick strokes. She was excited. Having just hung up the phone with her main contact at National Health's home office, she wanted to get in to see Robert Barker as soon as possible. She knew he was going to love what she had to tell him.

Stepping back from the mirror, Helen surveyed herself from both the right and the left. Satisfied, she closed the closet door and headed out of her office.

Her usual method of contacting Robert was merely to drop in on him. But she thought the information she now had justified a more formal approach; she'd ask one of the secretaries to call ahead. The secretary had reported back that Robert was available at that very moment, not that Helen was surprised.

Helen had been cultivating Robert for the last year. She started when it became apparent to her that Robert could ascend to the presidency. Sensing the man had a salacious streak, she'd deliberately fanned the fires of his imagination. It was easy, although she knew she trod a fine line. She wanted to encourage him, but not to the point where she would have to openly deny him. In reality, she found him physically unpleasant at best.

Helen's goal was Robert's position. She wanted to be executive director of accounts and could see no reason why she shouldn't be. Her only problem was that she was younger than the others in the department. She felt that was the handicap that her "cultivation" of Robert could overcome.

"Ah, Helen, my dear," Robert said as Helen demurely stepped into his office. He leaped to his feet and closed the door behind her.

Helen perched on the arm of the chair as was her custom. She crossed her legs and her skirt hiked up well above her knee. She noticed the photo of Robert's wife was lying facedown as usual.

"How about some coffee?" Robert offered, taking his seat and assuming his customary hypnotic stare.

"I've just spoken with Gertrude Wilson over at National Health," Helen began. "I'm sure you know her."

"Of course," Robert said. "She's one of the more senior vice presidents."

"She's also one of my most trusted contacts," Helen said. "And she is a fan of Willow and Heath."

"Uh-huh," Robert said.

"She told me two very interesting things," Helen said. "First of all, National Health's main hospital here in the city compares very favorably with other similar hospitals when it comes to hospital-based infections, or what they like to call nosocomial infections."

"Uh-huh," Robert repeated.

"National Health has followed all the recommendations of the CDC and the Joint Commission on Accreditation," Helen said.

Robert shook his head slightly, as if waking up. It had taken a moment for Helen's comments to penetrate his preoccupied brain. "Wait a second," he said. He looked away to organize his thoughts. "This doesn't sound like good news to me. I thought my secretary told me you had good news."

"Hear me out," Helen said. "Although they have an overall good nosocomial record, they've had some recent troubles in their New York facility that they're very sensitive about and would hate to be made public. There were three episodes in particular. One involved an extended outbreak of staph in the intensive-care units. That gave them a real problem until it was discovered a number of the nursing staff were carriers and had to be given courses of antibiotics. I tell you, this stuff is frightening when you hear about it."

"What were the other problems?" Robert asked. For the moment he tried to avoid looking at Helen.

"They had another kind of bacterial problem originate in their kitchen," Helen said. "A lot of patients got serious diarrhea. A few even died. And the last problem was an outbreak of hospital-based hepatitis. That killed several as well."

"That doesn't sound like such a good record to me," Robert said.

"It is when you compare it with some of the other hospitals," Helen said. "I tell you, it's scary. But the point is that National Health is sensitive about this nosocomial infection issue. Gertrude specifically told me that National Health would never in a million years consider running an ad campaign based on it."

"Perfect!" Robert exclaimed. "That is good news. What have you told Terese Hagen?"

"Nothing, of course," Helen said. "You told me to brief you first."

"Excellent job!" Robert said. He pushed himself up

onto his long, thin legs and paced. "This couldn't be better. I've got Terese just where I want her."

"What do you want me to tell her?" Helen asked.

"Just tell her that you have confirmed National Health has a excellent record vis-à-vis nosocomial infection," Robert said. "I want to encourage her to go ahead with her campaign, because it will surely bomb."

"But we'll lose the account," Helen said.

"Not necessarily," Robert said. "You've found out in the past that they are interested in 'talking heads' spots with celebrities. We've communicated that to Terese time and time again and she has ignored it. I'm going to go behind her back and line up a few of the stars from some of the current hospital-based TV dramas. They'd be perfect for testimonials. Terese Hagen will bomb and we'll be able to step in with our own campaign."

"Ingenious," Helen said. She slid off the arm of her chair. "I'll start the ball rolling by calling Terese Hagen immediately."

Helen scooted back to her own office and had a secretary put in a call to Terese. As she waited, she complimented herself on the conversation she'd just had with Robert. It couldn't have gone any better had she scripted it. Her position in the firm was looking better and better.

"Miss Hagen is downstairs in the arena," the secretary reported. "Do you want me to call down there?"

"No," Helen said. "I'll head down there in person."

Leaving the carpeted tranquility of the account executive area, Helen descended the stairs to the studio floor. Her pumps echoed loudly on the metal steps. She liked the idea of talking with Terese in person, although she'd not wanted to go to Terese's office, where she'd feel intimidated.

Helen rapped loudly on the doorjamb before entering. Terese was sitting at a large table covered with storyboards and tissues. Also present were Colleen Anderson, Alice Gerber, and a man Helen didn't know. He was introduced as Nelson Friedman.

"I've got the information you requested," Helen said to Terese. She forced her face into a broad smile.

"Good news or bad?" Terese asked.

"I'd say very good," Helen said.

"Let's have it," Terese said. She leaned back in her chair.

Helen described National Health's positive nosocomial record. She even told Terese something she hadn't told Robert: National Health's hospital infection rates were better than AmeriCare's at the General.

"Fabulous," Terese said. "That's just what I wanted to know. You've been a big help. Thank you."

"Glad to be of service," Helen said. "How are you coming with the campaign?"

"I feel good about it," Terese said. "By Monday we'll have something for Taylor and Brian to see."

"Excellent," Helen said. "Well, if I can do anything else, just let me know."

"Certainly," Terese said. She walked Helen to the door, then waved as Helen disappeared into the stairwell.

Terese returned to the table and sat back down.

"Do you believe her?" Colleen asked.

"I do," Terese said. "Accounts wouldn't risk lying about stats that we could presumably get elsewhere."

"I don't see how you can trust her," Colleen said. "I hate that plastic smile. It's unnatural."

"Hey, I said I believed her," Terese said. "I didn't say I trusted her. That's why I didn't share with her what we are doing here."

"Speaking of what we are doing here," Colleen said, "you haven't exactly said you like it."

Terese sighed as her eyes ranged around at the scattered storyboards. "I like the Hippocrates sequence," she said. "But I don't know about this Oliver Wendell Holmes and this Joseph Lister material. I understand how important washing hands is even in a modern hospital, but it's not zippy."

"What about that doctor who was up here with you last night?" Alice asked. "Since he suggested this handwashing stuff, maybe he'll have more of an idea now that we've sketched it out."

Colleen glanced up at Terese. She was dumbfounded. "You and Jack came here last night?" she asked.

"Yeah, we stopped by," Terese said casually. She reached out and adjusted one of the storyboards so she could see it better.

"You didn't tell me that," Colleen said.

"You didn't ask," Terese said. "But it's no secret, if that's what you are implying. My relationship with Jack is not romantic."

"And you guys talked about this ad campaign?" Colleen asked. "I didn't think you wanted him to know about it, especially since he'd been kinda responsible for the idea."

"I changed my mind," Terese said. "I thought he might like it since it deals with the quality of medical care."

"You're full of surprises," Colleen commented.

"Having Jack and Chet take a look at this is not a bad idea," Terese said. "A professional response might be helpful."

"I'd be happy to make the call," Colleen offered.

CHAPTER EIGHTEEN

Friday, 2:45 P.M., March 22, 1996

Jack had been on the phone for over an hour, calling the next of kin of the day's three infectious disease cases. He'd talked with Laurie before calling Joy Hester's sister and roommate. Jack didn't want Laurie to think he was trying to take over her case, but she assured him she didn't mind.

Unfortunately Jack did not learn anything positive. All he was able to do was to confirm a series of negatives, such as that none of the patients had had contact with wild animals in general or wild rabbits in particular. Only Donald Lagenthorpe had had contact with a pet, and that was his girlfriend's newly acquired cat, which was alive and well.

Hanging up at the end of the final call, Jack slouched down in his chair and stared moodily at the blank wall. The adrenaline rush he'd felt earlier with the tentative diagnosis of Rocky Mountain spotted fever had given way to frustration. He seemed to be making no headway.

The phone startled Jack and pulled him out of his gloom. The caller identified himself as Dr. Gary Eckhart, a microbiologist at the city reference lab.

"Are you Dr. Stapleton?"

"Yes, I am," Jack said.

"I'm reporting a positive reaction for *Rickettsia*

rickettsii," Dr. Eckhart said. "Your patient had Rocky Mountain spotted fever. Will you be reporting this to the Board of Health or do you want me to do it?"

"You do it," Jack said. "I'm not even sure I'd know whom to call."

"Consider it done," Dr. Eckhart said. He hung up.

Jack slowly replaced the receiver. That his diagnosis had been confirmed was as much of a shock as it had been when his diagnoses of the plague and tularemia had been confirmed. These developments were incredible. Within three days he'd seen three relatively rare infectious diseases.

Only in New York, he thought. In his mind's eye he saw all those planes Calvin had made reference to arriving at Kennedy Airport from all over the world.

But Jack's shock began to metamorphose to disbelief. Even with all the planes and all the people arriving from exotic locales carrying all manner of vermin, bugs and microbes, it seemed too much of a coincidence to see back-to-back cases of plague, tularemia, and now Rocky Mountain spotted fever. Jack's analytical mind tried to imagine what the probability of such an occurrence would be.

"I'd say about zero," he said out loud.

Suddenly Jack pushed back from his desk and stormed out of his office. His disbelief was now changing to something akin to anger. Jack was sure something weird was going on, and for the moment he was taking it personally. Believing that something had to be done, he headed downstairs and presented himself to Mrs. Sanford. He demanded to talk with the chief.

"I'm afraid Dr. Bingham is over at City Hall meeting

with the mayor and the chief of police," Mrs. Sanford said.

"Oh, hell!" Jack exclaimed. "Is he moving in over there or what?"

"There's a lot of controversy surrounding that gunshot case this morning," Mrs. Sanford said warily.

"When will he be back?" Jack demanded. Bingham's being unavailable was adding to his frustration.

"I just don't know," Mrs. Sanford said. "But I'll be sure to tell him you want to speak with him."

"What about Dr. Washington?"

"He's at the same meeting," Mrs. Sanford said.

"Oh, great!"

"Is there something I can help you with?" Mrs. Sanford asked.

Jack thought for a moment. "How about a piece of paper," he said. "I think I'll leave a note."

Mrs. Sanford handed him a sheet of typing paper. In block letters Jack wrote: *LAGENTHORPE HAD ROCKY MOUNTAIN SPOTTED FEVER.* Then he drew a half dozen large question marks and exclamation points. Beneath that he wrote: *THE CITY BOARD OF HEALTH HAS BEEN NOTIFIED BY THE CITY MICROBIOLOGICAL REFERENCE LAB.*

Jack handed the sheet to Mrs. Sanford, who promised that she'd personally see to it that Dr. Bingham got it as soon as he came in. Then she asked Jack where he'd be if the chief wanted to speak to him.

"Depends on when he gets back," Jack said. "I plan to be out of the office for a while. Of course, he might hear about me before he hears from me."

Mrs. Sanford regarded him quizzically, but Jack didn't elaborate.

Jack returned to his office and grabbed his jacket. Then he descended to the morgue and unlocked his bike. Bingham's exhortations notwithstanding, Jack was on his way to the Manhattan General Hospital. For two days he'd had the suspicion that something unusual was going on over there; now he was sure of it.

After a quick ride, Jack locked his bike to the same sign he'd used on his previous visits and entered the hospital. With visiting hours just beginning, the lobby was jammed with people, particularly around the information booth.

Jack wormed his way through the crowd and climbed the stairs to the second floor. He went directly to the lab and waited in line to speak with the receptionist. This time he asked to see the director, even though his impulse was to march right in.

Martin Cheveau made Jack wait for a half hour before seeing him. Jack tried to use the time to calm himself. He recognized that over the last four or five years he'd become less than tactful in the best of circumstances; when he was upset, as he was now, he could be abrasive.

A laboratory tech eventually came out and informed Jack that Dr. Martin Cheveau would see him now.

"Thanks for seeing me so promptly," Jack said as he entered the office. Despite his best intentions he couldn't avoid a touch of sarcasm.

"I'm a busy man," Martin said, not bothering to stand up.

"I can well imagine," Jack said. "With the string of rare infectious diseases emanating from this hospital on a daily basis, I'd think you'd be putting in overtime."

"Dr. Stapleton," Martin said in a controlled voice.

"I have to tell you that I find your attitude distinctly disagreeable."

"I find yours confusing," Jack said. "On my first visit you were the picture of hospitality. On my second visit, you were just the opposite."

"Unfortunately I don't have time for this conversation," Martin said. "Is there something in particular you wanted to say to me?"

"Obviously," Jack said. "I didn't come over here just for abuse. I wanted to ask your professional opinion about how you think three rare, arthropod-borne diseases have mysteriously occurred in this hospital. I've been cultivating my own opinion, but as the director of the lab I'm curious about yours."

"What do you mean three diseases?" Martin asked.

"I just got confirmation that a patient named Lagenthorpe who expired here in the General last night had Rocky Mountain spotted fever."

"I don't believe you," Martin said.

Jack eyed the man and tried to decide if he was a good actor or truly surprised.

"Well, then, let me ask you a question," Jack said. "What would I accomplish by coming over here and telling you something that wasn't true? Do you think of me as some sort of health-care provocateur?"

Martin didn't answer. Instead he picked up the phone and paged Dr. Mary Zimmerman.

"Calling in reinforcements?" Jack asked. "Why can't you and I have a talk?"

"I'm not sure you are capable of normal conversation," Martin said.

"Good technique," Jack commented. "When defense doesn't work, switch to offense. The problem is, strategies won't change the facts. Rickettsias are extremely dangerous in the laboratory. Maybe we should make sure whoever handled Lagenthorpe's specimens did so with proper precautions."

Martin pressed his intercom button and paged his chief microbiology tech, Richard Overstreet.

"Another thing I'd like to discuss," Jack said. "On my first visit here you told me how discouraging it was to run your lab with the budgets foisted on you by AmeriCare. On a scale of one to ten, how disgruntled are you?"

"What are you implying?" Martin demanded ominously.

"At the moment I'm not implying anything," Jack said. "I'm just asking."

The phone rang and Martin picked it up. It was Dr. Mary Zimmerman. Martin asked her if she could come down to the lab since something important had just come up.

"The problem as I see it is that the probability of these three illnesses popping up as they have is close to zero," Jack said. "How would you explain it?"

"I don't have to listen to this," Martin snarled.

"But I think you have to consider it," Jack said.

Richard Overstreet appeared in the doorway dressed as he'd been before, in a white lab coat over surgical scrubs. He appeared harried.

"What is it, Chief?" he asked. He nodded a greeting to Jack, who returned the gesture.

"I've just learned a patient by the name of Lagenthorpe expired from Rocky Mountain spotted fever," Martin said gruffly. "Find out who got the samples and who processed them."

Richard stood for a moment, obviously shocked by the news. "That means we had rickettsia in the lab," he said.

"I'm afraid so," Martin said. "Get right back to me." Richard vanished and Martin turned back to Jack. "Now that you have brought us this happy news, perhaps you could do us the favor and leave."

"I'd prefer to hear your opinion as to the origin of these diseases," Jack said.

Martin's face flushed, but before he could respond Dr. Mary Zimmerman appeared at his door.

"What can I do for you, Martin?" she asked. She started to tell him that she'd just been paged to the ER when she caught sight of Jack. Her eyes narrowed. She was obviously no happier than Martin to see Jack.

"Howdy, Doctor," Jack said cheerfully.

"I was assured we would not see you again," Dr. Zimmerman said.

"You can never believe everything you hear," Jack said.

Just then Richard returned, clearly distraught. "It was Nancy Wiggens," he blurted out. "She's the one who got the sample and processed it herself. She called in sick this morning."

Dr. Zimmerman consulted a note she held in her hand. "Wiggens is one of the patients I've just been called to see in ER," she said. "Apparently she's suffering from some sort of fulminant infection."

"Oh, no!" Richard said.

"What's going on here?" Dr. Zimmerman demanded.

"Dr. Stapleton just brought news that a patient of ours died from Rocky Mountain spotted fever," Martin said. "Nancy was exposed."

"Not here in the lab," Richard said. "I've been a bear about safety. Ever since the plague case I have insisted all infectious material be handled in the biosafety III cabinet. If she were exposed it had to be from the patient."

"That's not likely," Jack said. "The only other possibility is that the hospital is lousy with ticks."

"Dr. Stapleton, your comments are tasteless and inappropriate," Dr. Zimmerman said.

"They are a lot worse than that," Martin said. "Just before you got here, Dr. Zimmerman, he slanderously suggested that I had something to do with the spread of these latest illnesses."

"That's not true," Jack corrected. "I was merely implying that the idea of deliberate spread has to be considered when the probability of them occurring by chance is so negligible. It only makes sense. What's wrong with you people?"

"I think such thoughts are the product of a paranoid mind," Dr. Zimmerman said. "And frankly I don't have time for this nonsense. I've got to get to the ER. In addition to Miss Wiggens, there are two other employees with the same severe symptoms. Good-bye, Dr. Stapleton!"

"Just a minute," Jack said. "Let me guess what areas these two other stricken employees work in. Could they be from nursing and central supply?"

Dr. Zimmerman, who was already several steps away from Martin's door, paused and looked back at Jack. "How did you know that?" she asked.

"I'm beginning to see a pattern," Jack said. "I can't explain it, but it's there. I mean, the nurse is regrettable but understandable. But someone from central supply?"

"Listen, Dr. Stapleton," Dr. Zimmerman said. "Perhaps we're in your debt for once again having alerted us to a dangerous disease. But we will take over from here, and we certainly don't need any of your paranoid delusions. Good day, Dr. Stapleton."

"Hold on a minute," Martin called out to Dr. Zimmerman. "I'll come with you to the ER. If this is ricketts-sial disease I want to be sure all samples are handled safely."

Martin grabbed his long white lab coat from a hook behind the door and ran after Dr. Zimmerman.

Jack shook his head in disbelief. Every visit he'd made to the General had been strange and this one was no exception. On previous occasions he'd been chased out. This time he'd been all but deserted.

"Do you really think these illnesses could have been spread deliberately?" Richard asked.

Jack shrugged. "To tell you the truth, I don't know what to think. But there certainly has been some defensive behavior, particularly on the part of those two who just left. Tell me, is Dr. Cheveau generally mercurial? He seemed to turn on me rather suddenly."

"He's always been a gentleman with me," Richard said.

Jack got to his feet. "It must be me, then," he said. "And I suppose our relations won't improve after today. Such is life. Anyway, I'd better be going. I sure hope Nancy is okay."

"You and me both," Richard said.

Jack wandered out of the lab debating what to do next. He thought about either going to the emergency room to see about the three sick patients or heading up to central supply for another visit. He decided on the emergency room. Even though Dr. Zimmerman and

Dr. Cheveau had headed down there, Jack thought the chance of another run-in was remote, given the size of the ER and the constant activity there.

As soon as he arrived he detected a general panic. Charles Kelley was anxiously conferring with several other administrators. Then Clint Abelard came dashing through the main ambulance entry only to disappear down the central corridor.

Jack went over to one of the nurses who was busy behind the main counter. He introduced himself and asked if the hubbub was about the three sick hospital staff.

"It most certainly is," she said. "They're trying to decide how best to isolate them."

"Any diagnosis?" Jack asked.

"I just heard they suspect Rocky Mountain spotted fever," the nurse said.

"Pretty scary," Jack said.

"Very," the nurse said. "One of the patients is a nurse."

Out of the corner of his eye Jack saw Kelley approaching. Jack quickly faced away. Kelley came to the desk and asked the nurse for the phone.

Jack left the bustling ER. He thought about going up to central supply, but decided against it. Having come close to another confrontation with Charles Kelley, he thought it best to head back to the office. Although he hadn't accomplished anything, at least he was leaving of his own volition.

"Uh-oh! Where have you been?" Chet asked as Jack came into their office.

"Over at the General," Jack admitted. He started organizing the clutter on his desk.

"At least you must have behaved yourself; there haven't been any frantic calls from the front office."

"I was a good boy," Jack said. "Well, reasonably good. The place is in an uproar. They have another outbreak. This one is Rocky Mountain spotted fever. Can you believe it?"

"That's incredible," Chet said.

"That's my feeling exactly," Jack said. He went on to tell Chet how he'd implied to the head of the lab that outbreaks of three rare, infectious, arthropod-borne diseases in as many days couldn't occur naturally.

"I bet that went over well," Chet said.

"Oh, he was indignant," Jack said. "But then he got preoccupied with some fresh cases and forgot about me."

"I'm surprised you weren't thrown out again," Chet said. "Why do you do this to yourself?"

"Because I'm convinced that there's 'something rotten in the state of Denmark,'" Jack said. "But enough about me. How did your case go?"

Chet gave a short, scornful laugh. "And to think I used to like gunshot cases," he said. "This one is kicking up a storm. Three of the five bullets entered through the back."

"That's going to give the police department a headache," Jack said.

"And me too," Chet said. "Oh, by the way, I got a call from Colleen. She wants you and me to come by their studio when we leave work tonight. Listen to this: They want our opinion about some ads. What do you say?"

"You go," Jack said. "I've got to get some of these cases of mine signed out. I'm so far behind it's scaring me."

"But they want both of us," Chet said. "Colleen specifically said that. In fact, she said they particularly wanted you there because you had helped already. Come on, it will be fun. They are going to show us a bunch of sketches outlining some potential TV commercials."

"Is that really your idea of fun?" Jack asked.

"Okay," Chet admitted. "I've an ulterior motive. I'm enjoying spending time with Colleen. But they want both of us. Help me out."

"All right," Jack said. "But for the life of me I don't understand why you think you need me."

CHAPTER NINETEEN

Friday, 9:00 P.M., March 22, 1996

Jack had insisted on working late. Chet had obliged by fetching a Chinese takeout so Jack could continue. Once Jack got started, he hated to stop. By eight-thirty Colleen had called, wondering where they were. Chet had to nag Jack to get him to turn off his microscope and lay down his pen.

The next problem was Jack's bike. After much discussion it was decided that Chet would take a taxi and Jack would ride as he normally did. They then met in front of Willow and Heath after having arrived almost simultaneously.

A night watchman opened the door for them and made them sign in. They boarded the only functioning elevator, and Jack promptly pressed the eleventh floor.

"You really were here," Chet said.

"I told you I was," Jack said.

"I thought you were pulling my leg," Chet remarked.

When the doors opened Chet was as surprised as Jack had been the night before. The studio was in full swing, as if it were still sometime between nine and five, instead of almost nine in the evening.

The two men stood for a few minutes watching the bustle. They were totally ignored.

"Some welcoming party," Jack commented.

"Maybe someone should tell them it's after quitting time," Chet said.

Jack peered into Colleen's office. The lights were on but no one was there. Turning around, he recognized Alice toiling at her drawing board. He walked over to her, but she didn't look up.

"Excuse me?" Jack said. She was working with such concentration he hated to bother her. "Hello, hello."

Finally Alice's head bobbed up, and when she caught sight of him, her face reflected instant recognition.

"Oh, gosh, sorry," she said, wiping her hands on a towel. "Welcome!" She acted self-conscious; she'd not seen them arrive as she stood and motioned them to follow her. "Come on! I'm supposed to take you down to the arena."

"Uh-oh," Chet said. "That doesn't sound good. They must think we're Christians."

Alice laughed. "Creatives are sacrificed in the arena, not Christians," she explained.

Terese and Colleen greeted them with air kisses: the mere touching of cheeks accompanied by a smacking sound. It was the kind of ritual that made Jack feel distinctly uncomfortable.

Terese got right to business. She had the men sit at the table while she and Colleen began putting storyboards in front of them, maintaining a running commentary on what the storyboards represented.

Both Jack and Chet were entertained from the start. They were particularly taken by the humorous sketches involving Oliver Wendell Holmes and Joseph Lister visiting the National Health hospital and inspecting the hospital's hand-washing protocols. At the conclusion of each commercial these famous characters in the history of medicine commented on how much more scrupulously the National Health hospital followed their teaching than that "other" hospital.

"Well, there you have it," Terese said after the last storyboard was explained and withdrawn. "What do you men think?"

"They're cute," Jack admitted. "And probably effective. But they are hardly worth the money that's going to be spent on them."

"But they deal with something associated with the quality of care," Terese said defensively.

"Barely," Jack said. "The National Health subscribers would be better off if the millions spent on this were put into actual health care."

"Well, I love them," Chet said. "They're so fresh and delightfully humorous. I think they're great."

"I assume the 'other' hospital refers to the competition," Jack said.

"Most assuredly," Terese said. "We feel it would be in bad taste to mention the General by name, especially in light of the problems it's been having."

"Their problems are getting worse," Jack said. "They've had an outbreak of another serious disease. This makes three in three days."

"Good God!" Terese exclaimed. "That's awful. I certainly hope this gets to the media, or is this one going to be a secret?"

"I don't know why you keep making this an issue," Jack snapped. "There's no way it can be kept a secret."

"It would be if AmeriCare had its way," Terese said heatedly.

"Hey, are you guys at it again?" Chet said.

"It's an ongoing argument," Terese said. "I just can't

get over the fact that Jack does not feel it is his job as a public servant to let the media and hence the public know about these awful diseases."

"I told you I've been specifically informed it is not my job," Jack shot back.

"Wait! Time out," Chet called out. "Listen, Terese, Jack is right. We can't go to the media ourselves. That's the chief's domain via the PR office. But Jack is no slouch in all this. Today he went flying over to the General and implied right to their faces that these recent outbreaks aren't natural."

"What do you mean, not 'natural'?" Terese asked.

"Exactly that," Chet said. "If they are not natural, then they are deliberate. Somebody is causing them."

"Is that true?" Terese asked Jack. She was shocked.

"It's gone through my mind," Jack admitted. "I'm having trouble explaining scientifically everything that has been going on over there."

"Why would someone do that?" Terese wondered. "It's absurd."

"Is it?" Jack asked.

"Could it be the work of some crazy person?" Colleen offered.

"That I'd doubt," Jack said. "There is too much expertise involved. And these bugs are dangerous to handle. One of the current victims is a lab technician."

"What about a disgruntled employee?" Chet suggested. "Someone with the knowledge and a grudge who's snapped."

"That I think is more likely than some madman," Jack said. "In fact the director of the hospital lab is unhappy with the management of the hospital. He told me so himself. He's had to lay off twenty percent of his workforce."

"Oh my God," Colleen exclaimed. "Do you think it could be him?"

"Actually I don't," Jack said. "Frankly, too many arrows would point to the director of the lab. He'd be the first suspect. He's been acting defensive, but he's not stupid. I think that if this series of diseases has been spread deliberately it has to be for a more venal reason."

"Like what?" Terese said. "I think we're all jumping off the deep end here."

"Maybe so," Jack said. "But we have to remember that AmeriCare is first and foremost a business. I even know something about their philosophy. Believe me, it is bottom-line oriented all the way."

"You're suggesting that AmeriCare might be spreading disease in its own facility?" Terese asked incredulously. "That doesn't make any sense."

"I'm just thinking out loud," Jack explained. "For the sake of argument let's assume these illnesses have been deliberately spread. Now, let's look at the index case in each incidence. First, there was Nodelman, who had diabetes. Second, there was Hard, who had a chronic orthopedic problem, and lastly there was Lagenthorpe, who suffered from chronic asthma."

"I see what you're suggesting," Chet said. "All of the index cases were the type of patient prepaid plans hate because they lose money on them. They simply use too much medical care."

"Oh, come on!" Terese complained. "This is ridiculous. No wonder you doctors make such horrid businessmen. AmeriCare would never risk this kind of public relations disaster to rid itself of three problem patients. It would make no sense. Give me a break!"

"Terese is probably right," Jack admitted. "If Ameri-Care was behind all this, they certainly could have done it more expeditiously. What truly worries me is that infectious agents are involved. If these outbreaks have been deliberate, the individual behind them wants to start epidemics, not just eliminate specific patients."

"That's even more diabolical," Terese said.

"I agree," Jack said. "It kind of forces us back to considering the improbable idea of a crazy person."

"But if someone is trying to start epidemics, why hasn't there been one?" Colleen asked.

"For several reasons," Jack said. "First of all, the diagnosis has been made relatively rapidly in all three cases. Second, the General has taken these outbreaks seriously and has taken appropriate steps to control them. And third, the agents involved are poor choices for creating an epidemic here in New York in March."

"You'll have to explain," Colleen said.

"Plague, tularemia, and Rocky Mountain spotted fever can be transmitted by airborne spread, but it is not their usual routine. The usual route is through an arthropod vector, and those specific bugs are not available this time of year, especially not in a hospital."

"What do you think of all this?" Terese asked Chet.

"Me?" Chet asked with a self-conscious laugh. "I don't know what to think."

"Come on," Terese prodded. "Don't try to protect your friend here. What's your gut reaction?"

"Well, it is New York," Chet said. "We see a lot of infectious diseases, so I suppose I'm dubious about his notion of a deliberate spread. I guess I'd have to say it sounds a little paranoid to me. I do know that Jack dislikes AmeriCare."

"Is that true?" Terese asked Jack.

"I hate them," Jack admitted.

"Why?"

"I'd rather not talk about it," Jack said. "It's personal."

"Well," Terese said. She put her hand on top of the stack of storyboards. "Dr. Stapleton's disdain for medical advertising aside, you men think these sketches are okay?"

"I told you, I think they're great," Chet said.

"I imagine they will be effective," Jack grudgingly agreed.

"Do either of you have any other suggestions we could use regarding preventing hospital infections?" Terese asked.

"Maybe you could do something concerning steam sterilization for instruments and devices," Jack said. "Hospitals differ in their protocols. Robert Koch was involved with that advance, and he was a colorful character."

Terese wrote down the suggestion. "Anything else?" she asked.

"I'm afraid I'm not very good at this," Chet admitted. "But why don't we all head over to the Auction House for a couple of drinks. With the proper lubricant, who knows what I might come up with?"

The women declined. Terese explained that they had to continue working on the sketches. She said that by Monday they had to have something significant to show to the president and CEO.

"How about tomorrow night?" Chet suggested.

"We'll see," Terese said.

Five minutes later Jack and Chet were heading down in the elevator.

"That was the bum's rush," Chet complained.

"They are driven women," Jack said.

"How about you?" Chet asked. "Want to stop for a beer?"

"I think I'll head home and see if the guys are playing basketball," Jack said. "I could use some exercise. I feel wired."

"Basketball at this hour?" Chet questioned.

"Friday night is a big night in the neighborhood," Jack said.

The two men parted company in front of the Willow and Heath building. Chet jumped into a cab, and Jack undid his medley of locks. Climbing on his bike, Jack pedaled north on Madison, then crossed over to Fifth Avenue at Fifty-ninth Steet. From there he entered Central Park.

Although his usual style was to ride fast, Jack kept his pace slow. He was mulling over the conversation he'd just had. It had been the first time that he'd put his suspicions into words; he felt anxious as a result.

Chet had suggested he was paranoid, and Jack had to admit there must some truth in it. Ever since AmeriCare had effectively gobbled up his practice, Jack felt that death had been stalking him. First it had robbed him of his family, then it had threatened his own life with depression. It had even filled his daily routine with the second specialty he'd chosen. And now death seemed to be teasing him with these outbreaks, even mocking him with inexplicable details.

As Jack rode deeper into the dark, deserted park, its

gloomy and somber views added to his disquietude. In areas where he'd seen beauty that morning on his way to work, now he saw ghastly skeletons of leafless trees silhouetted against an eerily bleached sky. Even the distant sawtooth skyline of the city seemed ominous.

Jack put muscle into his pedaling, and his bike gained speed. For an irrational moment he was afraid to look back over his shoulder. He had the creepy feeling that something was bearing down on him.

Jack streaked into a puddle of light beneath a lonely streetlight, braked, and skidded to a stop. He forced himself to turn around and face his pursuer. But there was nothing there. Jack strained to see into the distant shadows, and as he did, he understood that what was threatening him was coming from inside his own head. It was the depression that had paralyzed him after his family's tragedy.

Angry with himself, Jack began pedaling again. He was embarrassed by his childlike fear. He thought he had more control. Obviously he was letting this episode with the outbreaks affect him far too much. Laurie had been right: he was too emotionally involved.

Having faced his fears, Jack felt better, but he noticed that the park still looked sinister. People had warned him about riding in the park at night, but Jack had always ignored their admonitions. Now, for the first time, he wondered if he was being foolish.

Emerging from the park into Central Park West was like escaping from a nightmare. From the dark, scary loneliness of the park's interior he was instantly thrust into a rallylike bustle of yellow cabs racing northward. The city had come alive. There were even people calmly walking on the sidewalks.

The farther north Jack rode the more the environment deteriorated. Beyond 100th Street the buildings became noticeably shabbier. Some were even boarded up and appeared abandoned. There was more litter in the street. Stray dogs plundered overturned trash cans.

Jack turned left onto 106th Street. As he rode along his street the neighborhood seemed more depressed than usual to him. The minor epiphany in the park had opened Jack's eyes to just how dilapidated the area was.

Jack stopped at the playground where he played basketball by grabbing onto the chain-link fence that separated it from the street. His feet remained snug in his toe clips.

As Jack had expected, the court was in full use. The mercury vapor lights that he'd paid to have installed were ablaze. Jack recognized many of the players as they surged up and down the court. Warren, by far the best player, was there, and Jack could hear him urging his teammates to greater effort. The team that lost would have to sit out, since a bevy of other players waited impatiently on the sidelines. The competition was always fierce.

While Jack was watching, Warren sank the final basket of the game and the losing team slunk off the court, momentarily disgraced. As the new game was being organized Warren caught sight of Jack. He waved and strutted over. It was the winning team walk.

"Hey, Doc, whatcha know?" Warren asked. "You coming out to run or what?"

Warren was a handsome African-American with a shaved head, a groomed mustache, and a body like one of the Greek statues in the Metropolitan Museum. It had taken Jack several months to cultivate Warren's acquaintance. They had developed a friendship of sorts, but it was based more on a shared love of street basketball than anything else. Jack didn't know much about Warren except that he was the best basketball player and also the de facto leader of the local gang. Jack suspected that the two positions went hand in hand.

"I was thinking about coming out for a run," Jack said. "Who's got winners?"

Getting into the game could be a tricky business. When Jack had first moved to the neighborhood, it had taken him a month of coming to the court and patiently waiting until he'd been invited to play. Then he'd had to prove himself. Once he'd demonstrated he was capable of putting the ball in the basket on a consistent basis, he'd been tolerated.

Things got a bit better when Jack had paid to have the lights installed and the backboards refurbished, but not a lot. There were only two other honkies besides Jack who were allowed to play. Being Caucasian was a definite disadvantage on the neighborhood playground: you had to know the rules.

"Ron's got winners and then Jake," Warren said. "But I can get you on my team. Flash's old lady wants him home."

"I'll be out," Jack said. He pushed off from the fence and rode the rest of the way to his building.

Jack got off his bike and hefted it up onto his shoulders. Before he entered his building he looked up at its facade. In his current critical state of mind he had to admit it wasn't pretty. In fact, it was a downright sorry structure, although at one time it must have been rather fancy, because a small segment of highly decorative cornice still clung precariously to the roofline. Two of the windows on the third floor were boarded up.

The building was six stories, constructed of brick, and had two apartments per floor. Jack shared the fourth floor with Denise, a husbandless teenager with two children.

Jack pushed the front door open with his foot. It had no lock. He started up the stairs, careful to avoid any debris. As Jack passed the second floor he heard the sorry sounds of a vehement argument, followed by the noise of breaking glass. Unfortunately, this was a nightly occurrence.

With the bike balanced on his shoulder, it took Jack some maneuvering to get himself situated in front of his apartment door. He was fumbling in his pocket for his key when he noticed he didn't need it. The doorjamb opposite his lock was splintered.

Jack pushed his door open. It was dark inside. He listened but only heard renewed yelling from 2A and the traffic out in the street. His apartment was eerily quiet. He put his bike down and reached in and turned on the overhead light.

The living room was in shambles. Jack didn't have much furniture, but what he had was either tipped over, emptied, or broken. He noticed that a small radio that usually stood on the desk was gone.

Jack wheeled the bike into the room and leaned it against the wall. He took off his jacket and draped it over the bike. Then he walked over to the desk. The drawers had been pulled out and dumped. Amid the rubble on the floor was a photo album; Jack bent down and picked it up. He opened the cover and breathed a sigh of relief.

It was unscathed. It was the only possession he cared about.

Jack placed the photo album on the windowsill and walked into the bedroom. He switched on the light and saw a similar scene. Most of his clothes had been pulled from his closet and from his bureau and tossed onto the floor.

The condition of the bathroom mirrored that of the living room and the bedroom. The contents of the medicine cabinet had been dumped into the bathtub.

Jack walked from the bedroom to the kitchen. Expecting more of the same, he flipped on the light. A slight gasp escaped from his lips.

"We were beginning to wonder about you," a large African-American male said. He was sitting at Jack's table, dressed totally in black leather, including gloves and a visorless hat. "We'd run out of your beer and we were getting antsy."

There were three other men dressed in identical fashion to the first. One was half sitting on the windowsill. The two others were to Jack's immediate right, leaning against the kitchen cabinet. On the table was an impressive array of weaponry, including machine pistols.

Jack didn't recognize any of these men. He was shocked that they were still there. He'd been robbed before but nobody had stayed to drink his beer.

"How about coming over and sitting yourself down?" the large black man said.

Jack hesitated. He knew the door to the hall was open. Could he make it before they picked up their guns? Jack doubted it, and he wasn't about to try.

"Come on, man," the black man said. "Get your white ass over here!"

Reluctantly Jack did as he was told. Warily he sat down and faced his uninvited visitor.

"We might as well be civilized about this," the black man said. "My name is Twin. This here's Reginald." Twin pointed to the man at the window.

Jack glanced in Reginald's direction. He was toying with a toothpick and sucking his teeth. He regarded Jack with obvious disdain. Although he wasn't quite as muscular as Warren, he was in the same category. Jack could see he had the words "Black Kings" tattooed on the volar surface of his right forearm.

"Now Reginald is pissed," Twin continued, "because you ain't got shit here in this apartment. I mean, there isn't even a TV. You see, part of the deal was that we'd have pickings over your stuff."

"What kind of deal are you talking about?" Jack asked.

"Let's put it this way," Twin said. "Me and my brothers are being paid some small change to come way the hell over here to rough you up a bit. Nothing major, despite the artillery you see on the table. It's supposed to be some kind of warning. Now, I don't know the details, but apparently you've been making a pain of yourself at some hospital and got a bunch of people all riled up. I'm supposed to remind you to do your job and let them do theirs. Does that make any more sense to you than it does to me? I mean, I've never done anything like this before."

"I think I catch your drift," Jack said.

"I'm glad," Twin said. "Otherwise we'd have to break a few fingers or something. We weren't supposed to hurt you bad, but when Reginald starts, it's hard to stop him, especially when he's pissed. He needs something. Are you sure you don't have a TV or something hidden around here?"

"He just came in with a bike," one of the other men said.

"What about that, Reginald?" Twin asked. "You want a new bike?"

Reginald leaned forward so he could see into the living room. He shrugged his shoulders.

"I think you got yourself a deal," Twin said. He stood up.

"Who's paying you to do this?" Jack asked.

Twin raised his eyebrows and laughed. "Now, it wouldn't be kosher of me to tell you that, now would it? But at least you've got the balls to ask."

Jack was about to ask another question when he was viciously cold-cocked by Twin. The force of the sucker punch knocked Jack over backward, and he sprawled limply on the floor. The room swam before his eyes. Hovering close to unconsciousness, he felt his wallet being pulled from his trousers. There was muffled laughter followed by a final agonizing kick in the stomach. Then there was absolute blackness.

CHAPTER TWENTY

The first thing Jack was aware of was a ringing in his head. Slowly he opened his eyes and found himself staring directly up at the ceiling fixture in the kitchen. Wondering what he was doing on the kitchen floor, he tried to get up. When he moved he felt a sharp pain in his jaw that made him lie back down. That was when he realized the ringing was intermittent and it wasn't in his head: it was the wall phone directly above him.

Jack rolled over onto his stomach. From that position he pushed himself up onto his knees. He'd never been knocked out before, and he couldn't believe how weak he felt. Gingerly he felt along his jawline. Thankfully he didn't feel any jagged edges of broken bones. Equally carefully he palpated his tender abdomen. That was less painful than the jaw, so he assumed there'd been no internal damage.

The phone continued to ring insistently. Finally Jack reached up and took it off the hook. As he said hello he eased himself into a sitting position on the floor with his back against the kitchen cabinets. His voice sounded strange even to himself.

"Oh, no! I'm sorry," Terese said when she heard his voice. "You've been asleep. I shouldn't have called so late."

"What time is it?" Jack asked.

"It's almost twelve," Terese said. "We're still here in the studio, and sometimes we forget that the rest of the world sleeps normal hours. I wanted to ask a question about sterilization, but I'll call you tomorrow. I'm sorry to have awakened you."

"Actually I've been unconscious on my kitchen floor," Jack said.

"Is that some kind of joke?" Terese asked.

"I wish," Jack said. "I came home to a ransacked apartment, and unfortunately the ransackers were still here. To add insult to injury they also kind of beat me up."

"Are you all right?" Terese asked urgently.

"I think so," Jack said. "But I think I chipped a tooth."

"Were you really unconscious?" Terese asked.

"I'm afraid so," Jack said. "I still feel weak."

"Listen," Terese said decisively. "I want you to call the police immediately, and I'm coming over."

"Wait a sec," Jack said. "First of all, the police won't do anything. I mean, what can they do? It was four gang members, and there's a million of them in the city."

"I don't care, I want you to call the police," Terese said. "I'll be over there in fifteen minutes."

"Terese, this isn't the best neighborhood," Jack said. He could tell she'd made up her mind, but he persisted. "You don't have to come. I'm okay. Honest!"

"I don't want to hear any excuses about not calling the police," Terese said. "I should be there in fifteen minutes."

Jack found himself holding a dead telephone. Terese had hung up.

Dutifully Jack dialed 911 and gave the information. When he was asked if he was in any current danger, he said no. The operator said the officers would be there as soon as possible.

Jack pushed himself up onto wobbly legs and walked out into his living room. Briefly he looked for his bike, but then vaguely remembered something about his attackers wanting it. In the bathroom he bared his teeth and examined them. As he'd suspected from touching it with his tongue, his left front tooth had a small chip. Twin must have had something like brass knuckles under his gloves.

To Jack's surprise the police arrived within ten minutes. There were two officers, an African-American by the name of David Jefferson and a Latino, Juan Sanchez. They listened politely to Jack's tale of woe, wrote down the particulars, including the make of the missing bike, and asked Jack if he'd care to come to the precinct to look at mug shots of various local gang members.

Jack declined. Through Warren he understood that the gangs did not fear the police. Consequently, Jack knew the police could not protect him from the gangs, so he decided not to tell the police everything. But at least he'd satisfied Terese's demand and would be able to collect insurance on his bike.

"Excuse me, Doc," David Jefferson said as the police were leaving. Jack had informed them he was a medical examiner. "How come you live in this neighborhood? Aren't you asking for trouble?"

"I ask myself the same question," Jack said.

After the police had left, Jack closed his splintered door and leaned against it while surveying his apartment.

Somehow he would have to find the energy to clean it up. At the moment it seemed like an overwhelming task.

A knock that he could feel more than hear made him reopen the door. It was Terese.

"Ah, thank God it's you," Terese said. She came into the apartment. "You weren't kidding when you said this wasn't the best neighborhood. Just climbing these stairs was a trauma. If it hadn't been you opening the door I might have screamed."

"I tried to warn you," Jack said.

"Let me look at you," Terese said. "Where's the best light?"

Jack shrugged. "You choose," he said. "Maybe the bathroom."

Terese dragged Jack into the bathroom and examined his face. "You have a tiny cut over your jawbone," she said.

"I'm not surprised," Jack said. He then showed her the chipped tooth.

"Why did they beat you up?" Terese said. "I hope you weren't playing hero."

"Quite the contrary," Jack said. "I was terrified into total immobility. I was sucker-punched. This was evidently some kind of warning for me to stay out of the Manhattan General."

"What on earth are you talking about?" Terese demanded.

Jack told her all the things he hadn't told the police. He even told her why he hadn't told the police.

"This is getting more and more unbelievable," Terese said. "What are you going to do?"

"To tell the truth, I haven't had a lot of time to think about it," Jack said.

"Well, I know one thing you are going to do," Terese said. "You are going to the emergency room."

"Come on!" Jack complained. "I'm fine. My jaw is sore, but big deal."

"You were knocked out," Terese reminded him. "You should be seen. I'm not even a doctor and I know that much."

Jack opened his mouth to protest further, but he didn't; he knew she was right. He should be seen. After a head injury serious enough to render him unconscious, there was the worry of intracranial hemorrhage. He should have a basic neurological exam.

Jack rescued his jacket from the floor. Then he followed Terese down the stairs to the street. To catch a cab they walked to Columbus Avenue.

"Where do you want to go?" Terese asked once they were in the taxi.

"I think I'll stay away from the General for the time being," Jack said with a smile. "Let's go uptown to Columbia-Presbyterian."

"Fine," Terese said. She gave directions to the cabdriver and settled back in her seat.

"Terese, I really appreciate your coming over," Jack said. "You didn't have to, and I certainly didn't expect it. I'm touched."

"You would have done it for me," Terese said.

Would he have? Jack wondered. He didn't know. The whole day had been confusing.

The visit to the emergency room went smoothly. They had to wait as auto accidents, knife wounds, and heart attacks were given priority. But eventually Jack was seen. Terese insisted on staying the whole time and even accompanied him into the examining room.

When the ER resident learned Jack was a medical examiner, he insisted Jack be seen by the neurology consultant. The neurology resident went over Jack with utmost care. He declared him fit and said he didn't even think an X ray was indicated unless Jack felt strongly otherwise. Jack didn't.

"The one thing I do recommend is that you be observed overnight," the neurology resident said. He then turned to Terese and said: "Mrs. Stapleton, just wake him up occasionally and make sure he behaves normally. Also check that his pupils remain the same size. Okay?"

"Okay," Terese said.

Later as they were walking out of the hospital Jack commented that he was impressed with her equanimity when she'd been addressed as Mrs. Stapleton.

"I thought it would have embarrassed the man to have corrected him," Terese said. "But I'm going to take his recommendations quite seriously. You are coming home with me."

"Terese . . ." Jack complained.

"No arguments!" Terese commanded. "You heard the doctor. There's no way I'd allow you to go back to that hellhole of yours tonight."

With his head mildly throbbing and his jaw aching and his stomach sore, Jack surrendered. "Okay," he said. "But this is all far beyond the call of duty."

Jack felt truly grateful as they rode up in the elevator in Terese's posh high-rise. No one had been as gracious to him as Terese in years. Between her concern and generosity he felt that he'd misjudged her.

"I've a guest room that I'm confident you'll find comfortable," she said as they walked down a carpeted hallway. "Whenever my folks come to town it is hard to get them to leave."

Terese's apartment was picture perfect. Jack was amazed how neat it was. Even the magazines were arranged carefully on the coffee table, as if she expected *Architectural Digest* to do a photo shoot.

The guest room was quaint with flower-print drapes, carpet, and bedspread that all matched. Jack joked that he hoped he didn't get disoriented since he might have trouble finding the bed.

After providing Jack with a bottle of aspirin, Terese left him to shower. After he'd finished, he donned a terry-cloth bathrobe, which she'd laid out. Thus attired, he poked his head out into the living room and saw her sitting on the couch reading. He walked out and sat across from her.

"Aren't you going to bed?" he asked.

"I wanted to be sure you were okay," she said. She leaned forward to stare directly into his face. "Your pupils look equal to me."

"To me too," Jack said. He laughed. "You are taking those doctor's orders seriously."

"You'd better believe it," she said. "I'll be coming in to wake you up, so be prepared."

"I know better than to argue," Jack said.

"How do you feel in general?" Terese asked.

"Physically or mentally?"

"Mentally," Terese said. "Physically I have a pretty good idea."

"To be truthful, the experience has scared me," Jack

admitted. "I know enough about these gangs to be afraid of them."

"That's why I wanted you to call the police," Terese said.

"You don't understand," Jack said. "The police can't really help me. I mean, I didn't even bother to tell them the possible name of the gang or the first names of the intruders. Even if the police picked them up, all they'd do is slap their wrists. Then they'll be back on the street."

"So what are you going to do?" Terese asked.

"I suppose I'm going to stay the hell away from the General," Jack said. "Seems like that's going to make everybody happy. Even my own boss told me not to go. I suppose I can do my job without going over there."

"I'm relieved," Terese said. "I was worried you'd try to be a hero and take the warning as a challenge."

"You said that before," Jack said. "But don't worry. I'm no hero."

"What about this bike-riding around this city?" Terese asked. "And riding through the park at night? And what about living where you do? The fact is, I do worry. I worry that you're either oblivious to danger or courting it. Which is it?"

Jack looked into Terese's pale blue eyes. She was asking questions that he strictly avoided. The answers were too personal. But after the concern that she'd demonstrated that evening and the effort she'd expended on his behalf, he felt she deserved some explanation. "I suppose I have been courting danger," he said.

"Can I ask why?"

"I guess I haven't been worried about dying," Jack said. "In fact, there was a time when I felt dying would be a relief. A few years back I had trouble with depression, and I suppose it's always going to be there in the background."

"I can relate to that," Terese said. "I had a bout with depression as well. Was yours associated with a particular event, if I may ask?"

Jack bit the inside of his lip. He felt uncomfortable talking about such issues, but now that he'd started it was hard to turn back.

"My wife died," Jack managed. He couldn't get himself to mention the children.

"I'm sorry," Terese said empathetically. She paused a moment and then said: "Mine was due to the death of my only child."

Jack turned his head away. Terese's admission brought instant tears to his eyes. He took a deep breath and then looked back at this complicated woman. She was a hard-driving executive; of that he was sure from the moment he'd met her. But now he knew there was more.

"I guess we have more in common than just disliking discos," he said in an attempt to lighten the atmosphere.

"I think we've both been emotionally scarred," Terese said. "And we've both overly invested ourselves in our careers."

"I'm not so sure we share that," Jack said. "I'm not as committed to my career as I once was, nor as I think you are. The changes that have come to medicine have robbed me of some of that."

Terese stood up. Jack did the same. They were standing close enough to appreciate each other physically.

"I guess I meant more that we both are afraid of emotional commitment," Terese said. "We've both been wounded."

"That I can agree to," Jack said.

Terese kissed the tips of her fingers and then touched them gently to Jack's lips.

"I'll be in to wake you in a few hours," she said. "So be prepared."

"I hate to be putting you through all this," Jack said.

"I'm enjoying this little bit of mothering," Terese said. "Sleep well."

They parted. Jack walked back toward the guest room, but before he got to the door, Terese called out: "One more question: Why do you live in that awful slum?"

"I guess I don't feel as if I deserve to be all that happy," Jack said.

Terese thought about that for a moment, then smiled. "Well, I shouldn't imagine I'd understand everything," she said. "Good night."

"Good night," Jack echoed.

CHAPTER TWENTY-ONE

Saturday, 8:30 A.M., March 23, 1996

True to her word, Terese had come into Jack's room and awakened him several times during the night. Each time they'd talked for a few minutes. By the time Jack awakened in the morning he felt conflicted. He was still thankful for Terese's ministrations, but he felt embarrassed by how much of himself he'd revealed.

As Terese made him breakfast, it became apparent that she felt as awkward as he. At eight-thirty, with mutual relief, they parted company in front of Terese's building. She was off to the studio for what she thought would be a marathon session. He headed for his apartment.

Jack spent a few hours cleaning up the debris left by the Black Kings. With some rudimentary tools he even repaired his door as best he could.

With his apartment taken care of, Jack headed to the morgue. He wasn't scheduled to work that weekend, but he wanted to spend more time on his backlog of autopsies that had yet to be signed out. He also wanted to check on any infectious cases that might have come in during the night from the General. Knowing that there had been three reportedly fulminant cases of Rocky Mountain spotted fever in the emergency room the day before, he was afraid of what he might find.

Jack missed his bike and thought about getting

another one. To get to work he took the subway, but it wasn't convenient. He had to change trains twice. The New York subway system was fine for getting from north to south, but west to east was another story entirely.

Even with the multiple train changing Jack still had to walk six blocks. With a light rain falling and no umbrella, he was wet by the time he got to the medical examiner's office at noon.

Weekends were far different than weekdays at the morgue. There was much less commotion. Jack used the front entrance and had the receptionist buzz him into the ID area. A distraught family was in one of the identification rooms. Jack could hear sobbing as he passed by.

Jack found the schedule that listed the doctors on call for the weekend and was pleased to see that Laurie was among them. He also found the master list of cases that had come in the previous night. Scanning it, he was sickened to see a familiar name. Nancy Wiggens had been brought in at four a.m.! The provisional diagnosis was Rocky Mountain spotted fever.

Jack found two more cases with the same diagnosis: Valerie Schafer, aged thirty-three, and Carmen Chavez, aged forty-seven. Jack assumed they were the other two cases in the General's emergency room the day before.

Jack went downstairs and peeked into the autopsy room. Two tables were in use. Jack couldn't tell who the doctors were, but judging by height he guessed one of them was Laurie.

After changing into scrubs and donning protective gear, Jack entered through the washroom.

"What are you doing here?" Laurie asked when she

caught sight of Jack. "You're supposed to be off enjoying yourself."

"Just can't keep away," Jack quipped. He leaned over to see the face of the patient Laurie was working on and his heart sank. Staring up at him with lifeless eyes was Nancy Wiggens. In death she appeared even younger than she had in life.

Jack quickly looked away.

"Did you know this individual?" Laurie asked. Her own emotional antennae had instantly picked up Jack's reaction.

"Vaguely," Jack admitted.

"It's a terrible thing when health-care workers succumb to their patients' illnesses," Laurie remarked. "The patient I did before this one was a nurse who'd ministered to the patient you did yesterday."

"I'd assumed as much," Jack said. "What about the third case?"

"I did her first," Laurie said. "She was from central supply. I couldn't quite figure how she contracted it."

"Tell me about it," Jack said. "I've done two other people from central supply. One with plague and one with tularemia. I can't understand it either."

"Somebody better figure it out," Laurie said.

"I couldn't agree more," Jack said. Then he pointed to Nancy's organs. "What'd you find?"

"It's all been consistent with Rocky Mountain spotted fever," Laurie said. "Are you interested to see?"

"I sure am," Jack said.

Laurie took time out to show all the relevant pathology to Jack. Jack told her the findings were the mirror image of those he'd seen with Lagenthorpe.

"It makes you wonder why just three got sick, since

they were so sick," Laurie said. "The interval from the onset of symptoms to the time of death was a lot shorter than usual. It suggests that the microbes were particularly pathogenic, yet if they were, where are the other patients? Janice told me that as far as the hospital knows there are no more cases."

"There was a similar pattern with the other diseases," Jack said. "I can't explain it, just like I can't explain so many other aspects of these outbreaks. That's why they've been driving me crazy."

Laurie glanced up at the clock and was surprised by the time. "I've got to get a move on here," she said. "Sal has to leave early."

"Why don't I help?" Jack offered. "Tell Sal he can go now."

"Are you serious?" Laurie asked.

"Absolutely," Jack said. "Let's get it done."

Sal was happy to leave a little early. Laurie and Jack worked well together and finished up the case in good time. They walked out of the autopsy room together.

"How about a bite up in the lunchroom?" Laurie asked. "My treat."

"You're on," Jack said.

They disposed of their isolation gear and disappeared into their respective locker rooms. When Jack was dressed, he went out into the hall and waited for Laurie to appear.

"You didn't have to wait for . . ." Laurie began to say, but stopped. "Your jaw is swollen," she said.

"That's not all," Jack said. He bared his teeth and pointed to his left incisor. "See the chip?" he asked.

"Of course I do," Laurie said. Her hands went onto her hips and her eyes narrowed. She looked like an irate mother confronting a naughty child. "Did you fall off of that bike?" she asked.

"I wish," Jack said with a mirthless laugh. He then told her the whole story minus the part about Terese. Laurie's expression changed from mock anger to disbelief.

"That's extortion," she said indignantly.

"I suppose it is in a way," Jack said. "But come on, let's not let it upset our gourmet lunch."

They did the best they could with the vending machines on the second floor. Laurie got a soup while Jack settled on a tuna-fish salad sandwich. They took their food to a table and sat down.

"The more I think about what you've told me, the crazier I think it sounds," Laurie said. "How's your apartment?"

"A bit dilapidated," Jack said. "But it wasn't so great before this happened, so it doesn't much matter. The worst thing is that they took my bike."

"I think you should move," Laurie said. "You shouldn't be living there anyway."

"It's only the second break-in," Jack said.

"I hope you're not planning on staying in tonight," Laurie said. "How depressing."

"No, I'm busy tonight," Jack said. "I've got a group of nuns coming into town who I'm supposed to show around."

Laurie laughed. "Hey, my folks are having a little dinner party tonight. Would you care to come along? It would be a lot more cheerful than sitting in your plundered apartment."

"That's very thoughtful of you," Jack said. As with

Terese's actions the night before, this invitation was totally unexpected. Jack was moved.

"I would enjoy your company," Laurie said. "What do you say?"

"You do realize that I'm not particularly social," Jack said.

"I'm aware of that," Laurie said. "I don't mean to put you on the spot. You don't even have to tell me now. The dinner is at eight and you can call me a half hour before if you decide to come. Here's my number." She wrote it on a napkin and handed it to him.

"I'm afraid I'm not such good company at dinner parties," Jack said.

"Well, it's up to you," Laurie said. "The invitation stands. Now, if you'll excuse me, I've got two more cases to do."

Jack watched Laurie leave. He'd been impressed with her from the first day, but he'd always thought of her as one of his more talented colleagues, nothing more. But now suddenly he saw how strikingly attractive she was with her sculptured features, soft skin, and beautiful auburn hair.

Laurie waved before slipping out the door, and Jack waved back. Disconcertedly he stood up, discarded his trash, and headed up to his office. In the elevator he wondered what was happening to him. It had taken him years to stabilize his life, and now his well-constructed cocoon seemed to be unraveling.

Once inside his office Jack sat down at his desk. He rubbed his temples to try to calm himself. He was becoming agitated again, and he knew that when he became agitated he could be impulsive.

As soon as he felt capable of concentrating he pulled

the closest folder toward him and flipped it open. Then he went to work.

By four o'clock Jack had accomplished as much paperwork as he could handle. Leaving the medical examiner's office, he took the subway. As he sat in the bouncing rail cars with the other silent, zombielike people, he told himself he had to get another bike. Commuting underground like a mole was not going to work for him.

Arriving home, Jack lost no time. He took his stairs two at a time. Finding a drunk, homeless person asleep on the first landing didn't faze him. He just stepped over the man and continued. With his anxiety Jack needed exercise, and the sooner he got out on the basketball court the happier he'd be.

Jack hesitated briefly at his door. It seemed to be in the same shape as he'd left it. He unlocked it and peered into the apartment. It, too, seemed undisturbed. Somewhat superstitiously Jack walked over to the kitchen and looked in. He was relieved to see that no one was there.

In the bedroom Jack pulled out his basketball gear: oversized sweat-pants, a turtleneck, and a sweater. He quickly changed. After lacing up his hightops, he grabbed a headband, a basketball, and was back out the door.

Saturday afternoon was always a big day at the playground, provided the weather cooperated. Usually twenty to thirty people showed up ready to run, and this particular Saturday was no exception. The morning rain had long since stopped. As Jack approached the court he counted fourteen people waiting to play. That meant he'd probably have to wait through two more games beyond the present match before he could hope to join.

Jack nodded subdued greetings to some of the people he recognized. The etiquette required that no emotion be shown. After he'd stood on the sidelines for the appropriate amount of time he asked who had winners. He was told that David had winners. Jack was acquainted with David.

Careful to suppress the eagerness he felt, Jack sidled up to David.

"You got winners?" Jack asked, pretending to be uninterested.

"Yeah, I got winners," David said. He went through some minor ducking and weaving that Jack had learned to recognize as posturing. Jack had also learned by sore experience not to imitate it.

"You got five?" Jack asked.

David already had his team lined up so Jack had to go through the same process with the next fellow who had winners. That was Spit, whose nick-name was based on one of his less endearing mannerisms. Luckily for Jack, Spit only had four players and since he knew Jack's outside shooting ability, he agreed to add Jack to his roster.

With his entrance into the game now assured, Jack took his ball to one of the unused side baskets and began warming up. He had a mild headache and his jaw ached, but otherwise he felt better than he'd expected. He'd been more concerned about his stomach once he started running around, but that didn't bother him in the slightest.

While Jack was busy shooting foul shots Warren showed up. After he'd gone through the same process that Jack had done in order to get into the game, he wandered over to where Jack was practicing.

"Hey, Doc, what's happening?" Warren asked. He snatched the ball from Jack's hands and quickly tossed in a shot that hit nothing but net. Warren's movements were uncannily fast.

"Not much," Jack said, which was the correct reply. Warren's question was really a greeting in disguise.

They shot for a while in a ritual fashion. First Warren would shoot until he missed, which wasn't often. Then Jack would do the same. While one was shooting the other rebounded.

"Warren, let me ask you a question," Jack said during one of his turns shooting. "You ever hear of a gang by the name of the Black Kings?"

"Yeah, I think so," Warren said. He fed Jack the ball after Jack had put in one of his patented long-distance jump shots. "I think they're a bunch of losers from down near the Bowery. How come you're asking?"

"Just curious," Jack said. He sank another long jump shot. He was feeling good.

Warren snatched the ball out of the air as it came through the basket. But he didn't pass it back to Jack. Instead he walked it to Jack.

"What do you mean, 'curious'?" Warren asked. He drilled Jack with his gun-barrel eyes. "You ain't been curious about any gangs before."

One of the other things that Jack knew about Warren was that he was keenly intelligent. Had he had the opportunity, Jack was sure he'd be a doctor or a lawyer or some other professional.

"I happened to see it tattooed on a guy's forearm," Jack said.

"The guy dead?" Warren asked. He was aware of what Jack did for a living.

"Not yet," Jack said. He rarely risked sarcasm with his playground acquaintances, but on this occasion it had just slipped out.

Warren regarded him warily and continued to hold the ball. "You pulling my chain, or what?"

"Hell no," Jack said. "I might be white, but I ain't stupid."

Warren smiled. "How come you got banged up on your jaw?"

Warren didn't miss a trick. "Just caught an elbow," Jack said. "I was in the wrong place at the wrong time."

Warren handed over the ball. "Let's warm up with a little one-on-one," he said. "Hit-or-miss for the ball."

Warren got in the game before Jack, but Jack eventually played, and played well. Spit's players seemed unbeatable, to the chagrin of Warren, who had to play against them on several occasions. By six o'clock Jack was exhausted and soaked to the skin.

Jack was perfectly happy to leave when everyone else departed en masse for dinner and their usual Saturday-night revelry. The basketball court would be empty until the following afternoon.

A long, hot postgame shower was a distinct pleasure for Jack. When he was finished he dressed in clean clothes and looked into his refrigerator. It was a sad scene. All his beer had been drunk by the Black Kings. As far as food was concerned he was limited to an old wedge of cheddar cheese and two eggs of dubious age. Jack closed the refrigerator. He wasn't all that hungry anyway.

In the living room Jack sat on his threadbare couch and picked up one of his medical journals. His usual evening routine was to read until nine-thirty or ten and then fall asleep. But tonight he was still restless despite the exercise, and he found he couldn't concentrate.

Jack tossed the journal aside and stared at the wall. He was lonely, and although he was lonely almost every night, he felt it more keenly at that moment. He kept thinking about Terese and how compassionate she'd been the night before.

Jack impulsively went to the desk, got out the phone book, and called Willow and Heath. He wasn't sure if the phones would be manned after hours, but eventually someone answered. After several wrong extensions he finally got Terese on the phone.

With his heart inexplicably pounding in his chest, Jack casually told her he was thinking of getting something to eat.

"Is this an invitation?" Terese questioned.

"Well," Jack said hesitantly. "Maybe you'd like to come along, provided you haven't eaten yet."

"This is the most roundabout invitation I've gotten since Marty Berman asked me to the junior prom," Terese said with a laugh. "You know what he did? He used the conditional. He said: 'What would you say if I asked you?' "

"I guess Marty and I have some things in common," Jack said.

"Hardly," Terese said. "Marty was a skinny runt. But as for dinner, I'll have to take a rain check. I'd love to see you, but you know about this deadline we have. We're hoping that we can get it under control tonight. I hope you understand."

"Absolutely," Jack said. "No problem."

"Call me tomorrow," Terese said. "Maybe in the afternoon we can get together for coffee or something."

Jack promised he'd call and wished her good luck. Then he hung up the phone, feeling even lonelier for having made an effort to be sociable after so many years and having been turned down.

Surprising himself anew, Jack found Laurie's number and called her. Trying to cover his nervousness with humor, he told her that the group of nuns he was expecting had to cancel.

"Does that mean you'd like to come to dinner?" Laurie asked.

"If you'll have me," Jack said.

"I'd be delighted," Laurie said.

CHAPTER TWENTY-TWO

Sunday, 9:00 A.M., March 24, 1996

Jack was poring over one of his forensic science journals when his phone rang. Since he had yet to speak that morning his voice was gravelly when he answered.

"I didn't wake you, did I?" Laurie asked.

"I've been up for hours," Jack assured her.

"I'm calling because you asked me to," Laurie said. "Otherwise I wouldn't call this early on a Sunday morning."

"It's not early for me," Jack said.

"But it was late when you went home," Laurie said.

"It wasn't that late," Jack said. "Besides, no matter what time I go to bed I always wake up early."

"Anyway, you wanted me to let you know if there were any infectious deaths from the General last night," Laurie said. "There weren't. Janice even told me before she left that there wasn't even anyone ill with Rocky Mountain spotted fever in the hospital. That's good news, isn't it?"

"Very good news," Jack agreed.

"My parents were quite impressed with you last night," Laurie added. "I hope you enjoyed yourself."

"It was a delightful evening," Jack said. "Frankly I'm embarrassed I stayed so long. Thank you for inviting me and thank your parents. They couldn't have been more hospitable."

"We'll have to do it again sometime," Laurie said.

"Absolutely," Jack said.

After they had said good-byes, Jack hung up the phone and tried to go back to reading. But he was momentarily distracted by thoughts of the previous evening. He had enjoyed himself. In fact he'd enjoyed himself much more than he could have imagined, and that confused him. He'd purposefully kept to himself for five years, and now without warning he found himself enjoying the company of two very different women.

What he liked about Laurie was how easy she was to be with. Terese, on the other hand, could be overbearing even while she was being warmly caring. Terese was more intimidating than Laurie, but she was also challenging in a way that was more consistent with Jack's reckless lifestyle. But now that he'd had the opportunity to see Laurie interact with her parents, he appreciated her open, warm personality all the more. He imagined having a pompous cardiovascular surgeon for a father couldn't have been easy.

Laurie had tried to engage Jack in personal conversation after the older generation had retired, but Jack had resisted, as was his habit. Yet he'd been tempted. Having opened up a little with Terese the night before, it had surprised him how good it felt to talk with someone caring. But Jack had fallen back on his usual stratagem of turning the conversation back to Laurie, and he'd learned some unexpected things.

Most surprising was that she was unattached. Jack had just assumed someone as desirable and sensitive as Laurie would have been involved with someone, but Laurie insisted she didn't even date much. She'd explained that she'd had a relationship with a police detective for a time, but it hadn't worked out.

Eventually Jack got back to his journal. He read until hunger drove him to a neighborhood deli. On his way home from lunch he saw that a group of guys was already beginning to appear on the basketball court. Eager for more physical activity, Jack dashed home, changed, and joined them.

Jack played for several hours. Unfortunately his shot wasn't as smooth or accurate as on the previous day. Warren teased him unmercifully, especially when he guarded Jack during several of the games. Warren was making up for the ignominy of the previous day's defeats.

At three o'clock after another loss, which meant Jack would be sitting out for at least three games, maybe more, he gave up and returned to his apartment. After a shower he sat down to try to read again, but found himself thinking about Terese.

Concerned about being rejected a second time, Jack had not planned on calling her. But by four he relented; after all, she had asked him to call. More important, he truly wanted to talk with her. Having partially opened up to her, he felt curiously disturbed not to have told her the whole story. He felt he owed her more.

Even more anxious than he had been the evening before, Jack dialed the number.

This time Terese was much more receptive. In fact, she was ebullient.

"We made great progress last night," she announced proudly. "Tomorrow we're going to knock the socks off the president and the CEO. Thanks to you this idea of hospital cleanliness and low infection rate is a great hook. We're even having some fun with your sterilization idea."

Finally Jack got around to asking her if she'd like to get together for some coffee. He reminded her it had been her suggestion.

"I'd love it," Terese said without hesitation. "When?"

"How about right now?" Jack said.

"Fine by me," Terese said.

They met at a small French-style café on Madison Avenue between Sixty-first and Sixty-second conveniently close to the Willow and Heath building. Jack got there ahead of Terese and took a table in the window and ordered an espresso.

Terese arrived soon after. She waved through the window, and after entering, she forced Jack into a repeat of the cheek-pressing routine. She was vibrant. She ordered a decaf cappuccino from the attentive waiter.

As soon as they were alone, she leaned across the table and grasped Jack's hand. "How are you?" she asked. She looked directly into his eyes and then at his jawline. "Your pupils are equal, and you look okay. I thought you'd be black and blue."

"I'm better than I would have expected," Jack admitted.

Terese then launched into an excited monologue about her upcoming review and how wonderfully everything was falling into place. She explained what a "ripomatic" was and how they had managed to put one together with tape sequences from their previous National Health campaign. She said it was terrific and gave a good impression of the Do-No-Harm Hippocrates idea.

Jack let her carry on until she'd exhausted the subject.

After taking a few gulps of her cappuccino, she asked him what he'd been doing.

"I've been thinking a lot about the conversation we had Friday night," he said. "It's been bothering me."

"How so?" Terese asked.

"We were being open with each other, but I wasn't completely forthright," Jack said. "I'm not accustomed to talking about my problems. The truth is: I didn't tell you the whole story."

Terese put her coffee cup down and studied Jack's face. His dark blue eyes were intense. His face was stubbled; he'd obviously not shaved that day. She thought that under different circumstances Jack could appear intimidating, maybe even scary.

"My wife wasn't the only person who died," Jack said haltingly. "I lost my two daughters as well. It was a commuter plane crash."

Terese swallowed with difficulty. She'd felt a welling of emotion clog her throat. Jack's story was hardly what she'd expected.

"The problem is, I've always felt so damn responsible," he continued. "If it hadn't been for me they wouldn't have been on that plane."

Terese felt an intense stab of empathy. After a few moments she said: "I wasn't entirely forthright either. I told you I'd lost my child. What I didn't say is that it was an unborn child, and at the same time I lost the child, I lost my ability to have any more. To add insult to injury, the man I'd married deserted me."

For a few emotionally choked minutes neither Jack nor Terese spoke. Finally, Jack broke the silence: "It sounds like we're trying to outdo each other with our personal tragedies," he said, managing a smile.

"Just like a couple of depressives," Terese agreed. "My therapist would love this."

"Of course, what I've told you is for your ears only," Jack said.

"Don't be silly," Terese assured him. "Same goes for you. I haven't told my story to anyone but my therapist."

"I haven't told anybody," Jack said. "Not even a therapist."

Feeling a sense of relief from having both bared their innermost secrets, Jack and Terese went on to talk about happier things. Terese, who'd grown up in the city, was shocked to hear how little of the area Jack had visited since he'd been there. She talked about taking him to the Cloisters when spring had truly arrived.

"You'll love it," she promised.

"I'll look forward to it," Jack said.

CHAPTER TWENTY-THREE

Jack was irritated at himself. He'd had time to buy a new bike on Saturday, but he'd failed to do so. Consequently, he had to use the subway again to commute to work, although he'd considered jogging. The problem with jogging was that he'd have to have a change of clothes in his office. To give him the option in the future he brought some to work in a small shoulder bag.

Coming in from First Avenue, Jack again entered the medical examiner's facility through the front entrance. As he passed through the glass door, he was impressed with the number of families waiting in the outer reception area. It was highly unusual for so many people to be there that early. Something must be up, he surmised.

Jack had himself buzzed in. He walked into the scheduling room and saw George Fontworth sitting at the desk Laurie had occupied each morning the previous week.

Jack was sorry Laurie's week as supervisor was over. George had rotated to the position. He was a short, moderately overweight doctor of whom Jack had a low opinion. He was perfunctory and often missed important findings.

Ignoring George, Jack headed over to Vinnie and pushed down the edge of his newspaper.

"Why are there so many people out in the ID area?" Jack asked.

"Because there's a minor disaster over at the General," George said, answering for Vinnie. Vinnie treated Jack to a jaunty but disdainful expression and went back to his paper.

"What kind of disaster?" Jack asked.

George patted the top of a stack of folders. "A whole bunch of meningococcal deaths," he said. "Could be an epidemic in the making. We've got eight so far."

Jack rushed over to George's desk and snapped up a folder at random. He opened it and shuffled through its contents until he came to the investigative report. Scanning it quickly, he learned that the patient's name was Robert Caruso, and that he had been a nurse on the orthopedic floor at the General.

Jack tossed the folder back onto the desk and literally ran through communications to the offices of the PAs. He was relieved to see Janice was still there, putting in overtime as usual.

She looked terrible. The dark circles under her eyes were so distinct, she resembled a battered woman. She put her pen down and leaned back. She shook her head. "I might have to get another job," she said. "I can't keep this up. Thank God I have tomorrow and the next day off."

"What happened?" Jack asked.

"It started on the shift before mine," Janice said. "The first case was called in around six-thirty. Apparently the patient had died about six p.m."

"An orthopedic patient?" Jack asked.

"How'd you know?"

"I just saw a folder from an orthopedic nurse," Jack said.

"Oh, yeah, that was Mr. Caruso," Janice said with a yawn. She excused herself before continuing. "Anyway, I started getting called shortly after I arrived at eleven. Since then it's been nonstop. I've been back and forth all night. In fact, I just got back here twenty minutes ago. I tell you, this is worse than the other outbreaks. One of the patients is a nine-year-old girl. What a tragedy."

"Was she related to the first case?" Jack asked.

"She was a niece," Janice said.

"Had she been in to visit her uncle?" Jack asked.

"Around noon yesterday," Janice said. "You don't think that could have contributed to her death, do you? I mean, that was only about twelve hours before her death."

"Under certain circumstances meningococcus has a frightful capacity to kill, and kill incredibly swiftly," Jack said. "In fact, it can kill in just a few hours."

"Well, the hospital is in a panic."

"I can imagine," Jack said. "What was the name of the first case?"

"Carlo Pacini," Janice said. "But that's about all I know. He came in on the shift before mine. Steve Mariott handled it."

"Could I ask a favor?" Jack asked.

"That depends," Janice said. "I'm awfully tired."

"Just leave word for Bart that I want you PAs to get all the charts of the index case in each of these outbreaks. Let's see, that's Nodelman with the plague, Hard with tularemia, Lagenthorpe with Rocky Mountain spotted fever, and Pacini with meningococcus. Do you think that will be a problem?"

"Not at all," Janice said. "They are all active ME cases."

Jack stood up and gave Janice a pat on the back. "Maybe you should go over to the clinic on your way home," he said. "Some chemoprophylaxis might not be a bad idea."

Janice's eyes widened. "You think that is necessary?"

"Better safe than sorry," Jack said. "Anyway, discuss it with one of the infectious disease gurus. They know better than I. There's even a tetravalent vaccine, but that takes a few days to kick in."

Jack dashed back to the ID room and asked George for Carlo Pacini's folder.

"It's not here," George said. "Laurie came in early, and when she heard about what was going on, she requested the case. She's got the folder."

"Where is she?" Jack asked.

"Up in her office," Vinnie responded from behind his paper.

Jack hustled up to Laurie's office. Contrary to the way Jack worked, she liked to go over each folder in her office before doing the autopsy.

"Pretty frightening, I'd say," Laurie said as soon as she saw Jack.

"It's terrifying," Jack said. He grabbed Laurie's officemate's chair, pulled it over to Laurie's desk, and sat down. "This is just what I've been worrying about. This could be a real epidemic. What have you learned about this index case?"

"Not much," Laurie admitted. "He'd been admitted Saturday evening with a fractured hip. Apparently he'd had a brittle bone problem; he'd had a whole string of fractures over the last few years."

"Fits the pattern," Jack said.

"What pattern?" Laurie asked.

"All the index cases from these recent outbreaks have had some sort of chronic illness," Jack said.

"A lot of people who are hospitalized have chronic illnesses," Laurie said. "In fact, most of them. What does that have to do with anything?"

"I'll tell you what's on his paranoid, sick mind," Chet said. Chet had appeared at Laurie's door. He stepped into the room and leaned against the second desk. "He's got this thing about AmeriCare and wants to see conspiracy behind all this trouble."

"Is that true?" Laurie asked.

"I think it's less that I want to see conspiracy than it's staring me in the face," Jack said.

"What do you mean by 'conspiracy'?" Laurie asked.

"He has this notion that these unusual illnesses are being spread deliberately," Chet said. Chet summarized Jack's theory that the culprit was either someone at AmeriCare trying to protect its bottom line or some crazy person with terrorist inclinations.

Laurie looked questioningly at Jack. Jack shrugged.

"There are a lot of unanswered questions," Jack offered.

"As there are in just about any outbreak," Laurie said. "But really! This is all a bit far-fetched. I hope you didn't mention this theory to the powers that be over at the General."

"Yeah, I did," Jack said. "In fact I sort of asked the director of the lab if he was involved. He's rather disgruntled with his budget. He immediately informed the infection-control officer. I imagine they've let the administration know."

Laurie let out a short, cynical laugh. "Oh, brother," she said. "No wonder you've become persona non grata around there."

"You have to admit there's been an awful lot of questionable nosocomial infection at the General," Jack said.

"I'm not even so sure about that," Laurie said. "Both the tularemic patient and the patient with Rocky Mountain spotted fever developed their illnesses within forty-eight hours of admission. By definition, they are not nosocomial infections."

"Technically that's true," Jack admitted. "But . . ."

"Besides, all these illnesses have been seen in New York," Laurie said. "I've done some recent reading myself. There was a serious outbreak of Rocky Mountain spotted fever in eighty-seven."

"Thank you, Laurie," Chet said. "I tried to tell Jack the same thing. Even Calvin has told him."

"What about the series of cases coming from central supply?" Jack asked Laurie. "And what about the rapidity with which the patients with Rocky Mountain spotted fever developed their illnesses? You were questioning that just this Saturday."

"Of course I'd question those things," Laurie said. "They're the type of questions that have to be asked in any epidemiological situation."

Jack sighed. "I'm sorry," he said. "But I'm convinced something highly unusual is going on. All along I've been worried that we might see a real epidemic crop up. This outbreak of meningococcus may be it. If it peters out like the other outbreaks, I'll be relieved, of course, in human terms. But it will only add to my suspicions.

This pattern of multiple fulminant cases, then nothing, is highly unusual in itself."

"But this is the season for meningococcus," Laurie said. "It's not so unusual."

"Laurie's right," Chet said. "But regardless, my concern is that you're going to get yourself into real trouble. You're like a dog with a bone. Calm down! I don't want to see you fired. At least reassure me you're not going back to the General."

"I can't say that," Jack said. "Not with this new outbreak. This one doesn't depend on some arthropods that aren't around. This is an airborne problem, and as far as I'm concerned, it changes the rules."

"Just a moment," Laurie said. "What about that warning you got from those thugs?"

"Now what?" Chet questioned. "What thugs?"

"Jack had a cozy visit from some charming members of a gang," Laurie said. "It seems that at least one of the New York gangs is going into the extortion business."

"Somebody has to explain," Chet said.

Laurie told Chet what she knew of Jack's beating.

"And you're still thinking of going over there?" Chet asked when she was through.

"I'll be careful," Jack said. "Besides, I haven't exactly decided to go yet."

Chet rolled his eyes to the ceiling. "I think I would have preferred you as a suburbanite ophthalmologist."

"What do you mean, ophthalmologist?" Laurie questioned.

"Come on, you guys," Jack said. He stood up. "Enough is enough. We've got work to do."

*

Jack, Laurie, and Chet did not emerge from the autopsy room until after one in the afternoon. Although George had questioned the need to post all the meningococcal cases, the triumvirate had insisted; George relented in the end. Doing some on their own and some together, they autopsied the initial patient, one orthopedic resident, two nurses, one orderly, two people who'd visited the patient, including the nine-year-old girl, and particularly important as far as Jack was concerned, one woman from central supply.

After the marathon they all changed back to their street clothes and met up in the lunchroom. Relieved to be away from the mayhem and a bit overwhelmed by the findings, they didn't talk at first. They merely got their selections from the vending machines and sat down at one of the free tables.

"I haven't done many meningococcal cases in the past," Laurie said finally. "But these today were a lot more impressive than the ones I did do."

"You won't see a more dramatic case of the Waterhouse-Friderichsen syndrome," Chet said. "None of these people had a chance. The bacteria marched through them like a Mongol horde. The amount of internal hemorrhage was extraordinary. I tell you, it scares the pants off me."

"It was one time that I actually didn't mind being in the moon suit," Jack agreed. "I couldn't get over the amount of gangrene on the extremities. It was even more than on the recent plague cases."

"What surprised me was how little meningitis was involved," Laurie said. "Even the child had very little, and I would have thought at least she would have had extensive involvement."

"What puzzles me," Jack said, "is the amount of pneumonitis. Obviously it is an airborne infection, but it usually invades the upper part of the respiratory tree, not the lungs."

"It can get there easily enough once it gets into the blood," Chet said. "Obviously all these people had high levels coursing through their vascular systems."

"Have either of you heard if any more cases have come in today?" Jack asked.

Chet and Laurie exchanged glances. Both shook their heads.

Jack scraped back his chair and went to a wall phone. He called down to communications and posed the same question to one of the operators. The answer was no. Jack walked back to the table and reclaimed his seat.

"Well, well," he said. "Isn't this curious. No new cases."

"I'd say it was good news," Laurie said.

"I'd second that," Chet said.

"Does either of you know any of the internists over at the General?" Jack asked.

"I do," Laurie said. "One of my classmates from medical school is over there."

"How about giving her a call and seeing if they have many meningococcal cases under treatment?" Jack asked.

Laurie shrugged and went to use the same phone Jack had just used.

"I don't like that look in your eye," Chet said.

"I can't help it," Jack said. "Just like with the other outbreaks, little disturbing facts are beginning to appear. We've just autopsied some of the sickest meningococcal patients any of us has ever seen and then, boom! No more cases, as if a faucet had been turned off. It's just what I was talking about earlier."

"Isn't that characteristic of the disease?" Chet asked. "Peaks and valleys."

"Not this fast," Jack said. Then he paused. "Wait a second," he added. "I just thought of something else. We know who the first person was to die in this outbreak, but who was the last?"

"I don't know, but we've got all the folders," Chet said.

Laurie returned. "No meningococcal cases presently," she said. "But the hospital doesn't consider itself out of the woods. They've instituted a massive campaign of vaccination and chemoprophylaxis. Apparently the place is in an uproar."

Both Jack and Chet merely grunted at this news. They were preoccupied with going through the eight folders and jotting down notations on their napkins.

"What on earth are you guys doing?" Laurie asked.

"We're trying to figure out who was the last to die," Jack said.

"What on earth for?" Laurie asked.

"I'm not sure," Jack said.

"This is it," Chet said. "It was Imogene Philbertson."

"Honest?" Jack questioned. "Let me see."

Chet turned around the partially filled-out death certificate that listed the time of death.

"I'll be damned," Jack said.

"Now what?" Laurie asked.

"She was the one who worked in central supply," Jack said.

"Is that significant?" Laurie asked.

Jack pondered for a few minutes, then shook his head.

"I don't know," he said. "I'll have to look back at the other outbreaks. As you know, each outbreak has included someone from central supply. I'll see if it is a pattern I'd missed."

"You guys weren't particularly impressed with my news that there are currently no more cases of meningococcal disease over at the General."

"I am," Chet said. "Jack sees it as confirmation of his theories."

"I'm worried it is going to frustrate our hypothetical terrorist," Jack said. "It's also going to teach him an unfortunate lesson."

Both Laurie and Chet rolled their eyes to the ceiling and let out audible groans.

"Come on, you guys," Jack said. "Hear me out. Let's just say for the sake of argument that I'm right about some weirdo spreading these microbes in hopes of starting an epidemic. At first he picks the scariest, most exotic diseases he can think of, but he doesn't know that they won't really spread patient to patient. They are spread by arthropods having access to an infected reservoir. But after a few flops he figures this out and turns to a disease that is spread airborne. But he picks meningococcus. The problem with meningococcus is that it really isn't a patient-to-patient disease either: it's a carrier disease that's mainly spread by an immune individual walking around and giving it to others. So now our weirdo is really frustrated, but he truly knows what he needs. He needs a disease that is spread mainly patient-to-patient by aerosol."

"And what would you choose in this hypothetical scenario?" Chet asked superciliously.

"Let's see," Jack said. He pondered for a moment.

"I'd use drug-resistant diphtheria, or maybe even drug-resistant pertussis. Those old standbys are making some devastating comebacks. Or you know what else would be perfect? Influenza! A pathological strain of influenza."

"What an imagination!" Chet commented.

Laurie stood up. "I've got to get back to work," she said. "This conversation is too hypothetical for me."

Chet did the same.

"Hey, isn't anybody going to comment?" Jack said.

"You know how we feel," Chet said. "This is just mental masturbation. It seems like the more you think and talk about this stuff the more you believe it. I mean, really, if it were one disease, okay, but now we're up to four. Where would someone get these microbes? They are not the kind of thing you can go into your neighborhood deli and order. I'll see you upstairs."

Jack watched Laurie and Chet dispose of their trash and leave the lunchroom. He sat for a few moments and considered what Chet had said. Chet had a good point, one that Jack had not even considered. Where would someone get pathological bacteria? He really had no idea.

Jack got up and stretched his legs. After discarding his tray and sandwich wrappings, he followed the others up to the fifth floor. By the time he got to the office, Chet was already engrossed and didn't look up.

Sitting down at his desk, Jack got all the folders together plus his notes and looked up the time of death of each of the women victims from central supply. To date, central supply had lost four people. Jack imagined that the departmental head would have to be actively recruiting to keep up with that type of attrition.

Next Jack looked up the time of death of each of the

other infectious cases. For the times of death of the few he'd not autopsied, he called down to Bart Arnold, the chief PA.

When Jack had all the information it became immediately apparent that with each outbreak, it had been the woman from central supply to be the last to succumb. That suggested, but certainly didn't prove, that in each instance those from central supply were the last to become infected. Jack asked himself what that meant, but couldn't come up with an answer. Still, it was an extremely curious detail.

"I have to go back to the General," Jack said suddenly. He stood up.

Chet didn't even bother to look up. "Do what you have to do," he said with resignation. "Not that my opinion counts."

Jack pulled on his bomber jacket. "Don't take it personally," he said. "I appreciate your concern, but I've got to go. I've got to look into this strange central supply connection. It could just be a coincidence, I agree, but it seems unlikely."

"What about Bingham and what about those gang members Laurie mentioned?" Chet asked. "You're taking a lot of risk."

"Such is life," Jack said. He gave Chet a tap on the shoulder on his way to the hallway. Jack had just reached the threshold when his phone rang. He debated whether to take the time to answer it. It was usually someone from one of the labs.

"Want me to get it?" Chet offered when he saw Jack hesitate.

"No, I'm here, and I might as well," Jack said. He returned to his desk and picked up the receiver.

"Thank God you are there!" Terese said with obvious relief. "I was terrified I wouldn't get you, at least not in time."

"What on earth is the matter?" Jack asked. His pulse quickened. He could tell by the sound of her voice that she was acutely upset.

"There's been a catastrophe," she said. "I have to see you immediately. Can I come over to your office?"

"What happened?" Jack asked.

"I can't talk now," Terese said. "I can't risk it with everything that has happened. I've just got to see you."

"We're sort of in the middle of an emergency ourselves," Jack said. "And I'm just on my way out."

"It's very important," Terese said. "Please!"

Jack immediately relented, especially with Terese's selfless response to his emergency Friday night.

"All right," Jack said. "Since I was just leaving, I'll come to you. Where would you like to meet?"

"Were you going uptown or downtown?" Terese asked.

"Uptown," Jack said.

"Then let's meet at the café where we had coffee on Sunday," Terese said.

"I'll be right there," Jack said.

"Wonderful!" Terese asserted. "I'll be waiting." Then she hung up.

Jack replaced the receiver and self-consciously looked over at Chet. "Did you hear any of that?" Jack asked.

"It was hard not to," Chet said. "What do you think happened?"

"I haven't the faintest idea," Jack said.

True to his word, Jack left immediately. Exiting from the front of the medical examiner facility, he caught a cab on First Avenue. Despite the normal afternoon traffic, he made it uptown in reasonable time.

The café was crowded. He found Terese sitting toward the rear on a small banquette. He took the seat opposite her. She didn't make any motion to get up. She was dressed as usual in a smart suit. Her jaw was clenched. She looked angry.

She leaned forward. "You are not going to believe this," she said in a forced whisper.

"Did the president and the CEO not like your presentation?" Jack asked. It was the only thing he could think of.

Terese made a motion of dismissal with her hand. "I canceled the presentation," she said.

"Why?" Jack asked.

"Because I'd had the sense to schedule an early breakfast with a woman acquaintance at National Health," Terese said. "She's a vice president in marketing who I happened to have gone to Smith College with. I'd had a brainstorm about leaking the campaign to some higher-ups through her. I was so confident. But she shocked me by telling me that under no circumstances would the campaign fly."

"But why?" Jack asked. As much as he disliked medical advertising, he'd considered the ads Terese had come up with the best he'd seen.

"Because National Health is deathly afraid of any reference to nosocomial infections," Terese said angrily. Then she leaned forward again and whispered. "Apparently they have had some of their own trouble lately."

"What kind of trouble?" Jack asked.

"Nothing like the Manhattan General," Terese said. "But serious nonetheless, even with a few deaths. But the real point is that our own account executive people, specifically Helen Robinson and her boss, Robert Barker, knew all this and didn't tell me."

"That's counterproductive," Jack said. "I thought you corporate types were all working toward the same end."

"Counterproductive!" Terese practically shouted, causing the nearby diners to turn their heads. Terese closed her eyes for a moment to collect herself.

" 'Counterproductive' is not the term I'd use," Terese said, keeping her voice down. "The way I'd describe it would make a sailor blush. You see, this was not an oversight. It was done deliberately to make me look bad."

"I'm sorry to hear this," Jack said. "I can see it's upsetting for you."

"That's an understatement," Terese said. "It's the death of my presidential aspirations if I don't come up with an alternative campaign in the next couple of days."

"A couple of days?" Jack questioned. "From what you've shown me about how this process works, that's a mighty tall order."

"Exactly," Terese said. "That's why I had to see you. I need another hook. You came up with this infection idea, or at least you were the source of it. Can you come up with another concept? Something that I can construct an ad campaign around. I'm desperate!"

Jack looked off and tried to think. The irony of the situation didn't escape him; as much as he despised medical advertising, here he was racking his brains for some sort of an idea. He wanted to help; after all, Terese had been willing to help him.

"The reason I think medical advertising is such a waste of money is that it ultimately has to rely on superficial amenities," he said. "The problem is that without quality being an issue there just isn't enough difference between AmeriCare and National Health or any of the other big conglomerates."

"I don't care," Terese said. "Just give me something I can use."

"Well, the only thing that comes to my mind at the moment is the issue about waiting," Jack said.

"What do you mean, 'waiting'?" Terese asked.

"You know," Jack said. "Nobody likes waiting for the doctor, but everybody does. It's one of those irritating universal annoyances."

"You're right!" Terese said excitedly. "I love it. I can already see a tag line like: No waiting with National Health! Or even better: We wait for you, you don't wait for us! God, that's great! You're a genius at this. How about a job?"

Jack chuckled. "Wouldn't that be a trip," he said. "But I'm having enough trouble with the one I have."

"Is there something wrong?" Terese asked. "What did you mean when you said you were in the middle of an emergency?"

"There's more trouble at the Manhattan General," Jack said. "This time it's an illness caused by meningococcus bacteria. It can be extremely deadly, as it has been in this instance."

"How many cases?"

"Eight," Jack said. "Including a child."

"How awful," Terese said. She was appalled. "Do you think it will spread?"

"I was worried at first," Jack said. "I thought we were going to have a bona fide epidemic on our hands. But the cases just stopped. So far it hasn't spread beyond the initial cohort."

"I hope this isn't going to be kept a secret like whatever killed the people at National Health," Terese said.

"No worry on that account," Jack said. "This episode is no secret. I've heard the hospital is in an uproar. But I'll find out firsthand. I'm on my way over there."

"Oh, no you're not!" Terese commanded. "Is your memory so short that Friday night is already a blur?"

"You sound like several of my colleagues," Jack said. "I appreciate your concern, but I can't stay away. I have a sense that these outbreaks are deliberate, and my conscience won't let me ignore them."

"What about those people who beat you up?" she demanded.

"I'll have to be careful," Jack said.

Terese made a disparaging sound. "Being careful hardly sounds adequate," she said. "It's certainly not consistent with how you described those hoodlums Friday night."

"I'll just have to take my chances and improvise," Jack said. "I'm going over to the General no matter what anybody says."

"What I can't understand is why you are so agitated about these infections. I've read that infectious diseases are generally on the rise."

"That's true," Jack said. "But that's not due to deliberate spread. That's from the injudicious use of antibiotics, urbanization, and the invasion of primeval habitats."

"Give me a break," Terese commented. "I'm concerned about you getting yourself hurt or worse, and you're giving me a lecture."

Jack shrugged. "I'm going to the General," he said.

"Fine, go!" Terese said. She stood up. "You're being that ridiculous hero I was afraid you'd be." Then she softened. "Do what you must, but if you need me, call me."

"I will," Jack said. He watched her hurry out of the restaurant, thinking that she was a bewildering blend of ambition and solicitude. It was no wonder he was confused by her: one minute attracted, the next minute mildly put off.

Jack tossed down the remains of his coffee and stood up. After leaving an appropriate tip, he, too, hurried out of the café.

CHAPTER TWENTY-FOUR

Monday, 2:30 P.M., March 25, 1996

Jack walked rapidly toward the General. After the conversation with Terese he needed some fresh air. She had a way of agitating him. Not only was she emotionally confusing, but she was also right about the Black Kings. As much as Jack didn't want to think about it, he was taking a chance defying their threat. The questions were: Whom had he irritated enough to send a gang to threaten him, and did the threat confirm his suspicions? Unfortunately there was no way to know. As he'd told Terese, he would have to be careful. The problem with that flippant answer, of course, was that he had no idea with whom he had to be careful. He assumed it would have to be Kelley, Zimmerman, Cheveau, or Abelard because those were the people he'd irritated. The trick was to avoid them all.

As Jack rounded the final corner, it was immediately apparent that things were abnormal at the hospital. Several wooden police sawhorses stood on the sidewalk, and two New York City uniformed policemen lounged on either side of the main door. Jack stopped to watch them for a moment, since they seemed to be spending more time talking with each other than anything else.

Feeling confused about their role, Jack went up to them and asked.

"We were supposed to discourage people from going into the hospital," one officer said. "There was some kind of epidemic in there, but they think it's under control."

"We're really here more for crowd control," the other officer admitted. "They were expecting trouble earlier when they were toying with the idea of quarantining the facility, but things have settled down."

"For that we can all be thankful," Jack said. He started forward, but one of the officers restrained him.

"You sure you want to go in?" he asked.

"Afraid so," Jack said.

The officer shrugged and let Jack pass.

The minute Jack entered through the door he was confronted by a uniformed hospital security officer wearing a surgical mask.

"I'm sorry," the officer said. "No visitors today."

Jack pulled out his medical examiner's badge.

"Sorry, Doctor," the officer said. He stepped aside.

Although calm outside, the inside of the hospital was still in a minor furor. The lobby was filled with people. What gave the scene a surrealistic aura was that everyone was wearing a mask.

With the sudden cessation of new meningococcal cases some twelve hours earlier, Jack was reasonably confident that a mask was superfluous. Yet he wanted one, not so much for protection as for disguise. He asked the security officer if they were available. He was directed to the unmanned information desk, where he found several boxes. Jack took one out and put it on.

Next he located the doctors' coatroom. He entered when one of the staff doctors was exiting. Inside he took off his bomber jacket and searched for an appropriately sized long white coat. When he found one, he put it on, then returned to the lobby.

Jack's destination was central supply. He felt that if he was to learn anything on this visit, it would be there. He got off the elevator on the third floor and was impressed with how much less patient traffic there was than there had been on his visit the previous Thursday. A glance through the glass portal on the OR suite doors told him why. Apparently the OR's had been temporarily shut down. With some knowledge of hospital cash flow, Jack surmised that AmeriCare must be having a financial stroke.

Jack pushed through the swinging doors into central supply. Even there the level of activity was a quarter of what it had been on his first visit. He only saw two women near the end of one of the long aisles between the floor-to-ceiling shelving. Like everyone else he'd seen so far, they were wearing masks. Obviously the hospital was taking this last outbreak particularly seriously.

Avoiding the aisle with the women, Jack set off for Gladys Zarelli's office. She'd been receptive on his first visit, and she was the supervisor. Jack couldn't think of a better person with whom to talk.

As he walked through the department, Jack eyed the myriad hospital supplies and equipment stacked on the shelves. Seeing such a profusion of items made him wonder if there had been anything unique sent from central supply to the index cases. It was an interesting thought, he reasoned, but he couldn't imagine how it would matter. There was still the question of how the women in central supply could have come in contact with the patient and the infecting bacteria. As he'd been told, the employees rarely, if ever, even saw a patient.

Jack found Gladys in her office. She was on the phone, but when she saw him standing at her door, she motioned exuberantly for him to come in. Jack sat down on a straight-back chair opposite her narrow desk. With the size of the office, he could not help overhearing both sides of Gladys's conversation. As he might have imagined, she was busy recruiting.

"Sorry to keep you waiting," she said when she finished her call. Despite her problems she was as affable as the last time Jack had talked with her. "But I'm in desperate need of more help."

Jack reintroduced himself, but Gladys said she'd recognized him despite the mask. So much for the disguise, Jack thought glumly.

"I'm sorry about what's happened," Jack said. "It must be difficult for you for all sorts of reasons."

"It's been terrible," she admitted. "Just terrible. Who would have guessed? Four wonderful people!"

"It's shocking," Jack said. "Especially since it's so unusual. As you said last time I was here, no one in this department had ever caught anything serious before."

Gladys raised her hands. "What can you do?" she said. "It's in God's hands."

"It might be in God's hands," Jack said. "But usually there is some way to explain this kind of contagion. Have you given it any thought at all?"

Gladys nodded vigorously. "I've thought about it until I was blue in the face," she said. "I don't have a clue. Even if I didn't want to think about it, I've had to because everybody has been asking me the same question."

"Really," Jack said with a twinge of disappointment. He'd had the idea he was exploring virginal territory.

"Dr. Zimmerman was in here right after you on Thursday," Gladys said. "She came with this cute little man who kept sticking his chin out as if his collar button were too tight."

"That sounds like Dr. Clint Abelard," Jack said, realizing he truly was strolling a beaten path.

"That was his name," Gladys said. "He sure could ask a lot of questions. And they've been back each time someone else has gotten sick. That's why we're all wearing our masks. They even had Mr. Eversharp down here from engineering, thinking there might have been something messed up with our air-conditioning system, but apparently that's fine."

"So they haven't come up with any explanation?" Jack said.

"Nope," Gladys said. "Unless they haven't told me. But I doubt that. It's been like Grand Central in here. Used to be no one came. Some of these doctors, though, they're a little strange."

"How so?" Jack asked.

"Just weird," Gladys said. "Like the doctor from the lab. He's come down here plenty of times lately."

"Is that Dr. Cheveau?" Jack asked.

"I think so," Gladys said.

"In what way was he strange?" Jack asked.

"Just unfriendly," Gladys said. She lowered her voice as if telling a secret. "I asked him if I could help him a couple of times, and he bites my head off. He says he just wants to be left alone. But, you know, this is my department. I'm responsible for all this inventory. I don't like people wandering around, even doctors. I had to tell him."

"Who else has been around?" Jack asked.

"A bunch of the bigwigs," Gladys said. "Even Mr. Kelley. Usually I'd only see him at the Christmas party. Last couple of days he's been down here three or four times, always with a bunch of people. Once with that little doctor."

"Dr. Abelard?" Jack asked.

"That's the one," Gladys said. "I can never remember his name."

"I hate to ask you the same questions as the others," Jack said. "But did the women who died perform similar tasks? I mean, did they share some specific job?"

"Like I told you last time," Gladys said, "we all pitch in."

"None of them went up to the patients' rooms who died of the same illnesses?" Jack asked.

"No, nothing like that," Gladys said. "That was the first thing that Dr. Zimmerman checked."

"Last time I was here you printed out a big list of all the stuff that you'd sent up to the seventh floor," Jack said. "Could you make the same list for an individual patient?"

"That would be more difficult," Gladys said. "The order usually comes from the floor, and then it is the floor that enters it into the patient's data."

"Is there any way you could come up with such a list?" Jack asked.

"I suppose," Gladys said. "When we do inventory there is a way of double-checking through billing. I could tell billing I'm doing that kind of check even though we're not officially doing inventory."

"I'd appreciate it," Jack said. He took out one of his cards. "You could either call me or just send it over."

Gladys took the card and examined it. "I'll do anything that might help," she said.

"One other thing," Jack said. "I've had my own run-in with Dr. Cheveau and even a few of the other people around here. I'd appreciate it if this was just between you and me."

"Isn't he weird!" Gladys said. "Sure, I won't tell anybody."

Easing out from in front of Gladys's desk, Jack bid good-bye to the robust woman and exited central supply. He wasn't in the best of moods. After beginning with high expectations, the only thing of note he'd been told was something he already knew: Martin Cheveau was irascible.

Jack pushed the down button at the bank of elevators while he pondered his next move. He had two choices: either he could just leave and minimize his risk, or he could make a careful visit to the lab. Ultimately, he decided in favor of the lab. Chet's comment about the lack of availability of pathological bacteria carried the day, since it had raised a question Jack needed to answer.

When the elevator doors opened, Jack started to board, but then he hesitated. Standing directly in front of the crowded car was Charles Kelley. Jack recognized him instantly despite his mask.

Jack's first impulse was to back away and let the elevator go. But such a move would have only drawn attention. Instead he put his head down, proceeded onto the elevator, and immediately turned to face the closing door. The administrator was standing right behind him. Jack half expected a tap on the shoulder.

Luckily, Kelley had not recognized him. The administrator was deep in conversation with a colleague about

how much it was costing the hospital to transport the
ER patients by ambulance and the clinic patients by bus
to their nearest facility. Kelley's agitation was palpable.
He said their self-imposed semi-quarantine would have
to end.

Kelley's companion assured him that everything was
being done that could be done, since the city and state
regulatory people were all there making an evaluation.

When the doors opened on the second floor, Jack
exited with great relief, especially when Kelly didn't get
off as well. With such a close call, Jack wondered if he
was doing the right thing, but after a moment of indecision he elected to continue with a quick visit to the
lab. After all, he was right there.

In contrast to the rest of the hospital, the lab was in full
swing. The outer lobby area was thronged with hospital
personnel, all of whom were masked.

Jack was confused as to why so many hospital
employees were there but thankful because it was easy
to blend in with the crowd. With his mask and white lab
coat he fit in perfectly. Since Martin's office was just off
this main reception, Jack had worried that he'd be apt
to run into him. Now he felt the chances were next to
nil.

At the far end of the room was a series of cubicles
used by the technicians to draw blood or obtain other
samples from clinic patients. Near them the crowd con-
centrated. As Jack wormed his way past this area it
dawned on him what was going on. The entire hospital
staff was having throat cultures taken.

Jack was impressed. It was an appropriate response to
the current outbreak. Since most meningococcal epidemics resulted from a carrier state, there was always a

chance the carrier was a hospital employee. It had happened in the past.

A glance into the last cubicle made Jack do a double take. Despite a mask and even a surgical cap, Jack recognized Martin. He literally had his sleeves rolled up as he worked as a technician, swabbing throat after throat. Next to him on a tray the used swabs were piling up in an impressive pyramid. Obviously, everyone in the lab was pitching in.

Feeling even more confident, Jack slipped through the doors into the lab itself. No one paid him any attention. In sharp contrast to the comparative pandemonium in reception, the lab's interior was a study in automated solitude. The only sounds were a muted chorus of mechanical clicks and low-pitched beeps. There were no technicians in sight.

Jack made a beeline for the microbiology section. His hope was to run across either the head tech, Richard, or the vivacious Beth Holderness. But when he arrived he found no one. The micro area appeared as deserted as the rest of the lab.

Jack approached the spot where Beth had been working on his last visit. There he found something encouraging. A Bunsen burner was aflame. Next to it was a tray of throat culture swabs and a large stack of fresh agar plates. On the floor stood a plastic trash barrel brimming with discarded culture tubes.

Sensing that Beth must be in the immediate area, Jack began to explore. The microbiology section was a room about thirty feet square divided by two rows of countertop. Jack walked down the center aisle. Along the back wall were several biosafety cabinets. Jack rounded the lab bench to his right and glanced into a small office. It had a desk and a file cabinet. On a bulletin board he could see some photos. Without going into the room, Jack recognized Richard, the head tech, in several of them.

Moving on, Jack came abreast of several polished aluminum insulated doors that looked like walk-in refrigerators. Glancing over to the opposite side of the room, he saw a regular door that he thought could lead into a storeroom. As he was about to head in that direction one of the insulated doors opened with a loud click that made him jump.

Beth Holderness emerged along with a waft of warm, moist air and nearly collided with Jack. "You scared me to death," she said, pressing a hand to her chest.

"I'm not sure who scared whom more," Jack said. He then reintroduced himself.

"Don't worry, I remember you," Beth said. "You caused quite a stir, and I don't think you should be here."

"Oh?" Jack questioned innocently.

"Dr. Cheveau is really mad at you," Beth said.

"Is he now?" Jack said. "I've noticed he's been rather grumpy."

"He can be cranky," Beth admitted. "But Richard said something about your accusing him of spreading the bacteria that we've been experiencing here at the General."

"Actually, I didn't accuse your boss of anything," Jack said. "It was only an implication I made after he irritated me. I'd come over here just to have a conversation with him. I really wanted his opinion about the plausibility of all these relatively rare illnesses having appeared so close together and at this time of year. But for reasons unknown to me, he was in as inhospitable a mood as he'd been on my previous visit."

"Well, I must admit I was surprised how he treated you the day we met," Beth said. "Same with Mr. Kelley and Dr. Zimmerman. I just thought you were trying to help."

Jack had to restrain himself from giving this lively young woman a hug. It seemed as if she were the only person on the planet who appreciated what he was doing.

"I was so sorry about your co-worker, Nancy Wiggens," Jack said. "I imagine it's been difficult for you all."

Beth's cheerful face clouded over to the point just shy of tears.

"Maybe I shouldn't have said anything," Jack said when he noticed her reaction.

"It's all right," Beth managed. "But it was a terrible shock. We all worry about such a thing, but hope it will never happen. She was such a warm person, although she could be a bit reckless."

"How so?" Jack asked.

"She just wasn't as careful as she should have been," Beth said. "She took chances, like not using one of the hoods when it was indicated or not wearing her goggles when she was supposed to."

Jack could understand that attitude.

"She didn't even take the antibiotic Dr. Zimmerman prescribed for her after the plague case," Beth said.

"How unfortunate," Jack said. "That might have protected her against the Rocky Mountain spotted fever."

"I know," Beth said. "I wish that I had tried harder to convince her. I mean, I took it, and I don't think I was exposed."

"Did she happen to say she did anything different when she got samples from Lagenthorpe?" Jack asked.

"No, she didn't," Beth said. "That's why we feel she was exposed down here in the lab when she processed the samples. Rickettsia are notoriously dangerous in the lab."

Jack was about to respond when he noticed that Beth had begun to fidget and look over his shoulder. Jack glanced in the direction she was looking, but there was no one there.

"I really should be getting back to work," Beth said. "And I shouldn't be talking with you. Dr. Cheveau told us specifically."

"Don't you find that strange?" Jack said. "After all, I am a medical examiner in this city. Legally I have a right to investigate the deaths of the patients assigned to us."

"I guess I do," Beth admitted. "But what can I say? I just work here." She stepped around Jack and went back to her workstation.

Jack followed her. "I don't mean to be a pest," he said. "But my intuition tells me something weird is going on here; that's why I keep coming back. A number of people have been acting defensive, including your boss. Now there could be an explanation. AmeriCare and this hospital are a business, and these outbreaks have been tremendously disruptive economically. That's reason enough for people to be acting strangely. But from my point of view it's more than that."

"So what do you want from me?" Beth asked. She'd taken her seat and gone back to transferring the throat cultures to the agar plates.

"I'd like to ask you to look around," Jack said. "If pathological bacteria are being deliberately spread they have to come from somewhere, and the microbiology lab would be a good place to start looking. I mean, the equipment is here to store and handle the stuff. It's not as if plague bacteria is something you'd find anywhere."

"It wouldn't be so strange to find it on occasion in any standard lab," Beth said.

"Really?" Jack questioned. He'd assumed that outside of the CDC and maybe a few academic centers, plague bacteria would be a rarity.

"Intermittently labs have to get cultures of all different bacteria to test the efficacy of their reagents," Beth said as she continued to work. "Antibodies, which are often the main ingredients in many modern reagents, can deteriorate, and if they do the tests would give false negatives."

"Oh, of course," Jack said. He felt stupid. He should have remembered all this. All laboratory tests had to be constantly checked.

"Where do you get something like plague bacteria?"

"From National Biologicals in Virginia," Beth said.

"What's the process for getting it?" Jack asked.

"Just call up and order it," Beth said.

"Who can do that?" Jack asked.

"Anybody," Beth said.

"You're joking," Jack said. Somehow he'd thought the security at a minimum would be comparable to that involved in getting a controlled drug like morphine.

"I'm not joking," Beth said. "I've done it many times."

"You don't need some special permit?" Jack asked.

"I have to get the signature of the director of the lab on the purchase order," Beth said. "But that's just to guarantee that the hospital will pay for it."

"So let me get this straight," Jack said. "Anyone can call these people up and have plague sent to them?"

"As long as their credit is okay," Beth said.

"How do the cultures come?" Jack said.

"Usually by mail," Beth said. "But if you pay extra and need it faster you can get overnight service."

Jack was appalled, but he tried to hide his reaction. He was embarrassed at his own naïveté. "Do you have this organization's phone number?" he asked.

Beth pulled open a file drawer to her immediate right, leafed through some files, and pulled out a folder. Opening it up, she took out a sheet and indicated the letterhead.

Jack wrote the number down. Then he pointed to the phone. "Do you mind?" he asked.

Beth pushed the phone in his direction but glanced up at the clock as she did so.

"I'll just be a second," Jack said. He still couldn't believe what he'd just been told.

Jack dialed the number. The phone was answered and a recording gave him the name of the company and asked him to make a selection. Jack pressed two for sales. Presently a charmingly friendly voice came on the line and asked if she could be of assistance.

"Yes," Jack said. "This is Dr. Billy Rubin and I'd like to place an order."

"Do you have an account with National Biologicals?" the woman asked.

"Not yet," Jack said. "In fact, for this order I'd just like to use my American Express card."

"I'm sorry, but we only accept Visa or MasterCard," the woman said.

"No problem," Jack said. "Visa will be fine."

"Okay," the woman said cheerfully. "Could I have your first order?"

"How about some meningococcus," Jack said.

The woman laughed. "You'll have to be more specific," she said. "I need the serologic group, the serotype, and the subtype. We have hundreds of meningococcus subspecies."

"Uh-oh!" Jack said, pretending to have been suddenly paged. "An emergency has just come up! I'm afraid I'll have to call back."

"No problem," the woman said. "Call anytime. As you know, we're here twenty-four hours a day to serve your culture needs."

Jack hung up the phone. He was stunned.

"I have the feeling you didn't believe me," Beth said.

"I didn't," Jack admitted. "I didn't realize the availability of these pathogens. But I'd still like you to look around here and see if these offending bugs might somehow be stashed here now. Could you do that?"

"I suppose," Beth said without her usual enthusiasm.

"But I want you to be discreet," Jack said. "And careful. I want this just between you and me."

Jack took out one of his cards and wrote his home number on the back. He handed it to her. "You can call me anytime, day or night, if you find anything or if you get into any trouble because of me. Okay?"

Beth took the card, examined it briefly, and then stuck it into her lab coat pocket. "Okay," she said.

"Would you mind if I asked for your number?" Jack said. "I might have some more questions myself. Obviously microbiology isn't my forte."

Beth thought for a moment, then relented. She got

out a piece of paper and wrote her phone number down. She handed it to Jack, who put it into his wallet.

"I think you'd better go now," she said.

"I'm on my way," Jack said. "Thanks for your help."

"You're welcome," Beth said. She was her old self again.

Preoccupied, Jack walked out of the microbiology section and headed across the main portion of the lab. He still couldn't believe how easy it was to order pathological cultures.

About twenty feet from the double swinging doors that connected the lab to the reception area, Jack stopped dead in his tracks. Backing through the doors was a figure that looked alarmingly like Martin. The individual was carrying a tray loaded with prepared throat swabs ready for plating.

Jack felt like a criminal caught in the act. For a fraction of a second he contemplated fleeing or trying to hide. But there was no time. Besides, irritation at the absurdity of his fear of being recognized inspired him to stand his ground.

Martin held the door open for a second figure Jack recognized as Richard. He, too, was carrying a tray of throat swabs. It was Richard who saw Jack first.

Martin was a quick second. He recognized Jack immediately, despite the mask.

"Hi, folks," Jack said.

"You . . .!" Martin cried.

"It is I," Jack said cheerfully. He grabbed the end of his face mask with his thumb and forefinger and pulled it away from his face to give Martin an unobstructed look.

"You've been warned about sneaking around in here," Martin snapped. "You're trespassing."

"Not so," Jack said. He produced his medical examiner badge and pointed it toward Martin's face. "Just making an official site visit. There've been a few more regrettable infectious deaths over here at the General. At least this time you were able to make the diagnosis on your own."

"We'll see whether this is a legitimate site visit," Martin said. He heaved the tray of throat swabs onto the countertop and snatched up the nearest phone. He told the operator to put him through to Charles Kelley.

"Couldn't we just discuss this like grown-ups?" Jack asked.

Martin ignored the question as he waited for Kelley.

"Out of curiosity, maybe you could just tell me why you were so accommodating on my first visit and so nasty on my next," Jack said.

"In the interim Mr. Kelley informed me what your attitude had been on that first day," Martin said. "And he told me he had learned that you were here without authorization."

Jack was about to respond when it became clear that Kelley had come on the line. Martin informed the administrator that he'd again found Dr. Stapleton lurking in the lab.

While Martin listened to an apparent monologue from Kelley, Jack moved over and leaned casually against the nearest countertop. Richard, on the other hand, stood rooted in place, still supporting his tray of throat swabs.

Martin punctuated Kelley's apparent tirade with a few strategically placed yeses and a final "Yes sir!" at the end of the conversation. As he hung up the phone he treated Jack to a supercilious smile.

"Mr. Kelley told me to inform you," Martin said haughtily, "that he will be personally calling the mayor's office, the Commissioner of Health, and your chief. He'll be lodging a formal complaint concerning your harassment of this hospital while we've been making every effort to deal with a state of emergency. He also told me to inform you that our security will be up here in a few moments to escort you off the premises."

"That's terribly considerate of him," Jack said. "But I really don't need to be shown the way out. In fact, I was on my way when we happened to bump into each other. Good day, gentlemen."

CHAPTER TWENTY-FIVE

"So there you have it," Terese said as she looked out on the expanded team of creatives for the National Health account. In the present emergency she and Colleen had pulled key people away from other projects. Right now they needed all the man- and womanpower they could muster to concentrate on the new campaign.

"Any questions?" Terese asked. The entire group was squeezed into Colleen's office. With no room to sit they were wedged in like sardines, cheek by jowl. Terese had outlined the "no wait" idea in an expanded form that she and Colleen had devised based on Jack's initial suggestion.

"We only have two days for this?" Alice questioned.

"I'm afraid so," Terese said. "I might be able to squeeze out another day, but we can't count on it. We've got to go for broke."

There was a murmur of incredulity.

"I know I'm asking a lot," Terese said. "But the fact of the matter is, as I've told you, we were sabotaged by the accounts department. We've even got confirmation that they are expecting to present a 'talking heads' spot with one of the *ER* stars. They are counting on us to self-destruct with the old idea."

"Actually I think the 'no wait' concept is better than

the 'cleanliness' concept," Alice said. "The 'cleanliness' idea was getting too technical with that asepsis malarkey. People are going to understand 'no waiting' much better."

"There's also a lot more opportunity for humor," another voice commented.

"I like it too," someone else said. "I hate waiting for the gynecologist. By the time I get in there I'm as tense as a banjo wire."

A wave of tension-relieving laughter rippled through the group.

"That's the spirit," Terese said. "Let's get to work. Let's show them what we can do when our backs are against the wall."

People started to leave, eager to get to their drawing boards.

"Hold up!" Terese shouted over the buzz of voices that had erupted. "One other thing. This has to stay quiet. Don't even tell other creatives unless absolutely necessary. I don't want accounts to have any inkling of what's going on. Okay?"

A murmur of agreement arose.

"All right!" Terese yelled. "Get to it!"

The room emptied as if there had been a fire. Terese flopped back into Colleen's chair, exhausted from the emotional effort of the day. Typical of her life in advertising, she'd started out that morning on a high, then sunk to a new low, and was now somewhere in between.

"They're enthusiastic," Colleen said. "You made a great presentation. I kind of wish someone from National Health were here."

"At least it's a good idea for a campaign," Terese

said. "The question is whether they can put it together enough for a real presentation."

"They'll certainly give it their best shot," Colleen said. "You really motivated them."

"God, I hope so," Terese said. "I can't let Barker have a free field with his stupid 'talking heads' junk. That's like taking advertising back to pre-Bernbach days. It would be an embarrassment for the agency if the client liked it, and we had to actually do it."

"God forbid," Colleen said.

"We'll be out of a job if that happens," Terese said.

"Let's not get too pessimistic," Colleen warned.

"Ah, what a day," Terese complained. "On top of everything else I've got to worry about Jack."

"How so?" Colleen asked.

"When I met with him and he gave me the 'no wait' idea he told me he was going back to the General."

"Uh-oh," Colleen said. "Isn't that where those gang members warned him against going?"

"Exactly," Terese said. "Talk about a Taurus, he's the epitome. He's so damn bullheaded and reckless. He doesn't have to go over there. They have people at the medical examiner's office whose job it is to go out to hospitals. It must be some male thing, like he has to be a hero. I don't understand it."

"Are you starting to get attached to him?" Colleen asked gingerly, aware it was a touchy subject with Terese. Colleen knew enough about her boss to know that she eschewed romantic entanglements, though she had no idea why.

Terese only sighed. "I'm attracted to him and put off by him at the same time," she said. "He got me to open up a little, and apparently I coaxed him out a little too.

I think both of us felt good talking to someone who seemed to care."

"That sounds encouraging," Colleen said.

Terese shrugged, then smiled. "We're both carrying around a lot of emotional baggage," she said. "But enough about me. How about you and Chet?"

"It's going great," Colleen said. "I could really fall for that guy."

Jack felt as if he were sitting through the same movie for a third time. Once again he was literally on Bingham's carpet enduring a protracted tirade about how his chief had been called by every major civil servant in the city to complain bitterly about Jack Stapleton.

"So what do you have to say for yourself?" Bingham demanded, finally running out of steam with his ranting. He was literally out of breath.

"I don't know what to say," Jack admitted. "But in my defense, I haven't gone over there with the intention of irritating people. I was just looking for information. There's a lot about this series of outbreaks that I don't understand."

"You're a goddamn paradox," Bingham remarked as he visibly calmed down. "At the same time you've been such a pain in the butt you've made some commendable diagnoses. I was impressed when Calvin told me about the tularemia and the Rocky Mountain spotted fever. It's like you're two different people. What am I to do?"

"Fire the irritating one and keep the other?" Jack suggested.

Bingham grunted a reluctant chuckle, but any sign of amusement quickly faded. "The main problem from my perspective," he grumbled, "is that you are so god-damned contumacious. You've specifically disobeyed my orders to stay away from the General, not once but twice."

"I'm guilty," Jack said, raising his hands as if to surrender.

"Is all this motivated by that personal vendetta you have against AmeriCare?" Bingham demanded.

"No," Jack said. "That was a minor factor to begin with, but my interest in the matter has gone way beyond that. I told you last time that I thought something strange was going on. I feel even more strongly now, and the people over there are continuing to act defensive."

"Defensive?" Bingham questioned querulously. "I was told that you accused the General's lab director of spreading these illnesses."

"That story has been blown way out of proportion," Jack said. He then explained to Bingham that he'd merely implied as much by reminding the lab director that he, the director, was disgruntled about the budget AmeriCare was giving him.

"The man was acting like an ass," Jack added. "I was trying to ask his opinion about the possible intentional spread of these illnesses, but he never gave me a chance, and I got mad at him. I suppose I shouldn't have said what I did, but sometimes I can't help myself."

"So you're convinced about this idea yourself?" Bingham asked.

"I don't know if I'm convinced," Jack admitted. "But it is hard to ascribe them all to coincidence. On top of that is the way people at the General have been acting, from the administrator on down." Jack thought about telling Bingham about his being beaten up and threatened, but he decided against it. He feared it might get him grounded altogether.

"After Commissioner Markham called me," Bingham said, "I asked her to have the chief epidemiologist, Dr. Abelard, get in touch with me. When he did, I asked him what he thought of this intentional spread idea. You want to know what he said?"

"I can't wait," Jack said.

"He said except for the plague case, which he still cannot explain but is working on with the CDC, he feels the others all have very reasonable explanations. The Hard woman had been in contact with wild rabbits, and Mr. Lagenthorpe had been out in the desert in Texas. And as far as meningococcus is concerned, it's the season for that."

"I don't think the time sequences are correct," Jack said. "Nor are the clinical courses consistent with—"

"Hold on," Bingham interrupted. "Let me remind you that Dr. Abelard is an epidemiologist. He's got a Ph.D. as well as an M.D. His whole job is to figure out the where and the why of disease."

"I don't doubt his credentials," Jack said. "Just his conclusions. He didn't impress me from the start."

"You certainly are opinionated," Bingham said.

"I might have ruffled feathers on past visits to the General," Jack admitted, "but this time all I did was talk to the supervisor of central supply and one of the microbiology techs."

"From the calls I got you were deliberately hampering their efforts to deal with the meningococcal outbreak," Bingham said.

"God is my witness," Jack said, holding up his hand.

"All I did was talk to Ms. Zarelli and Ms. Holderness, who happen to be two pleasant, cooperative people."

"You do have a way of rubbing people the wrong way," Bingham said. "I suppose you know that."

"Usually, I only have that effect on those I intend to provoke," Jack said.

"I get the feeling I'm one of those people," Bingham snapped.

"Quite the contrary," Jack said. "Irritating you is entirely unintentional."

"I wouldn't have known," Bingham said.

"In speaking with Ms. Holderness, the lab tech, I did uncover an interesting fact," Jack said. "I learned that just about anyone with reasonable credit can call up and order pathological bacteria. The company doesn't do any background check."

"You don't need a license or a permit?" Bingham asked.

"Apparently not," Jack said.

"I suppose I'd never thought about it," Bingham said.

"Nor had I," Jack said. "Needless to say, thought-provoking."

"Indeed," Bingham said. He appeared to ponder this for a moment as his rheumy eyes glazed over. But then they quickly cleared.

"Seems to me you've managed to get this conversation off track," he said, regaining his gruff posture. "The issue here is what to do with you."

"You could always send me on vacation to the Caribbean," Jack suggested. "It's nice down there this time of year."

"Enough of your impertinent humor," Bingham snapped. "I'm trying to be serious with you."

"I'll try to control myself," Jack said. "My problem is that during the last five years of my life cynicism has led to reflex sarcasm."

"I'm not going to fire you," Bingham announced. "But I've got to warn you again, you've come very close. In fact when I hung up the phone from the mayor's office, I was going to let you go. I've changed my mind for now. But there is one thing that we have to be clear on: You are to stay away from the General. Do we have an understanding?"

"I think it's finally getting through," Jack said.

"If you need more information, send the PAs," Bingham said. "For chrissake that's what they're here for."

"I'll try to remember that," Jack said.

"All right, get out of here," Bingham said with a sweep of his hand.

With relief Jack stood up and left Bingham's office. He went straight up to his own. When he arrived he found Chet talking with George Fontworth. Jack squeezed by the two of them and draped his coat over the back of his chair.

"Well?" Chet asked.

"Well what?" Jack asked back.

"The daily question," Chet said. "Are you still employed here?"

"Very funny," Jack said. He was perplexed by the stack of four large manila envelopes at the center of his desk. He picked one up. It was about two inches thick. There were no markings on the exterior. Opening the latch, he slid out the contents. It was a copy of Susanne Hard's hospital chart.

"You've seen Bingham?" Chet asked.

"I just came from there," Jack said. "He was sweet. He wanted to commend me on my diagnoses of tularemia and Rocky Mountain spotted fever."

"Bull!" Chet exclaimed.

"Honest," Jack said with a chuckle. "Of course, he also bawled me out for going over to the General." While Jack was talking, he took the contents out of all the manila envelopes. He now had copies of the hospital charts of the index cases of each outbreak.

"Was your visit worth it?" Chet asked.

"What do you mean, 'worth it'?" Jack asked.

"Did you learn enough to justify stirring up the pot once more?" Chet said. "We heard you got everyone over there angry again."

"Not a lot of secrets around here," Jack commented. "But I did learn something that I didn't know." Jack explained to Chet and George about the ease of ordering pathological bacteria.

"I knew that," George said. "I worked in a micro lab during summers while I was in college. I remember the supervisor ordering a cholera culture. When it came in I picked it up and held it. It gave me a thrill."

Jack glanced at George. "A thrill?" he questioned. "You're weirder than I thought."

"Seriously," George said. "I know other people who had the same reaction. Comprehending how much pain, suffering, and death the little buggers had caused and could cause was both scary and stimulating at the same time, and holding it in my hand just blew me away."

"I guess my idea of a thrill and yours are a bit

different," Jack said. He went back to the charts and organized them chronologically so that Nodelman was on top.

"I hope the mere availability of pathological bacteria doesn't encourage your paranoid thinking," Chet said. "I mean, that's hardly proof of your theory."

"Umm hmm," Jack murmured. He was already beginning to go over the charts. He planned to read through them rapidly to see if anything jumped out at him. Then he would go back over them in detail. What he was looking for was any way the cases could have been related that would suggest they were not random occurrences.

Chet and George went back to their conversation when it was apparent Jack was preoccupied. Fifteen minutes later George got up and left. As soon as he did Chet went to the door and closed it.

"Colleen called me a little while ago," he said.

"I'm happy for you," Jack said, still trying to concentrate on the charts.

"She told me what had happened over there at the agency," Chet said. "I think it stinks. I can't imagine one part of the same company undermining another. It doesn't make sense."

Jack looked up from his reading. "It's the business mentality," he said. "Lust for power is the major motivator."

Chet sat down. "Colleen also told me that you gave Terese a terrific idea for a new campaign."

"Don't remind me," Jack said. He redirected his attention to the charts. "I really don't want to be a part of it. I don't know why she asked me. She knows how I feel about medical advertising."

"Colleen also said that you and Terese are hitting it off," Chet said.

"Really now?" Jack said.

"She said that you two had gotten each other to open up. I think that is terrific for both of you."

"Did she give any specifics?" Jack asked.

"I didn't get the sense she had any specifics," Chet said.

"Thank God," Jack said without looking up.

When Jack answered Chet's next few questions with mere grunts, it dawned on Chet that Jack was again engrossed in his reading. Chet gave up trying to have a conversation and turned his attention to his own work.

By five-thirty Chet was ready to call it a day. He got up and stretched noisily, hoping that Jack would respond. Jack didn't. In fact, Jack had not moved for the last hour or so except to turn pages and jot down more notes.

Chet got his coat from the top drawer of his file cabinet and cleared his throat several times. Still Jack did not respond. Finally Chet resorted to speech.

"Hey, old sport," Chet called out. "How long are you going to work on that stuff?"

"Until I'm done," Jack said without looking up.

"I'm meeting Colleen for a quick bite," Chet said. "We're meeting at six. Are you interested? Maybe Terese could join us. Apparently they are planning to work most of the night."

"I'm sticking here," Jack said. "Enjoy yourselves. Say hello for me."

Chet shrugged, pulled on his coat, and left.

Jack had been through the charts twice. So far the only genuine similarity among the four cases was the fact

that their infectious disease symptoms had started after
they had been admitted for other complaints. But as
Laurie had pointed out, by definition, only Nodelman
was a nosocomial case. In the other three situations
the symptoms had come on within forty-eight hours of
admission.

The only other possible similarity was the one that
Jack had already considered: namely that all four patients
were people who'd been hospitalized frequently and
hence were economically undesirable in a capitated
system. But other than that, Jack found nothing.

The ages ranged from twenty-eight to sixty-three.
Two had been on the medical ward, one in OB-GYN,
and one in orthopedics. There were no medications
common to them all. Two were on "keep open" IVs.
Socially they ranged from lower- to upper-middle class,
and there was no indication that any of the four knew
any of the others. There was one female and three males.
Even their blood types differed.

Jack tossed his pen onto his desk and leaned back in
his chair to stare at the ceiling. He didn't know what he
expected from the charts, but so far he hadn't learned
anything.

"Knock, knock," a voice called.

Jack turned to see Laurie standing in the doorway.

"I see you made it back from your foray to the General," she said.

"I don't think I was in any danger until I got back
here," Jack said.

"I know what you mean," Laurie said. "Rumor had
it that Bingham was fit to be tied."

"He wasn't happy, but we managed to work it out,"
Jack said.

"Are you worried about the threat from the people who beat you up?" Laurie asked.

"I suppose," Jack said. "I haven't thought too much about it. I'm sure I'll feel differently when I get to my apartment."

"You're welcome to come over to mine," Laurie said. "I have a sad couch in my living room that pulls out into a decent bed."

"You're kind to offer," Jack said. "But I have to go home sometime. I'll be careful."

"Did you learn anything to explain the central supply connection?" Laurie asked.

"I wish," Jack said. "Not only didn't I learn anything, but I found out that a number of people, including the city epidemiologist and the hospital infection control officer, have been in there beating the bushes for clues. I had the mistaken notion it was a novel idea."

"Are you still thinking of the conspiracy slant?" Laurie asked.

"In some form or fashion," Jack admitted. "Unfortunately, it seems to be a lonely stance."

Laurie wished him good luck. He thanked her, and she left. A minute later she was back.

"I'm planning on getting a bite on the way home," Laurie said. "Are you interested?"

"Thanks, but I've started on these charts, and I want to keep at it while the material is fresh in my mind."

"I understand. Good night."

"Good night, Laurie," Jack said.

No sooner had Jack opened Nodelman's chart for the third time than the phone rang. It was Terese.

"Colleen is about to leave to meet up with Chet,"

Terese said. "Can I talk you into coming out for a quick dinner? We could all eat together."

Jack was amazed. For five years he'd been avoiding social attachments of any kind. Now suddenly two intelligent, attractive women were both asking him to dine with them on the same night.

"I appreciate the offer," Jack said. He then told Terese the same thing he'd told Laurie about the charts he was working on.

"I keep hoping you'll give up on that crusade," Terese said. "It hardly seems worth the risks, since you've already been beaten up and threatened with the loss of your job."

"If I can prove someone is behind this affair it will certainly be worth the risks," Jack said. "My fear is that there might be a real epidemic."

"Chet seems to think you're acting foolishly," Terese persisted.

"He's entitled to his opinion," Jack said.

"Please be careful when you go home," Terese intoned.

"I will," Jack said. He was getting weary of everyone's solicitude. The danger of going home that evening was something he'd considered as early as that morning.

"We'll be working most of the night," she added. "If you need to call, call me at work."

"Okay," Jack said. "Good luck."

"Good luck to you," Terese said. "And thanks for this 'no waiting' idea. Everyone loves it so far. I'm very grateful. 'Bye!"

Jack went back to Nodelman's chart as soon as he put the phone down. He was attempting to get through the reams of nurses' notes. But after five minutes of reading the same paragraph over and over, he acknowledged he wasn't concentrating. His mind kept mulling over the irony of both Laurie and Terese asking him to dine with them. Thinking about the two women led to pondering again the similarities and differences in their personalities, and once he started thinking about personality, Beth Holderness popped into his mind. As soon as he thought about Beth, he began musing about the ease of ordering bacteria.

Jack closed Nodelman's chart and drummed his fingers on his desk. He began to wonder. If someone had obtained a culture of a pathological bacteria from National Biologicals and then intentionally spread it to people, could National Biologicals tell it had been their bacteria?

The idea intrigued him. With the advances of DNA technology he thought it was scientifically possible for National Biologicals to tag their cultures, and for reasons of both liability and economic protection, he thought it was a reasonable thing to do. The question then became whether they did it or not.

Jack searched for the phone number. Once he found it, he put through a second call to the organization.

Early that afternoon on Jack's first call he'd pressed "two" for sales. This time he pressed "three" for "support." After being forced to listen to a rock music station for a few minutes, Jack heard a youthful-sounding male voice give his name, Igor Krasnyansky, and ask how he could be of assistance.

Jack introduced himself properly on this occasion and inquired if he could pose a theoretical question.

"Of course," Igor said with a slight Slavic accent. "I will try to answer."

"If I had a culture of bacteria," Jack began, "is there any way that I could determine that it had originally come from your company even if it had gone through several passages in vivo?"

"That's an easy one," Igor said. "We phage-type all our cultures. So, sure, you could tell it came from National Biologicals."

"What's the identification process?" Jack asked.

"We have a fluorescein-labeled DNA probe," Igor said. "It's very simple."

"If I wanted to make such an identification, would I have to send the sample to you?" Jack asked.

"Either that or I could send you some of the probe," Igor said.

Jack was pleased. He gave his address and asked for the probe to be shipped via overnight express. He said he wanted it as soon as possible.

Hanging up the phone, Jack felt pleased with himself. He thought he'd come up with something that might lend considerable weight to his theory of intentional spread if any of the patients' bacteria tested positive.

Jack looked down at the charts and considered giving up on them for the time being. After all, if the opposite turned out to be the case, and none of the bacteria was from National Biologicals, perhaps he would have to rethink the whole affair.

Jack scraped back his chair and stood up. He'd had enough for one day. Pulling on his jacket, he prepared to head home. Suddenly the idea of some vigorous exercise had a strong appeal.

CHAPTER TWENTY-SIX

Monday, 6:00 P.M., March 25, 1996

Beth Holderness had stayed late to get all the throat cultures of the hospital employees planted. The evening crew had come in at the usual time, but at that moment they were down in the cafeteria having their dinner. Even Richard had disappeared, although Beth wasn't sure if he'd left for the day or not.

Since the micro section of the lab was deserted except for her, Beth thought that if she were to do any clandestine searching, this was as good a time as any. Sliding off her stool, she walked over to the door to the main part of the lab. She didn't see a soul, which encouraged her further.

Turning back to microbiology, Beth headed over to the insulated doors. She wasn't sure she should be doing what she was doing, but having said she would, she felt some obligation. She was confused about Dr. Jack Stapleton, but she was even more confused about her own boss, Dr. Martin Cheveau. He'd always been temperamental, but lately that moodiness had reached ridiculous proportions.

That afternoon he'd stormed in after Dr. Stapleton had left, demanding to know what she had told the medical examiner. Beth had tried to say that she'd told him nothing of consequence and had tried to get him to leave, but Dr. Cheveau wouldn't listen. He even threatened to fire Beth for willfully disobeying him. His ranting had brought her close to tears.

After he'd left Beth had thought about Dr. Stapleton's comment that people at the hospital, including her boss, had been acting defensively. Considering Dr. Cheveau's behavior, she'd thought Dr. Stapleton might be right. It made her even more willing to follow up on Dr. Stapleton's request.

Beth stood in front of the two insulated doors. The one on the left was the walk-in freezer, the other the walk-in incubator. She debated which one to search first. Since she'd been in and out of the incubator all day with the throat cultures, she decided to tackle that first. After all, there was only a small area in the incubator where the contents were unfamiliar to her.

Beth pulled open the door and entered. Immediately she was enveloped by the moist, warm air. The temperature was kept close to body temperature, at 98.6° Fahrenheit. Many bacteria and viruses, especially those that affected humans, had understandably evolved to grow best at human body temperature.

The door behind Beth closed automatically to seal in the heat. The compartment was about eight by ten. The lighting came from two bulbs covered with wire mesh mounted on the ceiling. The shelving was perforated stainless steel. It extended floor to ceiling on both walls, along the back, and down the center, creating two narrow aisles.

Beth made her way to the rear of the compartment. There were stainless-steel boxes back there that she'd seen on numerous occasions but had never examined.

Grasping one of the boxes with both hands, Beth slid

it out from its shelf and put it on the floor. It was about the size of a shoe box. When she tried to open it, she realized it had a latch that was secured with a miniature padlock!

Beth was amazed and instantly suspicious. Few things in the lab were kept under lock and key. Picking the box up, Beth slid it back into place. Moving along the shelf, she reached around each box in turn. Every one of them had the same type of lock.

Bending down, Beth did the same on the lower shelf. The condition of the fifth box was different. As Beth stuck her hand around its back, she could feel that the padlock's clasp had not been closed.

Insinuating her fingers between the unlocked box and its neighbors, Beth was able to slide it out. As she lifted it, she could tell it wasn't quite as heavy as the first locked box; she feared it would be empty. But it wasn't. As she lifted its cover, she saw that it contained a few petri dishes. She also noted that the petri dishes did not bear the customary label that was used in the lab. Instead they only had grease-pencil alphanumeric designators.

Beth gingerly reached into the box and lifted out a petri dish labeled A-81. She lifted the top and looked in at expanding bacterial colonies. They were transparent and mucoid and they were growing on a medium she recognized as chocolate agar.

A sharp mechanical click of the insulated door opening startled Beth. Her pulse raced. Like a child caught in a forbidden act, she frantically tried to get the petri dish back in the box and the box back on the shelf before whoever was entering saw what she was doing.

Unfortunately, there wasn't enough time. She'd only had a chance to close the box and pick it up before she found herself face-to-face with Dr. Martin Cheveau. Ironically, he was at that moment carrying a box identical to the one she was holding.

"What are you doing?" he snarled.

"I'm . . ." Beth voiced, but that was all she could say. Under the pressure of the circumstance, no potential explanation came to mind.

Dr. Cheveau noisily stashed his box on one of the shelves, then grabbed Beth's away from her. He looked at the open latch.

"Where's the lock?" he growled.

Beth extended her hand and then opened it. In her palm was the open padlock. Martin snatched it and examined it.

"How did you get it open?" he demanded.

"It was open," Beth asserted.

"You're lying," Martin snapped.

"I'm not," Beth said. "Honest. It was open and it made me curious."

"Likely story," Martin yelled. His voice reverberated around the confined space.

"I didn't disturb anything," Beth said.

"How do you know you didn't disturb anything?" Martin said. He opened the box and glanced inside. Seemingly satisfied, he closed it and locked it. He tested the lock. It held.

"I only lifted the cover and looked at one culture dish," Beth said. She was beginning to regain some composure, although her pulse was still racing.

Martin slipped the box into its position. Then he counted them all. When he was finished, he ordered her out of the incubator.

"I'm sorry," Beth said after Martin had closed the

insulated door behind them. "I didn't know that I wasn't supposed to touch those boxes."

At that moment Richard appeared in the doorway. Martin ordered him over, then angrily related how he'd caught Beth handling his research cultures.

Richard acted as upset as Martin when he heard. Turning to Beth, he demanded to know why she would do such a thing. He wondered whether they weren't giving her enough work to do.

"No one told me not to touch them," Beth protested. She was again close to tears. She hated confrontations and had already weathered a previous one only hours earlier.

"No one told you to handle them either," Richard snapped.

"Did that Dr. Stapleton put you up to this?" Martin demanded.

Beth hesitated, not knowing how to respond. As far as Martin was concerned her hesitation was incriminating. "I thought as much," he snapped. "He probably even told you about his preposterous idea that the plague cases and the others were started on purpose."

"I told him I wasn't supposed to talk with him," Beth cried.

"But talk he did," Martin said. "And obviously you listened. Well, I'm not going to stand for it. You are fired, Miss Holderness. Take your things and get out. I don't want to see your face again."

Beth sputtered a protest and with it came tears.

"Crying is not going to get you anywhere," Martin spat out. "Nor are excuses. You made your choice, now live with the consequences. Get out."

*

Twin reached across the scarred desk and hung up the phone. His real name was Marvin Thomas. He'd gotten the nickname "Twin" because he'd had an identical twin. No one had been able to tell the two of them apart until one of them got killed in a protracted disagreement between the Black Kings and a gang from the East Village over crack territories.

Twin looked across the desk at Phil. Phil was tall and skinny and hardly imposing, but he had brains. It had been his brains, not his bravado or muscles, that had caused Twin to elevate him to number-two man in the gang. He had been the only person to know what to do with all the drug money they'd been raking in. Up until Phil took over, they'd been burying the greenbacks in PVC pipe in the basement of Twin's tenement.

"I don't understand these people," Twin said. "Apparently that honky doctor didn't get our message, and he's been out doing just what he damned well pleases. Can you believe it? I hit that sucker with just about everything I got, and three days later he's giving us the finger. I don't call that respect, no way."

"The people want us to talk to him again?" Phil asked. He'd been on the visit to Jack's apartment and witnessed how hard Twin had hit the man.

"Better than that," Twin said. "They want us to ice the bastard. Why they didn't have us do it the first time is anybody's guess. They're offering us five big ones." Twin laughed. "Funny thing is, I would have done it for nothing. We can't have people ignoring us. We'd be out of business."

"Should we send Reginald?" Phil asked.

"Who else?" Twin questioned. "This is the kind of activity he loves."

Phil got to his feet and ground out his cigarette. He left the office and walked down the litter-strewn hallway to the front room, where a half dozen members were playing cards. Cigarette smoke hung heavily in the air.

"Hey, Reginald," Phil called out. "You up for some action?"

Reginald glanced up from his cards. He adjusted the toothpick protruding from his mouth. "It depends," he said.

"I think you'd like this one," Phil said. "Five big ones to do away with the doctor whose bike you got."

"Hey, man, I'll do it," BJ said. BJ was the nickname for Bruce Jefferson. He was a stocky fellow with thighs as thick as Phil's waist. He'd also been on the visit to Jack's.

"Twin wants Reginald," Phil said.

Reginald stood up and tossed his cards on the table. "I had a crap hand anyway," he said. He followed Phil back to the office.

"Did Phil tell you the story?" Twin asked when they entered.

"Just that the doctor goes," Phil said. "And five big ones for us. Anything else?"

"Yeah," Twin said. "You gotta do a white chick too. Might as well do her first. Here's the address."

Twin handed over a scrap of paper with Beth Holderness's name and address written on it.

"You care how I do these honkies?" Reginald asked.

"I couldn't care less," Twin said. "Just be sure you get rid of them."

"I'd like to use the new machine pistol," Reginald said. He smiled with the toothpick still stuck in the corner of his mouth.

"It'll be good to see if it's worth the money we paid for it," Twin said. Twin opened up one of the desk drawers and withdrew a new Tec pistol. It still had some packing grease on the handle. He gave the gun a shove across the desk. Reginald snapped it up before it got to the edge. "Enjoy yourself," Twin added.

"I intend to," Reginald said.

Reginald made it a point never to show any emotion, but that didn't mean he didn't feel it. As he walked out of the building, his mood was soaring. He loved this kind of work.

He unlocked the driver's-side door of his jet-black Camaro and slipped in behind the wheel. He put the Tec pistol on the passenger seat and covered it with a newspaper. As soon as the motor was humming, he turned on his tape deck and pushed in his current favorite rap cassette. The car had a sound system that was the envy of the gang. It had enough subwoofer power to loosen ceramic tile in whatever neighborhood Reginald cruised.

With one last glance at Beth Holderness's address and with his head bobbing with the music, Reginald pulled away from the curb and headed uptown.

Beth hadn't gone directly home. In her distressed state, she needed to talk with someone. She'd stopped at a friend's house and even had a glass of wine. After talking the situation over, she felt somewhat better, but was still depressed. She couldn't believe she'd been fired. There was also the gnawing possibility that she'd stumbled onto something significant in the incubator.

Beth lived in a five-story tenement on East Eighty-third Street between First and Second Avenues. It wasn't the greatest neighborhood, but it wasn't bad either. The only problem was that her building was not one of the best. The landlord did the least possible in terms of repair, and there was always trouble with something. As Beth arrived, she saw there was a new problem. The outer front door had been sprung open with a crowbar. Beth sighed. It had happened before and it had taken three months for the landlord to fix it.

For several months Beth had been intending to move out of the building, and had been saving her money for a deposit on a new apartment. Now that she was out of work, she'd have to dip into her savings. She probably couldn't move, at least not for the foreseeable future.

As she climbed the last flight of stairs she told herself that as bad as things seemed, they could be worse. She reminded herself that at least she was healthy.

Outside of her door, Beth fumbled with the clutter in the depths of her purse to find her apartment key, which she kept separate from the building key. Her idea was that if she lost one, she wouldn't necessarily lose the other.

Finally coming up with the key, she let herself into her apartment. She closed and locked the door, as was her habit. After taking off her coat and hanging it up, Beth again searched through her purse for Jack Stapleton's card. When she found it, she sat on the couch and gave him a call.

Although it was after seven, Beth called the medical examiner's office. An operator told her that Dr. Stapleton had left for the day. Turning the card over, she tried Jack's home number. She got his answering machine.

"Dr. Stapleton," Beth said after Jack's beep sounded.

"This is Beth Holderness. I have something to tell you." Beth choked back tears from a sudden surge of emotion. She considered hanging up to collect herself, but instead she cleared her throat and continued haltingly: "I have to talk with you. I did find something. Unfortunately I was also fired. So please call."

Beth depressed the disconnect and then hung up the phone. For a second she debated calling back to describe what she found, but she decided against it. She'd wait for Jack to call her.

Beth was about to stand up when a tremendous crash shocked her into complete immobility. The door to her apartment had burst open, and it slammed back against the wall hard enough to drive the doorknob into the plaster. The deadbolt that she'd felt so secure about had splintered the doorjamb as if the jamb had been made of balsa wood.

A figure stood on the threshold like a magician appearing out of a cloud of smoke. He was dressed from head to foot in black leather. He glanced at Beth, then turned and yanked the door closed. Quiet returned to the apartment with the same suddenness as the explosive crash. At the moment only the muffled sound of TV in a neighboring apartment could be heard.

If Beth could have envisioned this situation she would have thought she'd scream or flee or both, but she didn't do either. She'd been paralyzed. She'd even been holding her breath, which she now let out with an audible sigh.

The man advanced towards her. His face was expressionless. A toothpick jauntily stuck out of his mouth. In his left hand he brandished the largest pistol Beth had ever seen. Its ammunition clip protruded down almost a foot.

The man stopped directly in front of Beth. He didn't say a word. Instead he slowly raised the pistol and pointed it at her forehead. Beth closed her eyes . . .

Jack exited the subway at 103rd Street and jogged north. The weather was fine and the temperature reasonable. He expected a big turnout at the playground, and he wasn't disappointed. Warren saw him through the chain-link fence and told him to get his ass in gear and get over there.

Jack jogged the rest of the way home. As he approached his building, thoughts of Friday night and his uninvited visitors unwelcomely entered his mind. Having been at the General that day and having been discovered, Jack thought it was very possible that the Black Kings would be back. If they were, Jack wanted to know about it.

Instead of going in the front door, Jack descended a few steps and walked down a dank tunnel that connected the front and the back of his building. It reeked of urine. He emerged in the backyard, which looked like a junkyard. In the half-light he could make out the twisted remains of discarded bedsprings, broken baby carriages, bald car tires, and other unwanted trash.

Against the back of the building was a fire escape. It didn't descend all the way to the ground. The last segment was a metal ladder with a cement counterweight. By turning over a garbage can and standing on its base, Jack was able to reach up and grab the lowest rung. As soon as he put his weight on it, it came down with a clatter.

Jack climbed up the ladder. When he stepped off onto

the grate of the first landing, the ladder retracted to its original position with equal clamor. Jack stood still for a few minutes to be sure that the din didn't disturb anyone. When no one stuck their head out of a window to complain, Jack continued climbing.

On each floor Jack had ample opportunity to glance in at the various domestic scenes, but he assiduously avoided doing so. It wasn't pretty. When he saw it close-up, Jack found true poverty enervating. Jack also kept his eyes elevated to avoid looking down. He'd always been afraid of heights, and climbing the fire escape was a test of his fortitude.

As Jack approached his own floor he slowed down. The fire escape serviced both his kitchen window and his bedroom window, both of which were ablaze with light. When he'd left that morning, he'd left all the lights on.

Jack sidled up to the kitchen window first and peered in. The room was empty. A grouping of fruit he'd left on the table was undisturbed. From where he was standing he could also see through to his door to the common hall. His repair was still in place. The door had not been forced open.

Moving to the second window, Jack made sure that the bedroom was as he'd left it. Satisfied, he opened the window and climbed in. He knew he'd been taking a chance leaving the bedroom window unlocked, but he thought it worth the risk. Once inside his apartment, he made a rapid final check. It was empty with no sign of any unexpected visitors having been there.

Jack quickly changed into his basketball gear and exited the same way he'd entered. Given his acrophobia, descent was more difficult than ascent, but Jack forced himself to do it. Under the circumstances, he wasn't wild about stepping out of his front door unprotected.

When Jack got to the street end of the tunnel, he paused in the shadows to view the area immediately in front of his building. He was particularly concerned about seeing any groups of men sitting in cars. When he was reasonably confident there were no hostile gang members waiting for him, he jogged down to the playground.

Unfortunately, during the time he'd taken to climb up and down the fire escape and change clothes the crowd at the playground had swelled. It took Jack even longer than usual to get into the game, and when he did, he ended up on a comparatively poor team.

Although Jack's shot was on, particularly his long jumper, his teammates' weren't. The game was a rout, to Warren's delight; his team had been winning all night.

Disgusted with his luck, Jack went to the sidelines and picked up his sweatshirt. Pulling it over his head, he started for the gate.

"Hey, man, you leaving already?" Warren called out. "Come on, stick around. We'll let you win one of these days." Warren guffawed. He wasn't being a bad sport; ridiculing the defeated was part of the accepted playground behavior. Everybody did it and everybody expected it.

"I don't mind getting whipped if it's by a decent team," Jack shot back. "But losing to a bunch of pansies is embarrassing."

"Ohhhh," Warren's teammates crooned. Jack's retort had been a good one.

Warren strutted over to Jack and stuck his index finger into Jack's chest. "Pansies, huh?" he said. "I tell you what. My five would devastate any five you could put together right now! You pick, we play."

Jack's eyes swept around the court. Everybody was looking in their direction. Jack considered the challenge and weighed the pluses and the minuses. First of all, he wanted more exercise so he did want to play, and he knew that Warren could make it happen.

At the same time, Jack understood that picking four people out of the crowd would irritate the ones he didn't pick. These were people Jack had been painstakingly cultivating over the past months to accept him. Beyond that, the people who were supposed to have winners would be especially vexed, not at Warren, who was insulated from such emotion, but at Jack. Considering all the angles, Jack decided it wasn't worth it.

"I'm going running in the park," Jack said.

Having bested Jack's retort and willing to accept Jack's refusal to meet his challenge as another victory, Warren bowed in recognition of his team's cheering. He high-fived with one of them and then swaggered back onto the court. "Let's run!" he yelled.

Jack smiled to himself, thinking how much the dynamics of the playground basketball court revealed about current intra-city society. Vaguely he wondered if any psychologist had ever thought about studying it from an academic point of view. He thought it would be fruitful indeed.

Jack stepped through the chain-link gate onto the sidewalk and started jogging. He ran due east. Ahead, at the end of the block he could see the dark silhouettes of jagged rocks and leafless trees. He knew that in a few minutes he'd leave behind the bustle of the city and enter the placid interior of Central Park. It was his favorite place to run.

Reginald had been stymied. There was no way he could have walked out into a playground in a hostile neighborhood. Having found the doc playing b-ball, he'd resigned himself to waiting in his Camaro. His hope was that Jack would separate himself from the crowd, perhaps by heading for one of the nearby delis for a drink.

When he'd seen Jack quit the game and pull on his sweater, he'd been encouraged enough to reach under the newspaper and snap the safety off the Tec. But then he heard Warren's challenge and was sure he'd be sitting through at least another game.

He was wrong. To his delight, a few minutes later Jack came out of the playground. But he didn't head west in the direction of the shops as Reginald had anticipated. Instead he headed east!

Cursing under his breath, Reginald had to make a U-turn right in the middle of all the traffic. A cabdriver complained bitterly by leaning on his horn. It was all Reginald could do to keep from reaching for the Tec. The cabdriver was one of those guys from the Far East whom Reginald would have loved to surprise with a couple of bursts.

Reginald's disappointment turned back to delight when he became aware of Jack's destination. As Jack sprinted across Central Park West, Reginald quickly parked. Leaping from the car, he grabbed the Tec along with the newspaper. Cradling the package in his hands, he, too, dashed across Central Park West, dodging the traffic.

At that point an entrance to the park's West Drive
continued eastward into the park. Nearby was a sweeping
stone stairway that rose up around a rocky outcropping.
Lampposts partially lit the walkway before it disappeared
into the blackness.

Reginald started up the stairs where he'd seen Jack go
seconds earlier. Reginald was pleased. He couldn't
believe his luck. In fact, chasing his prey into the dark,
deserted park was making the job almost too easy.

From Jack's point of view at that moment the park's
desolate darkness was more a source of comfort than
uneasiness, unlike when he'd crossed the park on his
bike Friday night. He felt consolation in the fact that
although his vision was hampered, so was everyone
else's. He firmly believed if the Black Kings were to
harass him it would be in and around his apartment.

The terrain where Jack's run began was surprisingly
hilly and rocky. The area was called the Great Hill for
good reason. He was following an asphalt walkway that
twisted, turned, and tunneled beneath the leafless
branches of the surrounding trees. The lights from the
lampposts illuminated the branches in an eerie fashion,
giving the impression the park was covered by a giant
spider's web.

Although he felt winded at first, Jack settled into a
comfortable pace and began to relax. With the city out
of view, he had a chance to think more clearly. He began
to wonder if his crusade was based on his hatred for
AmeriCare, as Chet and Bingham had implied. From his
present perspective Jack had to agree it was possible.
After all, the idea of the intentional spread of the four

diseases was implausible if not preposterous. And if he found the people at the General defensive, maybe he'd made them respond that way. As Bingham had reminded him: Jack could be abrasive.

In the middle of his musings Jack became aware of a new sound that coincided with his own footfalls. It was a metallic click, as if his basketball shoes had heel-savers. Perplexed, Jack altered his pace. The sound went out of sync for a moment but then gradually merged back.

Jack hazarded a glance behind him. When he did, he saw a figure running in his direction and closing. At the moment Jack spotted the figure, the man was passing under a lamppost. Jack could see he was not dressed as a jogger. In fact, he was wearing black leather, and in his hand he brandished a gun!

Jack's heart leaped in his chest. Aided by an adrenaline rush, he put on a burst of speed. Behind him he could hear his pursuer do likewise.

Jack frantically tried to figure the fastest way out of the park. If he was able to get among traffic and other people he might have a chance. All he knew for sure was that the closest way to the city was through the foliage to his right. He had no idea how far. It could have been a hundred feet or a hundred yards.

Sensing his pursuer was staying with him and perhaps even gaining, Jack veered right and plunged into the forest. Within the woods it was considerably darker than on the walkway. Jack could barely see where he was going as he stumbled up a steep grade. He was in a full panic, crashing over underbrush and scrambling through dense evergreens.

The hill leveled off at the summit and Jack burst through to an area with considerably less undergrowth.

It was just as dark, but there were only dead leaves to contend with as he ran between the closely spaced tree trunks.

Happening upon a massive oak tree, Jack slipped behind and leaned against its rough surface. He was breathing hard. He tried to control his panting to listen. All he could hear was the sound of distant traffic that reverberated like the muffled roar of a waterfall. Only occasional car horns and undulating sirens punctuated the night.

Jack stayed behind the broad trunk of the oak for several minutes. Hearing no more footfalls, he pushed off the tree and continued heading west. Now he moved slowly and as silently as possible, nudging his feet forward in the leaves to keep the noise down. His heart was racing.

Jack's foot hit up against something soft, and to his horror it seemed to explode in front of him. For a second Jack had no idea what was happening. With great commotion a phantom figure swathed in rags lurched out of the ground as if resurrecting itself from the dead. The creature whirled about like a dervish, flailing at the air and shouting "Bastards" over and over again.

Instantly another figure loomed up as well, equally frantic. "You're not gonna get our shopping cart," the second man yelled. "We'll kill you first."

Jack had only managed to take a single step backward when the first figure threw himself at him, smothering him with a wretched stench and ineffectual blows. Jack tried to push him away, but the man reached up and drew his fingernails down Jack's face.

Jack marshaled his strength to rid himself of this fetid vagrant who clung to his chest. Before Jack could shake him loose, a burst of gunfire shattered the night. Jack felt himself sprayed with fluid as the tramp stiffened, then collapsed forward. Jack had to push him aside to keep from being knocked over backward.

The other vagrant's keening brought forth a second burst of gunfire. His wails of grief were cut off suddenly with a gurgle.

Having seen the direction from which the second burst of gunfire had come, Jack turned and fled in the opposite direction. Once again he was in headlong flight despite the darkness and the obstacles. Suddenly the ground dropped off, and Jack stumbled down a steep hillside, barely keeping his feet under him until he plunged into a dense undergrowth of vines and thornbushes.

Jack clawed his way through the thick bushes until he burst out onto a walkway with such suddenness, he fell to his hands and knees. Ahead he could see a flight of dimly lit, granite stairs. Scrambling to his feet, he dashed toward the stairs and took them two at a time. As he neared the top a single shot rang out. A bullet ricocheted off the stone to Jack's right and whined off into the night.

Trying to duck and weave, Jack reached the top of the stairs and emerged onto a terrace. A fountain that had been turned off for the winter stood empty in its center. Three sides of the terrace were enclosed by an arcade. In the center of the rear arcade was another stone stairway leading to another level.

Jack heard the rapid metallic clicks of his pursuer's shoes start up the stone stairway behind him. He would be there in an instant. Jack knew he had no time to make it to the second stairway, so he ran into the interior of the arcade. Within the arched space the darkness was complete. Jack advanced blindly by holding his hands out in front of him.

The pounding footfalls on the first stairway abruptly stopped. Jack knew his pursuer had reached the terrace. Jack continued forward, moving faster, heading for the second run of stairs. To his horror he collided in the blackness with a metal trash can. The noise was loud and unmistakable as the can tipped over and rolled to a stop. Almost immediately a burst of gunfire sounded. The bullets entered the arcade and ricocheted wildly off the granite walls. Jack lay flat, clasping his arms over his head until the final shell whined off into the night.

Standing up again, Jack continued forward, more slowly this time. When he reached the corner he encountered more obstacles: bottles and beer cans were strewn on the floor with no way for Jack to avoid them.

Jack winced every time one of his feet struck an object and the resulting noise echoed in the arcade. But there was no stopping. Ahead a faint glow indicated where the second stairway rose up to the next level. As soon as Jack reached it, he started climbing, moving more quickly now that there was light enough to see where to put his feet.

Jack was almost to the top when a sharp, authoritative command rang out in the stillness.

"Hey, man, hold up or you're gone!"

Jack could tell from the sound of the man's voice that he was at the foot of the stairs. At that range Jack had no choice. He stopped.

"Turn around!"

Jack did as he was told. He could see that his pursuer had a huge pistol leveled at him.

"Remember me? I'm Reginald."

"I remember you," Jack said.

"Come down here!" Reginald ordered in between breaths. "I'm not climbing another stair for you. No way."

Jack descended slowly. When he got to the third stair he stopped. The only light was a suffused glow from the surrounding city reflected off the cloud cover. Jack could barely make out the man's features. His eyes appeared to be bottomless holes.

"Man, you got balls," Reginald said. Slowly he let his hand holding the Tec pistol fall until it was dangling at his side. "And you're in shape. I gotta hand you that."

"What do you want from me?" Jack asked. "Whatever it is you can have it."

"Hey, I'm not expecting anything," Reginald said. "'Cause I can tell you ain't got much. Certainly not in those threads, and I've already been to that shithole apartment of yours. To be honest, I'm just supposed to ice you. Word has it you didn't take Twin's recommendation."

"I'll pay you," Jack said. "Whatever you're being paid to do this, I'll pay you more."

"Sounds interesting," Reginald said. "But I can't deal. Otherwise I'd have to answer to Twin, and you couldn't pay me enough to take on that kind of shit. No way."

"Then tell me who's paying you," Jack said. "Just so I know."

"Hey, to tell you the truth, I don't even know," Reginald said. "All I know is that the money's good. We're getting five big ones just for me to chase you around the park for fifteen minutes. I'd say that's not bad."

"I'll pay a thousand," Jack said. He was desperate to keep Reginald talking.

"Sorry," Reginald said. "Our little rap is over and your number's up." As slowly as Reginald had lowered the gun, now he raised it.

Jack couldn't believe he was going to be shot at point-blank range by someone he didn't know and who didn't know him. It was preposterous. Jack knew he had to get Reginald talking, but as glib as Jack was, he couldn't think of anything more to say. His gift for repartee had deserted him as he watched the gun rise up to the point where he was staring directly down the barrel.

"My bad," Reginald said. It was a comment that Jack understood from his street basketball. It meant that Reginald was taking responsibility for what he was about to do.

The gun fired, and Jack winced reflexively. Even his eyes closed. But he didn't feel anything. Then he realized that Reginald was toying with him like a cat with a captured mouse. Jack opened his eyes. As terrorized as he felt, he was determined not to give Reginald any satisfaction. But what he saw shocked him. Reginald had disappeared.

Jack blinked several times, as if he thought his eyes were playing tricks on him. When he looked more closely he could just make out Reginald's body sprawled on the paving stones. A dark stain like an octopus's ink was spreading out from his head.

Jack swallowed but didn't move. He was transfixed. Out of the shadows of the arcade stepped a man. He was wearing a baseball hat backward. In his hand a pistol similar to the one Reginald had been carrying. He went first to Reginald's gun, which had skidded ten feet away, and picked it up. He examined it briefly, then thrust it into the top of his trousers. He stepped over to the dead

man and with the tip of his foot turned Reginald's head
over to look at the wound. Satisfied, he bent down and
frisked the body until he found a wallet. He pulled it
out, pocketed it, then stood up.

"Let's go, Doc," the man said.

Jack descended the last three steps. When he got to
the bottom he recognized his rescuer. It was Spit!

"What are you doing here?" Jack asked in a forced
whisper. His throat had gone bone dry.

"This ain't no time for rapping, man," Spit said. He
then indulged in the act that had been the source of his
sobriquet. "We gotta get the hell out of here. One of
those bums back on the hill was only winged, and he's
going to have this place crawling with cops."

From the moment Spit's gun had gone off in the arcade,
Jack's mind had been spinning. Jack had no idea how
Spit happened to be there at such a crucial time, or why
he was now hustling him out of the park.

Jack tried to protest. He knew leaving a murder scene
was a felony, and there had been two murders, not one.
But Spit was not to be dissuaded. In fact, when Jack
finally stopped running and started to explain why they
shouldn't flee, Spit slapped him. It wasn't a gentle slap;
it was a blow with vengeance.

Jack put his hand to his face. His skin was hot where
he'd been struck.

"What the hell are you doing?" Jack asked.

"Trying to knock some sense into you, man," Spit
said. "We got to get our asses over to Amsterdam. Here,
you carry this mother." Spit thrust Reginald's machine
pistol into Jack's hands.

"What am I supposed to do with it?" Jack asked. As far as he was concerned it was a murder weapon that should be handled with latex gloves and treated as evidence.

"Stick it under your sweater," Spit said. "Let's get."

"Spit, I don't think I can run away like this," Jack said. "You go if you must, and take this thing." Jack extended the gun toward Spit.

Spit exploded. He grabbed Reginald's gun out of Jack's hand and immediately pressed the barrel against Jack's forehead. "You're pissing me off, man," he said. "What's the matter with you? There still could be some of these Black King assholes hanging around here. I tell you what: If you don't get your ass in gear I'm going to waste you. You understand? I mean I wouldn't be out here risking my black ass if it hadn't been for Warren telling me to do it."

"Warren?" Jack questioned. Everything was getting too complicated. But he believed Spit's threat, so he didn't try to question him further. Jack knew Spit to be an impulsive man on the basketball court with a quick temper. Jack had never been willing to argue with him.

"Are you coming or what?" Spit demanded.

"I'm coming," Jack said. "I'm bowing to your better judgment."

"Damn straight," Spit said. He handed the machine pistol back to Jack and gave Jack a shove to move out.

On Amsterdam Spit used a pay phone while Jack waited nervously. All at once the ubiquitous sirens heard in the distance in New York City had a new meaning for Jack. So did the concept of being a felon. For years Jack had been thinking of himself as a victim. Now he was the criminal.

Spit hung up the phone and gave Jack a thumbs-up sign. Jack had no idea what the gesture meant, but he smiled anyway since Spit seemed to be content.

Less than fifteen minutes later a lowered maroon Buick pulled up to the curb. The intermittent thud of rap music could be heard through the tinted windows. Spit opened the back door and motioned for Jack to slide in. Jack complied. Events were clearly not in his control.

Spit gave a final look around before climbing into the front seat. The car shot away from the curb.

"What's happening?" the driver asked. His name was David. He was also a regular on the b-ball court.

"A lot of shit," Spit said. He rolled his window down and noisily expectorated.

Jack winced each time the bass sounded in one of the many stereo speakers. He slipped the machine pistol out from under his sweater. Having the thing close to his body gave him a distinctly unpleasant feeling. "What do you want me to do with this?" Jack asked Spit. He had to talk loudly to be heard over the sound of the music.

Spit swung around and took the gun. He showed it to David, who whistled in admiration. "That's the new model," he commented.

With little talk the threesome drove north to 106th Street and turned right. David braked across from the playground. The basketball game was still in progress.

"Wait here," Spit said. He got out of the car and headed into the playground.

Jack watched Spit as he walked to the basketball court and stood on the sidelines as the game swept back and forth in front of him. Jack was tempted to ask David what was happening, but his intuition told him to keep still. Eventually Spit got Warren's attention and Warren stopped the game.

After a brief conversation during which Spit passed Reginald's wallet to Warren, the two men came back to David's car. David lowered the window. Warren stuck his head in and looked at Jack. "What the hell have you been doing?" he demanded angrily.

"Nothing," Jack said. "I'm the victim here. Why be angry with me?"

Warren didn't answer. Instead, he ran his tongue around the inside of his dry mouth while he thought. Perspiration lined his forehead. All at once he stood up and opened the door for Jack. "Get out," he said. "We have to talk. Let's go up to your place."

Jack slid out of the car. He tried to look Warren in the eye, but Warren avoided his stare. Warren started out across the street, and Jack followed. Spit came behind Jack.

They climbed Jack's stairs in silence.

"You got anything to drink?" Warren asked once they were inside.

"Gatorade or beer," Jack said. He had restocked his refrigerator.

"Gatorade," Warren said. He walked over to Jack's couch and sat heavily.

Jack offered Spit the same choices. He took beer.

After Jack had provided the drinks he sat in the chair opposite the couch. Spit preferred to lean against the desk.

"I want to know what's going on," Warren said.

"You and I both," Jack said.

"I don't want to hear any shit," Warren said. "'Cause you haven't been straight with me."

"What do you mean?" Jack asked.

"Saturday you asked me about the Black Kings," Warren reminded him. "You said you were just curious. Now tonight one of those mothers tries to knock you off. Now I know something about those losers. They're into drugs big time. You catch my drift? What I want you to know is if you're mixed up with dealing, I don't want you in this neighborhood. It's as simple as that."

Jack let out a short laugh of incredulity. "Is that what this is about?" he asked. "You think I'm dealing drugs?"

"Doc, listen to me," Warren said. "You're a strange dude. I never understood why you're living here. But it's okay as long as you don't screw up the neighborhood. But if you're here because of drugs, you gotta rethink your situation."

Jack cleared his throat. He then admitted to Warren that he'd not been truthful with him when he'd asked about the Black Kings. He told him that the Black Kings had beaten him up, but that it involved something concerning his work that even he didn't totally understand.

"You sure you're not dealing?" Warren asked again. He looked at Jack out of the corner of his eye. "'Cause if you're not straight with me now you're going to be one sorry shit."

"I'm being entirely truthful," Jack assured him.

"Well, then you're a lucky man," Warren said. "Had David and Spit not recognized that dude who came cruising around the neighborhood in his Camaro, you'd be history right now. Spit says he was fixing to blow you away."

Jack looked up at Spit. "I'm very grateful," he said.

"It was nothing, man," Spit said. "That mother was so fixed on getting you that he never once looked behind him. We'd been on his tail almost the moment he turned on a Hundred and Sixth."

Jack rubbed his head and sighed. Only now was he truly beginning to calm down. "What a night," he said. "But it's not over. We've got to go to the police."

"Hell we do," Warren said, his anger returning. "Nobody's going to the police."

"But there's someone dead," Jack said. "Maybe two or three, counting those homeless guys."

"There'll be four if you go," Warren warned. "Listen, Doc, don't get yourself involved in gang business, and this has become gang business. This Reginald dude knew he wasn't supposed to be up here. No way. I mean, we can't have them thinking they can just breeze into our neighborhood and knock somebody off, even if it is only you. Next they'd be icing one of the brothers. Leave it be, Doc. The police don't give a shit anyway. They're happy when us brothers are knocking each other off. All you can do is cause you and us trouble, and if you go to the police, you're no friend of ours, no way."

"But leaving the scene of a crime is a—" Jack began.

"Yeah, I know," Warren interrupted. "It's a felony. Big deal. Who the hell cares? And let me tell you something else. You still got a problem. If the Black Kings want you dead, you'd better be our friend, because we're the only ones who can keep you alive. The cops can't, believe me."

Jack started to say something, but he changed his mind. With his knowledge of gang life in New York City, he knew that Warren was right. If the Kings wanted him dead, which they apparently did – and would all the more now with Reginald's death – there was no way for the police to prevent it short of secret-service-type twenty-four-hour guard.

Warren looked up at Spit. "Somebody's going to have to stick tight to Doc for the next few days," he said.

Spit nodded. "No problem," he said.

Warren stood up and stretched. "What pisses me off is that I had the best team I've had in weeks tonight, and this shit has cut it short."

"I'm sorry," Jack said. "I'll let you win next time I play against you."

Warren laughed. "One thing I can say about you, Doc," he said. "You can sure rap with the best of them."

Warren motioned to Spit to leave. "We'll be seeing you, Doc," Warren said at the door. "Now don't do anything foolish. You going to run tomorrow night?"

"Maybe," Jack said. He didn't know what he was going to do in the next five minutes, much less the following night.

With a final wave Warren and Spit departed. The door closed behind them.

Jack sat for a few minutes. He felt shell-shocked. Then he got up, went into the bathroom. When he looked into the mirror he cringed. At the time he and Spit had been waiting for David to arrive with the car, a few people had glanced at Jack, but no one had stared. Now Jack wondered why they hadn't. Jack's face and sweater were spattered with blood, presumably from the vagrant. There was also a nasty series of parallel scratches from the vagrant's fingernails down his forehead and over his nose. A cross-hatching of scratches marred his cheeks, from the underbrush, no doubt. He looked like he'd been in a war.

Jack climbed into his tub and took a shower. By then

his mind was going a mile a minute. He couldn't remember ever being in such a state of confusion, except after his family had perished. But that was different. He'd been depressed then. Now he was just confused.

Jack got out of the shower and dried himself off. He was still half debating whether or not to contact the police. In a state of indecision, he went to the phone. That's when he noticed that his answering machine was blinking. He pushed the play button and listened to Beth Holderness's disturbing message. Instantly he called her back. He let her phone ring ten times before giving up. What could she have found? he wondered. He also felt responsible for her having been fired. Somehow he was sure he was to blame.

Jack got a beer and took it into the living room. Sitting on the windowsill, he could see a sliver of 106th Street. There was the usual traffic and parade of people. He watched with unseeing eyes as he wrestled with his dilemma regarding calling the police.

Hours passed. Jack realized that by not making a decision he was in essence making one. By not calling the police he was agreeing with Warren. He'd become a felon.

Jack went back to the phone and tried Beth for the tenth time. It was now after midnight. The phone rang interminably. Jack started to worry. He hoped she'd simply fled to a friend's house for solace after losing her job. Yet not being able to get in touch with her nagged at him along with everything else.

CHAPTER TWENTY-SEVEN

Tuesday, 7:30 A.M., March 26, 1996
New York City

The first thing Jack did when he woke up was to try calling Beth Holderness. When she'd still not answered he'd tried to be optimistic about her visiting a friend, but in the face of everything that had happened, the inability to get ahold of her was progressively more distressing.

Still without a bike, Jack was forced back into the subway for his commute. But he wasn't alone. From the moment Jack had emerged from his tenement he'd been trailed by one of the younger members of the local gang. His name was Slam, in deference to his dunking ability with the basketball. Even though he was Jack's height, he could outjump Jack by at least twelve inches.

Jack and Slam did not talk during the train ride. They sat opposite each other, and although Slam didn't try to avoid eye contact, his expression never changed from one of total indifference. He was dressed like most of the young African-Americans in the city, with oversized clothes. His sweatshirt was tentlike, and Jack preferred not to imagine what it concealed. Jack didn't believe that Warren would have sent the young man out to protect Jack without some significant weaponry.

As Jack crossed First Avenue and mounted the steps in front of the medical examiner's office, he glanced behind him. Slam had paused on the sidewalk, obviously confused as to what he should do. Jack hesitated as well. The unreasonable thought went through Jack's mind of inviting the man in so that he could pass the time in the second-floor canteen, but that was clearly out of the question.

Jack shrugged. Although he appreciated Slam's efforts on his behalf, it was Slam's problem what he was going to do for the day.

Jack turned back to the building, steeling himself for the possibility of having to face one or more bodies in whose death he somehow felt complicit.

Gathering his courage, Jack pulled open the door and entered.

Even though he was scheduled for a "paper day" and no autopsies, Jack wanted to see what had come in during the night. Not only was he concerned about Reginald and the vagrants, he was also concerned about the possibility of more meningococcus cases.

Jack had the receptionist buzz him into the ID area. Walking into the scheduling room, Jack knew instantly that it was not going to be a normal day. Vinnie was not sitting in his usual location with his morning newspaper.

"Where's Vinnie?" Jack asked George.

Without looking up, George told Jack that Vinnie was already in the pit with Bingham.

Jack's pulse quickened. Given his guilt about the previous evening's events, he had the irrational thought that Bingham could have been called in to do Reginald. At this stage of his career Bingham rarely did autopsies unless they were of particular interest or importance.

"What's Bingham doing in this early?" Jack asked, trying to sound uninterested.

"It's been a busy night," George said. "There was another infectious death over at the General. Apparently it's got the city all worked up. During the night the city epidemiologist called the Commissioner of Health, who called Bingham."

"Another meningococcus?" Jack asked.

"Nope," George said. "They think this one is a viral pneumonia."

Jack nodded and felt a chill descend his spine. His immediate concern was hantavirus. He knew there had been a case on Long Island the previous year in the early spring. Hantavirus was a scary proposition, although it was still not an illness with much patient-to-patient spread.

Jack could see there were more than the usual number of folders on the desk in front of George. "Anything else interesting last night?" Jack asked. He shuffled through the folders looking for Reginald's name.

"Hey," George complained. "I got these things in order." He looked up, then did a double take. "What the hell happened to you?"

Jack had forgotten how bad his face looked.

"I tripped when I was out jogging last night," Jack said. Jack didn't like to lie. What he said was true, but hardly the whole story.

"What did you fall into?" George asked. "A roll of barbed wire?"

"Any gunshot wounds last night?" Jack asked, to change the subject.

"You'd better believe it," George said. "We got four. Too bad it's a paper day for you. I'd give you one."

"Which ones are they?" Jack asked. He glanced around the desk.

George tapped the top of one of his stacks of folders.

Jack reached over and picked up the first one. When he opened the cover, his heart sank. He had to reach out and steady himself against the desk. The name was Beth Holderness.

"Oh, God, no," Jack murmured.

George's head shot up again. "What's the matter?" he asked. "Hey, you're as white as a sheet. You okay?"

Jack sat in a nearby chair and put his head down between his legs. He'd felt dizzy.

"Is it someone you know?" George asked with concern.

Jack straightened up. The dizziness had passed. He took a deep breath and nodded. "She was an acquaintance," he said. "But I'd spoken with her just yesterday." Jack shook his head. "I can't believe it."

George reached over and took the folder from Jack's hands. He opened it up. "Oh, yeah," he said. "This is the lab tech from over at the General. Sad! She was only twenty-eight. Supposed to be shot through the forehead for a TV and some cheap jewelry. What a waste."

"What are the other gunshot wounds?" Jack asked. For the moment he remained seated.

George consulted his master sheet. "I've got a Hector Lopez, West Hundred and Sixtieth Street, a Mustafa Aboud, East Nineteenth Street, and Reginald Winthrope, Central Park."

"Let me see Winthrope," Jack said.

George handed Jack the folder.

Jack opened it up. He wasn't looking for anything in particular, but his sense of involvement made him want to check the case. The strangest thing was that had it not been for Spit, Jack himself would have been represented there on George's desk with his own folder. Jack shuddered. He handed Reginald's folder back to George.

"Is Laurie here yet?" Jack asked.

"She came in just before you did," George said. "She wanted some folders, but I told her that I'd not made out the schedule yet."

"Where is she?" Jack asked.

"Up in her office, I guess," George said. "I really don't know."

"Assign her the Holderness and the Winthrope cases," Jack said. He stood up. He anticipated feeling dizzy again, but he didn't.

"How come?" George asked.

"George, just do it," Jack said.

"All right, don't get mad," George said.

"I'm sorry," Jack said. "I'm not mad. Just pre-occupied."

Jack walked back through communications. He passed Janice's office, where she was putting in her usual over-time. Jack didn't bother her. He was too absorbed by his own thoughts. Beth Holderness's death made him feel unhinged. Feeling guilty about his complicity in her losing her job was bad enough; the idea that she might have lost her life because of his actions was unthinkable.

Jack pressed the button for the elevator and waited. The attempt on his own life the night before had given more weight to his suspicions. Someone had tried to kill him after he refused to heed the warning. The very same night Beth Holderness had been murdered. Could it have been in the course of an unrelated robbery or could it have been because of Jack, and, if so, what did that mean about Martin Cheveau? Jack didn't know. But what he did know was that he could not involve anyone else in this affair for fear of putting them in jeopardy. From that moment on, Jack knew he had to keep everything to himself.

As George had surmised, Laurie was in her office. While waiting for George to assign the day's cases, she was using the time profitably, working on some of her uncompleted cases. She took one look at Jack and recoiled. Jack offered the same explanation he'd given George, but he could tell that Laurie wasn't quite convinced.

"Did you hear that Bingham is down the pit?" Jack asked, to move the conversation away from his previous night's experiences.

"I did," Laurie said. "I was shocked. I didn't think there was anything that could get him here before eight, much less in the autopsy room."

"Do you know anything about the case?" Jack asked.

"Just that it was atypical pneumonia," Laurie said. "I spoke with Janice for a moment. She said they'd had preliminary confirmation it was influenza."

"Uh-oh!" Jack said.

"I know what you're thinking," Laurie said, wagging her finger. "Influenza was one of the diseases you said you'd use if you were a terrorist type trying to start an epidemic. But before you go jumping off using this as confirmation of your theory, just remember that it is still influenza season."

"Primary influenza pneumonia is not very common," Jack said, trying to stay calm. The mention of the word "influenza" had his pulse racing again.

"We see it every year," Laurie said.

"Maybe so," Jack said. "But I tell you what. How

about calling that internist friend of yours and asking if there are any more cases?"

"Right now?" Laurie asked. She glanced at her watch.

"It's as good a time as any," Jack said. "She'll probably be making her rounds. She can use the computer terminal at one of the nurses' stations."

Laurie shrugged and picked up her phone. A few minutes later she had her friend on the line. She asked the question, then waited. While she waited she looked up at Jack. She was worried about him. His face was not only scratched up, it was now flushed.

"No cases," Laurie repeated into the phone when her friend came back on the line. "Thanks, Sue. I appreciate it. Talk to you soon. Bye."

Laurie hung up the phone. "Satisfied?" she said.

"For the moment," Jack said. "Listen: I asked George to assign you two particular cases this morning. The names are Holderness and Winthrope."

"Is there some specific reason?" Laurie asked. She could see that Jack was trembling.

"Do it as a favor," Jack said.

"Of course," Laurie said.

"One thing I'd like you to do is look for any hairs or fibers on the Holderness woman's body," Jack said. "And find out if homicide had a criminologist on the scene to do the same. If there are any hairs, see if there is a DNA match with Winthrope."

Laurie didn't say anything. When she found her voice, she asked: "You think that Winthrope killed Holderness?" Her voice reflected her disbelief.

Jack looked off and sighed. "There's a chance," he said.

"How would you know?" Laurie asked.

"Let's call it a disturbing hunch," Jack said. He would have liked to tell Laurie more, but with the new pact he had with himself, he didn't. He wasn't about to put anyone else at risk in any form or fashion.

"Now you really have my curiosity going," Laurie said.

"I'd like to ask one more favor," Jack said. "You told me that you had a relationship with a police detective who's now a friend."

"That's true," Laurie said.

"Do you think you could give him a call?" Jack said. "I'd like to talk with him sorta off the record."

"You are scaring me," Laurie said. "Are you in some kind of trouble?"

"Laurie," Jack said. "Please don't ask any questions. The less you know right now the better off you are. But I think I should talk to someone high up in law enforcement."

"You want me to call him now?"

"Whenever is convenient," Jack said.

Laurie blew out through pursed lips as she dialed Lou Soldano's number. She'd not talked to him in a few weeks, and she felt it was a little awkward calling about a situation she knew so little about. But she was definitely worried about Jack and wanted to help.

When police headquarters answered and Laurie asked for Lou, she was told the detective wasn't available. She left a message on his voice mail for him to call her.

"That's the best I could do," Laurie said as she hung up. "Knowing Lou, he'll be back as soon as he can."

"I appreciate it," Jack said. He gave her shoulder a squeeze. He had the comforting sense she was a true friend.

Jack went back to his own office just in time to run into Chet. Chet took one look at Jack's face and whistled.

"And what did the other guy look like?" Chet asked jokingly.

"I'm not in the mood," Jack said. He took off his jacket and hung it over his chair.

"I hope this doesn't have anything to do with those gang members who visited you Friday," Chet said.

Jack gave the same explanation he'd given to the others.

Chet flashed a wry smile as he stowed his coat in his file cabinet. "Sure, you fell while jogging," he said. "And I'm dating Julia Roberts. But, hey, you don't have to tell me what happened; I'm just your friend."

That was exactly the point, Jack mused. After checking to see if he had any phone messages, he started back out of the office.

"You missed a nice little dinner last night," Chet said. "Terese came along. We talked about you. She's a fan of yours, but she's as concerned as I am about your monomania concerning these infectious cases."

Jack didn't even bother to answer. If Chet or Terese knew what had really happened last night, they'd be more than concerned.

Returning to the first floor, Jack looked into Janice's office. Now he wanted to ask her about the influenza case that was being posted by Bingham, but she'd left. Jack descended to the morgue level and changed into his isolation gear.

He went into the autopsy room and walked up to the only table in operation. Bingham was on the patient's right, Calvin on the left, and Vinnie at the head. They were almost done.

"Well, well," Bingham said when Jack joined them. "Isn't this convenient? Here's our in-house infectious expert."

"Perhaps the expert would like to tell us what this case is," Calvin challenged.

"I've already heard," Jack said. "Influenza."

"Too bad," Bingham said. "It would have been fun to see if you truly have the nose for this stuff. When it came in early this morning there was no diagnosis yet. The suspicion was some sort of viral hemorrhagic fever. It had everybody up in arms."

"When did you learn it was influenza?" Jack asked.

"A couple of hours ago," Bingham answered. "Just before we started. It's a good case, though. You want to see the lungs?"

"I would," Jack said.

Bingham reached into the pan and lifted out the lungs. He showed the cut surface to Jack.

"My God, the whole lung is involved!" Jack commented. He was impressed. In some areas there was frank hemorrhage.

"Even some myocarditis," Bingham said. He put the lung back and lifted up the heart and displayed it for Jack. "When you can see the inflammation grossly like this, you know it's extensive."

"Looks like a virulent strain," Jack said.

"You'd better believe it," Bingham said. "This patient's only twenty-nine years old, and his first symptoms occurred around six last night. He was dead at four a.m. It reminds me of a case I did back in my residency during the pandemic of fifty-seven and fifty-eight."

Vinnie rolled his eyes. Bingham had a mind-numbing habit of comparing every case to one that he'd had in his long career.

"That case was also a primary influenza pneumonia," Bingham continued. "Same appearance of the lung. When we looked at it histologically we were amazed at the degree of damage. It gave us a lot of respect for certain strains of influenza."

"Seeing this case concerns me," Jack said. "Especially in light of the other diseases that have been popping up."

"Now, don't head off into left field!" Bingham warned, remembering some of Jack's comments the day before. "This isn't out of the ordinary, like the plague case or even the tularemia. It's flu season. Primary influenza pneumonia is a rare complication, but we see it. In fact we had a case just last month."

Jack listened, but Bingham wasn't making him feel any more comfortable. The patient in front of them had had a lethal infection with an agent that had the capability of spreading from patient to patient like wildfire. Jack's only consolation was the call Laurie had made to her internist friend who'd said there were no other cases in the hospital.

"Mind if I take some washings?" Jack asked.

"Hell no!" Bingham said. "Be my guest. But be careful what you do with them."

"Obviously," Jack said.

Jack took the lungs over to one of the sinks, and with Vinnie's help prepared some samples by washing out some of the small bronchioles with sterile saline. He then sterilized the outside of the containers with ether.

Jack was on his way out when Bingham asked him what he was going to do with the samples.

"Take them up to Agnes," Jack said. "I'd like to know the subtype."

Bingham shrugged and looked across at Calvin.

"Not a bad idea," Calvin said.

Jack did exactly what he said he would. But he was disappointed when he presented the bottles to Agnes up on the third floor.

"We don't have the capability of subtyping it," she said.

"Who does?" Jack asked.

"The city or state reference lab," Agnes said. "Or even over at the university lab. But the best place would be the CDC. They have a whole section devoted to influenza. If it were up to me, I'd send it there."

Jack got some viral transport medium from Agnes and transferred the washings into it. Then he went up to his office. Sitting down, he placed a call to the CDC and was put through to the influenza unit. A pleasant-sounding woman answered, introducing herself as Nicole Marquette.

Jack explained what he wanted, and Nicole was accommodating. She said she'd be happy to see that the influenza was typed and subtyped.

"If I manage to get the sample to you today," Jack said, "how long would it take for you to do the typing?"

"We can't do this overnight," Nicole said, "if that's what you have in mind."

"Why not?" Jack asked impatiently.

"Well, maybe we could," Nicole corrected herself. "If there is a sufficient viral titer in your sample, meaning enough viral particles, I suppose it is possible. Do you know what the titer is?"

"I haven't the faintest idea," Jack said. "But the sample was taken directly from the lung of a patient who passed away from primary influenza pneumonia. The strain is obviously virulent, and I'm worried about a possible epidemic."

"If it is a virulent strain, then the titer might be high," Nicole said.

"I'll find a way to get it to you today," Jack promised. He then gave Nicole his telephone number both at the office and at home. He told her to call anytime she had any information.

"We'll do the best we can," Nicole said. "But I have to warn you, if the titer is too low it might be several weeks before I get back to you."

"Weeks!" Jack complained. "Why?"

"Because we'll have to grow the virus out," Nicole explained. "We usually use ferrets, and it takes a good two weeks for an adequate antibody response which guarantees we'll have a good harvest of virus. But once we have the virus in quantity, we can tell you a lot more than just its subtype. In fact, we can sequence its genome."

"I'll keep my fingers crossed that my samples have a high titer," Jack said. "And one other question. What subtype would you think was the most virulent?"

"Whoa!" Nicole said. "That's a hard question. There are a lot of factors involved, particularly host immunity. I'd have to say the most virulent would be an entirely new pathological strain, or one that hasn't been around for a long time. I suppose the subtype that caused the pandemic of 1918 to 1919 that killed twenty-five million

people worldwide might get the dubious honor of having
been the most virulent."

"What subtype was that?" Jack asked.

"No one knows for sure," Nicole said. "The subtype
doesn't exist. It disappeared years ago, maybe right after
the epidemic wore itself out. Some people think it was
similar to the subtype that caused that swine-flu scare
back in seventy-six."

Jack thanked Nicole and again assured her he'd get
the samples to her that day. After he hung up, he called
Agnes back and asked her opinion on shipping. She told
him the name of the courier service they used, but she
said she didn't know if they shipped interstate.

"Besides," Agnes added, "it will cost a small fortune.
I mean overnight is one thing, but you're talking about
the same day. Bingham will never authorize it."

"I don't care," Jack said. "I'll pay for it myself."

Jack called the courier company. They were delighted
with the request and put Jack through to one of the
supervisors, Tony Liggio. When Jack explained what he
wanted, Tony said no problem.

"Can you come to pick it up now?" Jack asked. He
was encouraged.

"I'll send someone right away," Tony said.

"It will be ready," Jack said.

Jack was about to hang up when he heard Tony add:
"Aren't you interested in the cost? I mean, this is not
like taking something over to Queens. Also, there's the
question of how you plan to pay."

"Credit card," Jack said. "If that's okay."

"Sure, no problem, Doc," Tony said. "It's going to
take me a little while to figure out the exact charge."

"Just give me a ballpark figure," Jack said.

"Somewhere between one and two thousand dollars," Tony said.

Jack winced but didn't complain. Instead, he merely gave Tony his credit card number. He'd envisioned the cost would be two or three hundred dollars, but then he hadn't thought about the fact that someone might have to fly round-trip to Atlanta.

While Jack had been engaged in giving his credit card information, one of the secretaries from the front office had appeared at his door. She'd handed him an overnight Federal Express package and departed without saying a word. As Jack hung up from the courier service he saw that the parcel was from National Biologicals. It was the DNA probes he'd requested the day before.

Taking the probes and his viral samples, Jack went back down to Agnes. He told her about the arrangements he'd made with the courier service.

"I'm impressed," Agnes said. "But I'm not going to ask how much it's costing."

"Don't," Jack advised. "How should I package the samples?"

"We'll take over," she said. She called in the department secretary and commissioned her to do it with appropriate biohazard containers and labels.

"Looks like you have something else for me," she said, eyeing the vials containing the probes.

Jack explained what they were and what he wanted, namely to have the DNA lab use the probes to see if they reacted with the nucleoproteins of the cultures taken from any of the four recent infectious disease cases he'd been working on. What he didn't tell her was why he wanted it done.

"All I need to know is whether it is positive or not," Jack said. "It doesn't have to be quantitative."

"I'll have to handle the rickettsia and the tularemia agents myself," Agnes said. "I'm afraid to have any of the techs working with them."

"I really appreciate all this," Jack said.

"Well, it's what we're here for," Agnes said agreeably.

After leaving the lab Jack went downstairs to the scheduling room and helped himself to some coffee. He'd been so frantic since he'd arrived that he'd not had much time to think. Now, as he stirred his coffee, he realized that neither of the homeless men that he'd inadvertently run into in his flight from Reginald had been brought in. That meant that they were either in some hospital, or they were still out there in the park.

Carrying his coffee back upstairs, Jack sat down at his desk. With both Laurie and Chet in the autopsy room, he knew he could count on some peace and quiet.

Before he could enjoy his solitude, the phone interrupted. It was Terese.

"I'm mad at you," she said without preamble.

"That's wonderful," Jack said with his usual sarcasm. "Now my day is complete."

"I am angry," Terese maintained, but her voice had softened considerably. "Colleen just hung up from talking with Chet. He told her you were beaten up again."

"That was Chet's personal interpretation," Jack said. "The fact is, I wasn't beaten up again."

"You weren't?"

"I explained to Chet that I'd fallen while jogging," Jack said.

"But he told Colleen . . ."

"Terese," Jack said sharply. "I wasn't beaten up. Can we talk about something else?"

"Well, if you weren't assaulted, why are you sounding so irritable?"

"It's been a stressful morning," Jack admitted.

"Care to talk about it?" she asked. "That's what friends are for. I've certainly bent your ear about my problems."

"There's been another infectious death at the General," Jack said. He would have liked to tell her what was really on his mind – his sense of guilt about Beth Holderness – but he dared not.

"That's terrible!" Terese said. "What is wrong with that place? What is it this time?"

"Influenza," Jack said. "A very virulent case. It's the kind of illness I've been truly worried we'd see."

"But the flu is around," Terese said. "It's flu season."

"That's what everybody says," Jack admitted.

"But not you?"

"Put it this way," Jack said. "I'm worried, especially if it is a unique strain. The deceased was a young patient, only twenty-nine. In the face of what else has been popping up over there at the General, I'm worried."

"Are some of your colleagues worried as well?" Terese asked.

"At the moment, I'm on my own," Jack admitted.

"I guess we're lucky to have you," Terese said. "I have to admire your dedication."

"That's kind of you to say," Jack said. "Actually, I hope I'm wrong."

"But you're not going to give up, are you?"

"Not until I have some proof one way or the other,"

Jack said. "But let's talk about you. I hope you are doing better than I."

"I appreciate your asking," Terese said. "Thanks in no small part to you, I think we have the makings of a good ad campaign. Plus, I've managed to have the in-house presentation put off until Thursday, so we have another whole day of breathing room. At the moment things are looking reasonable, but in the advertising world that could change at any moment."

"Well, good luck," Jack said. He wanted to get off the phone.

"Maybe we could have a quick dinner tonight," Terese suggested. "I'd really enjoy it. There's a great little Italian restaurant just up the street on Madison."

"It's possible," Jack said. "I'll just have to see how the day progresses."

"Come on, Jack," Terese complained. "You have to eat. We both could use the relaxation, not to mention the companionship. I can hear the tension in your voice. I'm afraid I'm going to have to insist."

"All right," Jack said, relenting. "But it might have to be a short dinner." He realized there was some truth to what Terese was saying, although at the moment it was hard for him to think as far ahead as dinnertime.

"Fantastic," Terese said happily. "Call me later and we'll decide on the time. If I'm not here, I'll be home. Okay?"

"I'll call you," Jack promised.

After they exchanged good-byes, Jack hung up the phone. For a few minutes he stared at it. He knew that conventional wisdom held that talking about a problem was supposed to relieve anxiety. But at the moment, having talked about the case of influenza with Terese, he only felt more anxious. At least the viral sample was on its way to the CDC and the DNA lab was working with the probe from National Biologicals. Maybe soon he'd start to get some answers.

CHAPTER TWENTY-EIGHT

Phil came through the outer door of the abandoned building the Black Kings had taken over. The door was a piece of three-quarter-inch plywood bolted to an aluminum frame.

Phil passed the front room with the invariable pall of cigarette smoke and interminable card game and rushed directly back to the office. He was relieved to see Twin at the desk.

Phil waited impatiently for Twin to wrap up a payoff from one of their eleven-year-old pushers and send the kid away.

"There's a problem," Phil said.

"There's always a problem," Twin said philosophically. He was recounting the ragged stack of greenbacks the kid had brought in.

"Not like this one," Phil said. "Reginald's been tagged."

Twin looked up from the money with an expression as if he'd just been slapped. "Get out!" he said. "Where'd you hear that shit?"

"It's true," Phil insisted. He took one of the several beat-up straight-backed chairs standing against the wall and turned it around so he could sit on it backward. The

pose provided visual harmony with the backward baseball
cap he always wore.

"Who says?" Twin asked.

"It's all over the street," Phil said. "Emmett heard it
from a pusher up in Times Square. Seems that the doc is
being protected by the Gangsta Hoods from Manhattan
Valley on the Upper West Side."

"You mean one of the Hoods iced Reginald?" Twin
asked in total disbelief.

"That's the story," Phil said. "Shot him through the
head."

Twin slammed his open palm on the desk hard enough
to send the tattered stack of greenbacks wafting off into
the air. He leaped to his feet and paced. He gave the
metal wastebasket a hard kick.

"I can't believe this," he said. "What the hell is this
world coming to? I don't understand it. They'd do a
brother for some white honky doctor. It doesn't make
sense, no way."

"Maybe the doc is doing something for them," Phil
suggested.

"I don't care what the hell he's doing," Twin raged.
He towered over Phil, and Phil cringed. Phil was well
aware that Twin could be ruthless and unpredictable
when he was pissed, and he was royally pissed at the
moment.

Returning to the desk, Twin pounded it again. "I
don't understand this, but there is one thing that I do
know. It can't stand. No way! The Hoods can't go
around knocking off a Black King without a response.
I mean, at a minimum we gotta do the doc like we
agreed."

"Word is that the Hoods have a tail on the doc," Phil said. "They are still protecting him."

"It's unbelievable," Twin said as he retook his seat at the desk. "But it makes things easier. We do the doc and the tail at the same time. But we don't do it in the Hoods' neighborhood. We do it where the doc works."

Twin pulled open the center drawer of his desk and rummaged around. "Where the hell is that sheet about the doc," he said.

"Side drawer," Phil said.

Twin glared at Phil. Phil shrugged. He didn't want to aggravate Twin, but he remembered Twin putting the sheet in the side drawer.

Twin got the sheet out and read it over quickly. "All right," he said. "Go get BJ. He's been itching for action."

Phil disappeared for two minutes. When he reappeared he had BJ with him. BJ lumbered into the office, his pace belying his notorious quickness.

Twin explained the circumstances.

"Think you can handle this?" Twin asked.

"Hey, no problem," BJ said.

"You want a backup?" Twin asked.

"Hell, no," BJ said. "I'll just wait until the two mothers are together, then nail them both."

"You'll have to pick the doc up where he works," Twin said. "We can't risk going up into the Hoods' neighborhood unless we go in force. You understand?"

"No problem," BJ said.

"You got a machine pistol?" Twin asked.

"No," BJ said.

Twin opened the lower drawer of the desk and took

out a Tec like the one he'd given to Reginald. "Don't
lose this," he said. "We only have so many."

"No problem," BJ said. He took the gun and handled
it with reverence, turning it over slowly in his hands.

"Well, what are you waiting for?" Twin asked.

"You finished?" BJ asked.

"Of course I'm finished," Twin said. "What do you
want, me to come along and hold your hand? Get out
of here so you can come back and tell me it's done."

Jack could not concentrate on his other cases no matter
how hard he tried. It was almost noon, and he'd
accomplished a pitifully small amount of paperwork. He
couldn't stop worrying about the influenza case and
wondering what had happened to Beth Holderness.
What could she have found?

Jack threw down his pen in disgust. He wanted desperately to go to the General and visit Cheveau and his lab,
but he knew he couldn't. Cheveau would undoubtedly
call in the marines at a minimum, and Jack would get
himself fired. Jack knew he had to wait for the results
with the probe from National Biologicals to give him
some ammunition before he approached anyone in
authority.

Giving up on his paperwork, Jack impulsively went up
to the DNA lab on the sixth floor. In contrast to most
of the rest of the building, this lab was a state-of-the-art
facility. It had been renovated recently and outfitted with
the latest equipment. Even the white lab coats worn
by the personnel seemed crisper and whiter than in any
of the other labs.

Jack sought out the director, Ted Lynch, who was on his way to lunch.

"Did you get those probes from Agnes?" Jack asked.

"Yup," Ted said. "They're in my office."

"I guess that means there's no results yet," Jack said.

Ted laughed. "What are you talking about?" he questioned. "We haven't even gotten the cultures yet. Besides, I think you might be underestimating what the process is going to be. We don't just throw the probes into a soup of bacteria. We have to isolate the nuclear protein, then run it through the PCR in order to have enough substrate. Otherwise we wouldn't see the fluorescence even if the probe reacted. It's going to take some time."

Sufficiently chastised, Jack returned to his office to stare at the wall behind his desk. Although it was lunchtime, he wasn't hungry in the slightest.

Jack decided to call the city epidemiologist. Jack was interested in the man's reaction to this case of influenza; he thought he could give the epidemiologist a chance to redeem himself.

Jack got the number from the city directory and placed the call. A secretary answered. Jack asked to speak with Dr. Abelard.

"Who should I say is calling?" the secretary asked.

"Dr. Stapleton," Jack said, resisting the temptation to be humorously sarcastic. Knowing Abelard's sensitive ego, Jack would have liked to have said he was the mayor or the Secretary of Health.

Jack twisted a paper clip mindlessly as he waited. When the phone was picked up again, he was surprised it was again the secretary.

"Excuse me," she said. "But Dr. Abelard told me to tell you that he does not wish to speak with you."

"Tell the good doctor that I am in awe of his maturity," Jack said.

Jack slammed the phone down. His first impression had been correct: the man was an ass. Anger now mixed with his anxiety, which made his current inaction that much more difficult to bear. He was like a caged lion. He had to do something. What he wanted to do was go to the General despite Bingham's admonitions. Yet if he went over there whom could he talk with? Jack made a mental checklist of the people he knew at the hospital. Suddenly he thought of Kathy McBane. She'd been both friendly and open, and she was on the Infection Control Committee.

Jack snatched up the phone again and called the Manhattan General. Kathy was not in her office, so he had her paged. She picked up the page from the cafeteria. Jack could hear the usual babble of voices and clink of tableware in the background. He introduced himself and apologized for interrupting her lunch.

"It doesn't matter," Kathy said agreeably. "What can I do for you?"

"Do you remember me?" Jack asked.

"Absolutely," Kathy said. "How could I forget after the reaction you got out of Mr. Kelley and Dr. Zimmerman?"

"They are not the only people I seem to have offended in your hospital," Jack admitted.

"Everybody has been on edge since these infectious cases," Kathy said. "I wouldn't take it personally."

"Listen," Jack said. "I'm concerned about the same cases, and I'd love to come over and talk to you directly.

Would you mind? But it will have to be just between the two of us. Is that too much to ask?"

"No, not at all," Kathy said. "When did you have in mind? I'm afraid I have meetings scheduled for most of the afternoon."

"How about right now?" Jack said. "I'll pass up lunch."

"Now that's dedication," Kathy said. "How can I refuse? My office is in administration on the first floor."

"Uh-oh," Jack voiced. "Is there a chance I'd run into Mr. Kelley?"

"The chances are slim," Kathy said. "There's a group of bigwigs in from AmeriCare, and Mr. Kelley is scheduled to be locked up with them all day."

"I'm on my way," Jack said.

Jack exited from the front entrance on First Avenue. He was vaguely aware of Slam straightening up from where he was leaning against a neighboring building, but Jack was too preoccupied to take much notice. He flagged a cab and climbed in. Behind him he saw Slam following suit.

BJ had not been entirely confident he'd recognize Jack from the visit to the doc's apartment, but the moment Jack appeared at the door of the medical examiner's office, BJ knew it was him.

While he'd been waiting BJ had tried to figure out who was supposedly protecting Jack. For a while a tall muscular dude had loitered on the corner of First Avenue and Thirtieth Street, smoking, and intermittently looking up at the medical examiner building's door. BJ had thought he was the one, but eventually he'd left. So BJ had been surprised when he'd seen Slam stiffen in response to Jack's appearance.

"He's no more than a goddamn kid," BJ had whispered to himself. He was disgusted. He'd expected a more formidable opponent.

No sooner had BJ gotten his hand around the butt of his machine pistol, which he had in a shoulder holster under his hooded sweatshirt, than he saw first Jack and then Slam jump into separate cabs. Letting go of his gun, BJ stepped out into the street and flagged his own taxi.

"Just head north," BJ told the cabdriver. "But push it, man."

The Pakistani cabdriver gave BJ a questioning look, but then did as he was told. BJ kept Slam's cab in sight, aided by the fact that it had a broken taillight.

Jack jumped out of the cab and dashed into the General and across the lobby. The masks had been dispensed with now that the meningococcal scare had passed, so Jack couldn't use one to hide behind. Concerned about being recognized, he wanted to spend the least time possible in the hospital's public places.

He pushed through the doors into the administrative area, hoping that Kathy had been right about Kelley's being occupied. The sounds of the hospital died away as the doors closed behind him. He was in a carpeted hall. Happily, he saw no one he recognized.

Jack approached the first secretary he came upon and asked for Kathy McBane's office. He was directed to the third door on the right. Losing no time, Jack hustled down there and stepped in.

"Hello," Jack called out as he closed the door behind

him. "I hope you don't mind my shutting us in like this. I know it's presumptuous, but as I explained there are a few people I don't want to see."

"If it makes you feel better, by all means," Kathy said. "Come and sit down."

Jack took one of the seats facing the desk. It was a small office with barely enough room for a desk, two facing chairs, and a file cabinet. The walls had a series of diplomas and licenses attesting to Kathy's impressive credentials. The decoration was spartan but comfortable. There were family photos on the desk.

Kathy herself appeared as Jack remembered her: friendly and open. She had a round face with small, delicate features. Her smile came easily.

"I'm very concerned about this recent case of primary influenza pneumonia," Jack said, losing no time. "What's been the reaction of the Infection Control Committee?"

"We've not met yet," Kathy said. "After all, the patient just passed away last night."

"Have you spoken about it with any of the other members?" Jack asked.

"No," Kathy admitted. "Why are you so concerned? We've seen a lot of influenza this season. Frankly, this case hasn't bothered me anywhere near the way the others did, particularly the meningococcus."

"It bothers me because of a pattern," Jack said. "It presented as a fulminant form of a pneumonia just like the other, rarer diseases. The difference is that with influenza the infectivity is higher. It doesn't need a vector. It spreads person to person."

"I understand that," Kathy said. "But as I've pointed out we've been seeing influenza all winter long."

"Primary influenza pneumonia?" Jack questioned.

"Well, no," Kathy admitted.

"This morning I had someone check to see if there were any other similar cases currently in the hospital," Jack said. "There weren't. Do you know if there are now?"

"Not that I am aware of," Kathy said.

"Could you check?" Jack asked.

Kathy turned to her terminal and punched in a query. The answer flashed back in an instant. There were no cases of influenza pneumonia.

"All right," Jack said. "Let's try something else. The patient's name was Kevin Carpenter. Where was his room in the hospital?"

"He was on the orthopedic floor," Kathy said.

"His symptoms started at six p.m.," Jack said. "Let's see if any of the orthopedic nurses on the evening shift are sick."

Kathy hesitated for a moment, then turned back to her computer terminal. It took her several minutes to get the list and the phone numbers.

"You want me to call them now?" Kathy asked. "They're due in for their shift in just a couple of hours."

"If you don't mind," Jack said.

Kathy started making the calls. On her second call, to a Ms. Kim Spensor, she discovered that the woman was ill. In fact, she'd just been preparing to call in sick. She admitted to severe flu symptoms with a temperature of almost 104°.

"Would you mind if I talked with her?" Jack asked.

Kathy asked Kim if she'd be willing to speak to a doctor who was in her office. Kim apparently agreed, because Kathy handed the phone to Jack.

Jack introduced himself, but not as a medical examiner. He commiserated with her about her illness, and then inquired about her symptoms.

"It started abruptly," Kim said. "One minute I was fine; the next minute I had a terrible headache and a shaking chill. Also, my muscles are aching, particularly my lower back. I've had the flu before, but this is the worst I've ever felt."

"Any cough?" Jack asked.

"A little," Kim said. "And it's been getting worse."

"How about substernal pain?" Jack asked. "Behind your breastbone when you breathe in?"

"Yes," Kim said. "Does that mean anything in particular?"

"Did you have much contact with a patient by the name of Carpenter?" Jack asked.

"I did," Kim said. "And so did the LPN, George Haselton. Mr. Carpenter was a demanding patient once he started complaining of headache and chills. You don't think my contact with him could be the cause of my symptoms, do you? I mean, the incubation period for the flu is more than twenty-four hours."

"I'm not an infectious disease specialist," Jack said. "I truly don't know. But I'd recommend you take some rimantadine."

"How is Mr. Carpenter?" Kim asked.

"If you give me the name of your local pharmacy I'll call in a prescription," Jack said, purposefully ignoring Kim's question. Obviously Carpenter's fulminant course started after Kim's shift had departed.

As soon as he could, Jack terminated the conversation. He handed the phone back to Kathy. "I don't like this," Jack said. "It's just what I was afraid of."

"Aren't you being an alarmist?" Kathy questioned. "I'd guess two to three percent of the hospital personnel are out with the flu currently."

"Let's call George Haselton," Jack said.

George Haselton turned out to be even sicker than Kim; he'd already called in sick to the floor supervisor. Jack didn't talk to him. He simply listened to Kathy's side of the conversation.

Kathy hung up slowly. "Now you're starting to get me worried," she admitted.

They called the rest of the evening shift for the orthopedic floor, including the ward secretary. No one else was ill.

"Let's try another department," Jack said. "Someone from the lab must have been in to see Carpenter. How can we check?"

"I'll call Ginny Whalen in personnel," Kathy said, picking up the phone again.

A half hour later they had the full picture. Four people had symptoms of a bad case of the flu. Besides the two nurses, one of the evening microbiology techs had abruptly experienced sore throat, headache, shaking chill, muscle pain, cough, and substernal discomfort. His contact with Kevin Carpenter had occurred about ten o'clock in the evening, when he'd visited the patient to obtain a sputum culture.

The final person from the evening shift who was similarly ill was Gloria Hernandez. To Kathy's surprise but not Jack's, she worked in central supply and had had no contact with Kevin Carpenter.

"She can't be related to the others," Kathy said.

"I wouldn't be too sure," Jack said. He then reminded her that someone from central supply had perished with each of the other recent infectious cases. "I'm surprised this hasn't been a topic of debate with the Infection Control Committee. I know for a fact that both Dr. Zimmerman and Dr. Abelard are aware of the connection, because they have been to central supply to talk to the supervisor, Mrs. Zarelli."

"We haven't had a formal committee meeting since all this started," Kathy said. "We meet on the first Monday of each month."

"Then Dr. Zimmerman is not keeping you informed," Jack said.

"It wouldn't be the first time," Kathy said. "We've never been on the best of terms."

"Speaking of Mrs. Zarelli," Jack said. "She'd promised me printouts of everything central supply had sent to each of the index cases. Could we see if she has them and, if so, have her bring them down?"

Having absorbed some of Jack's anxiety about the influenza, Kathy was eager to help. After talking briefly to Mrs. Zarelli and ascertaining that the printouts were available, Kathy had one of the administrative secretaries run up to get them.

"Let me have Gloria Hernandez's phone number," Jack said. "In fact, give me her address as well. This central supply connection is a mystery that for the life of me, I can't understand. It can't be coincidence and could be key to understanding what is going on."

Kathy got the information from the computer, wrote it down, and handed it to Jack.

"What do you think we should do here at the hospital?" she asked.

Jack sighed. "I don't know," he admitted. "I guess you'll have to discuss that with friendly Dr. Zimmerman.

She's the local expert. In general, quarantine is not very effective for influenza since it spreads so quickly. But if this is some special strain, perhaps it would be worth a try. I think I'd get those hospital personnel who are sick in here and isolate them: worst case, it's an inconvenience; best case, it could help avert a disaster."

"What about rimantadine?" Kathy asked.

"I'm all for it," Jack said. "I'll probably get some myself. It has been used to control some nosocomial influenza in the past. But again that should be up to Dr. Zimmerman."

"I think I'll give her a call," Kathy said.

Jack waited while Kathy spoke to Dr. Zimmerman. Kathy was deferential but firm in explaining the apparent connection between the sick personnel and the deceased, Kevin Carpenter. Once she had spoken, she was reduced to silence punctuated only by repetitions of "yes" at certain intervals.

Eventually, Kathy hung up. She rolled her eyes. "That woman is impossible," she said. "At any rate, she's reluctant to do anything extraordinary, as she puts it, with just one confirmed case. She's afraid Mr. Kelley and the AmeriCare executives would be against it for PR reasons until it was undeniably indicated."

"What about the rimantadine?" Jack asked.

"On that she was a little more receptive," Kathy said. "She said she'd authorize the pharmacy to order in enough for the staff, but she wasn't going to prescribe it just yet. At any rate, I got her attention."

"At least that's something," Jack agreed.

The secretary knocked and came in with the printouts Jack had wanted from central supply. He thanked the woman, and immediately began scanning them. He was impressed; it was rather extraordinary what each patient utilized. The lists were long and included everything short of medications, food, and linen.

"Anything interesting?" Kathy asked.

"Nothing that jumps out at me," Jack admitted. "Except how similar they are. But I realize I should have asked for a control. I should have asked for a similar list from a random patient."

"That shouldn't be hard to get," Kathy said. She called Mrs. Zarelli back and asked her to print one out.

"Want to wait?" Kathy said.

Jack got to his feet. "I think I've overstretched my luck as it is," he said. "If you could get it and have it sent over to the medical examiner's office, I'd be appreciative. As I mentioned, this central supply connection could be important."

"I'd be happy to do it," Kathy said.

Jack went to the door and furtively glanced out into the hall. Turning back to Kathy, he said, "It's hard to get used to acting like a criminal."

"I think we're in your debt for your perseverance," Kathy said. "I apologize for those who have misinterpreted your intentions."

"Thank you," Jack said sincerely.

"Can I ask you a personal question?" Kathy asked.

"How personal?" Jack asked.

"Just about your face," Kathy said. "What happened? Whatever it was, it looks like it must have been painful."

"It looks worse than it is," Jack said. "It's merely a reflection of the rigors of jogging in the park at night."

Jack walked quickly through administration and across the lobby. As he stepped out into the early-spring sunshine, he felt relief. It had been the first time he'd been able to visit the General without stirring up a hornet's nest of protest.

Jack turned right and headed east. On one of his prior visits he'd noticed a chain drugstore two blocks from the hospital. He went directly there. Kathy's suggestion of rimantadine was a good one, and he wanted to get some for himself, especially given his intention of visiting Gloria Hernandez.

Thinking of the Hernandez woman made Jack reach into his pocket to be sure he'd not misplaced her address. He hadn't. Unfolding the paper, he looked at it. She lived on West 144th Street, some forty blocks north of Jack.

Arriving at the drugstore, Jack pulled open the door and entered. It was a large store with a bewildering display of merchandise. Everything, including cosmetics, school supplies, cleaning agents, stationery, greeting cards, and even automotive products, was crammed onto metal shelving. The store had as many aisles as a supermarket.

It took Jack a few minutes to find the pharmacy section, which occupied a few square feet in the back corner of the store. With as little respect as pharmacy was given, Jack felt there was a certain irony they even called the establishment a drugstore.

Jack waited in line to speak to the pharmacist. When he finally did he asked for a prescription blank, which he quickly filled out for rimantadine.

The pharmacist was dressed in an old-fashioned white, collarless pharmacist jacket with the top button undone. He squinted at the prescription and then he told Jack it would take about twenty minutes.

"Twenty minutes!" Jack questioned. "Why so long? I mean, all you have to do is count out the tablets."

"Do you want this or don't you?" the pharmacist asked acidly.

"I want it," Jack muttered. The medical establishment had a way of bullying people; doctors were no longer immune.

Jack turned back to the main part of the store. He had to entertain himself for twenty minutes. With no goal in mind, he wandered down aisle seven and found himself before a staggering variety of condoms.

BJ liked the idea of the drugstore from the moment he saw Jack enter. He knew it would be close quarters, and as an added attraction, there was a subway entrance right out the door. The subway was a great place to disappear.

After a quick glance up and down the street, BJ pulled open the door and stepped inside. He eyed the glass-enclosed manager's office near the entrance, but experience told him it wouldn't be a problem. It might take a short burst from his machine pistol just to keep everybody's head down when he was on his way out, but that would be about it.

BJ advanced beyond the checkout registers and started glancing down the aisles, looking for either Jack or Slam. He knew if he found one, he'd quickly find the other. He hit pay dirt in aisle seven. Jack was at the very end, with Slam loitering less than ten feet away.

As BJ moved quickly down aisle six, he reached under his sweatshirt and let his hand wrap around the butt of his Tec pistol. He snapped off the safety with his thumb. When he arrived at the cross-aisle in the middle of the store, he slowed, stepped laterally, and stopped. Carefully he leaned around a display of Bounty paper towels and glanced down the remainder of aisle seven.

BJ felt his pulse quicken in anticipation. Jack was standing in the same spot, and Slam had moved over next to him. It was perfect.

BJ's heart skipped a beat when he felt a finger tap his shoulder. He swung around. His hand was still under his sweatshirt, holding on to the holstered Tec.

"May I help you?" a bald-headed man asked.

Anger seared through BJ at having been interrupted at precisely the wrong moment. He glared at the jowled clerk and felt like busting him in the chops, but instead he decided to ignore him for the moment. He couldn't pass up the opportunity with Jack and Slam standing nose to nose.

BJ spun back around, and as he did so he drew out the machine pistol. He started forward. He knew a single step would bring the aisle into full view.

The clerk was shocked by BJ's sudden movement, and he didn't see the gun. If he had, he never would have shouted "Hey" the way he did.

Jack felt on edge and jittery. He disliked the store, especially after his run-in with the pharmacist. The background elevator music and the smell of cheap cosmetics added to his discomfort. He didn't want to be there.

As wired as he was, when he heard the clerk yell, his head shot up, and he looked in the direction of the commotion. He was just in time to see a stocky African-American leaping into the center of the aisle brandishing a machine pistol.

Jack's reaction was pure reflex. He threw himself into the condom display. As his body made contact with the shelving an entire unit tipped over with a clatter. Jack found himself in the center of aisle eight on top of a mountain of disarranged merchandise and collapsed shelves.

While Jack leaped forward, Slam hit the floor, extracting his own machine pistol in the process. It was a skillful maneuver, suggesting the poise and expertise of a Green Beret.

BJ was the first to fire. Since he held his pistol in only one hand, the burst of shots went all over the store, ripping divots in the vinyl flooring and poking holes in the tin ceiling. But most of the shots screamed past the area where Jack and Slam had been standing seconds before, and pounded into the vitamin section below the pharmacy counter.

Slam let out a burst as well. Most of his bullets traveled the length of aisle seven, shattering one of the huge plate-glass windows facing the street.

BJ had pulled himself back the moment he'd seen the element of surprise had been lost. Now he stood, crouched over behind the Bounty paper towels, trying to decide what to do next.

Everyone else in the store was screaming, including the clerk who'd tapped BJ on the shoulder. They began rushing to the exits, fleeing for their lives.

Jack scrambled to his feet. He'd heard Slam's burst of gunfire, and now he was hearing another burst from BJ. Jack wanted out of the store.

Keeping his head down, he dashed back into the pharmacy area. There was a door that said "Employees Only," and Jack rushed through. He found himself in a lunchroom. A handful of open soft drinks and half-eaten packaged pastries on the table told him that people had just been there.

Convinced that there was a way out through the back, Jack began opening doors. The first was a bathroom, the second a storeroom.

He heard more sustained gunfire and more screams out in the main part of the store.

Panicked, Jack tried a third door. To his relief it led out into an alley lined with trash cans. In the distance he could see people running. Among those fleeing, he recognized the pharmacist's white coat. Jack took off after them.

CHAPTER TWENTY-NINE

Detective Lieutenant Lou Soldano pulled his unmarked Chevy Caprice into the parking area at the loading bay of the medical examiner's office. He parked behind Dr. Harold Bingham's official car and took the keys out of the ignition. He gave them to the security man in case the car had to be moved. Lou was a frequent visitor to the morgue, although he hadn't been there for over a month.

He got on the elevator and pushed five. He was on his way to Laurie's office. He'd gotten her message earlier but hadn't been able to call until a few minutes ago as he was on his way across the Queensboro Bridge. He'd been over in Queens supervising the investigation on a homicide of a prominent banker.

Laurie had been telling him about one of the medical examiners when Lou had interrupted to tell her he was in the neighborhood and could stop by. She'd immediately agreed, telling him she'd be waiting in her office.

Lou got off the elevator and walked down the hall. It brought back memories. There had been a time when he'd thought that he and Laurie could have had a future together. But it hadn't worked out. Too many differences in their backgrounds, Lou thought.

"Hey, Laur," Lou called out when he caught sight of

her working at her desk. Every time he saw her she looked better to him. Her auburn hair fell over her shoulders in a way that reminded him of shampoo commercials. "Laur" was the nickname his son had given her the first time he'd met her. The name had stuck.

Laurie got up and gave Lou a big hug.

"You're looking great," she said.

Lou shrugged self-consciously. "I'm feeling okay," he said.

"And the children?" Laurie asked.

"Children?" Lou commented. "My daughter is sixteen now going on thirty. She's boy crazy, and it's driving me crazy."

Laurie lifted some journals off the spare chair she and her officemate shared. She gestured for Lou to sit down.

"It's good to see you, Laurie," Lou said.

"It's good to see you too," she agreed. "We shouldn't let so much time go by without getting together."

"So what's this big problem you wanted to talk to me about?" Lou asked. He wanted to steer the conversation away from potentially painful arenas.

"I don't know how big it is," Laurie said. She got up and closed her office door. "One of the new doctors on staff would like to talk to you off the record. I'd mentioned that you and I were friends. Unfortunately, he's not around at the moment. I checked when you said you were coming over. In fact, no one knows where he is."

"Any idea what it's about?" Lou asked.

"Not specifically," Laurie said. "But I'm worried about him."

"Oh?" Lou settled back.

"He asked me to do two autopsies this morning. One

on a twenty-nine-year-old Caucasian woman who'd been a microbiology tech over at the General. She'd been shot in her apartment last night. The second was on a twenty-five-year-old African-American who'd been shot in Central Park. Before I did the cases he suggested that I try to see if the two were in any way related: through hair, fiber, blood . . ."

"And?" Lou asked.

"I found some blood on his jacket which preliminarily matches the woman's," Laurie said. "Now that's just by serology. The DNA is pending. But it's not a common type: B negative."

Lou raised his eyebrows. "Did this medical examiner give any explanation for his suspicion?" he asked.

"He said it was a hunch," Laurie said. "But there's more. I know for a fact that he'd been beaten up recently by some New York gang members – at least once, maybe twice. When he showed up this morning he looked to me like it might have happened again, although he denied it."

"Why was he beaten up?" Lou asked.

"Supposedly as a warning for him not to go to the Manhattan General Hospital," Laurie said.

"Whoa!" Lou said. "What are you talking about?"

"I don't know the details," Laurie said. "But I do know he's been irritating a lot of people over there, and for that matter, over here as well. Dr. Bingham has been ready to fire him on several occasions."

"How's he been irritating everyone?" Lou asked.

"He has it in his mind that a series of infectious diseases that have appeared over at the General have been spread intentionally."

"You mean like by a terrorist or something?" Lou asked.

"I suppose," Laurie said.

"You know this is sounding familiar," Lou said.

Laurie nodded. "I remember how I felt about that series of overdoses five years ago and the fact that no one believed me."

"What do you think of your friend's theory?" Lou said. "By the way, what's his name?"

"Jack Stapleton," Laurie said. "As to his theory, I don't really have all the facts."

"Come on, Laurie," Lou said. "I know you better than that. Tell me your opinion."

"I think he's seeing conspiracy because he wants to see conspiracy," Laurie said. "His officemate told me he has a long-standing grudge against the health care giant AmeriCare, which owns the General."

"But even so, that doesn't explain the gang connection or the fact that he might have knowledge of the woman's murder. What're the names of the homicide victims?"

"Elizabeth Holderness and Reginald Winthrope," Laurie said.

Lou wrote down the names in the small black notebook he carried.

"There wasn't much criminologist work done on either case," Laurie said.

"You of all people know how limited our personnel is," Lou said. "Did they have a preliminary motive for the woman?"

"Robbery," Laurie said.

"Rape?"

"No."

"How about the man?" Lou asked.

"He was a member of a gang," Laurie said. "He was shot in the head at relatively close range."

"Unfortunately, that's all too common," Lou said. "We don't spend a lot of time investigating those. Did the autopsies show anything?"

"Nothing unusual," Laurie said.

"Do you think your friend Dr. Stapleton comprehends how dangerous these gangs can be?" Lou asked. "I have a feeling that he's walking on the edge."

"I don't know much about him," Laurie said. "But he's not a New Yorker. He's from the Midwest."

"Uh-oh," Lou said. "I think I'd better have a talk with him about the realities of city life, and I'd better do it sooner rather than later. He might not be around long."

"Don't say that," Laurie said.

"Is your interest in him more than professional?" Lou asked.

"Now let's not get into that kind of discussion," Laurie said. "But the answer is no."

"Don't get steamed up," Lou said. "I just like to know the lay of the land." He stood up. "Anyway, I'll help the guy, and it sounds like he needs help."

"Thank you, Lou," Laurie said. She got up herself and gave the detective another hug. "I'll have him call you."

"Do that," Lou said.

Leaving Laurie's office, Lou took the elevator down to the first floor. Walking through the communications area, he stopped in to see Sergeant Murphy, who was permanently assigned to the medical examiner's office. After they talked for a while about the prospects of the

Yankees and the Mets in the upcoming baseball season, Lou sat down and put his feet up on the corner of the sergeant's desk.

"Tell me something, Murph," Lou said. "What's your honest take on this new doctor by the name of Jack Stapleton?"

After having fled from the drugstore, Jack had run the length of the alley and then another four blocks before stopping. When he had, he was winded from the exertion. In between breaths he heard the undulating wails of converging police sirens. He assumed the police were on their way to the store. He hoped that Slam had fared as well as he.

Jack walked until both his breathing and his pulse were back to a semblance of normal. He was still shaking. The experience in the store had unnerved him as much as the ordeal in the park, even though the store episode had taken only seconds. The knowledge that once again he'd been stalked in an attempt to kill him was mind numbing.

Additional sirens now competed with the normal clatter of the city, and Jack wondered if he should go back to the scene to talk to the police and perhaps help if anyone had been struck with a bullet. But Warren's admonitions about talking to the police about gang affairs came to mind. After all, Warren had been right about Jack needing his protection. If it had not been for Slam, Jack sensed he would have been killed.

Jack shuddered. There had been a time in the not-too-distant past when he'd not cared particularly if he lived or died. But now, having come close to death twice, he felt differently. He wanted to live, and that desire made him question why the Black Kings wanted him dead. Who was paying them? Did they think Jack knew something that he didn't, or was it just because of his suspicions concerning the outbreaks at the Manhattan General?

Jack had no answer to these questions, but this second attempt on his life made him more confident that his suspicions were correct. Now he had only to prove them.

In the middle of these musings Jack found himself in front of a second drugstore. But in contrast to the first, it was a small, neighborhood concern. Entering, Jack approached the pharmacist who was manning the store by himself. His name tag said simply "Herman."

"Do you carry rimantadine?" Jack asked.

"We did last time I looked," Herman said with a smile. "But it's a prescription item."

"I'm a doctor," Jack said. "I'll need a script."

"Can I see some identification?" Herman asked.

Jack showed him his New York State medical license. "How much do you want?"

"Enough for at least a couple of weeks," Jack said. "Why don't you give me fifty tablets. I might as well err on the plus side."

"You got it," Herman said. He started working behind a counter.

"How long will it take?" Jack asked.

"How long does it take to count to fifty?" Herman replied.

"The last store I was in told me it would take twenty minutes," Jack said.

"It was a chain store, right?" Herman said.

Jack nodded.

"Those chain stores don't care a whit about service," Herman said. "It's a crime. And for all their poor service, they're still forcing us independents out of business. It's got me angrier than hell."

Jack nodded. He knew the feeling well. These days no part of the medical landscape was sacrosanct.

Herman came out from behind his counter carrying a small plastic vial of orange tablets. He plunked it next to the cash register. "Is this for you?" he asked.

Jack nodded again.

Herman rattled off a list of possible side effects as well as contraindications. Jack was impressed. After Jack paid for the drug, he asked Herman for a glass of water. Herman gave him some in a small paper cup. Jack took one of the tablets.

"Come again," Herman said as Jack left the store.

With the rimantadine coursing through his system, Jack decided it was time to visit Gloria Hernandez from central supply.

Stepping out into the street, Jack caught a cab. At first the driver demurred about going up into Harlem, but he agreed after Jack reminded him of the rules posted on the back of the front seat.

Jack sat back as the taxi first headed north and then across town on St. Nicholas Avenue after passing Central Park. He looked out the window as Harlem changed from predominantly African-American neighborhoods to Hispanic ones. Eventually all the signs were in Spanish.

When the cab pulled up to his destination, Jack paid the fare and stepped out into a street alive with people. He looked up at the building he was about to enter. At one time it had been a fine, proud single-family home in the middle of an upscale neighborhood. Now it had seen better days, much like Jack's own tenement.

A few people eyed Jack curiously as he mounted the brownstone steps and entered the foyer. The black-and-white mosaic on the floor was missing tiles.

The names on a broken line of mailboxes indicated that the Hernandez family lived on the third floor. Jack pushed the doorbell for that apartment even though his sense was that it didn't work. Next he tried the inner door. Just as in his own building, the lock on the door had been broken long ago and never repaired.

Having climbed the stairs to the third floor, Jack knocked on the Hernandezes' door. When no one answered he knocked again, only louder. Finally he heard a child's voice ask who was there. Jack called out he was a doctor and wanted to speak with Gloria Hernandez.

After a short, muffled discussion that Jack could hear through the door, the door was pulled open to the limit of a chain lock. Jack saw two faces. Above was a middle-aged woman with disheveled, bleached-blond hair. Her eyes were red and sunken with dark shadows. She was wearing a quilted bathrobe and was coughing intermittently. Her lips had a slight purplish cast.

Below was a cherubic child of nine or ten. Jack wasn't sure if it was a boy or a girl. The child's hair was shoulder length, coal black, and combed straight back from the forehead.

"Mrs. Hernandez?" Jack questioned the blond-haired woman.

After Jack showed his medical examiner's badge and explained he'd just come from Kathy McBane's office at the Manhattan General, Mrs. Hernandez opened the door and invited him inside.

The apartment was stuffy and small, although an attempt had been made to decorate it with bright colors and movie posters in Spanish. Gloria immediately retreated to the couch where she'd apparently been resting when Jack knocked. She drew a blanket up around her neck and shivered.

"I'm sorry you are so sick," Jack said.

"It's terrible," Gloria said. Jack was relieved that she spoke English. His Spanish was rusty at best.

"I don't mean to disturb you," Jack said. "But as you know, lately people from your department have become ill with serious diseases."

Gloria's eyes opened wide. "I just have the flu, don't I?" she asked with alarm.

"I'm sure that's correct," Jack said. "Katherine Mueller, Maria Lopez, Carmen Chavez, and Imogene Philbertson had completely different illnesses than you have, that is certain."

"Thank the Lord," Gloria said. She made the sign of the cross with the index finger of her right hand. "May their souls rest in peace."

"What concerns me," Jack continued, "is that there was a patient by the name of Kevin Carpenter on the orthopedic floor last night who possibly had an illness similar to your own. Does that name mean anything to you? Did you have any contact with him?"

"No," Gloria said. "I work in central supply."

"I'm aware of that," Jack said. "And so did those other unfortunate women I just mentioned. But in each case there had been a patient with the same illness the women caught. There has to be a connection, and I'm hoping you can help me figure out what it is."

Gloria looked confused. She turned to her child, whom she addressed as "Juan." Juan began speaking in rapid Spanish. Jack gathered he was translating for him; Gloria had not quite understood what he'd said.

Gloria nodded and said "si" many times while Juan spoke. But as soon as Juan finished, Gloria looked up at Jack, shook her head, and said: "No!"

"No?" Jack asked. After so many yeses he didn't expect such a definitive no.

"No connection," Gloria said. "We don't see patients."

"You never go to patient floors?" Jack asked.

"No," Gloria said.

Jack's mind raced. He tried to think what else to ask. Finally he said: "Did you do anything out of the ordinary last night?"

Gloria shrugged and again said no.

"Can you remember what you did do?" Jack asked. "Try to give me an idea of your shift."

Gloria started to speak, but the effort brought on a serious bout of coughing. At one point Jack was about to pound her on her back, but she raised her hand to indicate she was all right. Juan got her a glass of water, which she drank thirstily.

Once she could speak, she tried to recall everything she'd done the evening before. As she described her duties, Jack struggled to think if any of her activities put her in contact with Carpenter's virus. But he couldn't. Gloria insisted she had not left central supply for the entire shift.

When Jack could not think of any more questions, he

asked if he could call if something else came to mind. She agreed. Jack then insisted she call Dr. Zimmerman at the General to let her know how sick she was.

"What could she do?" Gloria asked.

"She might want to put you on a particular medication," Jack said. "As well as the rest of your family." He knew that rimantadine not only could prevent flu, but if it was started early enough in an established case, it might reduce the duration and possibly the severity of symptoms by as much as fifty percent. The problem was, it wasn't cheap, and Jack knew that AmeriCare was loath to spend money on patient care it didn't feel it had to.

Jack left the Hernandez apartment and headed toward Broadway where he thought he could catch a cab. Now, on top of being agitated from the attempt on his life, he was also discouraged. The visit to Gloria had accomplished nothing other than to expose him to Gloria's influenza, which he feared might be the strain that so readily killed Kevin Carpenter.

Jack's only consolation was that he'd started his own course of rimantadine. The problem was, he knew rimantadine wasn't one hundred percent effective in preventing infection, particularly with a virulent strain.

It was late afternoon by the time Jack was dropped off at the medical examiner's office. Feeling stressed and despondent, he entered and allowed himself to be buzzed in. As he passed the ID area, he did a double take. In one of the small rooms set aside for families identifying their dead, Jack saw David. He didn't know David's last name, but it was the same David who had driven Jack and Spit back to the neighborhood after the episode in the park.

David also caught sight of Jack, and for the second their eyes made contact, Jack sensed anger and contempt.

Resisting the impulse to approach, Jack immediately descended to the morgue level. With his heels echoing loudly on the cement floor he walked around the refrigerated compartments, fearful of what he was going to find. There in the hall was a single gurney bearing a newly dead body. It was directly beneath the harsh glare of a hooded overhead light.

The sheets had been arranged so that only the face could be seen. It had been so posed for a Polaroid picture to be taken. Such a picture was the current method for families to identify their dead. Photographs were considered more humane than having the bereaved families view the often mutilated remains.

A lump formed in Jack's throat as he looked down on Slam's placid face. His eyes were closed; he truly appeared to be asleep. In death he looked even younger than he had in life. Jack would have guessed around fourteen.

Depressed beyond words, Jack took the elevator up to his office. He was thankful that Chet was not in. He slammed his door, sat down at his desk, and held his head in his hands. He felt like crying, but no tears came. He knew indirectly he was responsible for yet another individual's death.

Before he'd had a chance to wallow in guilt, there was a knock on his door. At first Jack ignored it, hoping whoever it was would go away. But then the would-be visitor knocked again. Finally he called out irritably for whoever it was to come in.

Laurie opened the door hesitantly. "I don't mean to be a bother," she said. She could sense Jack's agitation immediately. His eyes were fierce, like the needle ends of darts.

"What do you want?" Jack asked.

"Just to let you know that I spoke with Detective Lou Soldano," Laurie said. "As you asked me to do." She took several steps into the room and placed Lou's phone number on the edge of Jack's desk. "He's expecting your call."

"Thanks, Laurie," Jack said. "But I don't think at the moment I am in the mood to talk to anyone."

"I think he could help," Laurie said. "In fact—"

"Laurie!" Jack called out sharply to interrupt her. Then, in a softer tone, he said: "Please, just leave me alone."

"Sure," Laurie said soothingly. She backed out and closed the door behind her. For a second she stared at the door. Her concerns skyrocketed. She'd never seen Jack this way. It was a far cry from his normally flippant demeanor and reckless, seemingly carefree ways.

Hurrying back to her own office, Laurie closed her door and called Lou immediately.

"Dr. Stapleton just came in a few minutes ago," she said.

"Fine," Lou said. "Have him give me a call. I'll be here for at least another hour."

"I'm afraid he's not going to call," Laurie said. "He's acting worse now than he was this morning. Something has happened. I'm sure of it."

"Why won't he call?" Lou said.

"I don't know," Laurie said. "He won't even talk to me. And as we speak there is another apparent gang murder down in the morgue. The shooting took place in the vicinity of the Manhattan General."

"You think it involved him in some way?" Lou asked.

"I don't know what to think," Laurie admitted. "I'm just worried. I'm afraid something terrible is about to happen."

"All right, calm down," Lou advised. "Leave it up to me. I'll think of something."

"Promise?" Laurie asked.

"Have I ever let you down?" Lou questioned.

Jack rubbed his eyes forcibly, then blinked them open. He glanced around at the profusion of unfinished autopsy cases that littered his desk. He knew there was no chance he'd be able to concentrate enough to work on them.

Then his eyes focused on two unfamiliar envelopes. One was a large manila envelope, the other was business size. Jack opened the manila one first. It contained the copy of a hospital chart. There was also a note from Bart Arnold saying that he'd taken it upon himself to get a copy of Kevin Carpenter's chart to add to the others Jack had requested.

Jack was pleased and impressed. Such initiative was commendable and spoke well for the entire PA investigative team. Jack opened the chart and glanced through it. Kevin had been admitted for an ACL repair of the right knee, which had gone smoothly Monday morning.

Jack stopped reading and thought about the fact that Kevin had been immediately postoperative when he'd come down with his symptoms. Putting Kevin's chart aside, he picked up Susanne Hard's and confirmed that she, too, had been immediately post-op, having had a cesarean section. Looking at Pacini's, he confirmed the same.

Jack wondered if having had surgery had anything to do with their having contracted their respective illnesses. It didn't seem probable, since neither Nodelman nor Lagenthorpe had undergone surgery. Even so, Jack thought he'd keep the operative connection in mind.

Going back to Kevin's chart, Jack learned that the flu symptoms started abruptly at six p.m. and progressed steadily and relentlessly until a little after nine. At that time they were considered worrisome enough to warrant transferring the patient to the intensive-care unit. In the unit he developed the respiratory distress syndrome that ultimately led to his death.

Jack closed the chart and put it on the stack with the others. Opening the smaller envelope – addressed simply to "Dr. Stapleton" – Jack found a computer printout and a Post-it note from Kathy McBane. The note simply thanked him again for his attention to the affairs of the General. In a short postscript Kathy added that she hoped the enclosed printout would help him.

Jack opened the printout. It was a copy of everything that had been sent from central supply to a patient by the name of Broderick Humphrey. The man's diagnosis wasn't mentioned, but his age was: forty-eight.

The list was just as long as the lists he had for the infectious disease index cases. Like the other lists, it appeared to be random. It was not in alphabetical order, nor were similar products or equipment lumped together. Jack guessed the list was generated in the sequence the items were ordered. That idea was bolstered by the fact that all five lists started out identically, presumably because as each patient was admitted, he required standard, routine equipment.

The random nature of the lists made them hard to

compare. Jack's interest was finding any ways that the control list differed from the others. After spending fifteen wasted minutes going back and forth among the lists, Jack decided to use the computer.

The first thing he did was create separate files for each patient. Into each file he copied each list. Since he was hardly the world's best typist, this activity took him a considerable amount of time.

Several hours drifted by. In the middle of the transcription process Laurie again knocked on his door to say good night and see if she could do anything for him. Jack was preoccupied, but he assured her that he was fine.

When all the data were entered, Jack asked the computer to list the ways the infectious cases differed from the control case. What he got was disheartening: another long list! Looking at it, he realized the problem. In contrast to the control case, all five infectious cases had had sojourns in the intensive-care unit. In addition, all five infectious cases had died and the control hadn't.

For a few minutes Jack thought that his painstaking efforts had been for naught, but then he got another idea. Since he'd typed the lists into the computer in the same order they'd been in originally, he asked the computer to make the comparison prior to the first product used in the ICU.

As soon as Jack pushed his execute button the computer flashed its answer. The word "humidifier" appeared on the screen. Jack stared. Apparently the infectious cases had all used humidifiers from central supply; the control hadn't. But was it a significant difference? From Jack's childhood, he remembered his mother had put a humidifier in his room when he'd had the croup. He remembered the device as a small, boiling cauldron that sputtered and steamed at his bedside. So Jack could not imagine a humidifier having anything to do with spreading bacteria. At 212° Fahrenheit, it would boil bacteria.

But then Jack remembered the newer type of humidifier: the ultrasonic, cold humidifier. That, he realized, could be a totally different story.

Jack snatched up his phone and called the General. He asked to be put through to central supply. Mrs. Zarelli was off, so he asked to speak to the evening supervisor. Her name was Darlene Springborn. Jack explained who he was and then asked if central supply at the General handled the humidifiers.

"Certainly do," Darlene said. "Especially during the winter months."

"What kind does the hospital use?" Jack asked. "The steam type or the cold type?"

"The cold type almost exclusively," Darlene said.

"When a humidifier comes back from a patient room what happens to it?" Jack asked.

"We take care of it," Darlene said.

"Do you clean it?" Jack asked.

"Certainly," Darlene said. "Plus we run them for a while to be sure they still function normally. Then we empty them and scrub them out. Why?"

"Are they always cleaned in the same location?" Jack asked.

"They are," Darlene said. "We keep them in a small storeroom that has its own sink. Has there been a problem with the humidifiers?"

"I'm not sure," Jack said. "But if so, I'll let you or Mrs. Zarelli know."

"I'd appreciate it," Darlene said.

Jack disconnected but kept the phone in the crook of his shoulder while he got out Gloria Hernandez's phone number. He punched in the digits and waited. A man answered who could speak only Spanish. After Jack struggled with a few broken phrases, the man told Jack to wait.

A younger voice came on the line. Jack assumed it was Juan. He asked the boy if he could speak to his mother.

"She's very sick," Juan said. "She's coughing a lot and having trouble breathing."

"Did she call the hospital like I urged?" Jack asked.

"No, she didn't," Juan said. "She said she didn't want to bother anybody."

"I'm going to call an ambulance to come and get her," Jack said without hesitation. "You tell her to hold on, okay?"

"Okay," Juan said.

"Meanwhile, could you ask her one question," Jack said. "Could you ask her if she cleaned any humidifiers last night? You know what humidifiers are, don't you?"

"Yeah, I know," Juan said. "Just a minute."

Jack waited nervously, tapping his fingers on top of Kevin Carpenter's chart. To add to his guilt, he thought he should have followed up on his suggestion for Gloria to call Zimmerman. Juan came back on the line.

"She says thank you about the ambulance," Juan said. "She was afraid to call herself because AmeriCare doesn't pay unless a doctor says okay."

"What about the humidifiers?" Jack asked.

"Yeah, she said she cleaned two or three. She couldn't remember exactly."

After Jack hung up from talking to the Hernandez boy he called 911 and dispatched an ambulance to the Hernandez residence. He told the dispatcher to inform the EMTs that it was an infectious case and that they should at least wear masks. He also told her that the patient should go to the Manhattan General and no place else.

With growing excitement, Jack placed a call to Kathy McBane. As late as it was, he didn't expect to get her, but he was pleasantly surprised. She was still in her office. When Jack commented on the fact that she was still there after six, she said she'd probably be there for some time.

"What's going on?" Jack asked.

"Plenty," Kathy said. "Kim Spensor has been admitted into the intensive care unit with respiratory distress syndrome. George Haselton is also in the hospital and is worsening. I'm afraid your fears were well grounded."

Jack quickly added that Gloria Hernandez would be coming to the emergency room soon. He also recommended that the contacts of all these patients be immediately started on rimantadine.

"I don't know if Dr. Zimmerman will go for the rimantadine for contacts," Kathy said. "But at least I've talked her into isolating these patients. We've set up a special ward."

"That might help," Jack said. "It's certainly worth a try. What about the microbiology tech?"

"He's on his way in at the moment," Kathy said.

"I hope by ambulance rather than public transportation," Jack said.

"That was my recommendation," Kathy said. "But Dr. Zimmerman followed up on it. I honestly don't know what the final decision was."

"That printout you sent over was helpful," Jack said, finally getting around to why he'd called. "Remember when you told me about the General's nebulizers getting contaminated in the intensive-care unit three months ago? I think there might have been a similar problem with the hospital's humidifiers."

Jack told Kathy how he'd come to this conclusion, particularly about Gloria Hernandez having admitted to handling humidifiers the previous evening.

"What should I do?" Kathy said with alarm.

"At the moment I don't want you to do anything," Jack said.

"But I should at least take the humidifiers out of service until their safety is assured," Kathy said.

"The problem is I don't want you to become involved," Jack said. "I'm afraid doing something like that might be dangerous."

"What are you talking about?" Kathy demanded angrily. "I am already involved."

"Don't get upset," Jack said soothingly. "I apologize. I'm afraid I'm handling this badly." Jack had not wanted to draw anyone else into the web of his suspicions for fear of their safety, yet at the moment he didn't seem to have any choice. Kathy was right: the humidifiers had to be taken out of service.

"Listen, Kathy," Jack said. Then, as succinctly as possible, he explained his theory about the recent illnesses being intentionally spread. He also told her there was a possibility Beth Holderness had been killed because he'd asked her to search the microbiology lab for the offending agents.

"That's a rather extraordinary story," Kathy said haltingly. Then she added: "It's a little hard to swallow all at once."

"I'm not asking you necessarily to subscribe to it,"

Jack said. "My only interest in telling you now is for your safety. Whatever you do or say to anyone, please keep what I have told you in mind. And for God's sake, don't mention my theory to anyone. Even if I'm right, I have no idea who's behind it."

"Well," Kathy said with a sigh. "I don't know what to say."

"You don't have to say anything," Jack said. "But if you want to help, there is something you could do."

"Like what?" Kathy asked warily.

"Get some bacterial culture medium and viral transport medium from the microbiology lab," Jack said. "But don't tell anyone why you want them. Then get someone from engineering to open the elbow drain below the sink in the storeroom where the humidifiers are kept. Put aliquots from the trap into the two mediums and take them to the city reference lab. Ask them to see if they can isolate any one of the five agents."

"You think some of the microorganisms would still be there?" Kathy asked.

"It's a possibility," Jack said. "It's a long shot, but I'm trying to find proof whatever way I can. At any rate, what I'm suggesting you do is not going to hurt anyone except possibly yourself if you are not careful."

"I'll think about it," Kathy said.

"I'd do it myself except for the reception I invariably get over there," Jack said. "I was able to get away with visiting your office, but trying to get bacterial samples out of a trap in central supply is another thing entirely."

"I'd have to agree with you there," Kathy said.

After he hung up, Jack wondered about Kathy's reaction to his revelations. From the moment he'd voiced his suspicions she'd sounded subdued, almost wary. Jack shrugged. At the moment there wasn't anything else he could say to convince her. All he could do was hope she'd heed his warnings.

Jack had one more call to make, and as he dialed the long-distance number he superstitiously crossed the middle and index fingers of his left hand. He was calling Nicole Marquette at the CDC, and Jack was hoping for two things. First, he wanted to hear that the sample had arrived. Second, he wanted Nicole to say that the titer was high, meaning there were enough viral particles to test without having to wait to grow it out.

As the call went through Jack glanced at his watch. It was nearing seven p.m. He scolded himself for not having called earlier, thinking he'd have to wait until morning to reach Nicole. But after dialing the extension for the influenza unit, he got Nicole immediately.

"It arrived here fine," Nicole said in response to his query. "And I have to give you credit for packing it so well. The refrigerant pack and the Styrofoam kept the sample well preserved."

"What about the titer?" Jack asked.

"I was impressed with that too," Nicole said. "Where was this sample from?"

"Bronchiole washings," Jack said.

Nicole gave a short whistle. "With this concentration of virus it's got to be one hell of a virulent strain. Either that, or a compromised host."

"It's a virulent strain all right," Jack said. "The victim was a young healthy male. Besides that, one of the nurses taking care of him is already in the ICU herself in acute respiratory distress. That's in less than twenty-four hours after exposure."

"Wow! I'd better do this typing immediately. In fact,

I'll stay here tonight. Are there any more cases besides the nurse?"

"Three others that I know about," Jack said.

"I'll call in the morning," Nicole said. Then she hung up.

Jack was mildly taken aback by the precipitous end to the conversation, but he was pleased that Nicole was as motivated as she'd apparently become.

Jack replaced the phone receiver, and as he did so, he noticed the tremble of his hand. He took a few deep breaths and tried to decide what to do. He was concerned about going home. He had no way of gauging Warren's reaction to Slam's death. He also wondered if yet another assassin would be sent after him.

The unexpected ring of the telephone interrupted his thoughts. He reached for the phone but didn't pick it up while he tried to think who it could be. As late as it was, he had to shake off some irrational thoughts, like the worry it might be the man who'd tried to kill him that afternoon.

Finally, Jack picked up the phone. To his relief, it was Terese.

"You promised you would call," she said accusingly. "I hope you're not going to tell me you forgot."

"I've been on the phone," Jack said. "In fact, I just this second got off."

"Well, all right," Terese said. "But I've been ready to eat for an hour. Why don't you come to the restaurant directly from work?"

"Oh, jeez, Terese," Jack voiced. With everything that had happened he'd totally forgotten about their dinner plans.

"Don't tell me you are going to try to cop out," Terese said.

"I've had a wicked day," Jack said.

"So have I," Terese countered. "You promised, and as I said this morning, you have to eat. Tell me, did you have lunch?"

"No," Jack said.

"Well, there you go," Terese said. "You can't skip dinner as well as lunch. Come on! I'll understand if you have to go back to work. I might myself."

Terese was making a lot of sense. He needed to eat something even if he wasn't hungry, and he needed to relax. Besides, knowing Terese's persistence he didn't expect she'd take no for an answer, and Jack did not have the energy for an argument.

"Are you thinking or what?" Terese asked impatiently. "Jack, please! I've been looking forward to seeing you all day. We can compare war stories and have a vote whose day was the worst."

Jack was weakening. Suddenly having dinner with Terese sounded wonderfully appealing. He was concerned about putting her at risk simply through proximity, but he doubted anyone was trailing him now. If they were, he could certainly shake them on the way to the restaurant.

"What's the name of the restaurant?" Jack asked finally.

"Thank you," Terese said. "I knew you'd come through. It's called Positano. It's just up the street from me on Madison. You'll love it. It's small and very relaxing. Very un-New-Yorkish."

"I'll meet you there in a half hour," Jack said.

"Perfect," Terese said. "I'm really looking forward to this. It's been a stressful few days."

"I can attest to that," Jack said.

Jack locked up his office and went down to the first floor. He did not know how to ensure that no one followed him, but he thought that he should at least glance out the front to see if anyone suspicious was lurking there. As he passed through communications he noticed that Sergeant Murphy was still in his cubbyhole talking with someone Jack didn't recognize.

Jack and the sergeant exchanged waves. Jack wondered if there had been an unusual number of unidentified dead over the last several days. Murphy usually left at five like clockwork.

Reaching the front door, Jack scanned the area outside. He immediately recognized the futility of what he was doing. Particularly with the homeless facility next door in the old Bellevue Hospital building, there were any number of people loitering who could have qualified as suspicious.

For a few moments Jack watched the activity on First Avenue. Rush hour was still in full swing with bumper-to-bumper traffic heading north. The buses were all filled to overflowing. All the cabs were occupied.

Jack debated what to do. The idea of standing in the street, trying to catch a taxi, had no appeal whatsoever. He'd be too exposed. Someone might even attack him right there, especially if they had been willing to try to shoot him in a drugstore.

A passing delivery van gave Jack an idea. Turning back into the building, he descended to the morgue floor and walked into the mortuary office. Marvin Fletcher, one of the evening mortuary techs, was having coffee and doughnuts.

"Marvin, I have a favor to ask," Jack said.

"What's that?" Marvin asked, washing down a mouthful with a gulp of his coffee.

"I don't want you to tell anyone about this," Jack said. "It's personal."

"Yeah?" Marvin questioned. His eyes opened wider than usual. He was interested.

"I need a ride up to New York Hospital," Jack said. "Could you take me in one of the mortuary vans?"

"I'm not supposed to drive—" Marvin began.

"There's a good reason," Jack said, interrupting Marvin. "I'm trying to duck a girlfriend, and I'm afraid she's outside. I'm sure a good-looking guy like you has had similar problems."

Marvin laughed. "I suppose," he said.

"It will only take a second," Jack said. "We shoot up First and cut over to York. You'll be back here in a flash, and here's a ten-spot for your trouble." Jack laid a ten-dollar bill on the desk.

Marvin eyed the bill and looked up at Jack. "When do you want to go?"

"Right now," Jack said.

Jack climbed into the passenger-side door of the van and then stepped back into the van's cargo area. He held on to whatever handhold he could find while Marvin backed out onto Thirtieth Street. As they waited for the light at the corner of First Avenue, Jack made sure he stayed well out of sight.

Despite the traffic they made good time to New York Hospital. Marvin dropped Jack off at the busy front entrance, and Jack immediately went inside. Within the lobby he stood off to the side for five minutes. When no one even vaguely suspicious entered, Jack headed for the emergency room.

Having been in the hospital on multiple occasions, Jack had no trouble finding his way. Once in the emergency room he stepped out on the receiving dock and waited for a cab to bring in a patient. He didn't have to wait long.

As soon as the patient got out of the cab, Jack got in. He told the cab-driver to take him to the Third Avenue entrance of Bloomingdale's.

Bloomingdale's was as crowded as Jack assumed it would be. Jack rapidly traversed the store's main floor, emerging on Lexington where he caught a second cab. He had this taxi drop him off a block away from Positano.

To be a hundred percent certain he was safe, Jack stood within the entrance of a shoe store for another five minutes. The vehicular traffic on Madison Avenue was moderate, as was the number of pedestrians. In contrast to the area around the morgue, everyone was dressed nattily. Jack saw no one he would have thought was a gang member.

Feeling confident and patting himself on the back for his ingenuity, Jack set out for the restaurant. What he didn't know was that two men sat waiting inside a shiny black Cadillac that had recently parked between the shoe store and Positano. As Jack walked past he couldn't see inside because the windows were tinted dark enough to make them appear like mirrors.

Jack opened the door to the restaurant and entered a canvas tent of sorts designed to keep the winter chill away from the people seated near the entrance.

Pulling a canvas flap aside, Jack found himself in a
warm, comfortable environment. To his left was a small
mahogany bar. The dining tables were grouped to the
right and they extended back into the depths of the restaurant. The walls and ceiling were covered with white
lattice into which was woven silk ivy that looked astonish-
ingly real. It was as if Jack had suddenly walked into a
garden restaurant in Italy.

From the savory aroma that informed the place, Jack
could tell that the chef had the same respect for garlic
that he had. Earlier Jack had felt he wasn't hungry. Now
he was famished.

The restaurant was crowded but without the frenzied
atmosphere of many New York restaurants. With the
lattice on the ceiling the sounds of the patrons' conversations and the clink of the china were muted. Jack
assumed that the peacefulness of the place was what
Terese had meant when she said it was un-New-Yorkish.

The maître d' greeted Jack and asked if he could be
of assistance. Jack said he was to meet a Ms Hagen. The
waiter bowed and gestured for Jack to follow him. He
showed Jack to a table against the wall just beyond the
bar.

Terese rose to give Jack a hug. When she saw his face,
she paused.

"Oh, my!" she said. "Your face looks painful."

"People have been saying that my whole life," Jack
quipped.

"Jack, please," Terese said. "Don't joke. I'm being
serious. Are you really okay?"

"To tell you the honest truth," Jack said, "I'd totally
forgotten about my face."

"It looks like it would be so tender," Terese said. "I'd like to give you a kiss, but I'm afraid."

"Nothing wrong with my lips," Jack said.

Terese shook her head, smiled, and waved her hand at him. "You are too much," she said. "I considered myself adept at repartee until I met you."

They sat down.

"What do you think of the restaurant?" Terese asked as she repositioned her napkin and moved her work aside.

"I liked it immediately," Jack said. "It's cozy, and you can't say that about too many restaurants in this city. I never would have known it was here. The sign outside is so subtle."

"It's one of my favorite places," Terese said.

"Thanks for insisting I come out," Jack said. "I hate to admit you were right, but you were. I'm starved."

Over the next fifteen minutes they studied their respective menus, listened to a remarkably long list of special entrées from their waiter, and placed their orders.

"How about some wine?" Terese asked.

"Why not," Jack said.

"Do you want to pick?" Terese asked, extending the wine list in his direction.

"I have a suspicion that you'll know better than I what to order," Jack said.

"Red or white?" Terese asked.

"I can go either way," Jack said.

With the wine opened and two glasses poured, both Terese and Jack leaned back and tried to relax. Both were tense. In fact, Jack wondered if Terese wasn't more tense than he. He caught her furtively glancing at her watch.

"I saw that," Jack said.

"Saw what?" Terese asked innocently.

"I saw you looking at your watch," Jack said. "I thought we were supposed to be relaxing. That's why I've been purposefully avoiding asking about your day or telling you about mine."

"I'm sorry," Terese said. "You're right. I shouldn't be doing it. It's just reflex. I know Colleen and the crew are still in the studio working, and I suppose I feel guilty being out here enjoying myself."

"Should I ask how the campaign is going?" Jack asked.

"It's going fine," Terese said. "In fact, I got nervous today and called my contact over at National Health and had lunch with her. When I told her about the new campaign she was so excited she begged me to allow her to leak it to her CEO. She called back this afternoon to say that he liked it so much that he's thinking of upping the advertising budget by another twenty percent."

Jack made a mental calculation of what a twenty percent increase meant. It was millions, and it made him ill since he knew the money would essentially be coming from patient-care funds. But not wishing to spoil their evening, he did not let Terese know his thoughts. Instead, he congratulated her.

"Thank you," she said.

"It hardly sounds like you had a bad day," Jack commented.

"Well, hearing that the client likes the concept is just the beginning," Terese said. "Now there is the reality of actually putting the presentation together and then actually doing the campaign itself. You have no idea of the problems that arise making a thirty-second TV spot."

Terese took a sip of her wine. As she set her glass back on the table she again glanced at her watch.

"Terese!" Jack said with mock anger. "You did it again!"

"You're right!" Terese said, slapping a hand to her forehead. "What am I going to do with myself. I'm an impossible workaholic. I admit it. But wait! I do know what I can do. I can take the damn thing off!" She unbuckled her wristwatch and slipped it into her purse. "How's that?" she asked.

"Much better," Jack said.

"The trouble is this dude is probably thinking he's some kind of superman or something," Twin said. "He's probably saying those brothers don't know what the hell they are doing. I mean, it's all pissing me off. You know what I'm saying?"

"So why don't you do this yourself?" Phil asked. "Why me?" Dots of perspiration stood out like cabochon diamonds along his hairline.

Twin was draped over the steering wheel of his Cadillac. Slowly he turned his head to regard his heir apparent in the half-light of the car's interior. Headlights of the passing vehicles alternately illuminated Phil's face.

"Be cool," Twin warned. "You know I can't walk in there. The doc would recognize me right off and the game would be over. The element of surprise is important."

"But I was there in the doc's apartment too," Phil complained.

"But the mother wasn't looking you in the eye," Twin

said. "Nor did you tag him with a sucker punch. He won't remember you. Trust me."

"But why me," Phil whined. "BJ wanted to do it, especially after things got screwed up in the drugstore. He wants another chance."

"After the drugstore the doc might recognize BJ," Twin said. "Besides, it's an opportunity for you. Some of the brothers have been complaining that you've never done anything like this and that you shouldn't be next in line in the gang. Trust me, I know what I'm doing."

"But I'm not good at this stuff," Phil complained. "I've never shot anyone."

"Hey, it's easy," Twin said. "First time maybe you wonder, but it's easy. Pop! It's over. In a way it's kinda a letdown, because you get yourself all keyed up."

"I'm keyed up, all right," Phil admitted.

"Relax, kid," Twin said. "All you have to do is walk in there and not say a word to anyone. Keep the gun in your pocket and don't take it out until you are standing right in front of the doc. Then draw it out and pop! Then get your black ass outta there and away we go. It's that easy."

"What if the doc runs?" Phil asked.

"He won't run," Twin said. "He'll be so surprised he won't lift a finger. If a dude thinks he might be knocked off he has a chance, but if it comes out of the blue like a sucker punch, there's no way. Nobody moves. I've seen it done ten times."

"I'm nervous, though," Phil admitted.

"Okay, so you're a little nervous," Twin said. "Let me look at you." Twin reached over and pushed Phil's shoulder back. "How's your tie?"

Phil reached up and felt the knot in his tie. "I think it's okay," he said.

"You look great," Twin said. "Looks like you're on your way to church, man. You look like a damn banker or lawyer." Twin laughed and slapped Phil repeatedly on the back.

Phil winced as he absorbed the blows. He hated this. It was the worst thing he'd ever done, and he wondered if it was worth it. Yet at this point he knew he didn't have much choice. It was like going on the roller coaster and clanking up that first hill.

"Okay, man, it's time to blow the mother away," Twin said. He gave Phil a final pat, then reached in front of him to open the passenger-side door.

Phil got out onto rubbery legs.

"Phil," Twin called.

Phil bent down and looked into the car.

"Remember," Twin said. "Thirty seconds from the time you go in the door, I'll be pulling up to the restaurant. You get out of there fast and into the car. Got it?"

"I guess so," Phil said.

Phil straightened up and began walking toward the restaurant. He could feel the pistol bumping up against his thigh. He had it in his right hip pocket.

When Jack had first met Terese he'd had the impression that she was so goal oriented, she'd be incapable of small talk. But he had to admit he'd been wrong. When he'd started to tease her unmercifully about her inability to leave her work behind, she'd not only borne the brunt of the gibes with equanimity but had been able to dish

out as good as he gave. By their second glasses of wine
they had each other laughing heartily.

"I certainly didn't think I'd be laughing like this earlier
today," Jack said.

"I'll take that as a compliment," Terese said.

"And indeed you should," Jack said.

"Excuse me," Terese said as she folded her napkin. "I
imagine our entrées will be out momentarily. If you
don't mind, I'd like to use the ladies' room before they
get here."

"By all means," Jack said. He grasped the edge of the
table and pulled it toward him to give Terese more room
to get out. There was not much space between tables.

"I'll be right back," Terese said. She gave Jack's
shoulder a squeeze. "Don't go away," she teased.

Jack watched her approach the maître d', who listened
to her and then pointed toward the rear of the restaurant.
Jack continued to watch her as she gracefully weaved her
way down the length of the room. As usual, she was
wearing a simple, tailored suit that limned her slim, ath-
letic body. It wasn't hard for Jack to imagine that she
approached physical exercise with the same dogged
determination she devoted to her career.

When Terese disappeared from view Jack turned his
attention back to the table. He picked up his wine and
took a sip. Someplace he'd read that red wine was capable
of killing viruses. That thought made him think of something he hadn't considered but perhaps should have.
He'd been exposed to influenza, and while he felt confident given the measures he was taking regarding his
health, he certainly didn't want to expose anyone else to
it, particularly not Terese.

Thinking about the possibility, Jack reasoned that

since he didn't have any symptoms, he could not be manufacturing virus. Therefore, he could not be infective. At least he hoped that to be the case. Thinking of influenza reminded him of his rimantadine. Reaching into his pocket, he took out the plastic vial, extracted one of the orange tablets, and took it with a swallow of water.

After putting the drug away, Jack let his eyes roam around the restaurant. He was impressed that every table was occupied, yet the waiters seemed to maintain a leisurely pace. Jack attributed it to good planning and training.

Looking to the right, Jack saw that there were a few couples and single men having drinks at the bar, possibly waiting for tables. Just then, he noticed that the canvas curtain at the entrance was thrown aside as a smartly dressed, young, African-American man stepped into the restaurant.

Jack wasn't sure why the individual caught his attention. At first he thought it might have been because the man was tall and thin; he reminded Jack of several of the men he played ball with. But whatever the reason was, Jack continued to watch the man as he hesitated at the door, then began to walk down the central aisle, apparently searching for friends.

The gait wasn't the high-stepping, springy, jaunty playground walk. It was more of a shuffle, as if the man were carrying a load on his back. His right hand was thrust into his trouser pocket while his left hung down stiffly at his side. Jack couldn't help but notice the left arm didn't swing. It was as if it were a prosthesis instead of a real arm.

Captivated by the individual, Jack watched as the

man's head swung from side to side. The man had advanced twenty feet when the maître d' intercepted him, and they had a conversation.

The conversation was short. The maître d' bowed and gestured into the restaurant. The man started forward once again, continuing his search.

Jack lifted his wineglass to his lips and took a sip. As he did so the man's eyes locked onto his. To Jack's surprise the man headed directly for him. Jack slowly put his wineglass down. The man came up to the table.

As if in a dream Jack saw the man start to raise his right hand. In it was a gun. Before Jack could even take a breath the barrel was aimed straight at him.

Within the confines of the narrow restaurant the sound of a pistol seemed deafening. By reflex Jack's hands had grasped the tablecloth and pulled it toward him as if he could hide behind it. In the process he knocked the wineglass and the wine bottle to the floor, where they shattered.

The concussion of the gunshot and the shattering of glass was followed by stunned silence. A moment later, the body fell forward onto the table. The gun clattered to the floor.

"Police," a voice called out. A man rushed to the center of the room, holding a police badge aloft. In his other hand he held a .38 detective special. "No one move. Do not panic!"

With a sense of disgust Jack pushed the table away. It was pinning him against the wall. When he did so the man rolled off the side and fell heavily to the floor.

The policeman holstered his gun and pocketed his badge before quickly kneeling at the side of the body.

He felt for a pulse, then barked an order for someone to call 911 for an ambulance.

Only then did the restaurant erupt with screams and sobs. Terrified diners began to stand up. A few in the front of the restaurant fled out the door.

"Stay in your seats," the policeman commanded to those remaining. "Everything is under control."

Some people followed his orders and sat. Others stood immobilized, their eyes wide.

Having regained a semblance of composure, Jack squatted beside the policeman.

"I'm a doctor," Jack said.

"Yeah, I know," the policeman said. "Give a check. I'm afraid he's a goner."

Jack felt for a pulse while wondering how the policeman knew he was a doctor. There was no pulse.

"I didn't have a lot of choice," the policeman said defensively. "It happened so fast and with so many people around, I shot him in the left side of his chest. I must have hit the heart."

Jack and the policeman stood up.

The policeman looked Jack up and down. "Are you all right?" he asked.

In shocked disbelief, Jack examined himself. He could have been shot without having felt it. "I guess so," he said.

The policeman shook his head. "That was a close one," he said. "I never expected anything to happen to you in here."

"What do you mean?" Jack asked.

"If there was to be trouble, I expected it to be after you left the restaurant," the policeman said.

"I don't know what you are talking about," Jack said. "But I'm awfully glad you happened to be here."

"Don't thank me," the policeman said. "Thank Lou Soldano."

Terese came out of the rest room, confused as to what was going on. She hurried back to the table. When she saw the body her hands flew to her face to cover her mouth. Aghast, she looked at Jack.

"What happened?" she asked. "You're as white as a ghost."

"At least I'm alive," Jack said. "Thanks to this policeman."

In confusion Terese turned to the policeman for an explanation, but the sound of multiple sirens could be heard converging on the restaurant, and the policeman began moving people out of the way and urging them to sit down.

CHAPTER THIRTY

Tuesday, 8:45 P.M., March 26, 1996

Jack looked out the window of the speeding car and watched the nighttime scenery flash by with unseeing eyes. Jack was in the front passenger seat of Shawn Magoginal's unmarked car as it cruised south on the FDR Drive. Shawn was the plainclothes policeman who had mysteriously materialized at the crucial moment to save Jack from sure death.

Over an hour had passed since the event, but Jack was no more relaxed. In fact, now that he'd had time to think about this third attempt on his life he was more agitated than right after the event. He was literally shaking. In an attempt to hide this belated reaction from Shawn he clutched both hands to his knees.

Earlier, when the police cars and the ambulance had arrived at the restaurant, chaos had reigned. The police wanted everyone's names and addresses. Some people balked, others complied willingly. At first Jack had assumed he'd be treated similarly, but then Shawn had informed him that Detective Lieutenant Lou Soldano wanted to talk with him at police headquarters.

Jack had not wanted to go, but he'd been given no choice. Terese had insisted on coming along, but Jack had talked her out of it. She'd only relented once he'd promised to call her later. She'd told him that she'd be at the agency. After such an experience she didn't want to be alone.

Jack ran his tongue around the inside of his mouth. A combination of the wine and tension had made it as dry as the inside of a sock. He didn't want to go to police headquarters for fear they might detain him. He'd failed to report Reginald's murder and he'd been at the scene of the drugstore homicide. To top it off, he'd said enough to Laurie to indicate a potential link between Reginald and Beth's murder.

Jack sighed and ran a worried hand through his hair. He wondered how he'd respond to the inevitable questions he'd be asked.

"You okay?" Shawn questioned. He glanced at Jack, sensing his anxiety.

"Yeah, fine," Jack said. "It's been a wonderful evening in New York. It's a city where you can never get bored."

"That's a positive way to look at it," Shawn agreed.

Jack shot a look at the policeman, who seemed to have taken his comment literally.

"I have a couple of questions," Jack said. "How the hell did you happen to be there at the restaurant? And how did you know I was a doctor? And how is it that I have Lou Soldano to thank?"

"Lieutenant Soldano got a tip you might be in danger," Shawn said.

"How'd you know I was at the restaurant?" Jack asked.

"Simple," Shawn said. "Sergeant Murphy and I tailed you from the morgue."

Jack again looked out at the dark city as it sped by and shook his head imperceptibly. He was embarrassed for having thought he'd been so clever to ensure he'd not been followed. It was painfully obvious that he was out of his league.

"You almost gave us the slip at Bloomies," Shawn said. "But I guessed what you were up to by then."

Jack turned back to the detective. "Who gave Lieutenant Soldano the tip?" he asked. He assumed it had to have been Laurie.

"That I don't know," Shawn said. "But you'll soon be able to ask him yourself."

The FDR Drive imperceptibly became the South Street Viaduct. Ahead Jack could see the familiar silhouette of the Brooklyn Bridge come into view. Against the pale night sky it looked like a gigantic lyre.

They turned off the freeway just north of the bridge and were soon pulling into police headquarters.

Jack had never seen the building and was surprised by its modernity. Inside he had to pass through a metal detector. Shawn accompanied him to Lou Soldano's office, then took his leave.

Lou stood up and offered his hand, then pulled over a straight-backed chair. "Sit down, Doc," Lou said. "This is Sergeant Wilson." Lou gestured toward a uniformed African-American police officer who got to his feet as he was introduced. He was a striking man, and his uniform was impeccably pressed. His well-groomed appearance stood in sharp contrast to Lou's rumpled attire.

Jack shook hands with the sergeant and was impressed with the man's grip. In contrast Jack was ashamed of his own trembling, damp palm.

"I asked Sergeant Wilson down because he's heading up our Anti-Gang Violence Unit in Special Ops," Lou said as he returned to his desk and sat down.

Oh, wonderful, Jack thought, concerned that this meeting might get back to Warren. Jack tried to smile, but it was hesitant and fake; he was afraid his nervousness was all too transparent. Jack worried that both these experienced law-enforcement people could tell he was a felon the moment he walked through the door.

"I understand you had a bad experience tonight," Lou said.

"That's an understatement," Jack said. He regarded Lou. The man was not what he'd expected. After Laurie had implied that she'd been involved with him, Jack assumed he'd be more physically imposing: taller and more stylish. Instead, Jack thought he was a shorter version of himself considering his stocky, muscular frame and close-cropped hair.

"Can I ask you a question?" Jack asked.

"By all means," Lou said, spreading his hands. "This isn't an inquisition. It's a discussion."

"What made you have Officer Magoginal follow me?" Jack asked. "Mind you, I'm not complaining. He saved my life."

"You have Dr. Laurie Montgomery to thank for that," Lou said. "She was worried about you and made me promise that I would do something. Putting a tail on you was the only thing I could think of."

"I'm certainly appreciative," Jack said. He wondered what he could say to Laurie to thank her.

"Now, Doc, there's a lot going on here that we'd like to know about," Lou said. He steepled his hands with his elbows on his desk. "Maybe you should just tell us what's happening."

"I truly don't know yet," Jack said.

"Okay, fair enough," Lou said. "But, Doc, remember! You can relax! Again, this is a discussion."

"As shaken up as I am, I'm not sure I'm capable of much of a conversation."

"Maybe I should let you know what I know already," Lou said. Lou quickly outlined what Laurie had told him. He emphasized that he knew that Jack had been beaten up at least once and now had had an attempt on his life made by a member of a Lower East Side gang. Lou mentioned Jack's dislike of AmeriCare and his tendency to see conspiracy in the recent series of outbreaks of infectious disease at the Manhattan General. He also mentioned that Jack had apparently irritated a number of people at that hospital. He concluded with Jack's suggestion to Laurie that two apparently unrelated homicides might be linked and that preliminary tests had substantiated this surprising theory.

Jack visibly swallowed. "Wow," he said. "I'm beginning to think you know more than I do."

"I'm sure that's not the case," Lou said with a wry smile. "But maybe all this information gives you a sense of what else we need to know to prevent any more violence to you and others. There was another gang-related killing in the vicinity of the General this afternoon. Is that anything you know about?"

Jack swallowed again. He didn't know what to say. Warren's admonition reverberated in his mind, as did his fleeing from two crime scenes and abetting a murderer. He was, after all, a felon.

"I'd rather not talk about this right now," Jack said.

"Oh?" Lou questioned. "And why is that, Doc?"

Jack's mind raced for answers, and he was loath to lie.

"I guess because I'm concerned about certain people's safety," he said.

"That's what we are here for," Lou said. "People's safety."

"I understand that," Jack said. "But this is a rather unique situation. There are a lot of things going on. I'm worried we might be on the brink of a real epidemic."

"Of what?" Lou asked.

"Influenza," Jack said. "A type of influenza with a high morbidity."

"Have there been a lot of cases?" Lou asked.

"Not a lot so far," Jack said. "But I'm worried none-theless."

"Epidemics scare me, but they are out of my area of expertise," Lou said. "But homicide isn't. When do you think you might be willing to talk about these murders we've been discussing if you're not inclined at the moment?"

"Give me a day," Jack said. "This epidemic scare is real. Trust me."

"Hmmmm . . ." Lou voiced. He looked at Sergeant Wilson.

"A lot can happen in a day," the sergeant said.

"That's my concern too," Lou said. He redirected his attention to Jack. "What worries us is that the two gang members who've been killed were from different gangs. We don't want to see a gang war erupt around here. Whenever they do, a lot of innocent people get killed."

"I need twenty-four hours," Jack repeated. "By then I hope to be able to prove what I'm trying to prove. If I can't, I'll admit I was wrong, and I'll tell you everything I know, which, by the way, is not much."

"Listen, Doc," Lou said. "I could arrest you right

now and charge you with accessory after the fact. You are willfully obstructing the investigation of several homicides. I mean, you do understand the reality of what you are doing, don't you?"

"I think I do," Jack said.

"I could charge you, but I'm not going to do that," Lou said. He sat back in his chair. "Instead I'm going to bow to your judgment concerning this epidemic stuff. In deference to Dr. Montgomery, who seems to think you are a good guy, I'll be patient about my area of expertise. But I want to hear from you tomorrow night. Understand?"

"I understand," Jack said. Jack looked from the lieutenant to the sergeant and then back. "Is that it?"

"For now," Lou said.

Jack got up and headed for the door. Before he reached it, Sergeant Wilson spoke up: "I hope you understand how dangerous dealing with these gangs is. They feel they have little to lose and consequently have little respect for life, either their own or others'."

"I'll keep that in mind," Jack said.

Jack hurried from the building. As he emerged into the night he felt enormous relief, as if he'd been granted a reprieve.

While he waited for a taxi to appear in Park Row in front of the police headquarters, he thought about what he should do. He was afraid to go home. At the moment he didn't want to see the Black Kings or Warren. He thought about going back to see Terese, but he feared endangering her more than he already had.

With few alternatives Jack decided to find a cheap hotel. At least he'd be safe and so would his friends.

CHAPTER THIRTY-ONE

Wednesday, 6:15 A.M., March 27, 1996

The first symptom Jack noticed was a sudden rash that appeared on his forearms. As he was examining it, the rash spread quickly to his chest and abdomen. With his index fingers he spread the skin at the site of one of the blotches to see if it would blanch with pressure. Not only did it not blanch, the pressure deepened the color.

Then, as quickly as the skin eruption appeared, it began to itch. At first Jack tried to ignore the sensation, but it increased in intensity to the point where he had to scratch. When he did, the rash began to bleed. Each blotch was transformed into an open sore.

With the bleeding and the sores came a fever. It started to rise slowly, but once it got past a hundred degrees, it shot up. Soon Jack's forehead was awash with perspiration.

When he looked at himself in the mirror and saw his face flushed and spotted with open sores, he was horrified. A few minutes later he began to experience difficulty breathing. Even with deep breaths he was gasping for air.

Then Jack's head began to pound like a drum with each beat of his heart. He had no idea what he'd contracted, but its seriousness was all too obvious. Intuitively

Jack knew he had only moments to make the diagnosis and determine treatment.

But there was a problem. To make the diagnosis he needed a blood sample, but he had no needle. Perhaps he could get a sample with a knife. It would be messy, but it might work. Where could he find a knife?

Jack's eyes blinked open. For a second he frantically searched the nightstand for a knife, but then he stopped. He was disoriented. A deep clang sounded again and again. Jack could not place it. He lifted his arm to look at his rash, but it had disappeared. Only then did Jack realize where he was and that he'd been dreaming.

Jack estimated the temperature in the hotel room to be ninety degrees. With disgust he kicked off the blankets. He was drenched in sweat. Sitting up, he put his legs over the side of the bed. The clanging noise was coming from the radiator, which was also steaming and sputtering. It sounded like someone was striking the riser with a sledgehammer.

Jack went to the window and tried to open it. It wouldn't budge. It was as if it had been nailed shut. Giving up, he went to the radiator. It was so hot he couldn't touch the valve. He got a towel from the bathroom, but then found the valve was stuck in the open position.

In the bathroom Jack was able to open a frosted window. A refreshing breeze blew in. For a few minutes he didn't move. The cool tiles felt good on his feet. He leaned on the sink and recoiled at the remembrance of his nightmare. It had been so frighteningly real. He even looked at his arms and abdomen again to make sure he didn't have a rash. Thankfully, he didn't. But he still had a headache, which he assumed was from being over-heated. He wondered why he hadn't awakened sooner.

Looking into the mirror, he noticed that his eyes were red. He was also in dire need of a shave. He hoped that there was a sundry shop in the lobby, because he had no toilet articles with him.

Jack returned to the bedroom. The radiator was now silent and the room temperature had dropped to a toler-able level, with cool air flowing in from the bathroom.

Jack began to dress so he could go downstairs. As he did so he recalled the events of the previous evening. The image of the gun barrel came back to his mind's eye with terrifying clarity. He shuddered. Another fraction of a second and he would have been gone.

Three times in twenty-four hours Jack had come close to death. Each episode made him realize how much he wanted to live. For the first time he began to wonder if his response to his grief for his wife and daughters – his reckless behavior – might be a disservice to their memory.

Down in the seedy lobby Jack was able to purchase a disposable razor and a miniature tube of toothpaste with a toothbrush attached. As he waited for the elevator to return to his room he caught sight of a bound stack of the *Daily News* outside of an unopened newsstand. Above the lurid headlines was: "Morgue Doc nearly Winds Up on the Slab in Trendy Restaurant Shoot-out! See page three."

Jack set down his purchases and tried to tease out a copy of the paper, but he couldn't. The securing band was too tough to snap.

Returning to the front desk, he managed to convince the morose night receptionist to come out from behind

his desk and cut the band with a razor blade. Jack paid
for the paper and saw the receptionist pocket the money.

On the way up in the elevator Jack was shocked to
see a picture of himself on page three coming out of the
Positano restaurant with Shawn Magoginal holding his
upper arm. Jack couldn't remember a picture being
taken. The caption read: "Dr. Jack Stapleton, a NYC
medical examiner, being led by plainclothes detective
Shawn Magoginal from the scene of the doctor's
attempted assassination. A NYC gang member was killed
in the incident."

Jack read the article. It wasn't long; he was finished
before he got back to his room. Somehow the writer
had learned that Jack had had run-ins with the same
gang in the past. There was an unmistakably scandalous
implication. He tossed the paper aside. He was disgusted
at the unexpected exposure and was concerned it could
hinder his cause. He expected to have a busy day, and
he didn't want interference resulting from this unwanted
notoriety.

Jack showered, shaved, and brushed his teeth. He felt
a world of difference from when he'd awakened, but he
did not feel up to par. He still had a headache and the
muscles of his legs were sore. So was his lower back.
He couldn't help but worry that he was having early
symptoms of the flu. He didn't have to remind himself
to take his rimantadine.

When Jack arrived at the medical examiner's office, he
had the taxi drop him off at the morgue receiving bay
to avoid any members of the press who might be lying
in wait.

Jack headed directly upstairs to scheduling. He was

worried about what had come in during the night. As he stepped into the room, Vinnie lowered his newspaper.

"Hey, Doc," Vinnie said. "Guess what? You're in the morning paper."

Jack ignored him and went over to where George was working.

"Aren't you interested?" Vinnie called out. "There's even a picture!"

"I've seen it," Jack said. "It's not my best side."

"Tell me what happened," Vinnie demanded. "Heck, this is like a movie or something. Why'd this guy want to shoot you?"

"It was a case of mistaken identity," Jack said.

"Aw, no!" Vinnie said. He was disappointed. "You mean he thought you were someone else?"

"Something like that," Jack said. Then, addressing George, he asked if there had been any more influenza deaths.

"Did someone actually fire a gun at you?" George asked, ignoring Jack's question. He was as interested as Vinnie. Other people's disasters hold universal appeal.

"Forty or fifty times," Jack said. "But luckily it was one of those guns that shoots Ping-Pong balls. Those I wasn't able to duck bounced off harmlessly."

"I guess you don't want to talk about it," George said.

"That's perceptive of you, George," Jack said. "Now, have any influenza deaths come in?"

"Four," George said.

Jack's pulse quickened.

"Where are they?" Jack asked.

George tapped one of his stacks. "I'd assign a couple of them to you, but Calvin already called to tell me he wants you to have another paper day. I think he saw the newspaper too. In fact, he didn't even know if you'd be coming in to work today."

Jack didn't respond. With as much as he had to do that day, having another paper day was probably a godsend. Jack opened the charts quickly to read the names. Although he could have guessed their identities, it was still a shock. Kim Spensor, George Haselton, Gloria Hernandez, and a William Pearson, the evening lab tech, had all passed away during the night with acute respiratory distress syndrome. The worry that the influenza strain was virulent was no longer a question; it was now a fact. These victims had all been healthy, young adults who'd died within twenty-four-plus hours of exposure.

All of Jack's anxiety came back in a rush. His fear of a major epidemic soared. His only hope was that if he was right about the humidifier being the source, all of these cases represented index cases in that all had been exposed to the infected humidifier. Hence, none of these deaths represented person-to-person transfer, the key element for the kind of epidemic he feared.

Jack rushed from the room, ignoring more questions from Vinnie. Jack didn't know what he should do first. From what had happened with the plague episode, he thought he should wait to talk to Bingham and have Bingham call the city and state authorities. Yet now that Jack's worry about a potential epidemic had increased, he hated to let any time pass.

"Dr. Stapleton, you've had a lot of calls," Marjorie Zankowski said. Marjorie was the night communications operator. "Some left messages on your voice mail, but here's a list. I was going to take them up to your office, but since you are here . . ." She pushed a stack of pink phone messages toward Jack. Jack snatched them up and continued on.

He scanned the list as he went up in the elevator. Terese had called several times, the last time being four o'clock in the morning. The fact that she'd called so many times gave Jack a stab of guilt. He should have called her from the hotel, but in truth he hadn't felt like talking with anyone.

To his surprise there were also messages from Clint Abelard and Mary Zimmerman. His first thought was that Kathy McBane might have told them everything he'd said. If she had, then Clint's and Mary's messages might be of the unpleasant sort. They had called one after the other just after six a.m.

Most intriguing and worrisome of all the calls were two from Nicole Marquette from the CDC. One was around midnight, the other at five forty-five.

Rushing into his office, Jack stripped off his coat, plopped himself at his desk, and returned Nicole's call. When he got her on the line, she sounded exhausted.

"It's been a long night," she admitted. "I tried to call you many times both at work and at home."

"I apologize," Jack said. "I should have called to give you an alternate number."

"One of the times I called your apartment the phone was answered by an individual called Warren," Nicole said. "I hope he's an acquaintance. He didn't sound all that friendly."

"He's a friend," Jack said, but the news disturbed him. Facing Warren was not going to be easy.

"Well, I don't know quite where to begin," Nicole said. "One thing I can assure you is that you've caused a lot of people to lose a night's sleep. The sample of influenza you sent has ignited a fire down here. We ran it against our battery of antisera to all known reference strains. It didn't react with any one of them to any significant degree. In other words, it had to be a strain that was either entirely new or had not been seen for as many years as we've been keeping antisera."

"That's not good news, is it?" Jack said.

"Hardly," Nicole said. "It was very scary news, particularly in light of the strain's pathogenicity. We understand there now have been five deaths."

"How did you know?" Jack asked. "I just found out myself there'd been four more victims last night."

"We've already been in contact with the state and local authorities during the night," Nicole said. "That was one of the reasons I tried so hard to get ahold of you. We consider this to be an epidemiological emergency; I didn't want you to feel you were out the loop. You see, we did finally find something that reacted with the virus. It was a sample of frozen sera we have that we suspect contains antisera to the influenza strain that caused the great epidemic in 1918 and 1919!"

"Good God!" Jack exclaimed.

"As soon as I discovered this, I called my immediate boss, Dr. Hirose Nakano," Nicole said. "He, in turn, called the director of the CDC. He's been on the phone with everyone from the Surgeon General on down. We're mobilizing to fight a war here. We need a vaccine, and we need it fast. This is the swine-flu scare of seventy-six all over again."

"Is there anything I can do?" Jack asked even though he already knew the answer.

"Not at this time," Nicole said. "We owe you a debt of gratitude for alerting us to the problem as soon as you did. I told as much to the director. I wouldn't be surprised if he gave you a call himself."

"So the hospital has been notified?" Jack asked.

"Most definitely," Nicole said. "A CDC team will be coming up there today to assist in any way it can, including helping the local epidemiologist. Needless to say, we'd love to find out where this virus came from. One of the mysteries of influenza is where the dormant reservoirs are. Birds, particularly ducks, and pigs are suspected, but no one knows for sure. It's astonishing, to say the least, that a strain that hasn't been seen for some seventy-five years comes back to haunt us."

A few minutes later, Jack hung up the phone. He was stunned, yet also relieved to a degree. At least his warnings of a possible epidemic had been heeded, and the proper authorities mobilized. If an epidemic was to be averted, the only people who could make that happen were now involved.

But there was still the question of where these infectious agents had come from. Jack certainly did not think it was a natural source like another animal or a bird for the influenza. He thought it was either a person or an organization, and now he could concentrate on that issue.

Before Jack did anything else, he called Terese. He found her at home. She was extremely relieved to hear his voice.

"What happened to you?" she asked. "I've been worried sick."

"I stayed the night in a hotel," Jack said.

"Why didn't you call like you said you would?" Terese asked. "I've called your apartment a dozen times."

"I'm sorry," Jack said. "I should have called. But by

the time I left the police headquarters and found a hotel, I wasn't feeling much like talking to anyone. I can't tell you how stressful the last twenty-four hours has been. I'm afraid I'm not myself."

"I suppose I understand," Terese said. "After that horrid incident last night I'm amazed you are functioning at all today. Didn't you consider just staying home? I think that's what I would have done."

"I'm too caught up in everything that is happening," Jack said.

"That's just what I was afraid of," Terese said. "Jack, listen to me. You've been beat up and now almost killed. Isn't it time to let other people take over, and you get back to your normal job?"

"It's already happening to an extent," Jack said. "Officials from the Centers for Disease Control are on their way up here in force to contain this influenza outbreak. All I have to do is make it through today."

"What is that supposed to mean?" Terese asked.

"If I don't solve this mystery of mine by tonight I'm giving up on it," Jack said. "I had to promise as much to the police."

"That's music to my ears," Terese said. "When can I see you? I have some exciting news to tell."

"After last night I would have thought you'd consider me dangerous to be around," Jack said.

"I'm assuming that once you stop this crusade of yours people will leave you alone."

"I'll have to call you," Jack said. "I'm not sure how the day is going to play out."

"You'd promised to call last night and didn't," Terese said. "How can I trust you?"

"You'll just have to give me another chance," Jack said. "And now I have to get to work."

"Aren't you going to ask me about my exciting news?" Terese asked.

"I thought you'd tell me if you wanted to," Jack said.

"National Health canceled their internal review," Terese said.

"Is that good?" Jack asked.

"Absolutely," Terese said. "The reason they canceled it is because they are so sure they'll like our 'no waiting' campaign that I leaked yesterday. So instead of having to throw the presentation together haphazardly we have a month to do it properly."

"That's wonderful," Jack said. "I'm pleased for you."

"And that's not all," Terese said. "Taylor Heath called me in to congratulate me. He also told me he'd learned what Robert Barker had tried to do, so Barker is out and I'm in. Taylor all but assured me I'll be the next president of Willow and Heath."

"That calls for a celebration," Jack said.

"Exactly," Terese said. "A good way to do it would be to have lunch today at the Four Seasons."

"You certainly are persistent," Jack said.

"As a career woman I have to be," Terese said.

"I can't have lunch, but maybe dinner," Jack said. "That is, unless I'm in jail."

"Now what does that mean?" Terese asked.

"It would take too long to explain," Jack said. "I'll call you later. Bye, Terese." Jack hung up before Terese could get in another word. As tenacious as she was, Jack had the feeling she'd keep him on the phone until she got her way.

Jack was about to head up to the DNA lab when Laurie appeared in his doorway.

"I can't tell you how glad I am to see you," Laurie said.

"And I have you to thank for my being here," Jack said. "A few days ago I might have thought of you as having interfered. But not now. I appreciate whatever you said to Lieutenant Soldano, because it saved my life."

"He called me last night and told me what happened," Laurie said. "I tried to call you at your apartment a number of times."

"You and everyone else," Jack said. "To tell you the truth, I was scared to go home."

"Lou also told me he thought you were taking a lot of risks with these gangs involved," Laurie said. "Personally, I think you should call off whatever you are doing."

"Well, you are siding with the majority if it is any consolation," Jack said. "And I'm sure my mother would agree if you were to call her in South Bend, Indiana, and ask her opinion."

"I don't understand how you can be flippant in light of everything that has happened," Laurie said. "Besides, Lou wanted me to make sure you understand that he can't protect you with twenty-four-hour security. He doesn't have the manpower. You're on your own."

"At least I'll be working with someone I've spent a lot of time with," Jack said.

"You are impossible!" Laurie said. "When you don't want to talk about something you hide behind your clever repartee. I think you should tell everything to Lou. Tell him about your terrorist idea and turn it over to him. Let him investigate it. He's good at it. It's his job."

"That might be," Jack said. "But this is a unique circumstance in a lot of ways. I think it requires knowledge that Lou doesn't have. Besides, I sense it might do a world of good for my self-confidence to follow this thing through. Whether it's obvious or not, my ego has taken a beating over the last five years."

"You are a mystery man," Laurie said. "Also stubborn, and I don't know enough about you to know when you are joking and when you are serious. Just promise to be more careful than you've been the last few days."

"I'll make you a deal," Jack said. "I'll promise if you agree to take rimantadine."

"I did notice there were more influenza deaths downstairs," Laurie said. "You think it warrants rimantadine?"

"Absolutely," Jack said. "The CDC is taking this outbreak very seriously, and you should as well. In fact, they think it might be the same strain that caused the disastrous influenza outbreak in 1918. I've started rimantadine myself."

"How could it be the same strain?" Laurie asked. "That strain doesn't exist."

"Influenza has a way of hiding out," Jack said. "It's one of the things that has the CDC so interested."

"Well, if that were the case, it sure shoots holes in your terrorist theory," Laurie said. "There's no way for someone to deliberately spread something that doesn't exist outside of some unknown natural reservoir."

Jack stared at Laurie for a minute. She was right, and he wondered why he hadn't thought of it.

"I don't mean to rain on your parade," Laurie said.

"That's okay," Jack said, preoccupied. He was busy

wondering if the influenza episode could be a natural phenomenon, while the other outbreaks were intentional. The problem with that line of thinking was that it violated a cardinal rule in medical diagnostics: single explanations are sought even for seemingly disparate events.

"Nevertheless, the influenza threat is obviously real," Laurie said. "So I'll take the drug, but to make sure you hold up your side of the bargain, I want you to keep in touch with me. I noticed that Calvin took you off autopsy, so if you leave the office you have to call me at regular intervals."

"Maybe you've been talking to my mother after all," Jack said. "Sounds remarkably like the orders she gave me during my first week at college."

"Take it or leave it," Laurie said.

"I'll take it," Jack said.

After Laurie left, Jack headed to the DNA lab to seek out Ted Lynch. Jack was glad to get out of his office. Despite the good intentions involved he was tiring of people giving him advice and he was afraid Chet would soon be arriving. Undoubtedly he'd voice the same concerns just expressed by Laurie.

As Jack mounted the stairs he thought more about Laurie's point concerning the influenza's source. He couldn't believe he'd not thought of it himself, and it undermined his confidence. It also underlined how much he was depending on a positive result with the probe National Biologicals had sent. If they were all negative he'd have scant hope of proving his theory. All he'd have left would be the improbable cultures he hoped Kathy McBane had obtained from the sink trap in central supply.

The moment Ted Lynch caught sight of Jack approaching, he pretended to hide behind his lab bench.

"Shucks, you found me," Ted joked when Jack came around the end of the counter. "I was hoping not to see you until the afternoon."

"It's your unlucky day," Jack said. "I'm not even on autopsy, so I've decided to camp out here in your lab. I don't suppose you've had a chance to run my probes . . ."

"Actually, I stayed late last night and even came in early to prepare the nucleoproteins. I'm ready to run the probes now. If you give me an hour or so, I should have some results."

"Did you get all four cultures?" Jack asked.

"Sure did," Ted said. "Agnes was on the ball as usual."

"I'll be back," Jack said.

With some time to kill, Jack went down to the morgue and changed into his moon suit before entering the autopsy room.

The morning routine was well under way. Six of the eight tables were in various stages of the autopsy procedure. Jack walked down the row until he recognized one of the cases. It was Gloria Hernandez. For a moment he looked at her pale face and tried to comprehend the reality of death. Having just spoken with her in her apartment the day before, it seemed an inconceivable transition.

The autopsy was being done by Riva Mehta, Laurie's officemate. She was a petite woman of Indian extraction who had to stand on a stool to do the procedure. At that moment she was just entering the chest.

Jack stayed and watched. When the lungs were

removed he asked to see the cut surface. It was identical to Kevin Carpenter's from the day before, complete with pinpoint hemorrhages. There was no doubt it was a primary influenza pneumonia.

Moving on, Jack found Chet, who was busy with the nurse, George Haselton. Jack was surprised; it was Chet's usual modus operandi to stop into the office before doing his day's autopsies. When Chet saw it was Jack, he seemed annoyed.

"How come you didn't answer your phone last night?" Chet demanded.

"It was too long a reach," Jack said. "I wasn't there."

"Colleen called to tell me what happened," Chet said. "I think this whole thing has gone far enough."

"Chet, instead of talking, how about showing me the lung," Jack said.

Chet showed Jack the lung. It was identical to Gloria Hernandez's and Kevin Carpenter's. When Chet started to talk again, Jack merely moved on.

Jack stayed in the autopsy room until he'd seen the gross on all the influenza cases. There were no surprises. Everyone was impressed by the pathogenicity of the virus.

Changing back into his street clothes, Jack went directly up to the DNA lab. This time Ted acted glad to see him.

"I'm not sure what you wanted me to find," Ted said. "But you are batting five hundred. Two of the four were positive."

"Just two?" Jack asked. He'd prepared himself for either all positive or all negative. Like everything else associated with these outbreaks, he was surprised.

"If you want I can go back and fudge the results," Ted joked. "How many do you want to be positive?"

"I thought I was the jokester around here," Jack said.

"Do these results screw up some theory of yours?" Ted asked.

"I'm not sure yet," Jack said. "Which two were positive?"

"The plague and the tularemia," Ted said.

Jack walked back to his office while he pondered this new information. By the time he was sitting down he'd decided that it didn't make any difference how many of the cultures were positive. That fact that any of them were positive supported his theory. Unless an individual was a laboratory worker it would be hard to come in contact with an artificially propagated culture of a bacteria.

Pulling his phone over closer to himself, Jack put in a call to National Biologicals. He asked to speak with Igor Krasnyansky, since the man had already been accommodating enough to send the probes.

Jack reintroduced himself.

"I remember you," Igor said. "Did you have any luck with the probes?"

"I did," Jack said. "Thank you for sending them. But now I have a few more questions."

"I'll try to answer them," Igor said.

"Does National Biologicals also sell influenza cultures?" Jack asked.

"Indeed," Igor said. "Viruses are a big part of our business, including influenza. We have many strains, particularly type A."

"Do you have the strain that caused the epidemic in

1918?" Jack asked. He just wanted to be one hundred percent certain.

"We wish!" Igor said with a laugh. "I'm sure that strain would be popular with researchers. No, we don't have it, but we have some that are probably similar, like the strain of the '76 swine-flu scare. It's generally believed that the 1918 strain was a permutation of H1N1, but exactly what, no one knows."

"My next question concerns plague and tularemia," Jack said.

"We carry both," Igor said.

"I'm aware of that," Jack said. "What I would like to know is who has ordered either of those two cultures in the last few months."

"I'm afraid we don't usually give that information out," Igor said.

"I can understand that," Jack said. For a moment Jack feared he would have to get Lou Soldano involved just to get the information he wanted. But then he thought he could possibly talk Igor into giving it to him. After all, Igor had been careful to say that such information wasn't "usually" given out.

"Perhaps you'd like to talk to our president," Igor suggested.

"Let me tell you why I want to know," Jack said. "As a medical examiner I've seen a couple of deaths recently with these pathogens. We'd just like to know which labs we should warn. Our interest is preventing any more accidents."

"And the deaths were due to our cultures?" Igor asked.

"That was why I wanted the probes," Jack said. "We suspected as much but needed proof."

"Hmm," Igor said. "I don't know if that should make me feel more or less inclined to give out information."

"It's just an issue of safety," Jack said.

"Well, that sounds reasonable," Igor said. "It's not as if it's a secret. We share our customer lists with several equipment manufacturers. Let me see what I can find here at my workstation."

"To make it easier for you, narrow the field to labs in the New York metropolitan area," Jack said.

"Fair enough," Igor said. Jack could hear the man typing on his keyboard. "We'll try tularemia first. Here we go."

There was a pause.

"Okay," Igor said. "We have sent tularemia to the National Health hospital and to the Manhattan General Hospital. That's it; at least for the last couple of months."

Jack sat more upright, especially knowing that National Health was the major competitor of AmeriCare. "Can you tell me when these cultures went out?"

"I think so," Igor said. Jack could hear more typing. "Okay, here we are. The National Health shipment went out on the twenty-second of this month, and the Manhattan General shipment went out on the fifteenth."

Jack's enthusiasm waned slightly. By the twenty-second he'd already made the diagnosis of tularemia in Susanne Hard. That eliminated National Health for the time being. "Does it show who the receiver was on the Manhattan General shipment?" Jack asked. "Or was it just the lab itself?"

"Hold on," Igor said as he switched screens again. "It says that the consignee was a Dr. Martin Cheveau."

Jack's pulse quickened. He was uncovering information that very few people would know could be discoverable. He doubted that even Martin Cheveau was aware that National Biologicals phage-typed their cultures.

"What about plague?" Jack asked.

"Just a moment," Igor said while he made the proper entries.

There was another pause. Jack could hear Igor's breathing.

"Okay, here it is," Igor said. "Plague's not a common item ordered on the East Coast outside of academic or reference labs. But there was one shipment that went out on the eighth. It went to Frazer Labs."

"I've never heard of them," Jack said. "Do you have an address?"

"Five-fifty Broome Street," Igor said.

"How about a consignee?" Jack asked as he wrote down the address.

"Just the lab itself," Igor said.

"Do you do much business with them?" Jack asked.

"I don't know," Igor said. He made another entry. "They send us orders now and then. It must be a small diagnostic lab. But there's one thing strange."

"What's that?" Jack asked.

"They always pay with a cashier's check," Igor said. "I've never seen that before. It's okay, of course, but customers usually have established credit."

"Is there a telephone number?" Jack asked.

"Just the address," Igor said, which he repeated.

Jack thanked Igor for his help and hung up the phone. Taking out the phone directory, he looked up Frazer Labs. There was no listing. He tried information but had the same luck.

Jack sat back. Once again he'd gotten information he
didn't expect. He now had two sources of the offending
bacteria. Since he already knew something about the lab
at the Manhattan General, he thought he'd better visit
Frazer Labs. If there was some way he could establish
an association with the two labs or with Martin Cheveau
personally, he'd turn everything over to Lou Soldano.

The first problem was the concern about being followed. The previous evening he'd thought he'd been so
clever but had been humbled by Shawn Magoginal. Yet
to give himself credit, he had to remember that Shawn
was an expert. The Black Kings certainly weren't. But
to make up for their lack of expertise, the Black Kings
were ruthless. Jack knew he'd have to lose a potential
tail rapidly since they had clearly demonstrated a total
lack of compunction about attacking him in public.

There was also the collateral worry about Warren and
his gang. Jack didn't know what to think about them.
He had no idea of Warren's state of mind. It was something Jack would have to face in the near future.

To lose any tail Jack wanted a crowded location with
multiple entrances and exits. Immediately Grand Central
Terminal and the Port Authority Bus Terminal came to
mind. He decided on the former since it was closer.

Jack wished there were some underground way of
getting over to the NYU Medical Center to help him
get away from the office, but there wasn't. Instead he
settled on a radio-dispatched taxi service. He directed
the dispatcher to have the car pick him up at the receiving
bay of the morgue.

Everything seemed to work perfectly. The car came
quickly. Jack slipped in from the bay. They managed to
hit the light at First Avenue; at no time was Jack a sitting

duck in a motionless car. Still, he hunched low in his seat, out of view, sparking the driver's curiosity. The cabbie kept stealing looks at Jack in his rearview mirror.

As they drove up First Avenue, Jack raised himself up and watched out the back. He saw nothing suspicious. No cars suddenly pulled into the traffic. No one ran out to flag a cab.

They turned left on Forty-second Street. Jack had the driver pull up directly in front of Grand Central. The moment the car came to a stop, Jack was out and running. He dashed through the entrance and merged quickly with the crowd. To be absolutely sure he was not being followed, he descended into the subway and boarded the Forty-second Street shuttle.

When the train was about to leave and the doors had started to close, Jack impeded their closing and jumped off the train. He ran up into the station proper and exited back onto Forty-second Street through a different entrance than he used when he arrived.

Feeling confident, Jack hailed a taxi. At first he told the driver to take him to the World Trade Center. During the trip down Fifth Avenue he watched to see if any cars, taxis, or trucks could have been following. When none seemed to be doing so, Jack told the driver to take him to 550 Broome Street.

Jack finally began to relax. He sat back in the seat and put his hands to his temples. The headache he'd awakened with in the overheated hotel room had never completely gone away. He'd been ascribing the lingering throb to anxiety, but now there were new symptoms. He had a vague sore throat accompanied by mild coryza. There was still a chance it was all psychosomatic, but he was still worried.

After rounding Washington Square, the taxi driver went south on Broadway before turning east on Houston Street. At Eldridge he made a right.

Jack looked out at the scenery. He'd not had any idea where Broome Street was, although he'd assumed it was someplace downtown, south of Houston. That entire section of the city was one of the many parts of New York he had yet to explore, and there were many street names with which he was unfamiliar.

The cab made a left-hand turn off Eldridge, and Jack caught a glimpse of the street sign. It was Broome Street. He looked out at the buildings. They were five and six stories tall. Many were abandoned and boarded up. It seemed an improbable place to have a medical lab.

At the next corner the neighbourhood improved slightly. There was a plumbing-supply store with thick metal grates covering its windows. Sprinkled down the rest of the block were other building-supply concerns. On the floors above the street-level stores were a few loft apartments. Otherwise, it seemed to be vacant commercial space.

In the middle of the following block, the cabdriver pulled to the side of the street. Five-fifty Broome Street was not Frazer Labs. It was a combination check-cashing place, mailbox rental, and pawnshop stuck between a package store and a shoe repair shop.

Jack hesitated. At first he thought he'd gotten the wrong address. But that seemed unlikely. Not only had he written it down, but Igor had mentioned it twice. Jack paid his fare and climbed from the cab.

Like all the other stores in the area, this one had an iron grille that could be pulled across its front at night and locked. In the window was a miscellaneous mixture of objects that included an electric guitar, a handful of cameras, and a display of cheap jewelry. A large sign over the door said: "Personal Mailboxes." Painted on the door glass were the words: "Checks Cashed."

Jack stepped up to the window. By standing directly in front of the electric guitar, he could see beyond the display into the store itself. There was a glass-topped counter that ran down the right side. Behind the counter was a mustached man with a punk-rock hairstyle. He was dressed in military camouflage fatigues. In the rear of the shop was a Plexiglas-enclosed cubicle that looked like a bank teller's window. On the left side of the store was a bank of mailboxes.

Jack was intrigued. The fact that Frazer Labs might be using this tacky shop as a mail drop was certainly suspicious if it was true. At first he was tempted to walk in and ask. But he didn't. He was afraid by doing so he might hinder other methods of finding out. He knew that such personal mailbox establishments were loath to give out any information. Privacy was the main reason people rented the boxes in the first place.

What Jack truly wanted was not only to find out if Frazer Labs had a box there, but to entice a Frazer Labs representative to come to the shop. Slowly an elaborate plan began to form in Jack's mind.

Being careful not to be seen by the clerk within the store, Jack quickly walked away. The first thing he needed was a telephone directory. Since the area around the pawnshop was comparatively deserted, Jack walked south to Canal Street. There he found a drugstore.

From the phone directory Jack copied down four addresses: a nearby uniform shop, a van rental agency, an office supply store, and a Federal Express office. Since the clothing shop was the closest, Jack went there first.

Once in the store Jack realized that he couldn't remember what Federal Express courier uniforms looked like. But he wasn't terribly concerned. If he couldn't remember, he didn't think the clerk in the pawnshop would know either. Jack bought a pair of blue cotton twill pants and a white shirt with flap pockets and epaulets. He also bought a plain black belt and blue tie.

"Would you mind if I put these on?" Jack asked the clerk.

"Of course not," the clerk said. He showed Jack to a makeshift dressing room.

The pants were slightly too long, but Jack was satisfied. When he looked at himself in the mirror he thought he needed something else. He ended up adding a blue peaked cap to his outfit. After Jack paid for his purchases, the clerk was happy to wrap up Jack's street clothes. Just before the package was sealed, Jack thought to rescue his rimantadine. With the symptoms he was feeling he didn't want to miss a dose.

The next stop was the office-supply store, where Jack selected wrapping paper, tape, a medium-sized box, string, and a packet of "rush" labels. To Jack's surprise he even found "biohazard" labels, so he tossed a box of them into his shopping cart. In another part of the store he found a clipboard and a pad of printed receipt forms. Once he had everything he wanted he took them to the checkout register and paid.

The next stop was the Federal Express office. From their supply stand Jack took several address labels with the clear plastic envelopes used to attach them to a parcel.

The final destination was a car rental agency, where Jack rented a cargo van. That took the most time, since Jack had to wait while someone went to another location to bring the van to the agency. Jack used the opportunity to prepare the parcel. First he put together the box. Wanting to give it the feeling of having contents, Jack eyed a triangular piece of wood on the floor near the entrance. He assumed it was a doorstop.

When no one at the rental counter was looking Jack picked up the object and slipped it into the box. He then crumpled up multiple sheets of a *New York Post* that he found in the waiting area. He hefted the box and gave it a shake. Satisfied, he taped it shut.

After the wrapping paper and the string were applied, Jack plastered the outside with "rush" and "biohazard" labels.

The final touch was the Federal Express label, which Jack carefully filled out, addressing it to Frazer Labs. For the return address Jack used National Biological's. After throwing away the top copy, Jack inserted one of the carbons into the plastic envelope and secured it to the front of the box. He was pleased. The package appeared official indeed, and with all the "rush" labels, he hoped it would have the desired effect.

When the van arrived, Jack went out and put the package, the remains of the wrapping material, and the parcel containing his clothes in the back. Climbing behind the wheel, he drove off.

Before going back to the pawnshop Jack made two stops. He returned to the drugstore where he'd used the phone book and bought some throat lozenges for his irritated throat, which seemed to be getting worse. He also stopped at a deli for some takeout. He wasn't hungry, but it was already afternoon, and he'd eaten nothing that day. Besides, after he delivered the package he had no idea how long he'd have to wait.

While driving back to Broome Street Jack opened one of the orange-juice containers he'd bought and used the juice to take a second dose of rimantadine. In view of his progressive symptoms he wanted to keep the drug's concentration high in his blood.

Jack pulled up directly in front of the pawnshop, leaving the engine running and the emergency blinkers blinking. Clutching his clipboard, he got out and went around to the rear to get the package. Then he entered the store.

The door had bells secured to the top edge, and Jack's entrance was heralded by a raucous ringing. As had been the case earlier, there were no customers in the shop. The mustached man in the camouflage fatigues looked up from a magazine. With his hair standing on end he had the look of perpetual surprise.

"I've got a rush delivery for Frazer Labs," Jack said. He plopped the parcel down on the glass counter and shoved the clipboard under the man's nose. "Sign there at the bottom," he added, while proffering his pen to the man.

The man took the pen but hesitated and eyed the box.

"This is the right address, isn't it?" Jack asked.

"I reckon," the man said. He stroked his mustache and looked up at Jack. "What's the rush?"

"I was told there was dry ice in there," Jack said. Then he leaned forward as if to tell a secret. "My supervisor thinks it's a shipment of live bacteria. You know, for research and all."

The man nodded.

"I was surprised I wasn't delivering this directly to the lab," Jack said. "It can't sit around. I mean, I don't think it will leak out or anything; at least I don't think so. But it might die and then it will be useless. I assume you have a way of getting in touch with your customers?"

"I reckon," the man repeated.

"I'd advise you to do that," Jack said. "Now sign and I'll be on my way."

The man signed his name. Reading upside down, Jack made out "Tex Hartmann." Tex pushed the clipboard back toward Jack, and Jack slipped it under his arm. "I'm sure glad to get that thing off my truck," Jack said. "I've never been much of a fan of bacteria and viruses. Did you hear about those cases of plague that were here in New York last week? They scared me to death."

The man nodded again.

"Take care," Jack said with a wave. He walked out of the store and climbed into his truck. He wished that Tex had been a bit more talkative. Jack wasn't sure if he would be calling Frazer Labs or not. But just as Jack was releasing the emergency brake he could see Tex through the window dialing his phone.

Pleased with himself, Jack drove several blocks down Broome Street, then circled the block. He parked about a half block from the pawn shop and turned off the motor. After locking the doors, he broke out the deli food. Whether he was hungry or not, he was going to make himself eat something.

"Are you sure we should be doing this?" BJ questioned.

"Yeah, man, I'm sure," Twin said. He was maneuvering his Cadillac around Washington Square Park looking for someplace to park. It wasn't looking good. The park was crammed full of people entertaining themselves in a bewildering variety of ways. There was skateboarding, in-line skating, Frisbee throwing, break dancing, chess playing, and drug dealing. Baby carriages dotted the park. It was a carnival-like atmosphere, which was exactly why Twin had suggested the park for the upcoming meeting.

"Shit, man, I feel naked without some kind of ordnance. It's not right."

"Shut your mouth, BJ, and look for a spot for this ride of mine," Twin said. "This is going to be a meeting of the brothers. There's no need for any firepower."

"What if they bring some?" BJ asked.

"Hey, man, don't you trust nobody?" Twin asked. At that moment he saw a delivery van pulling away from the curb. "What do you know, we're in luck."

Twin expertly guided his car into the spot and pushed on the emergency brake.

"It says for commercial vehicles only," BJ said. He had his face pressed up against the window to see the parking sign.

"With all the crack we've moved this year I think we qualify," Twin said with a laugh. "Come on, get your black ass in gear."

They got out of the car and crossed the street to enter the park. Twin checked his watch. They were a little early despite the trouble parking. That was how Twin liked it for this kind of meeting. He wanted a chance to scope the place out. It wasn't that he didn't trust the other brothers, it was just that he liked to be careful.

But Twin was in for a surprise. When his eyes swept the area for the agreed-upon meeting he found himself transfixed by the stare of one of the more physically imposing men he'd seen in some time.

"Uh-oh," Twin said under his breath.

"What's the matter?" BJ demanded, instantly alert.

"The brothers have gotten here before us," Twin said.

"What do you want me to do?" BJ asked. His own eyes raced around the park until they, too, settled on the same man Twin had spotted.

"Nothing," Twin said. "Just keep walking."

"He looks so goddamn relaxed," BJ said. "It makes me worried."

"Shut up!" Twin commanded.

Twin walked right up to the man whose piercing eyes had never left his. Twin formed his right hand into the form of a gun, pointed at the man, and said: "Warren!"

"You got it," Warren said. "How's it going?"

"Not bad," Twin said. He then ritualistically raised his right hand to head height. Warren did the same and they high-fived. It was a perfunctory gesture, akin to a couple of rival investment bankers shaking hands.

"This here's David," Warren said, motioning toward his companion.

"And this here's BJ," Twin said, mimicking Warren.

David and BJ eyed each other but didn't move or speak.

"Listen, man," Twin said. "Let me say one thing right off. We didn't know the doc was living in your hood. I mean, maybe we should have known, but we didn't think about it with him being white."

"What kind of a relationship did you have with the doc?" Warren asked.

"Relationship?" Twin questioned. "We didn't have no relationship."

"How come you've been trying to ice him?" Warren asked.

"Just for some small change," Twin said. "A white dude who lives down our way came to us and offered us some cash to warn the doc about something he was doing. Then, when the doc didn't take our advice, the dude offered us more to take him out."

"So you're telling me the doc hasn't been dealing with you people?" Warren asked.

"Shit no," Twin said with a derisive laugh. "We don't need no honky doctor for our operation, no way."

"You should have come to us first," Warren said. "We would have set you right about the doc. He's been running with us on the b-ball court for four or five months. He's not half bad neither. So I'm sorry about Reginald. I mean, it wouldn't have happened if we'd talked."

"I'm sorry about the kid," Twin said. "That shouldn't have happened neither. Trouble was, we were so pissed about Reginald. We couldn't believe a brother would get shot over a honky doctor."

"That makes us even," Warren said. "That's not counting what happened last night, but that didn't involve us."

"I know," Twin said. "Can you imagine that doc? He's like a cat with nine lives. How the hell did that cop react so fast? And why was he in there? He must think he's Wyatt Earp or something."

"The point is that we have a truce," Warren said.

"Damn straight," Twin said. "No more brother shooting brother. We've got enough trouble without that."

"But a truce means you lay off the doc too," Warren said.

"You care what happens to that dude?" Twin asked.

"Yeah, I do," Warren said.

"Hey, then it's your call, man," Twin said. "It wasn't like the money was that good anyway."

Warren stuck out his hand palm up. Twin slapped it. Then Warren slapped Twin's.

"Be good," Warren said.

"You too, man," Twin said.

Warren motioned to David that they were leaving. They walked back toward the Washington Arch at the base of Fifth Avenue.

"That wasn't half bad," David said.

Warren shrugged.

"You believe him?" David asked.

"Yeah, I do," Warren said. "He might deal in drugs, but he's not stupid. If this thing goes on, we all lose."

CHAPTER THIRTY-TWO

Wednesday, 5:45 P.M., March 27, 1996

Jack felt uncomfortable. Among other problems he was stiff and now all his muscles ached. He'd been sitting in the van for more hours than he cared to count, watching customers going in and out of the pawnshop. There'd never been a crowd, but it was steady. Most of the people looked seedy. It occurred to Jack that the shop was trafficking in illicit activities like gambling or drugs.

It was not a good neighborhood. Jack had sensed that the moment he'd arrived that morning. The point had been driven home as darkness fell and someone tried to break into the van with Jack sitting there. The man had approached the passenger-side door with a flat bar, which he proceeded to insert between the glass and the door frame. Jack had to knock on the glass and wave to get the man's attention. The moment he saw Jack he ran off.

Jack was now popping throat lozenges at a regular rate with little relief. His throat was worse, and to add to his increasing misery he'd developed a cough. It wasn't a bad cough, merely a dry hack. But it further irritated his throat and increased his anxiety that he had indeed caught the flu from Gloria Hernandez. Although two rimantadine tablets were recommended as the daily dose, Jack took a third when the coughing started.

Just about the time Jack was contemplating admitting to himself that his clever ploy with the package had been a failure, his patience paid off. The man involved did not attract Jack's attention initially. He'd arrived on foot, which was not what Jack expected. He was dressed in an old nylon ski parka with a hood just like a few of the individuals who'd preceded him. But when he came out he was carrying the parcel. Despite the failing light and the distance, Jack could see the "rush" and "biohazard" labels plastered haphazardly over the exterior.

Jack had to make a rapid decision as the man walked briskly toward the Bowery. He hadn't expected to be following a pedestrian, and he debated if he should get out of the van and follow on foot or stay in the van, circle around, and try to follow the man while driving.

Thinking that a slowly moving van would attract more attention than a pedestrian, Jack got out of the truck. He followed at a distance until the man turned right on Eldridge Street. Jack then ran until he reached the corner.

He peeked around just in time to see the man entering a building across the street, midway down the block.

Jack quickly walked to the building. It was five stories, like its immediate neighbors. Each floor had two large, storefront-sized windows with smaller, sashed windows on either side. A fire escape zigzagged down the left side of the facade to end in a counterweighted ladder pivoted some twelve feet from the sidewalk. The ground-floor commercial space was vacant with a For Rent sign stuck to the inside of the glass.

The only lights were in the second-floor windows. From where Jack was standing it appeared to be a loft apartment, but he couldn't be certain. There were no drapes or other obvious signs of domesticity.

While Jack was eyeing the building, vaguely wondering what to do next, the lights went on up on the fifth floor. While he watched he saw someone raise the sash of the smaller window to the left. Jack was unable to see if it had been the man he followed, but he suspected it was.

After making certain he wasn't being observed, Jack quickly moved over to the door where the man had entered. He tried it, and it opened. Stepping over the threshold, he found himself in a small foyer. A group of four mailboxes was set into the wall to the left. Only two had names. The second floor was occupied by G. Heilbrunn. The fifth-floor tenant was R. Overstreet. There was no Frazer Labs.

Four buzzers bordered a small grille which Jack assumed covered a speaker. He vaguely contemplated ringing the fifth floor but had trouble imagining what he could say. He stood there for a few minutes thinking, but nothing came to mind. Then he noticed that the mailbox for the fifth floor appeared to be unlocked.

Jack was about to reach up to the mailbox when the inner door to the building proper abruptly opened. It startled Jack and he jumped, but he had the presence of mind to keep himself turned away from whoever was exiting the building. The person hastily brushed by Jack with obvious distress. Jack caught a fleeting glimpse of the same nylon ski parka. A second later the man was gone.

Jack reacted quickly, getting his foot into the inner door before it closed. As soon as he was certain the man was not immediately returning, Jack entered the

building. He let the door close behind him. A stairway
wound up surrounding a wide elevator built of a steel
frame covered by heavy wire mesh. Jack assumed the
elevator had been for freight, not only because of its size
but also because its doors closed horizontally instead of
vertically, and its floor was rough-hewn planks.

Jack got into the elevator and pushed five.

The elevator was noisy, bumpy, and slow, but it got
Jack to the fifth floor. Getting off, he faced a plain,
heavy door. There was no name and no bell. Hoping
the apartment was empty, Jack knocked. When there was
no answer even after a second, louder rapping, Jack tried
the door. It was locked.

Since the stairway rose up another floor, Jack climbed
to see if he could get to the roof. The door opened but
would lock behind him once he was outside. Before the
ventured onto the roof he had to find something to
wedge between the door and doorjamb so he could
return to the stairwell. Just over the threshold he found
a short length of two-by-four, which he guessed was
there for that very purpose.

With the door propped open Jack stepped out onto
the dark roof and gingerly walked toward the front of the
building. Ahead of him he could see the arched handrails
of the fire-escape ladder silhouetted against the night
sky.

Arriving at the front parapet, Jack grasped the handrails and looked down. The view down to the street
awakened his fear of heights, and the idea of lowering
himself over the edge made him feel momentarily weak.
Yet just twelve feet down was the fire-escape landing for
the fifth floor. It was generously illuminated by the light
coming from within the apartment.

Despite his phobia, Jack knew this was a chance he couldn't pass up. He had to at least take a look into the window.

First he sat on the parapet facing the rear of the building. Then, holding on to the handrail, he stood up. Keeping his eyes fixed on each rung, Jack lowered himself down the short run of ladder. He moved slowly and deliberately until his foot hit up against the grate of the landing. Never once did he look down.

Maintaining one hand on the ladder, he leaned over and peered through the window. The space was indeed a loft as Jack had surmised, but he could see it was partially divided with six-foot-high partitions. Immediately in front of him was a living area with a bed to the right and a small kitchen against the left wall. On a round table was the open remains of Jack's parcel. The doorstop and the crumpled newspaper were strewn about the floor.

What interested Jack more was what he could just see over the partition: It was the top of a stainless-steel appliance that did not look as if it belonged in an apartment.

With the window in front of him invitingly open, Jack could not control his urge to climb into the apartment for a better look. Besides, he rationalized, he could exit into the stairwell rather than subject himself to climbing the fire-escape ladder again.

Although he continued to avoid looking down, it took Jack a moment to convince himself to let go of the ladder. By the time he had slithered into the apartment headfirst, he was perspiring heavily.

Jack quickly collected himself. Once inside with his feet planted on the floor, he had no compunction about peering back out the window and down at the street. He wanted to make sure the man in the ski parka wasn't coming back, at least not for the moment.

Satisfied, Jack turned back to the apartment. He went from the combination kitchen-bedroom into a living room dominated by a storefront-sized window. There were two couches facing each other and a coffee table on a small hooked rug. The walls of the partitions were decorated with posters announcing international microbiological symposia. The magazines on the coffee table were all microbiological journals.

Jack was encouraged. Perhaps he had found Frazer Labs after all. But there was also something that disturbed him. A large, glass-fronted gun cabinet stood against the far partition. The man in the ski parka was not only interested in bacteria; he was also a gun enthusiast.

Moving quickly, Jack passed through the living room intent on locating the door to the stairwell. But as soon as he passed beyond the living room's partition, he came to a stop. The entire rest of the large, multi-columned loft was occupied by a lab. The stainless-steel appliance he'd seen from the fire escape was similar to the walk-in incubator he'd seen in the General's lab. In the far right-hand corner was a type III biosafety hood whose exhaust vented out the top of the sashed window.

Although Jack had suspected he'd find a private lab when he climbed through the window, the comprehensiveness of the one he'd discovered stunned him. He knew that such equipment was not cheap, and the combination living quarters/lab was unusual to say the least.

A generous commercial freezer caught Jack's attention. Standing to the side were several large cylinders of compressed nitrogen. The freezer had been converted to using liquid nitrogen as its coolant, making it possible to take the interior temperature down into the minus-fifty degree range.

Jack tried to open the freezer, but it was locked.

A muffled noise that resembled a bark caught Jack's attention, and he looked up from the freezer. He heard it again. It came from the very back of the lab where there was a shed about twenty feet square. Jack walked closer to examine the odd structure. A vent duct exited from its rear and exhausted through the top of one of the rear windows.

Jack cracked the door. A feral odor drifted out as well as a few sharp barks. Opening the door farther, Jack saw the edges of metal cages. He flipped on a light. He saw a few dogs and cats, but for the most part the room was filled with rats and mice. The animals stared back at him blankly. A few dogs wagged their tails in hopeful anticipation.

Jack shut the door. In Jack's mind the man in the parka was becoming some kind of fiendish microbiological devotee. Jack didn't even want to think about what kind of experiments were in progress with the animals he'd discovered.

A sudden, distant high-pitched whine of electrical machinery made Jack's heart skip a beat. He knew instantly what it was: the elevator!

With rapidly mounting panic, Jack frantically searched for the door to the hall. The spectacle of the lab diverted his attention from locating it. It didn't take long to find, but by the time Jack reached it, he feared the elevator would be nearing the fifth floor.

Jack's initial thought had been to dash up the stairs to the roof and then exit the building after the man in the parka had entered his apartment. But now with the elevator fast approaching, Jack thought he'd be seen. That left exiting the apartment the way he'd entered. But when the elevator motor stopped and the metal doors clanged, he knew there wasn't time.

Jack had to hide quickly, preferably close to the door to the hall. About ten feet away was a blank door. Jack rushed to it and opened it. It was a bathroom. Jack jumped in and pulled the door closed behind him. He had to hope the man in the parka had other things on his mind than using the toilet or washing his hands.

Hardly had Jack shut the bathroom door than he heard keys turning the locks of the outer door. The man came in, locked the door after him, then walked briskly away. The sound of his footsteps receded, then disappeared.

For a second Jack hesitated. He gauged how much time he needed to get to the door to the hall and unlock it. Once he got to the stairs he felt confident he could outrun the man in the parka. With all his basketball playing, Jack was in better shape than most.

As quietly as possible, Jack opened the door. At first he only cracked it to be able to listen. Jack heard nothing. Slowly he opened the door further so that he could peer out.

From Jack's vantage point he could see a large part of the lab. The man was not to be seen. Jack pushed the door open just enough to squeeze through. He eyed the door to the hall. There was a deadbolt a few inches above the knob.

Glancing around the lab once more, Jack slipped out of the bathroom and rushed silently over to the outer door. He grasped the knob with his left hand while his right hand went to the deadbolt. But there was an agonizing problem. The deadbolt had no knob. A key was required from both inside and out. Jack was locked in!

Panicked, Jack retreated to the bathroom. He felt desperate, like one of the poor animals penned in the makeshift shelter. His only hope was that the man in the parka would leave before using the bathroom. But it was not to be. After only a few agonizing minutes, the bathroom door was suddenly whisked open. The man, sans parka, started in but collided with Jack. Both men gasped.

Jack was about to say something clever when the man stepped back and slammed the door hard enough to bring down the shower curtain and rod.

Jack immediately went for the door handle for fear of being locked in. Putting his shoulder into it, Jack rammed the door. Unexpectedly the door opened without hindrance. Jack stumbled out of the bathroom, struggling to stay on his feet. Once he had his balance, his eyes darted around the loft. The man had disappeared.

Jack headed for the kitchen and the open window. He had no other choice. But he only made it as far as the living room. The man had also run there to snatch a large revolver out of a drawer in the coffee table. As Jack appeared, the man leveled the gun at him and told him to freeze.

Jack immediately complied. He even raised his hands. With such a large gun pointing at him, Jack wanted to be as cooperative as possible.

"What the hell are you doing here?" the man snarled.

His hair fell across his forehead, making him snap his head back to keep it out of his eyes.

It was that gesture more than anything else that made Jack recognize the man. It was Richard, the head tech from the Manhattan General's lab.

"Answer me!" Richard demanded.

Jack raised his hands higher, hoping the gesture might satisfy Richard, while his mind desperately sought some reasonable explanation of why he was there. But none came to mind. Under the circumstances Jack couldn't even think of anything clever to say.

Jack kept his eyes riveted to the gun barrel, which had moved to within three feet of his nose. He noticed the tip trembled, suggesting that Richard was not only angry but also acutely agitated. In Jack's mind such a combination was particularly dangerous.

"If you don't answer me I'm going to shoot you right now," Richard hissed.

"I'm a medical examiner," Jack blurted out. "I'm investigating."

"Bull!" Richard snapped. "Medical examiners don't go bursting into people's apartments."

"I didn't break in," Jack explained. "The window was open."

"Shut up," Richard said. "It's all the same. You're trespassing and meddling."

"I'm sorry," Jack said. "Couldn't we just talk about this?"

"Were you the one who sent me that fake package?" Richard demanded.

"What package?" Jack asked innocently.

Richard's eyes left Jack's, and they swept down to Jack's feet and then back up to his face. "You've even got on a fake deliveryman outfit. That took thought and effort."

"What are you talking about?" Jack asked. "I dress like this all the time when I'm not at the morgue."

"Bull!" Richard repeated. He pointed toward one of the couches with the gun. "Sit down!" he yelled.

"All right already," Jack said. "You only have to ask nicely." The initial shock was passing and his wits were returning. He sat where Richard indicated.

Richard backed up to the gun cabinet without taking his eyes off Jack. He groped for keys in his pocket and then tried to get the gun cabinet open without looking at what he was doing.

"Can I give you a hand?" Jack asked.

"Shut up!" Richard yelled. Even his hand with the key was shaking. When he got the glazed door open, he reached in and pulled out a pair of handcuffs.

"Now, that's a handy item to have around," Jack said.

Handcuffs in hand, Richard started back toward Jack, keeping the gun pointed at his face.

"I tell you what," Jack said. "Why don't we call the police. I'll confess, and they can take me away. Then I'll be out of your hair."

"Shut up," Richard ordered. He then motioned for Jack to get to his feet.

Jack complied and lifted his hands again.

"Move!" Richard said, motioning toward the main part of the lab.

Jack backed up. He was afraid to take his eyes off the gun. Richard kept coming toward him, the handcuffs dangling from his left hand.

"Over by the column," Richard snapped.

Jack did as he was instructed. He stood against the column. It was about fifteen inches in diameter.

"Face it," Richard commanded.

Jack turned around.

"Reach around it with your hands and grasp them together," Richard said.

When he did what Richard had insisted, Jack felt the handcuffs snap over each wrist. He was now locked to the column.

"Mind if I sit down?" Jack asked.

Richard didn't bother to answer. He hurried back into the living area. Jack lowered himself to the floor. The most comfortable position was embracing the column with his legs wrapped around it as well as his arms.

Jack could hear Richard dialling a telephone. Jack considered yelling for help when Richard started his conversation, but quickly scrapped the idea as suicidal, considering how nervous Richard was acting. Besides, whomever Richard was calling probably wouldn't care about Jack's plight.

"Jack Stapleton is here!" Richard blurted without pre-amble. "I caught him in my goddamn bathroom. He knows about Frazer Labs and he's been snooping around in here. I'm sure of it. Just like Beth Holderness at the lab."

The hairs on the back of Jack's neck rose up when he heard Richard mention Beth's name.

"Don't tell me to calm down!" Richard shouted. "This is an emergency. I shouldn't have gotten myself involved in this. You'd better get over here fast. This is your problem as well as it is mine."

Jack heard Richard slam down the telephone. The

man sounded even more agitated. A few minutes later Richard appeared without his gun.

He came over to Jack and looked down at him. Richard's lips were quivering. "How did you find out about Frazer Labs?" he demanded. "I know you sent the phony package, so there's no use lying."

Jack looked up into the man's face. Richard's pupils were widely dilated. He looked half crazy.

Without warning, Richard slapped Jack with an open palm. The blow split Jack's lower lip. A trickle of blood appeared at the corner of his mouth.

"You'd better start talking," Richard snarled.

Jack gingerly felt the damaged part of his lip with his tongue. It was numb. He tasted the saltiness of his blood.

"Maybe we should wait for your colleague," Jack said, to say something. His intuition told him he would soon be seeing Martin Cheveau or Kelley or possibly even Zimmerman.

The slap must have hurt Richard as well because he opened and closed his hand a few times and then disappeared back into the living area. Jack heard what he thought was the refrigerator being opened, then an ice tray being dumped.

A few minutes later Richard reappeared to glare at Jack. He had a dish towel wrapped around his hand. He commenced pacing, pausing every now and again to glance at his watch.

Time dragged by. Jack would have liked to have been able to take one of his throat lozenges, but it was impossible. He also noticed that his cough was increasing and that now he felt just plain sick. He guessed he had a fever.

The distant, high-pitched sound of the elevator

brought Jack's head up from where it had slumped against the column. Jack considered the fact that the buzzer hadn't sounded. That meant that whoever was on their way up had a key.

Richard heard the elevator motor as well. He went to the door and opened it to wait in the hall.

Jack heard the elevator arrive with a thump. The motor switched off and the elevator door clanged open.

"Where is he?" an angry voice demanded.

Jack was facing away from the door when he heard Richard and his visitor come into the loft. He heard the door close and be locked.

"He's over there," Richard said with equal venom. "Handcuffed to the column."

Jack took a breath and turned his head as he heard footsteps close in on him. When he caught sight of who it was, he gasped.

CHAPTER THIRTY-THREE

Wednesday, 7:45 P.M., March 27, 1996

"You bastard!" Terese snapped. "Why couldn't you let sleeping dogs lie. You and your stubbornness! You're screwing everything up, just when things are finally starting to go right."

Jack was dumbstruck. He looked up into her blue eyes, which he had only recently seen as soft. Now they looked as hard as pale sapphires. Her mouth was no longer sensuous. Her bloodless lips formed a grim line.

"Terese!" Richard yelled. "Don't waste time trying to talk with him. We got to figure out what we're going to do. What if someone knows he is here?"

Terese broke off from glaring at Jack to look at Richard. "Are those stupid cultures of yours in this lab?" she demanded.

"Of course they're here," Richard said.

"Then get rid of them," Terese said. "Flush them down the toilet."

"But, Terese!" Richard cried.

"Don't 'but Terese' me. Get rid of them. Now!"

"Even the influenza?" Richard questioned.

"Especially the influenza!" Terese snapped.

Morosely Richard went over to the freezer, unlocked it, and began rummaging through its contents.

"What am I going to do with you?" Terese asked,

redirecting her attention back to Jack. She was thinking out loud.

"For starters you could take off these handcuffs," Jack said. "Then we could all go for a quiet dinner at Positano, and you can let your friends know we are there."

"Shut up!" Terese exclaimed. "I've had it with your repartee."

Abruptly Terese left Jack and moved over next to Richard. She watched him gathering a handful of frozen vials. "All of it, now!" she warned. "There cannot be any evidence here, you understand?"

"It was the worst decision of my life to help you," Richard complained. When he had all the vials he disappeared into the bathroom.

"How are you involved in all this?" Jack asked Terese.

Terese didn't answer. Instead she walked around the partition into the living room. Behind him Jack heard the toilet flush, and he hated to think what had just been sent into the city's sewers to infect the sewer rats.

Richard reappeared and followed Terese into the living area. Jack couldn't see them, but given the high, unadorned ceiling he could hear them as if they were right next to him.

"We've got to get him out of here immediately," Terese said.

"And do what?" Richard asked moodily. "Dump him in the East River?"

"No, I think he should just disappear," Terese said. "What about Mom and Dad's farmhouse up in the Catskills?"

"I never thought of that," Richard said. His voice brightened. "But, yeah, that's a good idea."

"How will we get him up there?" Terese asked.

"I'll bring around my Explorer," Richard said.

"The problem is getting him into it and then keeping him quiet," Terese said.

"I've got a ketamine," Richard said.

"What's that?" Terese asked.

"It's an anesthetic agent," Richard said. "It's used a lot in veterinary medicine. There are some uses for humans, but it can cause hallucinations."

"I don't care if it causes hallucinations," Terese said. "All I care about is whether it will knock him out or not. Actually, it would be best just to have him tranquilized."

"Ketamine is all I've got," Richard said. "I can get it because it's not a scheduled drug. I use it with the animals."

"I don't want to hear any of that," Terese said. "Is it possible just to give him enough to make him dopey?"

"I don't know for sure," Richard said. "But I'll try."

"How do you give it?" Terese asked.

"Injection," Richard said. "But it's short-acting, so we might have to do it several times."

"Let's give it a try," Terese said.

Jack found himself perspiring heavily when Terese and Richard reappeared from the living room. Jack didn't know if it was from a fever or from the worry engendered by the conversation he'd just overheard. He did not like the idea of being an unwilling experimental subject with a potent anesthetic agent.

Richard went to a cabinet and got out a handful of syringes. From another cabinet he got the drug, which came in a glass vial with a rubber top. He then stopped to figure out a dose.

"What do you think he weighs?" Richard asked Terese as if Jack were an uncomprehending animal.

"I'd guess about one-eighty, give or take five pounds," Terese said.

Richard did some simple calculations, then filled one of the syringes. As he came at Jack, Jack had to fight off a panic attack. He wanted to scream, but he didn't. Richard injected the ketamine into his right upper arm. Jack winced. It burned like crazy.

"Let's see what that does," Richard said, stepping away. He discarded the used syringe. "While we wait I'll go get my car."

Terese nodded. Richard got his ski parka and pulled it on. At the door he told Terese he'd be back in ten minutes.

"So this is a sibling operation," Jack commented when he and Terese were alone.

"Don't remind me," Terese said, shaking her head. She began to pace as Richard had earlier.

The first effect Jack experienced from the ketamine was a ringing in his ears. Then his image of Terese began to do strange things. Jack blinked and shook his head, and he was outside of himself watching it happen. Then he saw Terese at the end of a long tunnel. Suddenly her face expanded to an enormous size. She was speaking but the sound echoed interminably. Her words were incomprehensible.

The next thing Jack was aware of was that he was walking. But it was a strange, uncoordinated walk, since he had no idea where the various parts of his body were. He had to look down to see his feet sweep out of the periphery of his vision and then plant themselves. When he tried to look where he was going he saw a fragmented image of brightly colored shapes and straight lines that were constantly moving.

He felt mild nausea, but when he shook himself it passed. He blinked and the colored shapes came together and merged into a large shiny object. A hand came into his field of vision and it touched the object. That was when Jack realized it was his hand and the object was a car.

Other elements of his immediate environment became recognizable. There were lights and a building. Then he realized that there were people on either side of him holding him up. They were speaking but their voices had a deep, mechanical sound as if they were synthesized.

Jack felt himself falling, but he couldn't stop himself. It seemed as if he fell for several minutes before landing on a hard surface. Then he could only see dark shapes. He was lying on a carpeted surface with something firm jutting into his stomach. When he tried to move he found that his wrists were restrained.

Time passed. Jack had no idea how long. It could have been minutes or it could have been hours. But at last he'd regained orientation, and he was no longer hallucinating. He realized that he was on the floor of a moving car, and his hands were handcuffed to the undercarriage of the front passenger seat. Presumably they were on their way to the Catskills.

To relieve the discomfort of the driveshaft pressing against his stomach, Jack drew his knees underneath him to assume a crouched-over position. It was far from ideal but better than it had been. But his discomfort was from more than his cramped posture. The flu symptoms were much worse, and combined with a hangover from the ketamine, he felt about as bad as he'd ever felt.

Several violent sneezes caused Terese to look over the back of the seat.

"Good God!" she exclaimed.

"Where are we?" Jack asked. His voice was hoarse, and the effort of speaking caused him to cough repeatedly. He was having a problem with his nose running, but with his hands secured he couldn't do anything about it.

"I think you better just shut up or you'll choke to death," Richard said.

Terese turned to Richard: "Is this coughing and sneezing from the shot you gave him?"

"How the hell do I know? It's not as if I've ever given ketamine to a person before."

"Well, it's not so far-fetched to imagine you might have an idea," Terese snapped. "You use it on those poor animals."

"I resent that," Richard said indignantly. "You know I treat those animals like my pets. That's why I have the ketamine in the first place."

Jack sensed that the anxiety that Terese and Richard had evidenced earlier about his presence had metamorphosed into irritation. From the way they were speaking it seemed to be mostly directed at each other.

After a brief silence, Richard spoke up. "You know, this whole thing was your idea, not mine," he said.

"Oh no!" Terese voiced. "I'm not about to let you get away with that misconception. You were the one who suggested causing AmeriCare trouble with nosocomial infection. It never would have even crossed my mind."

"I only suggested it after you complained so bitterly about AmeriCare gobbling up National Health's market share despite your stupid ad campaign," Richard said. "You begged me to help."

"I wanted some ideas," Terese said. "Something to use with the ads."

"Hell you did!" Richard said. "You don't go to a grocery store and ask for hardware. I don't know squat about advertising. You knew my field was microbiology. You knew what I'd suggest. It was what you were hoping."

"I never thought about it until you mentioned it," Terese countered. "Besides, all you suggested was that you could arrange some bad press by nuisance infections. I thought you meant colds, or diarrhea, or the flu."

"I did use the flu," Richard said.

"Yes, you used the flu," Terese said. "But was it regular flu? No, it was some weird stuff that has everybody up in arms, including Doctor Detective in the back seat. I thought you were going to use common illnesses, not the plague, for chrissake. Or those other ones. I can't even remember their names."

"You didn't complain when the press jumped all over the outbreaks and the market share rapidly reversed," Richard said. "You were happy."

"I was appalled," Terese said. "And scared. I just didn't say it."

"You're full of crap!" Richard said heatedly. "I talked with you the day after the plague broke out. You didn't mention it once. It even hurt my feelings since it took some effort on my part."

"I was afraid to say anything about it," Terese said. "I didn't want to associate myself with it in any way. But as bad as it was, I thought that was it. I didn't know you were planning on more."

"I can't believe I'm hearing this," Richard said.

Jack became aware they were slowing down. He lifted his head as high as his handcuffed hands would allow. The glare of artificial light penetrated the car. They'd been driving in darkness for some time.

Suddenly there were bright lights, and they'd come to a complete stop under an overhang. When Jack heard the driver's side window going down, he realized they were at a tollbooth. He started to yell for help, but his voice was weak and raspy.

Richard reacted swiftly by reaching around and smacking Jack with a hard object. The blow impacted on Jack's head. He collapsed onto the floor.

"Don't hit him so hard," Terese said. "You don't want blood on the inside of the car."

"I thought shutting him up was more important," Richard said. He threw a handful of coins into the bin of the automatic gate.

Jack's headache was now worse from the blow. He closed his eyes. He tried to find the most comfortable position, but there weren't many choices. Mercifully, he finally fell into a troubled sleep despite being thrown from side to side. After the toll they were driving on a winding and twisting road.

The next thing Jack knew, they were stopped again. Carefully he raised his head. Again there were lights outside of the car.

"Don't even think about it," Richard said. He had the revolver in his hand.

"Where are we?" Jack asked groggily.

"At an all-night convenience store," Richard said. "Terese wanted to get some basics."

Terese came back to the car with a bag of groceries.

"Did he stir?" she asked, as she climbed in.

"Yeah, he's awake," Richard said.

"Did he try to yell again?"

"Nope," Richard said. "He didn't dare."

They drove for another hour. Terese and Richard intermittently continued to bicker about whose fault the whole mess was. Neither was willing to give in.

Finally they turned off the paved road and bounced along a rutted gravel drive. Jack winced as his tender body thumped against the floor and the driveshaft hump.

Eventually they made a sharp turn to the left and came to a stop. Richard switched off the motor. Both he and Terese then got out.

Jack was left in the car by himself. Lifting his head as high as he could, he was only able to see a swatch of night sky. It was very dark. Getting his legs under him, Jack tried to see if he could possibly rip the handcuffs from beneath the seat. But it wasn't possible. The handcuffs had been looped around a stout piece of steel.

Collapsing back down, he resigned himself to waiting. It was half an hour before they came back for him. When they did they opened both doors on the passenger side.

Terese unlocked one side of the handcuffs.

"Out of the car!" Richard commanded. He held his gun aimed at Jack's head.

Jack did as he was told. Terese then quickly stepped forward and recuffed Jack's free hand.

"In the house!" Richard said.

Jack started walking on wobbly legs through the wet grass. It was much colder than in the city, and he could see his breath. Ahead a white farmhouse loomed in the darkness. There were lights in the windows facing a balustraded porch. Jack could make out smoke and a few sparks issuing from the chimney.

As they reached the porch, Jack glanced around. To the left he could see the dark outline of a barn. Beyond that was a field. Then there were mountains. There were no distant lights; it was an isolated, private hideaway.

"Come on!" Richard said, poking Jack in the ribs with the barrel of the gun. "Inside."

The interior was decorated as a comfortable weekend/summer house with an English country flair. There were matching calico couches facing each other in front of a massive fieldstone chimney. In the fireplace was a roaring, freshly kindled fire. An oriental rug covered most of the wide-board floor.

Through a large arch was a country kitchen with a center table and ladder-back chairs. Beyond the table was a Franklin stove. Against the far wall was a large 1920s-style porcelain sink.

Richard marched Jack into the kitchen and motioned for him to get down on the rag rug in front of the sink. Sensing he was about to be shackled to the plumbing, Jack asked to use the rest room.

The request brought on a new argument between brother and sister. Terese wanted Richard to go into the bathroom with Jack, but Richard flatly refused. He told Terese she could do it, but she thought it was Richard's role. Finally they agreed to let Jack go in by himself, since the guest bathroom had only one tiny window, one that was too small for Jack to climb through.

Left to himself, Jack got out the rimantadine and took one of the tablets. He'd been discouraged that the drug had not prevented his infection, but he did think it was slowing down the flu's course. No doubt his symptoms would be far worse if he weren't taking it.

When Jack came out of the bathroom, Richard took him back to the kitchen, and as Jack had anticipated, locked the handcuffs around the kitchen drainpipe. While Terese and Richard retired to the couches in front of the fire, Jack eyed the plumbing with the intent of escaping. The problem was that the pipes were old-fashioned. They weren't PVC or even copper. They were brass and cast iron. Jack tried putting pressure on them, but they didn't budge.

Resigned for the moment, Jack assumed the most comfortable position. It was lying on his back on the rag rug. He listened to Terese and Richard, who for the moment had gotten past their attempts to blame each other for the present catastrophe. They were now being more rational. They knew they had to make some decisions.

Jack's position on his back made his nasal discharge run down the back of his throat. His coughing jags returned, as did a round of violent sneezes. When he finally got himself under control he found himself looking up into Terese's and Richard's faces.

"We have to know how you found out about Frazer Labs," Richard said, gun once again in hand.

Jack feared that if they found out he was the only person who knew about Frazer Labs, they'd probably kill him then and there.

"It was easy," Jack said.

"Give us a clue how easy," Terese said.

"I just called up National Biologicals and asked if anyone had recently ordered plague bacteria. They told me Frazer Labs had."

Terese reacted as if she'd been slapped. Angrily she turned to Richard. "Don't tell me you ordered the stuff," she said with disbelief. "I thought you had all these bugs in your so-called collection."

"I didn't have plague," Richard said. "And I thought plague would make the biggest media impact. But what difference does it make? They can't trace where the bacteria came from."

"That's where you are wrong," Jack said. "National Biologicals tags their cultures. We all found out about it at the medical examiner's office when we did the autopsy."

"You idiot!" Terese shouted. "You've left a goddamn trail right to your door."

"I didn't know they tagged their cultures," Richard said meekly.

"Oh, God!" Terese said, rolling her eyes to the ceiling. "That means everybody at the ME's office knows the plague episode was artificial."

"What should we do?" Richard asked nervously.

"Wait a second," Terese said. She looked down at Jack. "I'm not sure he's telling the truth. I don't think that fits with what Colleen said. Hang on. Let me call her."

Terese's conversation with Colleen was short. Terese told her underling that she was worried about Jack and asked if Colleen could call Chet to inquire about Jack's conspiracy theory. Terese wanted to know if anyone else at the medical examiner's office subscribed to it. Terese concluded by telling Colleen that she was unreachable but would call back in fifteen minutes.

During the interim, there was little conversation except for Terese asking Richard if he was sure he'd disposed of the cultures. Richard assured her that he'd flushed everything down the toilet.

When the fifteen minutes was up, Terese redialed Colleen as promised. At the end of their brief conversation Terese thanked Colleen and hung up.

"That's the first good news tonight," Terese said to Richard. "No one else at the ME's office gives any credence to Jack's theory. Chet told Colleen that everyone chalks it up to Jack's grudge against AmeriCare."

"So no one else must know about Frazer Labs and the tagged bacteria," Richard said.

"Exactly," Terese said. "And that simplifies things dramatically. Now all we have to do is get rid of Jack."

"And how are you going to do that?" Richard asked.

"First you are going to dig a hole," Terese said. "I think the best spot would be on the other side of the barn by the blueberry patch."

"Now?" Richard questioned.

"This isn't something we can blithely put off, you idiot," Terese said.

"The ground's probably frozen," Richard complained. "It will be like digging in granite."

"You should have thought of that when you dreamed up this catastrophe," Terese said. "Get out there and get it done. There should be a shovel and a pick in the barn."

Richard grumbled as he pulled on his parka. He took the flashlight and went out the front door.

"Terese," Jack called out. "Don't you think you've taken this a bit too far?"

Terese got off the couch and came into the kitchen. She leaned against the cabinet and eyed Jack.

"Don't try to make me feel sorry for you," she said.

"If I warned you once, I warned you a dozen times to leave well enough alone. You've only yourself to blame."

"I can't believe your career can be this important to you," Jack said. "People have died, and more people can die still. Not just me."

"I never intended that anybody die," Terese said. "That only happened thanks to my hairbrained brother, who's had this love affair with microbes ever since he was at high school. He's collected bacteria the way a survivalist collects guns. Just having them around was a weird turn-on for him. Maybe I should have known he'd do something crazy sometime; I don't know. Right now I'm just trying to get us out of this mess."

"You're rationalizing," Jack said. "You're an accomplice, just as guilty as he is."

"You know something, Jack?" Terese said. "At this moment I couldn't care less what you think."

Terese walked back to the fire. Jack could hear more logs being added. He rested his head on his forearm and closed his eyes. He was miserable, both sick and frightened. He felt like a condemned man vainly waiting for a reprieve.

When the door burst open an hour later Jack jumped. He'd fallen asleep again. He also noticed a new symptom: now his eyes hurt when he looked from side to side.

"Digging the hole was easier than I thought," Richard reported. He peeled off his coat. "Wasn't any frost at all. It must have been a bog in that area at one time, because there weren't even any rocks."

"I hope you made it deep enough," Terese said, tossing aside a book. "I don't want any screwups, like having him wash up in the spring rain."

"It's plenty deep enough," Richard said. He disappeared into the bathroom to wash his hands. When he came out Terese was putting on her coat. "Where are you going?"

"Out," Terese said. She headed for the door. "I'll go for a walk while you kill Jack."

"Wait a second," Richard said. "Why me?"

"You're the man," Terese said with a scornful smile. "That's a man's work."

"The hell it is," Richard said. "I'm not going to kill him. I couldn't. I couldn't shoot someone while he's handcuffed."

"I don't believe you," Terese yelled. "You're not making sense. You had no compunction about putting lethal bacteria into defenceless people's humidifiers, which sure as hell killed them."

"It was the bacteria that killed them," Richard said. "It was a fight between the bacteria and the person's immune system. I didn't do the killing directly. They had a chance."

"Give me patience!" Terese cried, rolling her eyes heavenward. She collected herself and took a breath. "Okay, fine. With the patients it wasn't you, it was the bacteria. In this case it will be the bullet, not you. How's that? Does that satisfy this weird sense of responsibility of yours?"

"This is different," Richard said. "It's not the same at all."

"Richard, we don't have any choice. Otherwise you'll go to jail for the rest of your life."

Richard looked hesitantly over at the gun on the coffee table.

"Get it!" Terese commanded when she saw him eyeing the pistol.

Richard wavered.

"Come on, Richard," Terese urged.

Richard went over and irresolutely picked up the gun. Holding it by the barrel as well as the handle, he cocked it.

"Good!" Terese said encouragingly. "Now go over there and do it."

"Maybe if we take off the handcuffs, and he tries to run, I can . . ." Richard began. But he stopped in midsentence when Terese strode over to him with her eyes blazing. Without warning she slapped him. Richard recoiled from the blow, and his own anger flared.

"Don't even talk like that, you fool," Terese spat. "We are not taking any more chances. Understand?"

Richard put a hand to his face and then looked at it as if he expected to see blood. His initial fury quickly abated. He realized that Terese was right. Slowly he nodded.

"Okay, now get to it," Terese said. "I'll be outside."

Terese strode to the door. "Do it quickly, but don't make a mess," she said. Then she was gone.

Silence settled over the room. Richard didn't move. He only turned the gun over slowly in his hands, as if he were inspecting it. Finally, Jack spoke up: "I don't know whether I'd listen to her. You might face prison for the outbreaks if they can prove it was you behind them, but killing me like this in cold blood means the death penalty here in New York."

"Shut up," Richard screamed. He rushed into the kitchen and assumed a shooting stance directly behind Jack.

A full minute went by which seemed like an hour to Jack. He'd been holding his breath. Unable to hold it any longer, he exhaled – and immediately began coughing uncontrollably.

The next thing he knew, Richard tossed the gun onto the kitchen table. Then he ran to the door. He opened it and shouted out into the night: "I can't do it!"

Almost immediately Terese reappeared. "You goddamned coward!" she told him.

"Why don't you do it yourself?" Richard spat back.

Terese started to respond, but instead she strode to the kitchen table, snapped up the gun, and walked around to face Jack. Holding the pistol in both hands, she pointed it at his face. Jack stared back at her, directly into her eyes.

The tip of the gun barrel began to waver. All at once Terese let out a barrage of profanity and threw the gun back onto the table.

"Ah, iron woman isn't as hard as she thought," Richard taunted.

"Shut up," Terese said. She stalked back to the couch and sat down. Richard sat across from her. They eyed each other irritably.

"This is becoming a bad joke," she said.

"I think we are all strung out," Richard said.

"That's probably the first thing you've said that's true," Terese said. "I'm exhausted. What time is it?"

"It's after midnight," Richard said.

"No wonder," Terese said. "I've got a headache."

"I'm not feeling so great myself," Richard admitted.

"Let's sleep," Terese said. "We'll deal with this

problem in the morning. Right now I can't even see straight."

Jack woke up at four-thirty in the morning, shivering. The fire had gone out and the temperature in the room had fallen. The rag rug had provided some warmth. Jack had managed to pull it over him.

The room was almost completely dark. Terese and Richard had not left on any lights when they'd retired to separate bedrooms. What little light there was drifted in from outside through the windows over the sink. It was just enough for Jack to discern the vague shapes of the furniture.

Jack didn't know what made him feel worse: fear or the flu. At least his cough had not worsened. The rimantadine had seemingly protected him from developing primary influenza pneumonia.

For a few minutes Jack allowed himself the luxury of contemplating being rescued. The problem was that the chances were minuscule. The only person who knew that the National Biologicals probe test was positive with the plague culture was Ted Lynch, not that he could know what it meant. Agnes might, but there was no reason for Ted to tell Agnes what he'd found.

If rescue was not a viable possibility, then he'd have to rely on escape. With numb fingers Jack felt up and down the length of the drainpipe to which he was shackled. He tried to feel for any imperfections, but there were none. He positioned the handcuffs at various heights and, with his feet against the pipes, pushed until the handcuffs cut into his skin. The pipes were there to stay.

If he were to escape it would have to occur when he was allowed to go to the bathroom. How he would actually do it, he had no idea. All he could hope was that they'd become careless.

Jack shuddered when he thought of what morning might bring. A good night's sleep would only toughen Terese's resolve. The fact that neither Terese nor Richard could shoot him in cold blood the night before was scant reassurance. As self-centered as they both were, he couldn't bank on that continuing indefinitely.

Using his legs, Jack succeeded in getting the rag rug to fold over him again. Settling down as best he could, he tried to rest. If an opportunity of escape presented itself, he hoped he'd be physically able to take full advantage of it.

CHAPTER THIRTY-FOUR

Thursday, 8:15 A.M. March 28, 1996
Catskill Mountains, New York

The hours had passed slowly and miserably for Jack. He'd not been able to fall back asleep. Nor could he even find a comfortable position with his shivering. When Richard finally staggered into the room with his hair standing on end, Jack was almost glad to see him.

"I've got to use the bathroom," Jack called out.

"You'll have to wait for Terese to get up," Richard said. He was busy rebuilding the fire.

The door to Terese's room opened a few minutes later. Terese was dressed in an old bathrobe; she didn't look any better than Richard. Her normal helmet of highlighted curls looked more like a mop. She was without makeup, and the contrast with her normal appearance made her seem exceptionally pale.

"I've still got my headache," Terese complained. "And I slept lousy."

"Me too," Richard said. "It's the stress, and we never really had any dinner."

"But I'm not really hungry," Terese said. "I can't understand it."

"I've got to go to the bathroom," Jack repeated. "I've been waiting for hours."

"Get the gun," Terese said to Richard. "I'll unlock the handcuffs."

Terese came into the kitchen and bent down to reach under the sink with the handcuff key.

"Sorry you didn't sleep well," Jack said. "You should have joined me out here in the kitchen. It's been delightful."

"I don't want to hear any more mouth from you," Terese warned. "I'm not in the mood."

The handcuff snapped open. Jack rubbed his chafed wrist as he stiffly got to his feet. A wave of dizziness spread over him, forcing him to lean against the kitchen table. Terese quickly relocked the handcuff around Jack's free wrist. Jack wouldn't have been able to resist even if he'd had the intention.

"Okay, march!" Richard said. He was training the gun on Jack.

"In a second," Jack said. The room was still spinning.

"No tricks!" Terese said. She stepped away from him.

As soon as he could, Jack walked to the bathroom on rubbery legs. The first order of business was to relieve himself. The second was to take a dose of the rimantadine with a long drink of water. Only then did he hazard a look in the mirror. What he saw surprised him. He wasn't sure he would have recognized himself. He looked like a vagrant. His eyes were bright red and slightly swollen. Dried blood was on the left side of his face and spattered on the shoulder of his uniform shirt, apparently from the blow he'd received in the car at the tollbooth. His lip was swollen where Richard had split it. Dried mucus stuck to his formidable stubble.

"Hurry up in there," Terese commanded through the door.

Jack ran water in the sink and washed his face. Using

his index finger, he brushed his teeth. Then with a little more water he smoothed his hair.

"It's about time," Terese said when Jack emerged.

Jack suppressed the urge to give a clever retort. He felt he was walking a tightrope with these people, and he didn't want to push his luck. He hoped they wouldn't lock him back to the kitchen drain, but the wish was in vain. He was marched right back to the sink and secured.

"We should eat something," Richard said.

"I got cold cereal last night," Terese said.

"Fine," Richard said.

They sat at the table a mere four feet away from Jack. Terese ate very little. She again mentioned that she just wasn't hungry. They didn't offer any cereal to Jack.

"Have you thought about what we're going to do?" Richard asked.

"What about those people who were supposed to kill Jack in the city? Who were they?"

"It's a gang from down where I live," Richard said.

"How do you contact them?" Terese asked.

"I usually call them up or just go over to the building they occupy," Richard said. "I've been dealing with a man called Twin."

"Well, let's get him the hell up here," Terese said.

"He might come," Richard said. "If the money is right."

"Call him," Terese said. "How much were you going to pay them?"

"Five hundred," Richard said.

"Offer him a thousand if you have to," Terese said. "But say it's a rush job and that he's got to come today."

Richard scraped back his chair and went into the living room to get the phone. He brought it back to the kitchen table. He wanted her to listen in case they had to up the ante; he didn't know how Twin would respond to the idea of coming all the way to the Catskills.

Richard dialed and Twin answered. Richard told him he wanted to talk once again about knocking off the doctor.

"Hey, man, we're not interested," Twin said.

"I know there was trouble in the past," Richard said. "But this time it will be a snap. We have him handcuffed and hidden away outside the city."

"If that's the case, you don't need us," Twin said.

"Wait!" Richard said hastily. He'd sensed Twin was about to hang up. "We still need you. In fact, to make it worth your while driving out here, we'll pay double."

"A thousand bucks?" Twin asked.

"You got it," Richard said.

"Don't come, Twin," Jack shouted. "It's a setup!"

"Shit!" Richard barked. He told Twin to hold the line for a second. In a fit of fury, Richard cracked Jack over the head with the butt of his gun.

Jack closed his eyes hard enough to bring tears. The pain in his head was intense. Again he felt blood drip down the side of his scalp.

"Was that the doc?" Twin asked.

"Yeah, that was the doc," Richard said angrily.

"What did he mean, 'setup'?" Twin asked.

"Nothing," Richard said. "He's just running off at the mouth. We've got him handcuffed to the kitchen drainpipe."

"Let me get this straight," Twin said. "You're paying a thousand bucks for us to come out and ice the doc while he's chained to a pipe."

"It'll be like a turkey shoot," Richard assured him.

"Where are you?" Twin asked.

"About a hundred miles north of the city," Richard said. "In the Catskills."

There was a pause.

"What do you say?" Richard asked. "It's easy money."

"Why don't you do it yourself?" Twin asked.

"That's my business," Richard said.

"All right," Twin said. "Give me directions. But if there is any funny stuff, you'll be one unhappy dude."

Richard gave directions to get to the farmhouse and told Twin they'd be waiting for him.

Richard slowly replaced the receiver while he looked triumphantly at Terese.

"Well, thank God!" Terese said.

"I'd better call in sick," Richard said, picking up the phone again. "I should have been at work already."

After he finished his call Terese made a similar one to Colleen. Then she went to take a shower. Richard went to fill the wood box.

Wincing against the pain, Jack pushed himself back to a sitting position. At least the bleeding had stopped. The prospect of the Black Kings' arrival spelled doom. From bitter experience, Jack knew these gang members would have no qualms about shooting him no matter what state he was in.

For a few seconds Jack lost total control of himself. Like a child in a temper tantrum he yanked inconsequentially at his shackles. All he managed to do was cut into his wrists and knock over some detergent containers. There was no way he was about to break either the drainpipe or the handcuffs.

After the fit had passed, Jack slumped over and cried. But even that didn't last long. Wiping his face on his left sleeve, he sighed and sat up. He knew he had to escape. On his next trip to the bathroom he'd have to try something. It was his only chance, and he didn't have much time.

Three-quarters of an hour later Terese reappeared in her clothes. She dragged herself to the couch and plopped down. Richard was on the other couch flipping through an old 1950s *Life* magazine.

"I really don't feel too good," Terese admitted. "My headache is still killing me. I feel like I'm coming down with a cold."

"Me too," Richard said without looking up.

"I have to use the bathroom again," Jack called out.

Terese rolled her eyes. "Give me a break!" she said.

No one moved or spoke for five minutes.

"I suppose I can just let loose right here," Jack said, breaking the silence.

Terese sighed and threw her legs over the side of the couch. "Come on, stalwart warrior," she said disparagingly to Richard.

They used the same method as before. Terese unlocked the handcuffs while Richard stood poised with the gun.

"Do I really need these handcuffs while I'm in the bathroom?" Jack asked when Terese started to relock them.

"Absolutely," Terese said.

Once inside the bathroom Jack took another rimantadine and a long drink of water. Then, leaving the water running, he stepped on the closed toilet seat, grasped the window trim with both hands, and began to pull. He increased the pressure to see if the window casing would come loose.

Just then the door opened.

"Get down from there!" Terese snarled.

Jack stepped down from the toilet and cringed. He was afraid that Richard was about to hit him on the head again. Instead Richard just crowded into the bathroom, holding the gun out in front of him trained on Jack's face. The gun was cocked.

"Just give me a reason to shoot," he hissed.

For a second no one moved. Then Terese ordered Jack back to the kitchen sink.

"Can't you think of another place?" Jack said. "I'm getting tired of the view."

"Don't push me," Terese warned.

With the cocked gun just a few feet away, there was nothing Jack could do. In a matter of seconds he was handcuffed to the drainpipe yet again.

A half hour later Terese decided to go out to the store to get some aspirin and some soup. She asked Richard if he wanted anything. He told her to get some ice cream; he thought it might feel good on his sore throat.

After Terese had left, Jack told Richard that he had to go to the bathroom again.

"Yeah, sure," Richard said without budging from the couch.

"I do," Jack averred. "I didn't get to go last time."

Richard gave a short laugh. "Tough shit," he said. "It was your own fault."

"Come on," said Jack. "It will only take a minute."

"Listen!" Richard yelled. "If I come in there it will be to crack you over the head again. Understand?"

Jack understood all too well.

Twenty minutes later Jack heard the unmistakable sound of a car approaching along the gravel drive. He felt a rush of adrenaline in his system. Was it the Black Kings? His panic returned, and he stared forlornly at the unbudgeable drainpipe.

The door opened. To Jack's relief it was Terese. She dropped a bag of groceries on the kitchen table, then retreated to the couch and lay down and closed her eyes. She told Richard to put the groceries away.

Richard got up without enthusiasm. He put what had to be kept cold in the refrigerator and the ice cream in the freezer. Then he placed the cans of soup in the cupboard. In the bottom of the bag he found aspirin and a bunch of small cellophane-wrapped packages of peanut-butter crackers.

"You might give some of the crackers to Jack," Terese said.

Richard looked down at Jack. "You want some?" he asked.

Jack nodded. Although he still felt ill, his appetite had returned. He'd not eaten anything since the deli food in the van.

Richard fed Jack peanut butter crackers whole, like a mother bird dropping food into a waiting chick's gaping mouth. Jack hungrily devoured five of them and then asked for water.

"For chrissake!" Richard voiced. He was annoyed this job had fallen to him.

"Give it to him," Terese said.

Reluctantly Richard did as he was told. After a long drink Jack thanked him. Richard told Jack to thank Terese, not him.

"Bring me a couple of aspirin and some water," Terese said.

Richard rolled his eyes. "What am I, the servant?"

"Just do it," Terese said petulantly.

Three-quarters of an hour later another car could be heard coming up the driveway.

"Finally," Richard said as he tossed a magazine aside and heaved himself off the couch. "They must have driven by way of Philadelphia, for chrissake." He headed for the door while Terese pushed herself up to a sitting position.

Jack swallowed nervously. He could feel his pulse pounding in his temples. He realized he didn't have long to live.

Richard pulled open the door. "Shit!" he voiced.

Terese sat bolt upright. "What's the matter?"

"It's Henry, the goddamn caretaker!" Richard croaked. "What are we going to do?"

"You cover Jack!" Terese barked in panic. "I'll talk to Henry." She stood up and swayed for a moment as a wave of dizziness overcame her. Then she went out the door.

Richard dashed over to Jack. En route he'd picked up the gun, which he now held by the barrel as if it were a hatchet. "One word and so help me I'll bash your head in," he growled.

Jack looked up at Richard. He could see the man's determination. Outside he could hear a car come to a stop followed by the muffled sound of Terese's voice.

Jack was faced with an unreasonable quandary. He could yell, but how much sound he could make before being incapacitated by Richard was questionable. Yet if he didn't try, he'd soon be facing the Black Kings and certain death. He decided to go for it.

Jack put his head back and started to scream for help. As expected, Richard brought the handle of his gun crashing down on Jack's forehead. Jack's scream was cut off before he could form any words. A merciful darkness intervened with the suddenness of a light being switched off.

Jack regained consciousness in stages. The first thing he was aware of was that his eyes wouldn't open. But after a struggle the right one did, and a minute later so did the left. When he wiped his face on his sleeve he realized that his lids had been sealed together with coagulated blood.

With his forearm, Jack could feel that he had a sizable lump centered at his hairline. He knew it was a good place to be hit if you had to take a wallop. That part of the skull was by far the thickest.

He blinked to clear his vision and looked at his watch. It was just after four, a fact confirmed by the anemic quality of the late-afternoon sunlight coming through the window over the sink.

Jack glanced around the living room, which he could see from under the kitchen table. The fire had burned down significantly. Terese and Richard were sprawled on their respective couches.

Jack changed his position and in the process tipped over a container of window cleaner.

"What's he doing now?" Richard asked.

"Who the hell cares," Terese said. "What time is it?"

"It's after four," Richard said.

"Where are these gang friends of yours?" Terese demanded. "Are they coming by bicycle?"

"Should I call and check?" Richard asked.

"No, let's just wait here for a week," Terese said irritably.

Richard put the phone on his chest and dialed. When the phone was answered he had to ask for Twin. After a long wait Twin came on the line.

"Why the hell aren't you here?" Richard complained. "We've been waiting all day."

"I'm not coming, man," Twin said.

"But you said you were," Richard rejoined.

"I can't do it, man," Twin said. "I can't come."

"Not even for a thousand dollars?"

"Nope," Twin said.

"But why?" Richard demanded.

"'Cause I gave my word," Twin said.

"You gave your word? What does that mean?" Richard asked.

"Just what I said," Twin said. "Don't you understand English?"

"But this is ridiculous," Richard said.

"Hey, it's your party," Twin said. "You have to do your own shit."

Richard found himself holding a dead telephone. He slammed the receiver down. "That worthless bum," he spat. "He won't do it. I can't believe it."

Terese pushed herself up into a sitting position. "So much for that idea. That puts us back to square one."

"Don't look at me. I'm not doing it," Richard snapped. "I've made that crystal clear. It's up to you, sister. Hell, all this was for your benefit, not mine."

"Supposedly," Terese retorted. "But you got some perverted enjoyment out of it. You finally got to use those bugs you've been playing with all your life. Yet now you can't do this simple thing. You're some sort of . . ." She struggled for the word: "Degenerate!" she said finally.

"Well, you're no Snow White yourself," Richard yelled. "No wonder that husband of yours left you."

Terese's face flushed. She opened her mouth but no words came out. Suddenly she lunged for the gun.

Richard took a step backward. He feared he'd overdone it by mentioning the unmentionable. For a second he thought Terese was about to use the gun on him. But instead she flew into the kitchen, cocking the gun as she went. She stepped up to Jack and pointed the gun at his bloodied face.

"Turn away!" she commanded.

Jack felt as if his heart had stopped. He looked up the quivering barrel and into Terese's arctic blue eyes. He was paralyzed, incapable of following her command.

"Damn you!" Terese said through a sudden flood of tears.

Uncocking the gun, she tossed it aside, then rushed back to the couch to bury her head in her hands. She was sobbing.

Richard felt guilty. He knew he shouldn't have said what he had. Losing her baby and then her husband was his sister's Achilles' heel. Meekly he went over to her and sat on the edge of the couch.

"I didn't mean it," Richard said, stroking her back gently. "It slipped out. I'm not myself."

Terese sat up and wiped her eyes. "I'm not myself either," she admitted. "I can't believe these tears. I'm a wreck. I feel awful too. Now my throat's sore."

"You want another aspirin?" Richard asked.

Terese shook her head. "What do you think Twin meant about giving his word?" she asked.

"I don't know," Richard said. "That's why I asked him."

"Why didn't you offer him more money?" Terese said.

"He didn't give me a chance," Richard said. "He hung up."

"Well, call him back," Terese said. "We have to get out of here."

"How much should I offer?" Richard said. "I don't have the kind of money you have."

"Whatever it takes," Terese said. "At this point money shouldn't be a limiting factor."

Richard picked up the phone and dialed. This time when he asked for Twin he was told Twin was out. He wouldn't be back for an hour. Richard hung up.

"We have to wait," he said.

"What else is new?" Terese commented.

Terese lay back on the couch and pulled a crocheted afghan over her. She shivered. "Is it getting cold in here or is it just me?" she asked.

"I had a couple of chills myself," Richard said. He went to the fire and piled on more logs. Then he got a blanket from his bedroom before reclining on his couch. He tried to read, but he couldn't concentrate. He was intermittently shivering despite the blanket. "I just thought of a new worry," he said.

"What now?" Terese asked. Her eyes were closed.

"Jack's been sneezing and coughing. You don't think he was exposed to my flu strain, the one I put in the humidifier?"

With the blanket wrapped around him, Richard got up and went into the kitchen and asked Jack about it. Jack didn't answer.

"Come on, Doc," Richard urged. "Don't make me have to hit you again."

"What difference does it make?" Terese called from the couch.

"It makes a lot of difference," Richard said. "There's a good chance my strain was the strain that caused the great flu epidemic of 1918. I got it in Alaska from a couple of frozen Eskimos who died of pneumonia. The time frame was right."

Terese joined him in the kitchen. "Now you're getting me worried," she said. "Do you think he has it and has exposed us?"

"It's possible," Richard said.

"That's terrifying!" She looked down at Jack. "Well?" she demanded. "Were you exposed?"

Jack wasn't sure if he should admit to his exposure or not. He didn't know which would anger them more. The truth or his silence.

"I don't like it that he's not answering," Richard said.

"He's a medical examiner," Terese said. "He had to have been exposed. They brought the dead people to him. He told me on the phone."

"I'm not afraid of that," Richard said. "The exposure to worry about is to a living, breathing, sneezing, coughing person, not a dead body."

"Medical examiners don't take care of live people," Terese said. "All their patients are dead."

"That's true," Richard admitted.

"Besides," Terese said, "Jack is hardly sick. He's got a cold. Big deal. Wouldn't he be really ill by now if he'd contracted your flu bug?"

"You're right," Richard said. "I'm not thinking

straight; if he had the 1918 flu bug he'd be flat out by now."

Brother and sister returned to their couches and collapsed.

"I can't take much more of this," Terese said. "Especially the way I feel."

At five-fifteen, exactly one hour after the previous call, Richard phoned Twin. This time Twin himself picked up.

"What the hell are you pestering me for?" Twin asked.

"I want to offer more money," Richard said. "Obviously a thousand wasn't enough. I understand. It's a long drive up here. How much are you looking for?"

"You didn't understand me, did you?" Twin said irritably. "I told you I couldn't do it. That's it. Game's over."

"Two thousand," Richard said. He looked over at Terese. She nodded.

"Hey, man, are you deaf or what?" Twin said. "How many times . . ."

"Three thousand," Richard said, and Terese again nodded.

"Three thousand bucks?" Twin repeated.

"That's correct," Richard said.

"You are sounding desperate," Twin said.

"We're willing to pay three thousand dollars," Richard said. "That should speak for itself."

"Hmmm," Twin said. "And you say you have the doc handcuffed."

"Exactly," Richard said. "It will be a piece of cake."

"I tell you what," Twin said. "I'll send someone up there tomorrow morning."

"You're not going to do what you did this morning, are you?" Richard asked.

"No," Twin said. "I guarantee I'll have someone up there to take care of things."

"For three thousand," Richard said. He wanted to be sure they understood each other.

"Three thousand will be just fine," Twin said.

Richard replaced the receiver and looked over at Terese.

"Do you believe him?" she asked.

"This time he guaranteed it," Richard said. "And when Twin guarantees something, it happens. He'll be here in the morning. I'm confident."

Terese sighed. "Thank God for small favors," she said.

Jack wasn't so relieved. His panic rekindled, he determined he had to find a way to escape that night. Morning would bring the apocalypse.

Afternoon dragged into evening. Terese and Richard fell asleep. Unattended, the fire died down. A chill came with the darkness. Jack wracked his brains for ideas of escape, but unless he was freed from the drainpipe, he didn't see how he could get away.

Around seven both Richard and Terese began to cough in their sleep. At first they seemed more to be clearing their throats than coughing, but soon the hacking became more forceful and productive. Jack considered the development significant. It gave support to a concern he'd been harboring since they both began complaining of chills: namely, that they had caught the dreaded flu from him just as Richard suspected.

Thinking back to the long car ride from the city, Jack realized it would have been hard for them not to have contracted his illness. During the ride Jack's symptoms were peaking, and symptoms of flu often peaked with maximum viral production. Each of Jack's sneezes and coughs had undoubtedly sent millions of the infective virions into the car's confined space.

Still, Jack couldn't be sure. Besides, his real worry was facing the Black Kings in the morning. He had more pressing concerns than the health of his captors.

Jack yanked futilely at the drain with the short chain between the handcuffs. All he succeeded in doing was to make a racket and abrade his wrists more than they already were.

"Shut up!" Richard yelled after having been awakened by the clamor. He switched on a table lamp, then was immediately overwhelmed by a fit of coughing.

"What's happening?" Terese asked groggily.

"The animal is restless," Richard rasped. "God, I need some water." He sat up, waited for a moment, then got to his feet. "I'm dizzy," he said. "I might even have a fever."

He walked hesitantly into the kitchen and got a glass. As he was filling it, Jack thought about knocking his legs out from under him. But he decided that would only win him another blow to the head.

"I have to go to the bathroom," Jack said.

"Shut up," Richard said.

"It's been a long time," Jack said. "It's not as if I'm asking to go for a run in the yard. And if I don't go, it's going to be unpleasant around here."

Richard shook his head in resignation. After he took a drink of water, he called out to Terese that her services were needed. Then he got the gun from the kitchen table.

Jack heard Richard cock the gun. The move narrowed Jack's options.

Terese appeared with the key. Jack noticed her eyes had a glazed, feverish look. She bent down under the sink and unlocked one side of the handcuffs without a word. She backed away as Jack got to his feet. As before, the room swam before his eyes. Some escape artist, he thought cynically. He was weak from lack of food, sleep, and liquids. Terese relocked the handcuffs.

Richard marched directly behind Jack with the gun at the ready. There was nothing that Jack could do. When he got to the bathroom he tried to close the door.

"Sorry," Terese said, using her foot to block it. "You lost that privilege."

Jack looked from one to the other. He could tell there was no use arguing. He shrugged and turned around to relieve himself. When he was finished he motioned towards the sink. "How about my washing my face," he asked.

"If you must," Terese said. She coughed but then held herself in check. It was obvious her throat was sore.

Jack stepped to the sink, which was out of the line of Terese's sight. After turning on the water, Jack surreptitiously got out his rimantadine and took one of the tablets. In his haste he almost dropped the vial before getting it back into his pocket.

He glanced at himself in the mirror and recoiled. He looked significantly worse than he had that morning, thanks to the new laceration high on his forehead. It was gaping and needed stitches if it was to heal without a scar. Jack laughed at himself. What a time to worry about cosmetics!

The trip back to the spot of Jack's internment was

without incident. There were a few moments when Jack was tempted to try something, but each time his courage failed him. By the time Jack was again locked up under the sink he felt disappointed in himself and correspondingly despondent. He had the disheartening sense that he'd just let his last chance of escape slip by.

"Do you want any soup?" Terese asked Richard.

"I'm really not hungry," Richard admitted. "All I want is a couple of aspirin. I feel like I've been run over by a truck."

"I'm not hungry either," Terese said. "This is more than a cold. I'm sure I have a fever too. Do you think we should be worried?"

"Obviously we've got what Jack has," Richard said. "I guess he's just more stoic. Anyway, we'll see a doctor tomorrow after Twin's visit if we think we should. Who knows, maybe a night's sleep is all we need."

"Let me have a couple of those aspirins," Terese said.

After taking their analgesic Terese and Richard returned to the living room. Richard spent a few moments building up the dying fire. Terese made herself as comfortable as possible on her couch. Soon Richard went back to his. They both seemed exhausted.

Jack was surer than ever that both his captors had the deadly strain of the flu. He didn't know what his ethics dictated he do. The problem was his rimantadine, and the fact that it possibly could thwart the flu's progress. Jack agonized silently over whether he should tell them of his exposure and talk them into taking the drug to potentially save their lives even though they were totally committed to ending his and were responsible for the deaths of other innocent victims. With that in mind, did he owe Terese and Richard compassion in the face of their callous indifference? Should his oath as a physician prevail?

Jack took no comfort at the notion of poetic justice being done. Yet if he shared the rimantadine with them, they might deny it to him. After all, they weren't choosy about the way he died as long as it wasn't directly by their hand.

Jack sighed. It was an impossible decision. He couldn't choose. But not making a decision was, in effect, a decision. Jack understood its ramifications.

By nine o'clock Terese's and Richard's breathing had become stertorous, punctuated by frequent coughing episodes. Terese's condition seemed worse than Richard's. Around ten a markedly violent fit of coughing woke Terese up, and she moaned for Richard.

"What's the matter?" Richard questioned lethargically.

"I'm feeling worse," Terese said. "I need some water and another aspirin."

Richard got up and woozily made his way into the kitchen. He gave Jack a halfhearted kick to move him out of the way. Needing little encouragement, Jack scrambled to the side as much as his shackled hands would allow. Richard filled a glass with water and stumbled back to Terese.

Terese sat up to take the aspirin and the water, while Richard helped support the glass. When she was finished with the water, she pushed the glass away and wiped her mouth with her hand. Her movements were jerky. "With the way I'm feeling, do you think we should head back to the city tonight?" she questioned.

"We have to wait for morning," Richard said. "As soon as Twin comes we'll be off. Besides, I'm too sleepy to drive now anyway."

"You're right," Terese said as she flopped back. "At the moment I don't think I could stand the drive either. Not with this cough. It's hard to catch my breath."

"Sleep it off," Richard said. "I'll leave the rest of the water right here next to you." He put the glass on the coffee table.

"Thanks," Terese murmured.

Richard made his way back to his couch and collapsed. He drew the blanket up around his neck and sighed loudly.

Time dragged, and with it Terese and Richard's congested breathing slowly got worse. By ten-thirty Jack noticed that Terese's respiration was labored. Even from as far away as the kitchen he could see that her lips had become dusky. He was amazed she'd not awakened. He guessed the aspirin had brought her fever down.

In spite of his ambivalence, Jack was finally moved to say something. He called out to Richard and told him Terese didn't sound or look good.

"Shut up!" Richard yelled back between coughs.

Jack stayed silent for another half hour. By then he was convinced he could hear faint popping noises at the end of each of Terese's inspirations that sounded like moist rales. If they were, it was an ominous sign, suggesting to Jack that Terese was slipping into acute respiratory distress.

"Richard!" Jack called out, despite Richard's warning to stay quiet. "Terese is getting worse."

There was no response.

"Richard!" Jack called louder.

"What?" Richard answered sluggishly.

"I think your sister needs to be in an intensive care unit," Jack said.

Richard didn't respond.

"I'm warning you," Jack called. "I'm a doctor, after all, and I should know. If you don't do something it's going to be your fault."

Jack had hit a nerve, and to his surprise Richard leaped off the couch in a fit of rage. "My fault?" he snarled. "It's your fault for giving us whatever we have!" Frantically he looked for the gun, but he couldn't remember what he'd done with it after Jack's last visit to the bathroom.

The search for the pistol only lasted for a few seconds. Richard suddenly grabbed his head with both hands and moaned about his headache. Then he swayed before collapsing back onto the couch.

Jack sighed with relief. Touching off a fit of rage in Richard had not been expected. He tried not to imagine what might have happened had the gun been handy.

Jack resigned himself to the horror of witnessing the spectacle of a virulently pathogenic influenza wreaking its havoc. With Terese's and Richard's rapidly worsening clinical state, he recalled stories that had been told about the terrible influenza pandemic of 1918–19. People were said to have boarded a subway in Brooklyn with mild symptoms, only to be dead by the time they'd reached their destination in Manhattan. When Jack had heard such stories he'd assumed they had been exaggerations. But now that he was being forced to observe Terese and Richard, he no longer thought so. Their swift deterioration was a frightening display of the power of contagion.

By one a.m. Richard's breathing was as labored as Terese's had been. Terese was now frankly cyanotic and barely breathing. By four Richard was cyanotic, and Terese was dead. At six a.m. Richard made a few feeble gurgling sounds and then stopped breathing.

CHAPTER THIRTY-FIVE

Friday, 8:00 A.M., March 29, 1996

Morning came slowly. At first pale fingers of sunlight limned the edge of the porcelain sink. From where Jack was sitting he could see a spiderweb of leafless tree branches against the gradually brightening sky. He hadn't slept a wink.

When the room was completely filled with morning light, Jack hazarded a look over his shoulder. It was not a pretty scene. Terese and Richard were both dead, with bloody froth exuding from their dusky blue lips. Both had started to bloat slightly, particularly Terese. Jack assumed it was from the heat of the fire, which was now reduced to mere embers.

Jack looked back despairingly at the drainpipe that so effectively nailed him to his spot. It was an inconceivable predicament. Twin and his Black Kings were probably now on their way. Even without the three thousand dollars, the gang had ample reason to kill him given his role in two of their members' deaths.

Throwing back his head, Jack screamed at the top of his voice for help. He knew it was futile and soon stopped when he was out of breath. He rattled the handcuffs against the brass pipe, and even put his head under the sink to examine the lead seal where the brass pipe joined the cast-iron pipe below the trap. With a fingernail he tried to dig into the lead, but without result.

Eventually Jack sat back. His anxiety was enervating, coupled with his lack of sleep, food, and water. It was hard to think clearly, but he had to try; he didn't have much time.

Jack considered the faint possibility that the Black Kings wouldn't show up as they'd failed to show the day before, yet that prospect wasn't any rosier. Jack would be sentenced to an agonizing death from exposure and lack of water. Of course, if he couldn't take his rimantadine, the flu might get him first.

Jack fought back tears. How could he have been so stupid as to have allowed himself to get caught in such an impossible situation? He chided himself for his inane heroic crusade idea, and the juvenile thought of wanting to prove something to himself. He'd been as reckless in this episode as he'd been each day he'd ridden his bike down Second Avenue thumbing his nose at death.

Two hours passed before Jack heard the faint beginnings of the dread sound: the crackling of car tires on gravel. The Black Kings had arrived.

In a fit of panic, Jack repeatedly kicked the drainpipe as he'd done numerous times over the previous day and a half with the same result.

He stopped and listened again. The car was closer. Jack looked at the sink. Suddenly an idea occurred to him. The sink was a huge, old cast-iron monstrosity with a large bowl and expansive drainage area for dishes. Jack imagined it weighed several hundred pounds. It was hung on the wall in addition to being supported by the heavy drain.

Getting his feet under him, Jack rested the underlip

of the sink on his biceps and tried to pry the sink upward. It moved slightly and bits of mortar at the sink's junction with the wall fell into the bowl.

Jack twisted like a contortionist to put his foot right against the sink's lip. He could hear the car come to a halt the moment he pushed with his leg. There was a cracking sound. Jack positioned himself so that both his feet were under the edge of the sink. Straining with all his might, he exerted the maximum force he could muster.

With a snap and a grinding sound the sink detached from the wall. A bit of plaster rained down on Jack's face. Unattached, the sink teetered on the drain.

With another thrust of his legs, Jack got the sink to fall forward. The copper water-supply pipes snapped off at their soldered ends and water began spraying. The drain remained intact until the lead seal gave way. At that moment the brass pipe slipped out of the cast iron. The sink made an enormous crashing noise as it crushed a ladder-back chair before thumping heavily on the wooden floor.

Jack was soaked from the spraying water, but he was free! He scrambled to his feet as heavy footfalls sounded on the front porch. He knew the door was unlocked and that the Black Kings would be inside in a moment. They'd undoubtedly heard the crash of the sink.

With no time to look for the pistol Jack lunged for the back door. Frantically he fumbled with the deadbolt and threw the door open. In an instant he was outside, hurling himself down the few steps to the dew-covered grass.

Hunching down to stay out of view, Jack ran from the house as fast as he could manage with his hands still handcuffed. Ahead was a pond. It occupied the area he'd imagined was a field on his arrival the previous night. To the left of the pond and about a hundred feet from the house stood the barn. Jack ran to it. It was his only hope of a hiding place. The surrounding forest was barren and leafless.

With heart pounding, Jack reached the barn door. To his relief it was unlocked. He yanked it open, dashed inside, and pulled it closed behind him.

The interior of the barn was dark, dank, and uninviting. The only light came through a single, west-facing window. The rusted remains of an old tractor loomed in the half-light.

With utter panic Jack stumbled around in the darkness searching for a hiding place. His eyes began to adjust. He looked into several deserted animal stalls, but there was no way to conceal himself. There was a loft above, but it was devoid of hay.

Looking down at the plank flooring, Jack vainly searched for a trapdoor, but there wasn't any. In the very back of the barn there was a small room filled with garden tools but still no place to hide. Jack was about to give up when he spotted a low wooden chest the size of a coffin. He ran to it and raised its hinged lid. Inside were malodorous bags of fertilizer.

Jack's blood ran cold. Outside he heard a male voice yell: "Hey, man, around here! There's tracks in the grass!"

With little other choice Jack emptied the chest of the bags of fertilizer. Then he climbed in and lowered the lid.

Shivering from fear and the damp cold, Jack was still perspiring. His breath was coming in short gasps. He tried to calm down. If the hiding place was to work, he'd have to be silent.

It wasn't long before he heard the door to the barn creak open followed by the sound of muffled voices. Footsteps sounded on the plank flooring. Then there was a crash as something was overturned. Jack heard curses. Then another crash.

"You got your machine pistol cocked?" one husky voice said.

"What d' you think I am, stupid?" another replied.

Jack heard footsteps approach. He held his breath, tried to contain his shivering, and fought the urge to cough. There was a pause, then the footsteps receded. Jack allowed himself to breathe out.

"Somebody's in here, I'm sure of it," a voice said.

"Shut up and keep looking," the other answered.

Without warning the cover to Jack's hiding place was whisked open. It happened with such unexpected suddenness, Jack was totally unprepared. He let out a muffled screech. The black man looking down at him did the same, letting the lid slam back into place.

The lid was quickly yanked open again. Jack could see that the man was holding a machine pistol in his free hand. On his head was a black knit cap.

Jack and the black man locked eyes for a moment, then the man looked toward his partner.

"It's the doc all right," he called out. "He's here in a box."

Jack was afraid to move. He heard footsteps approaching. He tried to prepare himself for Twin's mocking smile. But Jack's expectations weren't met. When he looked up, it wasn't Twin's face he saw; it was Warren's!

"Shit, Doc," Warren said. "You look like you fought the Vietnam War all by yourself."

Jack swallowed. He looked at the other man and now recognized him as one of the basketball regulars. Jack's eyes darted back to Warren. Jack was confused, afraid this was all a hallucination.

"Come on, Doc," Warren said, reaching a hand toward Jack. "Get the hell out of the box so we can see if the rest of you looks as bad as your face."

Jack allowed himself to be helped to stand up. He stepped out onto the floor. He was soaking wet from the broken water pipes.

"Well, everything else looks like it's in working order," Warren said. "But you don't smell great. And we've got to get these cuffs off."

"How did you get here?" Jack asked, finally finding his voice.

"We drove," Warren said. "How d' you think we got here? The subway?"

"But I expected the Black Kings," Jack said. "A guy by the name of Twin."

"Sorry to disappoint you, man," Warren said. "You've got to settle for me."

"I don't understand," Jack said.

"Twin and I made a deal," Warren said. "We called a truce so there'd be no more brothers shooting brothers. Part of the terms were that they wouldn't ice you. Then Twin called me and told me you were being held up here and that if I wanted to save your ass, I'd better get mine up to the mountains. So here we are: the cavalry."

"Good Lord!" Jack said, shaking his head. It was unsettling to learn how much one's fate was in the hands of others.

"Hey, those people back in the house don't look so good," Warren said. "And they smell worse than you. How'd they happen to die?"

"Influenza," Jack said.

"No shit!" Warren said. "So it's up here too. I heard about it on the news last night. There's a lot of people down in the city all revved up about it."

"And for good reason," Jack said. "I think you'd better tell me what you've heard."

EPILOGUE

The game to eleven was tied at ten apiece. The rules dictated a win by two, so a one-point layup wouldn't clinch it but a long two-pointer would. This was in the back of Jack's mind as he dribbled upcourt. He was being mercilessly hounded by an aggressive player by the name of Flash who Jack knew was faster then he.

The competition was fierce. Players on the sidelines waiting to play were loudly supporting the other team, a sharp contrast to their typical studied indifference. The reason for the change was the fact that Jack's team had been winning all night, mainly because Jack was teamed up with a particularly good mix of players that included Warren and Spit.

Jack normally didn't bring the ball downcourt. That was Warren's job. But on the previous play, to Jack's chagrin, Flash had made a driving layup to tie the game, and after the ball had passed through the basket it had ended up in Jack's hands. In order to get the ball downcourt as fast as possible, Spit had stepped out. When Jack gave him the ball, Spit gave it right back.

As Jack pulled up at the top of the key, Warren faked one direction and then made a rush for the basket. Jack saw this maneuver out of the corner of his eye and cocked his arm with the intent of passing the ball to Warren.

Flash anticipated the pass and dropped back in hopes of intercepting it. All at once Jack was in the clear, and he changed his mind about passing. Instead he let fly one of his normally reliable jumpers. Unfortunately the ball hit the back of the rim and bounded directly into Flash's waiting hands.

The tide then swept back in the other direction, to the glee of the onlookers.

Flash brought the ball rapidly downcourt. Jack was intent on denying him the opportunity of repeating his driving layup, but inadvertently gave him too much room. To Jack's surprise, since Flash was not an outside shooter, Flash pulled up and from "downtown" let fly his own jumper.

To Jack's horror it was "nothing-but-net" as the shot passed through the basket. A cheer rose up from the sidelines. The game had been won by the underdogs.

Flash high-stepped around the court holding his arms straight and stiffly to his sides with his palms out. All his teammates slapped his palms in a congratulatory ritual, as did some of the onlookers.

Warren drifted over to Jack with a disgusted look on his face.

"You should have passed the friggin' ball," Warren said.

"My bad," Jack said. He was embarrassed. He'd made three mistakes in a row.

"Shit," Warren said. "With these new kicks of mine I didn't think I could lose."

Jack looked down at the spanking-new pair of Nikes

Warren was referring to and then at his own scuffed and scarred Filas. "Maybe I need some new kicks myself."

"Jack! Hey, Jack!" a female voice called out. "Hello!"

Jack looked through the chain-link fence separating the playground from the sidewalk. It was Laurie.

"Hey, kid!" Warren said to Jack. "Looks like your shortie has decided to pay the courts a visit."

The game-winning celebration stopped. All eyes turned to Laurie. Girlfriends and wives didn't come to the courts. Whether they weren't inclined or whether they were actively excluded, Jack didn't know. But the infraction of Laurie's unexpected arrival made him feel uncomfortable. He'd always tried to play by the playground's mostly unspoken rules.

"I think she wants to rap," Warren said. Laurie was waving Jack over.

"I didn't invite her," Jack said. "We were supposed to meet later."

"No problem," Warren said. "She's a looker. You must be a better lover than you are a b-ball player."

Jack laughed in spite of himself, then walked over to Laurie. Behind him he heard the celebration recommence, and he relaxed a degree.

"Now I know the stories are all true," Laurie said. "You really do play basketball."

"I hope you didn't see the last three plays," Jack said. "You wouldn't have guessed I played much if you had."

"I know we weren't supposed to meet until nine, but I couldn't wait to talk to you," Laurie said.

"What's happened?" Jack asked.

"You got a call from a Nicole Marquette from the CDC," Laurie said. "Apparently she was so disappointed not to get you that Marjorie, the operator, put her through to me. Nicole asked me to relay a message to you."

"Well?" Jack questioned.

"The CDC is officially putting the crash vaccine program on hold," Laurie said. "There hasn't been a new case of the Alaska-strain influenza for two weeks. The quarantine efforts have worked. Apparently the outbreak has been contained just the way the seventy-six swine-flu was."

"That's great news!" Jack said. Over the past week he'd been praying that this would happen, and Laurie knew it. After fifty-two cases with thirty-four deaths there had been a lull. Everyone involved was holding his breath.

"Did she offer any explanations as to why they think this has occurred?" Jack asked.

"She did," Laurie said. "Their studies have shown that the virus is unusually unstable outside of a host. They believe that the temperature must have varied in the buried Eskimo hut and might have even approached thawing on occasion. That's a far cry from the usual minus fifty degrees at which viruses are typically stored."

"Too bad it didn't affect its pathogenicity as well," Jack said.

"But at least it made the CDC-engineered quarantine effective," Laurie said, "which everyone knows isn't the usual case with influenza. Apparently with the Alaska strain, contacts had to have relatively sustained close contact with an infected individual for transmission to occur."

"I think we were all very lucky," Jack said. "The pharmaceutical industry deserves a lot of credit too. They came through with all the rimantadine needed in record time."

"Are you finished playing basketball?" Laurie asked. She looked over Jack's shoulder and could see that another game had commenced.

"I'm afraid so," Jack said. "My team lost, thanks to me."

"Is that man you were talking with when I arrived Warren?" Laurie asked.

"That's right," Jack said.

"He's just as you described," Laurie said. "He looks impressive. But there's one thing I don't understand. How do those shorts of his stay on? They are so oversized and he has such narrow hips."

Jack let out a laugh. He looked back at Warren casually shooting foul shots like a machine. The funny thing was that Laurie was right: Warren's shorts defied Newton's law of gravity. Jack was just so accustomed to the hip-hop gear, he'd never questioned it.

"I guess it's a mystery to me too," Jack said. "You'll have to ask him yourself."

"Okay," Laurie said agreeably. "I'd like to meet him anyway."

Jack turned back to her with a quizzical look.

"I'm serious," she said. "I'd like to meet this man you are in awe of and who saved your life."

"Don't ask him about his drawers," Jack cautioned. He had no idea how that would go over.

"Please!" Laurie said. "I do have some social sense."

Jack called out to Warren and waved him over. Warren sauntered to the fence, dribbling his basketball. Jack was unsure of the situation and didn't know what to expect.

He introduced the two people, and to his surprise they got along well.

"It's probably not my place to say this . . ." Laurie began after they had spoken for a while. "And Jack might wish I didn't, but . . ."

Jack cringed. He had no idea what Laurie was about to say.

". . . I'd like to thank you personally for what you did for Jack."

Warren shrugged. "I might not have taken my ride all the way up there if I knew he wasn't going to pass me the ball tonight."

Jack formed his hand into a semi-fist and cuffed the top of Warren's head.

Warren flinched and ducked out of the way. "Nice meeting you, Laurie," he said. "I'm glad you stopped by. Me and some of the other brothers have been a bit worried about the old man here. We're glad to see that he has a shortie after all."

"What's a shortie?" Laurie asked.

"Girlfriend," Jack translated.

"Come anytime, Laurie," Warren said. "You sure are better-looking than this kid." He took a swipe at Jack and then dribbled back to where he'd been shooting foul shots.

" 'Shortie' for girlfriend?" Laurie questioned.

"It's just rap-talk," Jack said. "Shortie is a lot more flattering than some of the terms. But you're not supposed to take any of it literally."

"Don't get me wrong! I wasn't offended," Laurie said. "In fact, why don't you ask him and his 'shortie' to come to dinner with us. I'd like to get to know him better."

Jack shrugged and looked back at Warren. "That's an idea," he said. "I wonder if he'd come."

"You'll never know unless you ask," Laurie said.

"I can't argue with you there," Jack said.

"I assume he has a girlfriend," Laurie said.

"To tell you the truth, I don't know," Jack said.

"You mean to tell me you were quarantined with the man for a week and you don't even know if he has a girlfriend?" Laurie said. "What did you men talk about all the time?"

"I can't remember," Jack said. "Hold on. I'll be right back."

Jack walked over to Warren and asked him if he'd come to dinner with them and bring his "shortie."

"That is, if you have one," Jack added.

"Of course I have one," Warren said. He stared at Jack for a beat, then looked over at Laurie. "Was it her idea?"

"Yeah," Jack admitted. "But I think it's a good one. The reason I never asked in the past is because I never thought you'd come."

"Where?"

"A restaurant called Elios on the East Side," Jack said. "At nine. It's my treat."

"Cool," Warren said. "How you getting over there?"

"I suppose we'll take a taxi from my place," Jack said.

"No need," Warren said. "My ride's handy. I'll pick you up at quarter of nine."

"See you then," Jack said. He turned and started back toward Laurie.

"This doesn't mean I'm not still pissed that you didn't pass me the ball on that last run," Warren called out.

Jack smiled and waved over his shoulder. When he got back to Laurie he told her that Warren was coming.

"Wonderful," Laurie said.

"I agree," Jack said. "I'll be dining with two of the four people who saved my life."

"Where are the other two?" Laurie asked.

"Unfortunately, Slam is no longer with us," Jack said regretfully. "That's a story I have yet to tell you. Spit is the fellow over on the side-lines in the bright red sweatshirt."

"Why not ask him to dinner too," Laurie suggested.

"Another night," Jack said. "I'd rather this not be a party. I'm looking forward to the conversation. You learned more about Warren in two minutes than I've learned in months."

"I'll never understand what you men talk about," Laurie said.

"Listen, I've got to shower and dress," Jack said. "Do you mind coming up to my place?"

"Not at all," Laurie said. "I'm kind of curious, the way you've described it."

"It's not pretty," Jack warned.

"Lead on!" Laurie commanded.

Jack was pleased there were no homeless people asleep in the hall of his tenement, but to make up for that blessing the endless argument on the second floor was as loud as ever. Nevertheless, Laurie didn't seem to mind and had no comment until they were safely inside Jack's apartment. There she glanced around and said it looked warm and comfortable, like an oasis.

"It'll only take me a few minutes to get ready," Jack said. "Can I offer you something? Actually I don't have much. How about a beer?"

Laurie declined and told Jack to go ahead and shower. He tried to give her something to read, but she declined that as well.

"I don't have a TV," Jack said apologetically.

"I noticed," Laurie said.

"In this building a TV is too much of a temptation," Jack said. "It would walk out of here too fast."

"Talking about TV," Laurie said, "have you seen those National Health commercials everyone is talking about, the 'no wait' ones?"

"No, I haven't," Jack said.

"You should," Laurie said. "They're amazingly effective. One of them has become an overnight classic. It's the one with the tag line, 'We wait for you, you don't wait for us.' It's very clever. If you can believe it, it's even caused National Health's stock to go up."

"Could we talk about something else?" Jack said.

"Of course," Laurie said. She cocked her head to the side. "What's the matter? Did I say something wrong?"

"No, it's not you, it's me," Jack said. "Sometimes I'm overly sensitive. Medical advertising has always been a pet peeve of mine, and lately I feel even more strangely about it. But don't worry; I'll explain it later."

ROBIN COOK

Harmful Intent

£5.99

A routine spinal injection during a normal birth – and then the nightmare struck . . .

Before the doctor's unbelieving eyes a young, healthy woman suffers inexplicable seizures. And dies. Her child survives but is brain damaged and severely disabled. And the living nightmare begins for Dr Jeffrey Rhodes. . .

Sued for eleven million dollars, his career ruined, Rhodes suffers the final cruel blow of conviction and prison. If he is ever to face his future with confidence again he must discover what *really* caused that fatal error in the operating room.

A fugitive, desperately stalking the hospital he once proudly served, Rhodes stumbles upon a plot more evil than he ever suspected – and a crazed killer whose harmful intent is greedy for more than one life . . .

All Pan Books are available at your local bookshop or newsagent, or can be ordered direct from the publisher. Indicate the number of copies required and fill in the form below.

Send to: Macmillan General Books C.S.
                Book Service By Post
                PO Box 29, Douglas I-O-M
                IM99 1BQ

or phone: 01624 675137, quoting title, author and credit card number.

or fax: 01624 670923, quoting title, author, and credit card number.

or Internet: http://www.bookpost.co.uk

Please enclose a remittance* to the value of the cover price plus 75 pence per book for post and packing. Overseas customers please allow £1.00 per copy for post and packing.

*Payment may be made in sterling by UK personal cheque, Eurocheque, postal order, sterling draft or international money order, made payable to Book Service By Post.

Alternatively by Access/Visa/MasterCard

Card No. ▢▢▢▢▢▢▢▢▢▢▢▢▢▢▢▢▢▢▢

Expiry Date ▢▢▢▢▢▢▢▢▢▢▢▢▢▢▢▢▢▢▢

Signature   ——————————————————

Applicable only in the UK and BFPO addresses.

While every effort is made to keep prices low, it is sometimes necessary to increase prices at short notice. Pan Books reserve the right to show on covers and charge new retail prices which may differ from those advertised in the text or elsewhere.

NAME AND ADDRESS IN BLOCK CAPITAL LETTERS PLEASE

Name ——————————————————————

Address ——————————————————————

——————————————————————

——————————————————————

——————————————————————

8/95

Please allow 28 days for delivery.
Please tick box if you do not wish to receive any additional information. ▢